SCHUBERT STUDIES

Schubert Studies

Edited by
Brian Newbould

Ashgate
Aldershot • Brookfield USA • Singapore • Sydney

© The individual contributors, 1998

All rights reserved. No part of this publication may be reproduced, stored in a retrieval system, or transmitted in any for or by any means, electronic, mechanical, photocopying, recording, or otherwise without the prior permission of the publisher.

The editor and contributors have asserted their moral rights.

Published by
Ashgate Publishing Limited
Gower House
Croft Road
Aldershot
Hants GU11 3HR
England

Ashgate Publishing Company
Old Post Road
Brookfield
Vermont 05036–9704
USA

British Library Cataloguing-in-Publication data

Schubert studies
  1. Schubert, Franz, 1797–1828 – Criticism and interpretation
 I. Newbould, Brian
780.9'2

Library of Congress Cataloging-in-Publication data

Schubert studies / edited by Brian Newbould.
    Includes index.
    Contents: Schubert's tempo conventions / Clive Brown — Schubert's transitions / Susan Wollenberg — Schubert's string and piano duos in context / Elizabeth Norman McKay — 'Am Meer' reconsidered : strophic, binary, or ternary? / Edward T Cone — Schubert's 'Great' C major symphony : the autograph revisited / Brian Newbould — 'Biding his time' : Schubert among the Bohemians in the mid-nineteenth century / Jan Smaczny — Architecture as drama in late Schubert / Roy Howat — Schubert's piano sonatas : thoughts about interpretation and performance / András Schiff — Schubert and the Ungers : a preliminary study / Peter Branscombe — Schubert's relationship with women : an historical account / Rita Steblin — Adversity : Schubert's illnesses and their background / Peter Gilroy Bevan.
    1. Schubert, Franz, 1797–1828.   I. Newbould, Brian   .
ML410.S3S2995   1998
780'.92—dc21   98-12585
                                    CIP
                                    MN

ISBN 1 85928 253 9

Printed on acid-free paper

Typeset in Sabon by Raven Typesetters, Chester and printed in Great Britain at The University Press, Cambridge.

Contents

List of plates	vii
Notes on contributors	ix
Introduction	xi
1 Schubert's tempo conventions Clive Brown	1
2 Schubert's transitions Susan Wollenberg	16
3 Schubert's string and piano duos in context Elizabeth Norman McKay	62
4 'Am Meer' reconsidered: strophic, binary, or ternary? Edward T Cone	112
5 Schubert's 'Great' C major Symphony: the autograph revisited Brian Newbould	127
6 'Biding his time' – Schubert among the Bohemians in the mid-nineteenth century Jan Smaczny	153
7 Architecture as drama in late Schubert Roy Howat	166
8 Schubert's piano sonatas: thoughts about interpretation and performance András Schiff	191

9	Schubert and the Ungers: a preliminary study *Peter Branscombe*	209
10	Schubert's relationship with women: an historical account *Rita Steblin*	220
11	Adversity: Schubert's illnesses and their background *Peter Gilroy Bevan*	244

Index of Schubert's works 267

General Index 271

List of plates

between pages 146 and 147

1 Symphony No. 9, folio 13r (autograph score). Reproduced by permission of the Archiv der Gesellschaft der Musikfreunde, Wien.
2 Symphony in E, folio 57. Reproduced by permission of the Royal College of Music.
3 Symphony No. 9, folio 130v (autograph score). Reproduced by permission of the Archiv der Gesellschaft der Musikfreunde, Wien
4 Symphony in E, final page of last movement (sketch). Reproduced by permission of the Royal College of Music.
5 Engraving of Caroline Unger from O.E. Deutsch, *Franz Schubert. Sein Leben in Bildern* (München and Leipzig, 1913). Reproduced by permission of the British Library.
6 Portrait of Nikolaus Lenau from Nikolaus Lenau, *Sämtliche Werke Briefe* (Stuggart, 1959).
7 'Zur Unsinniade–5ter Gesang, 31 December 1817'. Watercolour by Carl Friedrich Zimmermann. Historisches Museum der Stadt Wien, I.N. 71.695/43.
8 'Schubert and the Kaleidoscope, Kupelwieser and the Draisine'. Watercolour by Leopold Kupelwieser, *Unsinnsgesellschaft* newsletter dated 16 July 1818. Weiner Stadt- und Landesbibliothek Handschriftensammlung, Jb 86, 126/7.
9 Watercolour portrait of Schubert by Wilhelm August-Rieder (1825) from O.E. Deutsch, *Schubert: A Documentary Biography* (London, 1946). Reproduced by kind permission of J.M. Dent and Sons.
10 Anonymous portrait of Schubert aged about 18 years from *Heritage of Music – The Romantic Era* (Oxford, 1989). Reproduced by kind permission of Oxford University Press.
11 A lancet used for bleeding in the nineteenth century. Photograph by Peter Gilroy Bevan. Reproduced by kind permission of the President and Council of the Royal College of Surgeons of England.

Notes on Contributors

Peter Branscombe is Emeritus Professor of Austrian Studies at the University of St Andrews. He is the author of the Cambridge Opera Handbook on *Die Zauberflöte*, and co-editor with Eva Badura-Skoda of *Schubert Studies: Problems of Style and Chronology* (Cambridge, 1982). He is currently editing the last six plays of Nestroy for the new Complete Edition (Vienna).

Clive Brown is Reader in Music at Bretton Hall College, University of Leeds. His publications include *Louis Spohr: A Critical Biography* (Cambridge, 1984), *A New Appraisal of the Sources of Beethoven's Fifth Symphony* (Wiesbaden, 1996), and many articles, as well as critical editions of music by Weber, Spohr and Beethoven. His latest book is *Classical and Romantic Performing Practice* (Oxford, 1998), and he is currently writing a book on Mendelssohn for Yale University Press.

Edward T. Cone is Professor Emeritus of the Music Department at Princeton University, where he taught from 1947 to 1965. He has composed numerous works for piano, voice, chamber groups and orchestra. A former editor of the periodical *Perspectives of New Music*, he is author of three books and numerous articles on musical critical and analytical subjects.

Peter Gilroy Bevan is Emeritus Consultant Surgeon and was Postgraduate Dean of Birmingham Medical School. He is a past President of the Association of Surgeons of Great Britain and Ireland, and Vice-President of the Royal College of Surgeons of England. Professor Gilroy Bevan is the author of books and articles on surgery and medical training. He has a special interest in the illnesses of eighteenth- and nineteenth-century composers.

Pianist *Roy Howat* has performed and broadcast Schubert's piano music worldwide, and has also recorded compact discs of music by Chabrier and Debussy. He is a co-founding editor of the *Œuvres Complètes de Claude Debussy*. Among his other publications are Urtext editions of Handel, Fauré and Chabrier, the book *Debussy in proportion*, and chapters and articles on various composers.

Brian Newbould is Professor of Music at the University of Hull. Author of *Schubert and the Symphony: a New Perspective* (London, 1992) and *Schubert: the Music and the Man* (London/California, 1997), he has made performing versions of sketched symphonies and other works left unfinished by Schubert.

Elizabeth Norman McKay was formerly Tutor in Piano and Visiting Professor at the Birmingham Conservatoire. Her publications include the books *Schubert's Music for the Theatre* (Tutzing, 1991) and *Franz Schubert: A Biography* (Oxford, 1996), and many contributions to journals, symposia and dictionaries.

Born in Budapest in 1953, pianist *András Schiff* studied with Elizabeth Vadász, Pál Kadosa, György Kurtág, Ferenc Rados and George Malcolm. He has performed and recorded a great deal of Schubert's music, including the piano sonatas, Lieder, chamber music and choral works. He has also made a documentary film about Schubert's life and music entitled 'The Wanderer' for BBC's Omnibus programme.

Jan Smaczny is Hamilton Harty Professor of Music at Queen's University, Belfast. He was educated at Oxford University and the Charles University, Prague. Well-known as a critic and broadcaster, he has published extensively on many aspects of Czech music, especially opera and the life and works of Dvořák.

Rita Steblin holds degrees in musicology from the Universities of British Columbia, Toronto and Illinois (Urbana). She also studied the harpsichord at the Vienna Hochschule für Musik. Her publications include *A History of Key Characteristics* (Ann Arbor, 1983; Rochester, 1996) and *Ein unbekanntes frühes Schubert Porträt?* (Tutzing, 1992). Since 1991 she has lived in Vienna researching Beethoven and Schubert iconography.

Susan Wollenberg is a University Lecturer on the Faculty of Music, University of Oxford, where she directs a course of seminars on Schubert's instrumental music. She has published on a variety of subjects, including Schubert, in musicological journals, symposia and reference works, and has contributed to numerous international conferences.

Introduction

The relationship between a composer's life and his music is one of the great imponderables of all time. We grope to flesh out our awareness of a piece by hunting down every biographical morsel that may have a bearing on it, yet the music – however profoundly it touches the sensibilities that make up the essential human condition – displays a momentum and dynamic of its own that seems to resist any such anchoring-to-reality urge and make all attempts to build bridges between music and other manifestations of existence seem simplistic. The dilemma is present enough when the composer enjoyed a degree of longevity and the parallel courses of his art and his life are reasonably well documented over a span of several decades.

How daunting, then, is the problem when the composer was compositionally active for less than two decades, and was so productive that a huge musical output has to be balanced against the paucity of those clues to his day-to-day existence he left himself time to bequeath! If a precise measure is ever established and applied, it will not be surprising to find that Schubert was the most prolific composer of all time. The crudest of yardsticks – about one thousand works in roughly eighteen years of composing – suggests this much. What testimony he left us as to what he did with the rest of his hours on earth – what he thought, felt and dreamed as a real-life man rather than a creative persona – is meagre. The witness of his friends, who tapped their memories long after the composer's death to construct a retrospective human picture of him, is a treasured resource; yet their knowledge of his daily existence (which is in any case restricted) cannot be matched by their acquaintance with his artistic personality, since they were exposed to a narrow range of his work – mostly songs, dances, a handful of piano and chamber works, some church music perhaps and many a partsong, rather than the accumulating corpus of symphonies, sonatas, quartets, trios and the like. They knew nothing of such quintessential products as the 'Unfinished' and 'Great' Symphonies, the String Quintet, *Fierabras*, or the Masses in A flat and E flat – to name but a few of the central planks of the edifice we now know and love as Schubert's *oeuvre*.

True it may be that Schubert was better known and celebrated (and funded, even) in his somewhat circumscribed world of Vienna and environs than has often been surmised. Yet it was not until many decades after his demise that the bulk of his life's work was published and performed; and only in consequence of that could the extent and value of our inheritance be fully appreciated. The music itself has presented its share of problematic aspects, often arising from the nature, status and interpretation of the musical sources; and many remain unsolved still. At the same time, stray pieces of the biographical jigsaw come to light from time to time, heightening controversy as often as they resolve it. The scattering of source material, much of it in private hands, does not help the historian or musicologist. On the other hand, the *oeuvre* now at our disposal is so vast that extensive study, listening, thinking and interpreting is needed as a secure basis for informed commentary on the music. Two centuries on, there are many diverse fronts on which we can still work to clarify and elucidate Schubert's art and life-story.

It is this diversity that the present set of essays aims to reflect. There was never any intention to impose a prescription or angle upon contributors, who were invited on the premise that they were research-active in the field and had already contributed something distinctive to furthering the Schubert cause or extending our knowledge of the composer or his music. Quizzed as to the way in which their research was developing, they spoke enthusiastically of imminent projects which might come to fruition within our time-scale. These, then, were essays waiting to be written, for which *Schubert Studies* presented the opportunity and platform.

While one writer might explore a less well-trodden part of the Schubert *oeuvre* in some depth (Elizabeth Norman McKay on the music for string-and-piano duo), another might make an initial study of some neglected biographical corner (Peter Branscombe on the Ungers). On the performance–practice front, one would broach issues of tempo in Schubert's music (Clive Brown) while another would pursue a strand of reception history that demanded critical exploration (Jan Smaczny on Dvořák and other mid-nineteenth-century Bohemians). A leading international pianist would consider aspects of the piano sonatas in performance (András Schiff) while a senior surgeon (Peter Gilroy Bevan) would present a medic's view of Schubert's ailing health. That doyen of American scholars, Edward T Cone, would come to grips with a vocal miniature, while a younger British Schubertian (Susan Wollenberg) would present a rationale of Schubert's transitions in a wide range of instrumental works. Close analysis informed by a knowledge of Schubert through the fingers as much as the ear would be Roy Howat's concern, while a questing historical review of a controversial biographical issue would occupy the young Canadian resident in Vienna, Rita Steblin. The editor himself would conduct a fresh examination of a precious autograph score, taking the standpoint of analyst and performer by turns.

Schubert Studies is addressed to the reader who has engaged with Schubert's music in one dimension or other, whether as performer or analyst or musicologist. To the non-professional Schubert-lover or student who it is hoped will explore it, it offers a conspectus of current concerns and approaches, demonstrating that, as we enter the third century of Schubert, his music has lost none of its unique potency; that there still remain manifold challenges to the understanding and interpretation of posterity; and that the commitment to opening windows which might allow access to new insights and perceptions is as strong as ever.

Brian Newbould

1 Schubert's tempo conventions
Clive Brown

Franz Schubert was eight years old when Friedrich Guthmann published the first of his 'Expectorations on Modern Music' in the *Allgemeine musikalische Zeitung*, with the subtitle 'On the all-too-great rapidity of allegro, and on tearing, excessive hurry in general'. Guthmann contrasted the spacious tempi adopted by Rode and other members of the Viotti school of string players in their own repertoire, with the fast *allegro* tempi that he generally heard in concerts and operas, which he considered to be so fast 'that the notes resemble the utterances of a dreamer and the ear is unable to follow them'; and he asked 'where will this end? – Only the most practised and greatest players are in a position to perform a moderately difficult piece with the necessary precision and the requisite expression, if it is taken so immoderately fast.'[1] Among the types of piece in which he identified the worst excesses were 'the so-called Minuets of symphonies and the allegro of overtures'.[2]

Guthmann's comments draw attention to two strongly contrasting styles, not only of performance, but also of composition. Each of these styles derived some of its most prominent characteristics from different aspects of 18th-century Italian music. The lively *allegros* to which Guthmann took exception reflect, among other things, the *buffa* tradition that had reached its highest artistic manifestations in the vocal and instrumental works of the Viennese Classical masters, but which was also to bear other fruit in the work of Rossini: the broader, more lyrical style of the Viotti school, whose preference for moderate tempi is well documented, took its inspiration from the great Italian tradition of string playing personified in the middle of the 18th century by Tartini and by Viotti's own master Pugnani. These divergent traditions were to find their first important point of synthesis in the style of Spohr and his immediate imitators, before blending more homogeneously in music of the generation of Mendelssohn and Schumann. It may nevertheless be noted that in Mendelssohn's and Schumann's own music there is a marked propensity for the fast tempi of the direct Classical tradition rather than the more spacious ones of the Viotti School.

At the time Guthmann committed his objections to paper, however, the contrast between the two divergent approaches was at its sharpest. By 1805

Beethoven had completed his first three symphonies, his Septet, and his first nine string quartets, to all of which he later gave metronome marks that appear to indicate a liking for extremely rapid tempi, sometimes bordering on the unplayable. There is no reason to suppose that Beethoven had radically changed his tempo preferences when, in 1818, he fixed the Menuetto/Scherzo movements of the first three symphonies (all containing quavers as their fastest notes) at $\mathe={108}$, 100 and 116 respectively, and the Scherzo of the Septet even faster at $\mathe={126}$, or the opening movements of his first two symphonies (both *allegro con brio*, containing semiquavers) at $\mathe={112}$ and 100, and the $\frac{3}{4}$ first movement of the 'Eroica' Symphony, which contains a considerable number of semiquavers, at $\mathe={60}$. Beethoven does not seem to have been alone among early 19th-century composers in his desire for far greater rapidity in *allegro* movements than has been customary in twentieth-century performances of this repertoire. Metronome marks for numbers in Rossini and Spontini operas often approach, though seldom reach, the fastest of Beethoven's tempi. Hummel's and Czerny's metronome marks for Haydn and Mozart also show this tendency and the Haslinger collected edition of Beethoven's works,[3] begun in the year of the composer's death, allotted metronome marks to works for which the composer had not fixed them that, in the case of *allegro*, are quite as fast as Beethoven's own. There are good grounds to believe that Franz Schubert, too, may have shared this predilection for very rapid tempi, which seems to have been particularly strong in Vienna, and that he may also have adhered to the same basic principles upon which, before the advent of the metronome, Beethoven, and probably Haydn and Mozart, relied for indicating their desired tempo. This depended on a subtle equation involving the tempo term, the metre and the note values employed in the music.

The fundamental consistency of the principles by which Mozart and Beethoven, in particular, attempted to convey their tempo conventions to performers has been discussed at length in a number of recent studies.[4] In Mozart's case it is possible to postulate persuasively, on the basis of circumstantial evidence, that he adhered to a coherent system, involving quite precise relationships between tempo term, metre and note values to indicate the tempo of his music; but, notwithstanding Jean-Pierre Marty's attempts to specify metronome tempi for Mozart's music, we have no firm information on which to base assumptions about the absolute speed he might have conceived for an *allegro*, *allegretto* or *andante* in a given set of conditions. In the case of Beethoven's music, the composer's own metronome marks make it possible not only to demonstrate that he employed a coherent system with a high degree of precision, but also to understand what this meant to him in terms of absolute tempo, and they make it feasible, furthermore, to extrapolate logically an approximate absolute tempo area for works he did not supply with metronome marks.

Schubert does not appear to have fixed metronome marks for any of his instrumental works, even for the few that were published during his lifetime. However, contemporary metronome marks exist, in association with German tempo directions, for a number of songs (opp. 1–7 and 'Drang in die Ferne', D770) and for the

Deutsche Messe. The opera *Alfonso und Estrella* is the only one of Schubert's works where metronome marks were used in conjunction with Italian tempo terms. In all these instances there is compelling evidence that the metronome marks derive from the composer himself. The songs opp. 1–7, engraved by Cappi and Diabelli in 1821, where the metronome marks appear in the first edition, although missing from the autograph, were printed by private subscription through the efforts of Leopold von Sonnleithner and others of Schubert's friends, and Schubert was directly involved in the process of publication. The metronome marks for the *Deutsche Messe* (unpublished until 1870), for which Philipp Neumann had provided the text, were, according to an entry in his son's diary, written into the score by his father 'as they were given to him by the composer when he once visited him and played the movements of the mass to him one after the other'.[5] With regard to the metronome marks for *Alfonso und Estrella*, it has been shown that those in the autograph manuscript are mostly, if not all, in the handwriting of Joseph Hüttenbrenner,[6] who during the years 1821–3 conducted much of the correspondence over *Alfonso und Estrella* for Schubert, dealt with publishers on his behalf and occasionally made copies of his manuscripts for the engravers. The metronome marks were certainly present in the autograph by December 1823 when a copyist reproduced those for the overture during the process of copying a first violin part for the production of *Rosamunde*, for which Schubert initially utilized the overture to his unperformed opera.[7] Walther Dürr has argued convincingly that the metronome marks were added to the autograph at the same time as a number of tempo modifications were made, and suggests that the pencil used by Schubert to add the instruction '*Voriges Tempo*' in No. 34 was the one with which Hüttenbrenner wrote the metronome mark for the Allegretto 14 bars later.[8] It seems probable that, as in the case of Beethoven and his nephew working out metronome marks for the Ninth Symphony, or the situation described by Neumann in the case of the *Deutsche Messe*, the composer played the work through on the piano while his companion operated the metronome and wrote the numbers and instructions into the score. Schubert's brother Ferdinand later included the metronome marks for the whole opera in his copy of the autograph, and those for the overture are also found in the composer's autograph of a piano duet version.[9]

There can be little doubt, therefore, that the metronome marks derive from Schubert, and that they probably represent his own performance of the opera at the keyboard on a particular occasion. Allowing for all the uncertainties that are raised by this method of determining tempo for such a work, the metronome marks indicate that Schubert used a very similar system for prescribing tempo by means of tempo term, metre and note values to that employed by his immediate Viennese predecessors, but significantly different from anything familiar to most of his Italian and French contemporaries. The characteristics of this system, propounded at length by mid- to late-18th-century German theorists such as Kirnberger and Schulz, have been discussed in some detail elsewhere,[10] but it will be useful here to review its essential features. Each metre was considered to have its *tempo giusto*, or natural rate of motion, which could be increased or decreased by means of a faster or slower tempo term; and shorter note values were felt to indicate lighter and faster performance than longer ones. Thus if the same music were notated first in 3/2 then in 3/4 and finally in 3/8, each time halving the note values, and the same tempo term (say *allegro*) were affixed to each version, the music would demand progressively faster and lighter performance, though halving the note values would not double the speed. Only if the tempo term were modified (say *allegro* 3/2, *allegro moderato* 3/4, *allegretto* 3/8) would the music have the same tempo, though the change of metre would still demand a different performance style. Some metres involved more complex problems than others. There were several different kinds of ¢ metre, as well as *alla breve* (2/2), that had bars to the value of four crotchets. And there were what theorists referred to as *zusammengesetzten* (literally, 'put together') metres: these consisted of bars that were made up of two bars of another metre combined, so that 4/4 could theoretically be two bars of 2/4, or 6/8 two bars of 3/8.[11] In addition, it was possible for there to be an *alla breve* type of relationship in metres such as 3/4, where crotchets rather than quavers would form the principal time units, so that a 3/4 *adagio* with crotchet movement might move approximately twice as fast as one with quaver movement. All these factors introduced complications into the system, which individual composers resolved in their own ways. In addition the note content of a particular piece and the extent to which this affected the listener's subjective impression of speed might be considered as modifying the equation to a limited extent.

The treatment of ¢ and C was a particular cause of confusion. Many late-18th- and 19th-century composers made no clear distinction; some used ¢ to indicate a slightly faster tempo than C, some used it to mean literally twice as fast as C, while others seem to have regarded ¢ and C as having a 2:1 ratio at slow tempo but converging progressively as the tempo increased. The latter treatment may have had something to do with the notion that longer note values naturally belonged to slower tempi and were therefore more resistant to faster tempo terms. It will be instructive therefore, before undertaking a more general consideration of the consistency of Schubert's tempo system, and the absolute levels of tempo indicated by the metronome marks for *Alfonso und Estrella*, to investigate what these metronome marks suggest about his conception of ¢ and C. On the whole, they imply that Schubert broadly shared Beethoven's view that at slow to moderate speeds there was a 2:1 relationship, but that to achieve faster tempi in *alla breve* normally required a faster tempo term than in common time. For example the Andante ¢ (♩=100) in No. 33 can be seen as an exact equivalent of the Andante ¢ in No. 35 (♩=50); the crotchet pulse in the former precisely matches the quaver pulse of the latter (Ex. 1.1). Up to *allegro moderato*, a similarly close relationship between a crotchet pulse in the one and a quaver pulse in the other can be seen, for instance with the *allegro moderatos* in Nos 10 (♩=116) and 35 (♩=120) (Ex. 1.2). However, in this intermediate tempo range, Schubert seems to have used two kinds of C metre (perhaps a relic of the theoretical notions, expounded by Schulz, Türk and others in the 18th century, that there were at least three different kinds

Ex 1.1

No. 33 **Andante** ♩ = 100

Froila: Kein Geist, ich bin am Le - ben, steh auf und sieh mich an;

No. 35 **Andante** ♩ = 50

Mauregato: Em - pfan - ge, lie - ber Sohn mein schön - stes Ei - gen - tum,

Ex 1.2

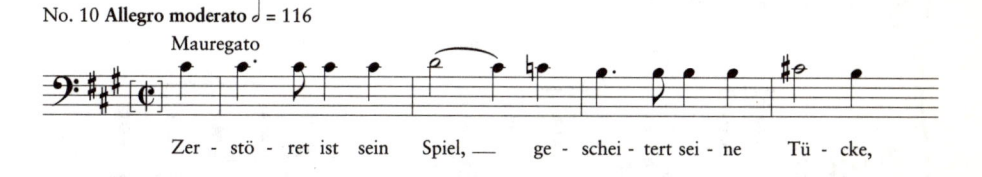

No. 10 **Allegro moderato** ♩ = 116

Mauregato: Zer - stö - ret ist sein Spiel, — ge - schei - tert sei - ne Tü - cke,

No. 35 **Allegro moderato** ♩ = 120

Jäger u. Krieger (Ten. I): Die Schwer - ter hoch ge - schwun - gen, der Sieg, er ist er - run - gen,

of C time, each of which had its own *tempo giusto*[12]). Thus Nos 16 and 28 contain *allegro moderato* sections in which the melody moves with a crotchet pulse, and the metronome marks (♩=138 and 132 respectively) are significantly higher, though nowhere near twice as fast as in No. 35. These sections are directly comparable with an *allegro assai* and an *allegro* in ₵ metre with metronome marks of ♩=138 and ♩=132 (Ex. 1.3). Table 1.1, showing sections in ₵ and C metre, continues in an ascending order of speed, for C metre, with the *allegro giusto* of No. 1 (♩=144) and the *allegro giusto* of No. 8 (♩=160); the latter seems rather too fast for the term, but this might be explained by an evident change in Schubert's idea of the tempo for this section which may never have been satisfactorily resolved: he originally headed it '*Mod*^{to} *maestoso*'. (It is difficult to escape the conviction that, in a number of cases, Schubert's conception of the tempo for a particular section changed, sometimes more than once, between his original composition of the opera and the fixing of metronome marks. Some of these modifications are documented by altered tempo terms, almost invariably made faster, and some are implied by metronome marks that seem too rapid for the given tempo terms.

Ex. 1.3

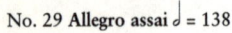

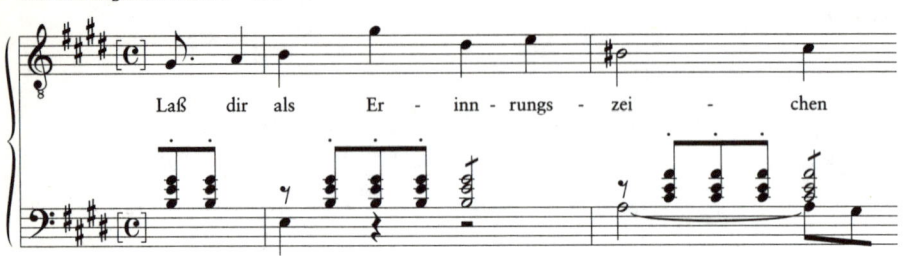

These alterations are listed in the notes to Table 1.1.) Several common-time sections marked *allegro*, most of which contain a substantial number of semiquavers, either in figurations or as repeated notes, received the metronome mark ♩=160; no 𝐂 *allegros* have a slower crotchet pulse. A couple of 𝐂 *allegros* were given faster metronome tempi: a section in No. 22 is ♩=176 (given as 𝅗𝅥=88 in the autograph) and one in No. 2 is ♩=184 (𝅗𝅥=92). One other 𝐂 *allegro* (No. 33) is of a different character, having a definite feeling of two beats in the bar, and apart from three

Table 1.1

¢				𝐂			
No.	Tempo term	MM mark	fastest notes	No.	Tempo term	MM mark	fastest notes
33*	andante	𝅗𝅥=100	♪	2	andante molto	♪=76	♬
4	andante	♩=58	♪₃	[3b	andante maestoso	♩=52	♬]
				35c	andante	♩=50	♬
				31	moderato	♩=96	♪₃
				3a	andantino	♩=100	♪₃
				27a	allegretto	♩=112	♪
				12	andantino	♩=116	♬
				15	andantino	♩=120	♪₃
				10	tempo di marcia	♩=132	♬
				35d	allegro molto moderato	♩=84	♪
10d	allegro moderato	𝅗𝅥=116	♪	[6	allegro moderato	♩=100	♪ (♬)]
7a	allegro moderato	𝅗𝅥=120	♪	35a	allegro moderato	♩=120	♬ (♬)
				[34b	allegro moderato	♩=120	
						(same music as 35a)]	
				5	allegro ma non troppo	♩=126	♬
31a	allegro	𝅗𝅥=132	♪	28	allegro moderato	♩=132	♬
29	allegro assai	𝅗𝅥=138	♪	16	allegro moderato	♩=138	♬
17	allegro agitato	𝅗𝅥=144	♪	1	allegro giusto	♩=144	♬
23**	allegro***	𝅗𝅥=160	♬	8a	allegro giusto†	♩=160	♬
ov††	allegro	𝅗𝅥=160	♪ (♬)	[8	allegro†††	♩=160°	♬]
17b	allegro molto	𝅗𝅥=160	♪	9a	allegro	♩=160	♬
				18	allegro	♩=160	♬
				35b	allegro	♩=160	♬
				35e	allegro	♩=160	♬
26	allegro molto	𝅝=84	♪				
				22	allegro	𝅗𝅥=88	♬
				2b	allegro	𝅗𝅥=92	♬

Table 1.1 concluded

¢				C			
No.	Tempo term	MM mark	fastest notes	No.	Tempo term	MM mark	fastest notes
				32	allegro agitato	♩=104**	♪
				17a	allegro assai	♩=104	♪
				33	allegro	♩=112***	♪(♪)₃
				20	allegro molto vivace	♩=112	♪
				19	allegro molto	♩=112	♪
				[10c	allegro assai	♩=116	♪]
				22b	allegro vivace	♩=120	♪

*Given as ¢ in the 1884–97 *Gesamtausgabe*
**This section and the *allegro* of the overture seem out of line with the other ¢ sections; they seem as if they ought to have a faster tempo term. But both are purely orchestral and this may suggest different criteria for orchestral and vocal music, just as there seems to have been in the case of sacred and secular music
***Originally *allegro moderato*, then *allegro ma non troppo*, and finally *allegro*. The separately bowed semiquaver runs in the violins would only be realistic at the original tempo and Schubert presumably omitted to alter these (by adding slurs) as his conception of the tempo increased
†Originally *mod^to maestoso*
††See note 3
†††Originally *All° mod^to*
•Incorrectly given as ♩=106 in the score (p. 177) in *NSA* and, equally incorrectly, as 100 in the *Quellen und Lesarten* (p. 797). It should be 160. Ferdinand Schubert's copy in the ÖNB also has 160
••The metronome mark is given in Ferdinand Schubert's copy simply as M.M. 104, without a note value and the editor of the 1884–97 *Gesamtausgabe* gave it as ♩=104. Schubert's autograph, however, clearly has '♩=104'
•••Given in the score of the *NSA* as ♩=112 (p. 723), though it is referred to in the *Quellen und Lesarten* (p. 825) as ♩=112. Ferdinand Schubert's copy has ♩=112. The 1884–97 *Gesamtausgabe* without any known authority, gave it as ¢ ♩=120. ♩=112 would be improbably slow; ♩=112, though slightly faster than might be expected, seems likelier to represent Schubert's intentions

bars with tremolando semiquavers in the violins at the end, it has quavers as its fastest notes; this received the metronome mark ♩=112.[13] Apart from that isolated instance, the C sections with metronome tempi ranging from ♩=208–240 (♩=104–120) have the tempo terms *allegro agitato*, *allegro assai*, *allegro (molto) vivace* and *allegro molto*. The fastest of these, in terms of absolute tempo, the *allegro vivace* in No. 22 has, like the *allegro* in No. 33, a two-in-the-bar pulse with quavers as its fastest notes; the subjective impression of speed in the *allegro molto* of No. 19, which has nearly continuous repeated semiquavers, is greater.

The *allegro molto* sections in ¢ metre (Nos. 17 and 26) correspond with *allegro* sections in C metre, and it is apparent from Table 1.1 that, with the exception of the *allegros* in the overture and in No. 23, sections in ¢ metre receive relatively slower metronome marks than similar tempo terms in C metre. The two exceptional *allegros* in ¢ metre, which in absolute and subjective terms contain some of the fastest music in the opera, are also exceptional in being purely orchestral sections, and it seems possible that there may have been a distinction in Schubert's mind between the tempo terms appropriate to attain a particular speed in orchestral music and those that would elicit the same speed in vocal music. Such a possibility is not inconceivable, for many writers of the period made distinctions between the tempo conventions appropriate to different types of music. The main distinction was between secular and sacred music (the latter generally requiring a slower *allegro* tempo than the former), but there were evidently subtler distinctions within these main genres. As Schubert's older namesake (but not relative) Johann Friedrich Schubert observed in 1804:

> An allegro in church style or in an oratorio must have a slower tempo than an allegro in theatre or chamber style. An allegro where the text has a solemn content and the character of the music is exalted or pathetic must have a more serious motion than an allegro with a joyful text and lightweight music. A well worked-out allegro with a powerful, full harmony must be performed more slowly than a hastily-written allegro with trivial harmony. ... Differences in compositional style or manner and national taste also necessitate a faster or slower tempo.[14]

Perhaps, however, these two anomalous ₵ *allegros* merely represent the ascendancy of convenience over consistency and should really be seen as *allegros* in C (or 2/4) that have been written in double note values to avoid the labour of notating many extra beams.

There are too few examples of most of the other metres in *Alfonso und Estrella* to draw firm conclusions about their relationship to the various kinds of common time in Schubert's scheme, but consideration of the ten sections in 3/4 (see Table 1.2) provides some instructive parallels. Leaving aside, for the moment, the *larghetto*, for which the metronome mark is ambiguous, and the *andante moto*, with which there are no directly comparable sections in C or ₵, it is evident that the crotchet

Table 1.2

3/4 No.	Tempo term	MM mark	fastest notes
5b	larghetto	♩=8 [sic! ?58]	♪
27	andante moto	♩=84	♪ (3)
9	andantino	♩=88	♪
10a	andantino	♩=88	♪ (3)
21	andantino	♩=80	♪
22a	allegretto agitato	♩=108	♪
14	allegro moderato	♩=108	♪ (3)
16a	allegro giusto	♩=126	♪
3	allegro	♩.=72	♪ (3)
25	allegro assai	♩.=84	♪ (3)

pulse of the three *andantinos* is in all cases slower than in 𝄴. A similar relationship is suggested by the ¾ *allegretto agitato* in No. 22 and the 𝄴 *allegretto* in No. 27; their metronome marks are ♩=108 and ♩=112 respectively despite the implication of greater speed in the designation *agitato*. (In fact, the accompaniment of repeated semiquavers in No. 22 does make it feel more urgent.) The tendency towards a somewhat slower crotchet pulse in ¾ is confirmed by the sections marked *allegro moderato* and *allegro giusto*; indeed the ¾ *allegro giusto* in No. 16 which is marked ♩=126 follows directly from a 𝄴 *allegro moderato* marked ♩=138 and both sections have the same range of note values and similar rhythmic patterns, though the *allegro moderato* actually contains a significantly larger number of semiquavers. In the case of the *allegro* in No. 3 and the *allegro assai* in No. 25, however, the situation is reversed, for with crotchets moving at 216 and 252 notes per minute respectively both these ¾ sections are faster than their equivalents in 𝄴. This may largely be explained by the fact that the ¾ sections contain nothing faster than triplet quavers, while the 𝄴 sections have semiquavers in the orchestra and substantially more active vocal lines.

The above investigation, despite all uncertainties, suggests a fundamentally logical relationship between tempo term, metre, note values and metronome tempi, which makes it possible to posit a number of hypotheses about the relative tempo implications of the various Italian terms that Schubert employed in this opera. Since there is only one example of a slow tempo (No. 10, Adagio), and this is in any case the sole instance of 2/4 metre in the opera, there is little to be deduced from these metronome marks about that part of his tempo range. This example may, however, help to illuminate his use of *andante*. It seems probable that Schubert's *andante* was, in general, somewhat more measured than that of many of his older contemporaries, who, in agreement with C. D. F. Schubart, seem to have considered *andante* as a tempo that 'kisses the borderline of Allegro'.[15] It is consistent with this that Schubert should have used a term like *andante molto* (No. 2) to elicit a slower tempo than the normal *andante*, not, as would have been the case in Mozart's or Beethoven's music, a faster tempo than *andante* alone. Thus Schubert's alterations of the tempo term of No. 2 in the autograph of *Alfonso und Estrella* from *andante* to *andante con moto*, and then to *andante molto*, would indicate that he first considered a faster tempo and finally decided upon a slower tempo than his original conception. This *andante molto*, with the metronome mark ♪=76, is certainly slower, both absolutely and subjectively, than the comparable *andante* in No. 35, with similar note values and rhythmic movement and a quaver pulse of 100 (Ex. 1.4). The pace of the *andante molto* is, indeed, scarcely different from that of the 2/4 *adagio* in No. 10, which is marked ♪=72. Even if Schubert regarded 2/4 as a metre with a significantly faster natural rate of motion than 𝄴 (or at least than the type of 𝄴 employed in No. 2), this seems to indicate that the two terms were nearly synonymous for him, at least in respect of absolute tempo; in fact, the 2/4 *adagio*, though it begins in an equally measured manner, quickly becomes significantly more active than the *andante molto*.

Schubert's notion of *larghetto*, represented in *Alfonso und Estrella* by only two

Ex. 1.4

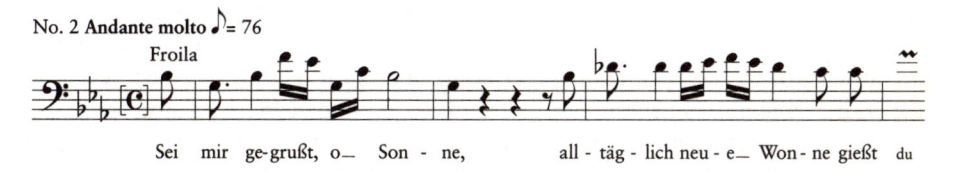

No. 35 **Andante** ♩ = 50
Mauregato
Em- pfan- ge, lie- ber Sohn, mein schön- stes Ei- gen- tum, es sei des Sie - gers Lohn

No. 2 **Andante molto** ♪ = 76
Froila
Sei mir ge- grüßt, o— Son - ne, all - täg - lich neu - e— Won- ne gießt du

examples, is difficult to estimate. The situation is further complicated by the fact that, for the ¾ Larghetto in No. 5, Hüttenbrenner clearly wrote down an incomplete number: the autograph contains, in red pencil, '8 ♩ 3 St[reiche]. 1 T[akt].'. This impossible marking is reproduced literally in Ferdinand Schubert's copy. Walther Dürr, in the *NSA*, has proposed that the 8 stands for 80 or 82 [*sic*!].[16] Such a rapid tempo, however, seems unlikely on two grounds. It would mean that Schubert regarded *larghetto* as faster than *andante*, indeed about the same as *andante [con] moto*, as comparison with No. 27 suggests (Ex. 1.5). A tempo of ♩=80 also seems implausible in the light of the metronome mark assigned to the ⁶⁄₈ Larghetto in No. 2, which at ♪=108, with accompaniment in semiquavers and a voice part moving mostly in crotchets and quavers with a few semiquavers, has a very much more leisurely feeling than No. 5 would have at ♩=80. If the 8 really represents part of the intended metronome mark, 58 would be a far likelier number. This supposition may derive support from comparison with two exactly contemporaneous operas for which the composers provided metronome marks: Weber's *Euryanthe* and Spohr's *Jessonda*. In *Euryanthe* a ⁶⁄₈ Larghetto (No. 19), with predominantly similar note values to Schubert's No. 2, has the metronome

Ex 1.5

No. 5 **Larghetto** ♩ = ?80 ?58
Alfonso
Schon, wenn es be- ginnt zu ta- gen, wird in mir die Sehn- sucht wach, Vö- gel— flie- gen

No. 27 **Andante moto** ♩ = 84
Alfonso
Doch nun wer - de deinem Ret - ter deine— Freude— offen - bar

mark ♪=100, while the ¾ Larghetto of No. 14 and the ¾ Larghetto non lento of No. 12, both with semiquavers as their fastest notes, like Schubert's ¾ Larghetto, were marked ♩=52 and ♩=54 respectively. In *Jessonda* nos 3 and 15 contain ¾ sections with the tempo direction *larghetto con moto*, having semiquavers as their fastest notes, to which, in both cases, Spohr gave the metronome mark ♩=58.

The vexed question of whether *andantino* was slower or faster than *andante* occupied the attention of many early 19th-century theorists, and it is clear that the two terms were used in quite contradictory ways by late-18th- and early-19th-century composers. The relatively fast *andante* of Mozart, Beethoven and others inclined them to regard *andantino* as somewhat slower, though Beethoven was generally reluctant to use the term because of its ambiguity.[17] Schubert's slower *andante* would of itself suggest that he might favour the faster interpretation of *andantino*. His employment of the term provides several examples in support of this view. In *Claudine von Villa Bella* No. 6 is marked *andantino quasi allegretto*, and the same direction is given for No. 2 in *Die Freunde von Salamanca*. The second movement of the Piano Sonata in A minor, D537, is marked *allegretto quasi andantino*. In the autograph of *Fierrabras*, No. 2 originally bore the heading *allegretto*, but Schubert subsequently replaced this with *andantino*. These and other similar instances suggest that he regarded *andantino* as coming between *andante* and *allegretto*. The metronome marks in *Alfonso und Estrella* leave no doubt about where he stood on the matter. All six *andantinos* in the opera (three in ₵ and three in ¾) are strikingly brisk. In ₵ the *andantinos* occupy the same tempo range as the *allegretto*, they exceed that of *moderato* and *allegro molto moderato* and, indeed, are scarcely distinguishable from the slower *allegro moderato* sections. In ¾ the *andantinos* may also border on *allegretto*, if we assume that *allegretto agitato* is faster than the normal *allegretto*. Spohr's music shows a similar correspondence between *andantino* and *allegretto* in ¾. Schubert's ¾ *andantinos* are only a little slower than the single example of *allegro moderato* in that metre, as comparison of the *andantino* in No. 9 at ♩=88 with the *allegro moderato* in No. 14 at ♩=108 indicates; both sections have triplet accompaniment (Ex. 1.6).

Ex 1.6

The single example of *allegro ma non troppo*, which occurs only for a short section of recitative accompaniment, probably implies that this tempo term was seen by Schubert as virtually synonymous with *allegro moderato*. The three examples of *allegro giusto* (about one of which, No. 8, some problematic aspects have already been discussed) indicate that this bridged the gap between *allegro moderato* and *allegro* in Schubert's scheme.

Although some of the metronome marks for unqualified *allegros* in *Alfonso und Estrella* are significantly faster than others, there are very few that appear anomalous in relation to those *allegros* that have tempo-intensifying qualifiers. In ₵ the two orchestral sections, which have faster metronome marks than might be expected, have already been discussed; similarly in ℭ, possible reasons for the rapid metronome mark for the *allegro* in No. 33 have been suggested. Leaving these three sections aside, the words *agitato, assai, vivace, molto vivace* and *molto* are, unsurprisingly, seen to indicate a more rapid tempo than the unqualified *allegro*, though on the basis of the available data it is difficult to suggest a hierarchy among them. Schubert probably regarded *allegro molto*, in accordance with generally recognized convention, as the fastest type of *allegro*, but it is not clear whether he saw *assai* in the sense of 'rather' or 'very' (a problem of language in Italian, French (*assez*) and German (*ziemlich*), which has led to this term being employed in quite various ways[18]), or whether he regarded *vivace* as requiring a greater or lesser intensification of the *allegro* than that term. With respect to the sections in question, the answer is almost immaterial, since the metronome marks for all of them indicate a tempo approaching the limits of performability.

Schubert's understanding of *allegro* seems, on the whole, much closer to Beethoven's than to Spohr's or Weber's. In *Euryanthe* Weber's unqualified *allegros* in ℭ metre, with semiquaver movement, range from ♩=116 to ♩=160 and they share this tempo area with sections designated *allegro fiero*, ♩=144 (No. 8), *allegro ma non troppo* ♩=144 (No. 14), *molto passionato* ♩=152 (No. 16), *vivace* ♩=152 (No. 23), *con tutto fuoco ed energia* ♩=160 (No. 14) and *allegro con fuoco* ♩=160 (No. 20). An *agitato* (𝅗𝅥=96) and a *presto* (𝅗𝅥=116) in No. 15 are among the few movements to attain a faster tempo. The implication that Weber's tempo terms are much less closely connected with a definite tempo seems clear. Spohr's unqualified *allegros* in ℭ metre with semiquaver movement (taken from a broad cross-section of his works), for which he gave metronome marks, range from ♩=126 to ♩=160; and only a few *allegro moltos* exceed this velocity. In Beethoven's music, on the other hand, all the unqualified *allegros* in ℭ metre, with semiquaver movement, range from ♩=160 to ♩=168 (𝅗𝅥=80–84), while the Allegro in Op. 59/1, which has triplet quavers, reaches ♩=176 (𝅗𝅥=88). Also with semiquavers, the Allegro vivace of op. 59/3 is marked 𝅗𝅥=88 (♩=176), while the Allegro con brio movements in Opp. 95 and 36 are marked 𝅗𝅥=92 and 𝅗𝅥=100 respectively. The parallel with the *allegros* in *Alfonso und Estrella* is striking.

It has been plausibly suggested that metronome marks determined in the head or by performance on the piano will often be faster than a composer might adopt in an actual performance. It seems unlikely, though, that any such discrepancies will have been significantly great, and if we accept that the metronome marks of Beethoven, Schubert, and a number of the other major composers from this period, accurately represent, or are even close to representing, the kind of tempi at which they expected their *allegros* to be performed, it is not difficult to see why Guthmann should have felt that tempi of this order could only be rendered adequately by 'the most practised and greatest players'. Regardless of whether we consider that composers were always fully conscious of the practical implications of the metronome marks they sanctioned, there was evidently a substantial number of skilled and less skilled musicians who, as the testimonies of Guthmann and others demonstrate, acknowledged that certain types of music required tempi which stretched the technique of the day to its limits, and who made more or less satisfactory attempts to realize the composers' explicit instructions or assumed intentions. In Schubert's case, the pattern indicated by the metronome marks in *Alfonso und Estrella*, apart from the light which it sheds on his conception of particular terms and his attitude towards metre and note values in general, may well suggest that many of the *allegro* movements in his instrumental works, executed in accordance with his own preference and the practice of the period, would have been performed at considerably faster speeds than is customary today.

Notes and references

1. Friedrich Guthmann 'Expectorationen über die heutige Musik. Erste Expectoration. Ueber die allzugrosse Geschwindigkeit des Allegro, und überhaupt über das eingerissene unmässige Eilen', *Allgemeine musikalische Zeitung* (1804–5), 773.
2. ibid, 175.
3. Ignaz Schuppanzigh, Carl Czerny and Carl Holz seem to have been concerned in deciding the metronome marks for this publication.
4. These include: Neal Zaslaw 'Mozart's Tempo Conventions', *Report of the Eleventh Congress Copenhagen 1972* pp. 720–33 Uri Toeplitz 'Über die Tempi in Mozarts Instrumentalmusik'; *Mozart Jahrbuch* ... p. 183 Jean-Pierre Marty *The Tempo Indications of Mozart* (Yale, 1988); Sandra Rosenblum *Performance Practices in Classic Piano Music* (Bloomington, 1988); Clive Brown, 'Historical Performance, Metronome Marks and Tempo in Beethoven's Symphonies', *Early Music* xix/2 (1991), 247ff.
5. 'wie sie ihm vom Komponisten angegeben wurden, als dieser bei ihm einmal zu Besuch war und die Sätze der Messe der Reihe nach vorspielte.' Cited in Peter Stadlen 'Können die Metronomisierung in Schuberts Werken als authentisch gelten? Weitere Bemerkungen', *Durch die Brille* 10 (1993), 93f.
6. Ernst Hilmar 'Können die Metronomisierung in Schuberts Werken als authentisch gelten?', *Durch die Brille* 8 (1992), 27–9.
7. See *Alfonso und Estrella* ed. Walther Dürr in *Franz Schubert Neue Ausgabe sämtlicher Werke* Series II, vol. 6a p. xviii and, for illustration of the copied violin part, p. xxiv.
8. ibid. p. xviii.
9. Both in the Österriechische Nationalbibliothek.
10. Clive Brown, 'Historical Performance, Metronome Marks and Tempo in Beethoven's Symphonies', *Early Music* xix/2 (1991), 247ff.

11. For further discussion of these issues see Clive Brown *Classical and Romantic Performing Practice*, OUP.
12. J. A. P. Schulz's articles in J. G. Sulzer's *Allgemeine Theorie der schönen Künste* 2 vols (Leipzig, 1771, 1774); D.G. Türk *Klavierschule oder Anweisung zum Klavierspielen für Lehrer und Lernende mit kritischen Anmerkungen* (Leipzig und Halle, 1789). The three types were usually described 'large four-four time', 'common four-four time', and 'combined four-four time' (*zusammengesetzten Vierviertaltakt*).
13. See Table 1.1 for discussion of confusion over the note value of the metronome mark.
14. Johann Friedrich Schubert *Neue Singe-Schule oder gründliche und vollständige Anweisung zur Singkunst in 3 Abtheilungen mit hinlänglichen Uebungsstücken* (Leipzig, [1804]), p. 124.
15. Carl Daniel Friedrich Schubart *Ideen über einer Aesthetik der Tonkünst* (Vienna, 1806) p. 360.
16. He gives 80 in the score, p. 129, and proposes 80 or 82 in the *Quellen und Lesarten* p. 793.
17. See Clive Brown *Classical and Romantic Performing Practice 1750–1900* (Oxford, forthcoming) for an extensive discussion of these two terms. Also Sandra Rosenblum *Performance Practice in Classic Piano Music* (Bloomington, 1988).
18. See Stewart Deas 'Beethoven's "Allegro assai" ', *Music and Letters*, xxxi (1950), 333.

2 Schubert's transitions
Susan Wollenberg

Introduction

'Magical' transitions

Schubert's transitions: the title evokes those characteristic moments in the instrumental works when a transitional move is effected almost imperceptibly from one key to another, with the potential to leave the listener astounded. Among these 'magical' transitions several types may be distinguished. In the first, the music departs from its original tonic to prepare a new key fitting 'Classical' expectations; at the 'magical moment' the key simply slips elsewhere, so that the new tonal area is not only more remote than might be classically expected, but also has been reached by a surprising route. This build-up to one key, then slipping to another, could be termed 'false transition'. But it is part of Schubert's tonal sleight-of-hand that such progressions are made to sound in fact entirely 'true'. A prime example is the first movement of the String Quintet in C major, D956 (? September 1828) bb 49–60, especially 58–9:[1] see Ex. 2.1. The reverse case is exemplified by the first movement of the String Quartet in G Major, D887 (June 1826) bb 54–65, especially 63–4:[2] see Ex. 2.2. Here the preparation is apparently for a 'non-Classical' choice of key (the mediant minor or major), but the second main theme enters classically in the dominant. A comparable example is the first movement of the Piano Trio in B flat major, D898 (October 1827)[3] bb 47–59, especially 55–8: see Ex. 2.3. If the first type discussed above represents a 'false transition', then this type presents a double deception: the 'right' key is in fact reached, but via the preparation for a more remote choice. The false move thus creates remote expectations (which are further strengthened by an awareness of Schubert's penchant for third-relationships) and these expectations are enjoyably thwarted by the arrival in the dominant. The effect of the classically expected key is greatly enhanced by such proceedings. Here the potentially 'ordinary' is transformed into the 'special'.

In a third category are those transitions where the key prepared is the one actually reached, but the move takes place so rapidly (possibly after some built-in

Ex. 2.1 D956 – i, 49–60

18 Schubert Studies

Ex. 2.1 concluded

Ex. 2.2   D887 – i, bb 54–65

20 *Schubert Studies*

Ex. 2.3   D898 – i, bb 47–59

Ex. 2.3   concluded

delay) as to create a sense of surprise. An example is the *Quartettsatz* in C minor, D703 (December 1820) bb 19–27, especially 23–6: see Ex. 2.4. Although there is no 'false transition' here, the effect is still of unexpectedness at the point where the second main theme enters in A flat major. A fourth category of 'magical transitions' covers those cases where a key is prepared neither through a false move nor through a quickly-effected 'true' move but by a totally unpredictable route. The prime example here must be the first movement of the Piano Sonata in B flat major, D960 (September 1828) bb 35/⁴–48, especially 43/⁴–47: see Ex. 2.5. Schubert's capacity for open-endedness in thematic construction leads the first theme here convincingly, on its reappearance in the tonic, from a dominant seventh to a diminished seventh harmony. In retrospect the placing of the second theme in F sharp minor can be logically derived from what has preceded it, but at the moment before the arrival of the new key, pure enigma is created by the diminished seventh pivot chord.

Ex. 2.4   D703, bb 19–27

Finally there is the case where apparently no new key is prepared. A sense of expectation is created, but the tonic is reaffirmed, as in the first movement of the 'Unfinished' Symphony in B minor, D759 (October 1822) bb 26–42, acting as departure point for a 'magical transition' (here enhanced by scoring with magical associations): see Ex. 2.6, especially bb 38–41. Whether the new key had been the classical choice (here D major) or a more distant area (as here with the choice of submediant major) the effect would still have been one of surprise. A comparable case is the first movement of the 'Great' C major Symphony, D944 (1825–6).

From all these examples it becomes clear that Schubert deploys a variety of transitional strategies to produce surprising effects.[4] In all five categories mentioned, the suddenness with which the new key enters gives it the quality of a revelation, whatever its status vis-à-vis the tonic. The sense that Schubert is working

Ex. 2.5 D960 – i, bb 35/⁴–48

24 *Schubert Studies*

Ex. 2.6 D759 – i, bb 26–42

Ex. 2.6   continued

26 *Schubert Studies*

Ex. 2.6   continued

Ex. 2.6   concluded

with a distillation of the transitional process is perhaps strongest in the Allegro in A minor for Piano Duet, 'Lebensstürme', D947 (May 1828), where sparse and purely melodic passages link the main key-areas, and remote modulatory change can be effected by such instant means as in the move to A flat by enharmonic respelling of a single note.

These rightly much-admired examples of Schubert's tonal conjuring prompt a closer look at his transitional passages in general. An understandable preoccupation with Schubert's tonal structures has dominated much of the analytical literature on the instrumental works,[5] while the transitional procedures linked with those structures have received less systematic attention. There are numerous points of interest arising in a survey of Schubert's transitions which have tended to be discussed, if at all, tangentially in accounts of individual works.[6] Some of these points are sketched below, indicating the directions in which this enquiry might lead, before proceeding to more detailed observations on specific examples. (Consideration will be given here to various early and unfinished works which traditionally have tended to be comparatively neglected in terms of analytical attention.)

Transitional questions

One question that has been generally overlooked is how transitional passages are treated in Schubert's 'three-key' expositions (where, presumably, the three keys will require two transitions).[7] With any transitional passage, but perhaps particularly with the categories of 'magical transitions' outlined in pp 16–28 above, an important sequel to the appreciation of the effect on its original appearance in the exposition must be a consideration of its role in subsequent sections of the movement, especially the recapitulation. Another interesting question is the treatment of the transition in cases of 'subdominant recapitulations' (Boyd's 'short cuts':[8] his main concern is to demonstrate that these represent in fact far from an 'easy way out'). It could be illuminating to consider the meaning of those passages in an exposition where 'the urge to move' is clearly felt, but transition of a decisive kind is not yet an issue. Although 'sonata form' transitions are my main concern here, Schubert's episodic forms may also provide enlightening insights into his transitional procedures. His retransitions (preceding either a recapitulatory return in 'sonata form' or a rondo return in episodic structures) may link up significantly with his transitions. These are among the points that help provide a context for the study of Schubert's transitions.[9]

An essential formulation is given by Hascher[10] during the course of his summary of Schubert's structural characteristics as defined in the critical literature. In this connection he offers the following statement on the transitions: [they show] 'a difficulty in departing from the tonic key, replaced by a brusque modulation' ('une difficulté de la transition à quitter le ton principal, remplacée par une modulation brutale': in a footnote Hascher introduces the synonym 'violence' for 'brutalité'). This coupling of failure (to achieve the necessary tonal move required by the structure) and success (in effecting the modulation, but by 'brutal' means) ties in with the idea traditionally promulgated by some writers on Schubert that he lacked intellectual control over his structures. Hascher quotes Whaples[11] on this point: 'Among musical myths none dies harder than that of the alleged poverty of Schubert's intellect'. The relationship between, on the one hand, the long-winded transition expressing the 'difficulty' of leaving the tonic, and, on the other hand, the brusque transition effecting the move with 'violence', will be explored here together with the question of whether the latter simply replaced the former. If intellectual control includes the ability to invest detail (of a kind that makes momentary effect) with significance in relation to the longer-term aspects of the structure, then material can be found in Schubert's handling of transitions to support the view of his acute intellectual powers as a composer which has emerged from more recent investigations.

Early works

Exploration of transitional procedures

The freedom of Schubert's structures in his first instrumental works (those of his early teens) may mean that transitional issues are simply evaded altogether. This is true of the String Quartet in 'mixed keys', D18 (1810–11) with its sectional movement-structures. However, amid the experimental elements of this fascinating work is a clear attempt at a 'brusque' modulation. The finale (like the first movement, constructed sectionally) displays two remarkable section-links. The first instance (bb 56/^{2}–63) leads from F minor to B flat minor with an uncomfortable progression that, although it misfires, creates an element of drama: see Ex. 2.7a. In the second instance (bb 137/^{2}–141) a reapproach to B flat minor is engineered with greatly intensified dramatic effect: see Ex. 2.7b. And, although again there is an obvious harmonic awkwardness here, the elliptical progression (suggesting a hypothetical major–minor link between bb 139 and 140, and containing a linear 'thread' of [enharmonic] flat vi to v)[12] adumbrates some of the characteristic constituents of Schubert's personal tonal language. It seems that the 'brusque' transitional strategy preceded the 'long-winded' transitional type in the early, experimental works.

With the (probably second surviving) String Quartet in D major, D94 (1811 or 1812?) the first movement's exposition certainly shows the reluctance to leave the tonic, in this case in the context of what Whaples[13] terms a 'unique essay in a one-key exposition'. The sub-tonic recapitulation (beginning at b. 168) has the equally unique task of effecting the return from C to D major, which it achieves awkwardly (bb 189–96) but again creating a 'brusque' modulation: see Ex. 2.8. The impression here of moving too far, too quickly is carried over into the second movement, Andante, in connection first with a late move to the dominant (D major) to close there at the double bar, and then in the parallel passage re-estab-

Ex. 2.7a D18 – iv, bb 56/2–63

lishing G major for the close of the movement (cf bb 27–37 and 57–68: Ex. 2.9a and b). In these instances it is as if an unnecessarily dramatic progression suddenly erupts, moving the music forcibly to E flat (flat vi of G) and B flat (flat vi of D) at *ff* dynamic in an extreme disruption of the settled surface and stable tonality. The key-move that follows is effected rapidly through an augmented VI chord in the first instance, and by a melodic passage in the second. In this early slow movement, simple key-change is associated with a dramatic context.

The earliest quartets show a variety of approaches to modulation, among them some repetitive and tautological passages which nevertheless represent tonal and transitional exploration, as in the irregular first movements of the String Quartets in C major, D32 (September–October 1812) and B flat major, D36 (1812–13). An important aspect of transitional procedure explored in the first movement of the String Quartet in C major, D 46 (March 1813) is the creation of a dramatically-

Ex. 2.7b   D18 – iv, bb 137/2–141

Ex. 2.8   D94 – i, bb 185–98 93

32 *Schubert Studies*

Ex. 2.9a   D94 – ii, bb 25–37

Ex. 2.9a   concluded

articulated passage with the capacity for neat adjustment in the recapitulation:[14] see Ex. 2.10a and b (cf bb 55–64, 202–11).[15] The discursive and experimental format of many of these early quartet movements may contain focused attention on the transition, as in the String Quartet in D major, D74 (August–September 1813) where in the first movement three main thematic statements[16] are connected by two transitions which are themselves interconnected: see Ex. 2.11a and b. (The 'x' motif is redeveloped in the recapitulation's second transition.) This is an early adumbration of the 'transition complex' (see further, below). Schubert's interest in the transition process *per se* is illustrated in the finale of D74, where a potentially bifocal close[17] is given a new twist in the recapitulation (again beginning in the dominant, at b. 189: cf bb 34–55, 198–223) to produce a 'false transition' – the first clear example of this strategy. The key-context is identical to that of D887–i, discussed in p. 16 above: see Ex. 2.12a and b.

In only one case among the earliest works is the 'difficulty' in departing from the tonic significantly noticeable (this condition can only validly be identified where the move to a new key is the goal: thus the 'one-key' exposition of D94 can not qualify). In the first movement of the String Quartet in B flat major, D112 (September 1814) a focus on transitional procedures is combined with a reluctance to leave the tonic, so that the (over-effortful) emphasis on G minor (potentially II of V) is negated by a return to B flat (cf bb 35–73: Ex. 2.13) before regaining G minor as a launching-point for the dominant. The complete (protracted and circular) set of progressions here takes up almost half of the 156-bar exposition. The recapitulation transition is of the parallel type, reproducing the whole series (cf. bb 35–102 and 243–310) following the subdominant counter-statement of theme I at b 226. One tiny detail is worth noting in the context of the transition. The recapitulatory version of theme I (returning in the tonic at b 207) incorporates the new chromatic passing-note F sharp", which – as well as reflecting the passing-note already contained in the complementary phrase – looks back

Ex. 2.9b D94 – ii, bb 53–~~58~~ 68

Ex. 2.9b   concluded

Ex. 2.10a   D46 – i, bb 55–64

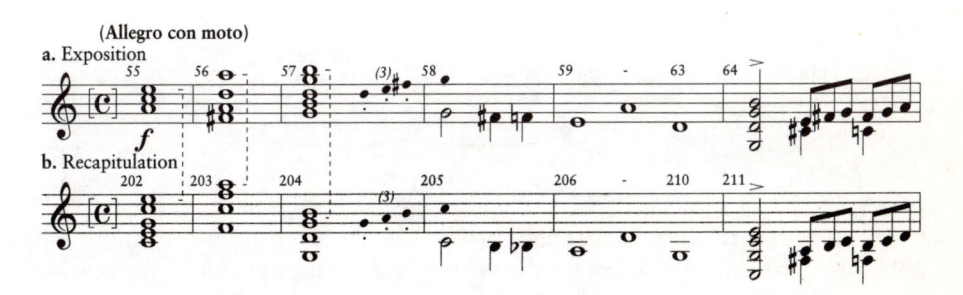

a. Exposition (Allegro con moto)

b. Recapitulation

36 Schubert Studies

Ex. 2.10b   D46 – i, bb 202–11 (example on previous page).

Ex. 2.11a   D74 – i, bb 53–76

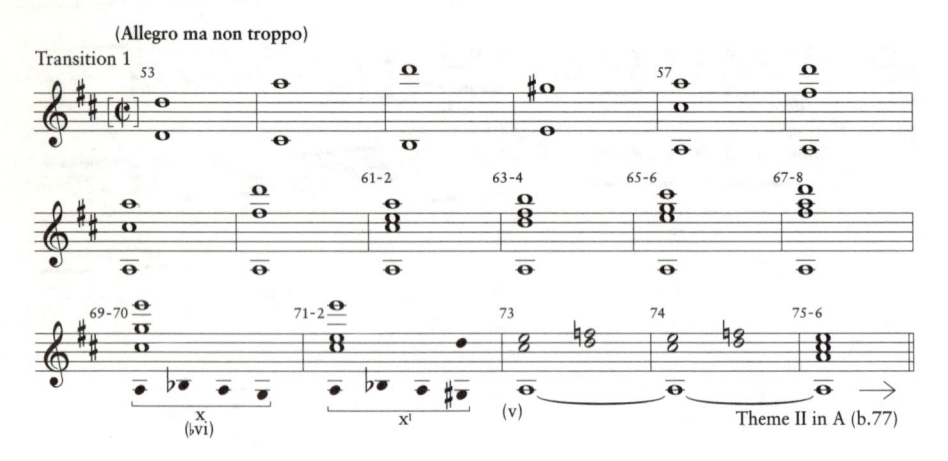

Ex. 2.11b   D74 – i, bb 141–174

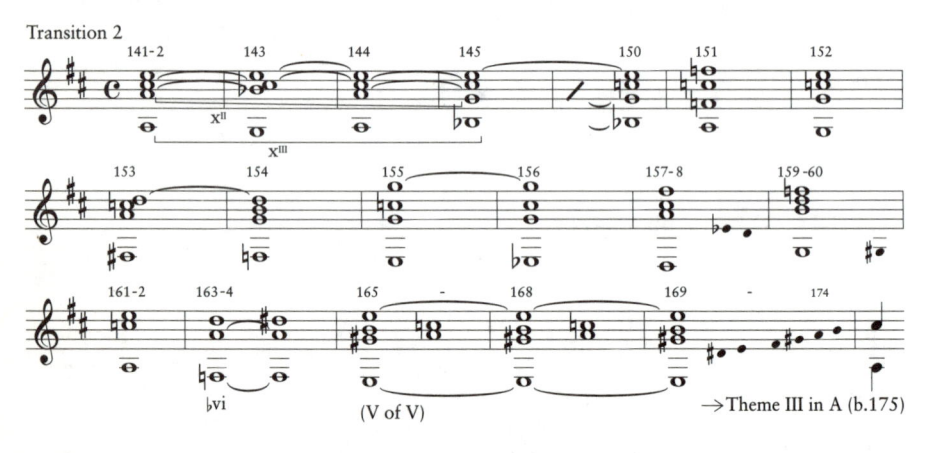

to the G minor tonality so strongly profiled in the exposition transition. It is noticeable that from the end of the exposition (in F) to the opening of the development section (in D flat at b 157) Schubert creates a rapid and elliptical transition by means of a melodic passage. And in the rondo finale the progression to the dominant via G minor works extremely effectively in the context of scherzo-like

Ex. 2.12a   D74 – iv, bb 51–56

material (bb 55–71) and is later adapted neatly to provide for a subdominant recall of the 'B' theme (bb 235–51).

From the evidence of the first movement of D112 it might appear that Schubert found it easier to move from F major to D flat in four bars than to go from B flat to F major in more than 70 bars. It is important to note the corollary, that Schubert was entirely capable of creating, in the early series of instrumental works, 'Classical' transitions to dominant or relative major within a disciplined framework.

'Classical' transitions

As early as 1813, in various instrumental works, Schubert showed himself fully conversant with a range of 'Classical' transitional gestures. These are used, for example – within a symphonic style comparable to Beethoven's earliest essays in

Ex. 2.12b D74 – iv, bb 214–224

the genre – to well-aimed dramatic effect in the first movement of the Symphony in D major, D82 (finished in October 1813: cf. bb 49–77) where II of V is tonicized (and dramatized) and the dominant is approached (from b 64) via Ic, minor, and V harmonies over the classical dominant pedalpoint. The woodwind link (bb 73–7) affirms the move into the dominant for theme II. In the recapitulation (bb 363–89) Schubert mixes 'parallel' with 'identical' procedures, replacing II of V by the relatively undramatic subdominant, but preparing identically thereafter for the halt on V, thus – convincingly – in the manner of a 'bifocal close'. The woodwind link is then reworked to lead into the tonic for theme II. Interestingly, in the finale it is the recapitulation transition that carries more drama with the plunge to B flat (b 249; cf b 52) which in Schubertian terms can predict D major, since it will take the augmented VI chord to resolve into that key. The approach to D here is again coloured by D minor, picking up this classical device from the first move-

Ex. 2.13   D112 – i, bb 35–73

40 *Schubert Studies*

Ex. 2.13   continued

Ex. 2.13   concluded

[musical score: string quartet, measures 65–73, with dynamics pp, sf, f, p]

ment. (A pertinent comparison may be made with Mozart's String Quartet in G major, K387 finale, bb 39–51: see Ex. 2.14 a and b, although there the pedalpoint is on the non-bifocal v of V.) Comparable devices are used in the first movement of the String Quartet in D major, D74 (August–September 1813). There is not a simple correlation between Classical style and Classical transition procedures: here the overall style is of a more modern discursive quality, with a leisurely lyricism new in the quartets.

The most settled in style and format among the early quartets, D87 (November 1813) deserves the epithet 'neo-Classical'. In its perfectly-realized Classical ideals it achieves Mozartian neatness with confidence and with the sense of recreating an eighteenth-century style viewed from a nineteenth-century perspective. In both the first movement and finale, a clearly-articulated transitional passage is fitted skilfully into its surroundings (partly through thematic means). Besides the characteristic pedalpoint techniques (first movement), secure harmonic thread (as in the

Ex. 2.14a   Mozart, K387 – iv, bb 39–51

Ex. 2.14b   D82 – i, bb 65–75

Ex. 2.14b   concluded

finale, bb 44 ff., approaching the dominant through II of V, eventually leading to V of V) and minor preparation for dominant major (first movement), the transitional passages here show the mixing of 'parallel' and 'identical' procedures, but also a new feature in the form of an overriding tonal motif. This is the emphasis on C minor which links the finale's exposition, transition, retransition and recapitulation. (It is notable that the transition here is used in the development section (bb 207 ff.) as an agent of modulation.) The retransition – altogether very skilful – rejoins C minor into E flat for the double return; the recapitulation transition then extends the role of C minor even further, inserting a passage of C minor following 18 bars of 'identical' procedure, and thereby dramatizing the proceedings before returning to an 'identical' design, given a neat new twist to lead to V of E flat (cf bb 62–5 and 316–19 ff.) The handling of the transitions in D87 demonstrates that Schubert could work successfully with Classical designs. Perhaps, then, the first movement of D112 (1814) misfired in its attempt to move to the dominant, not because Schubert lacked the competence to engineer such a move satisfactorily in principle, but because in practice here the essentially dramatic Classical procedures did not fit the more lyrical context. However, the element of reluctance to leave the tonic which appears in such awkward guise in this movement was transformed into a newly expressive means, as Schubert found his own way forward.

'Poetic' transitions

The range of possibilities in moving away from the tonic, and setting up the transition, in the earlier works of Schubert (those of *c*. 1810–15) can be summarized broadly under four headings. A first type could be characterized as 'losing his way', returning to retry and to find it again eventually (as displayed by the first movement of D112). At the opposite extreme, he may find the way decisively and unproblematically, as in both D82 and D87. Alternatively he may seek his way with considerable hesitation, as in the first movement transition of the Piano Sonata in E major, D157 (February 1815). The hesitations here are palpable, in the form of several bars' silence punctuating the series of tonal sallies that follow the crucial plunge to C sharp minor (II of V) at b 27 (the goal is in sight; it then takes a further 19 bars to approach the dominant, looking back at – rather than actually regaining – the tonic en route). The striking silences here are interpretable either in a spirit of *reculer pour mieux sauter* or as part of a rhetorical procedure, defeating the expectations of resolution. Their overall effect is to draw attention to the transition process: this could be categorized as a 'self-conscious' transition. The fourth type again forms an opposite extreme: in this case the transitional move is effected almost unobserved, drawing the minimum of attention to itself. Here we are in the realm of the 'poetic' transition.

The earliest example of 'poetic' transition is in the first movement of the String Quartet in G minor, D173 (March-April 1815). Stylistically, within the quartets this work represents the furthest Schubert could go in polishing the Mozart–Haydn quartet style to perfection. It takes its cue from the Symphony in B flat major, D125 (1814–15), sharing some of the same Mozartian models. (The neo-Classical style passes thereafter to the genre of sonata, with the three works for violin and piano, D384, 385 and 408 of 1816, and the solo piano sonatas D557 and 567 [568] as well as the String Trio, D581 of 1817.) But rather than a 'Classical' transition, the first movement of D173 – structurally very fine, and unusual[18] – features a lyrical transition, growing (as often) from a counterstatement of theme I, effectively extended. Also very effective is the pulling back towards the tonic (rather than paralysing in its effect, as in D112): the reluctance to leave the tonic here has a poetic quality. The move to B flat is achieved quickly yet definitively. This combination of brief nostalgia for the tonic at the point where the relative major could have been reached (bb 32–3 ff.) and a quick transition at the point where it is reached (bb 43–5) is expressive beyond the merely architectural or engineering aspects of transitional procedure. (The nostalgia for the tonic impinges on theme II.) The passage could be described as creating 'transitional imagery' (see Ex. 2.15a and b: the chromatic melodic thread serves as an expressive binding element). This imagery is not reproduced in the recapitulation: rather than subject it to 'parallel' or 'identical' use, Schubert cuts it so that the element of 'quick transition' is eliminated (the recapitulation here is altogether open to new possibilities, including some secondary development).

The 'poetic' transition makes its next appearance in the *Quartettsatz*, D703 (1820). In a series of string quartet first movements showing a preoccupation with unifying motifs[19] the *Quartettsatz* is the most intensely unified, transforming its basic 'cell' in different contexts. Unity and intensity also characterize the tonal structure, offering the possibility of integrating transitions profoundly within the whole. Transition 1 of D703 (see Ex. 2.4 on p. 22)[20] is linked with the D flat–A flat subtext that underlies the primary C–G axis of the movement.[21] The D flat efflorescence heard as a Neapolitan harmony in the first presentation of theme I is restored to the simple II b chord in the counterstatement, and on its repetition (the bass now disturbed by D flat) reverts to the D flat version reinterpreted as IV of A flat in a 'quick transition' comparable to D173. In D703 Schubert's unusualness of structural thinking includes, as in D173, the elimination of this 'quick transition' in the recapitulation, here because the recapitulation begins with theme II. (The retransition that precedes this return is significantly linked with Transition 2; see below.) In the eventual, much displaced, double return of theme I in the tonic minor that closes the movement, the crucial D flat harmony is now restored to its Neapolitan function to precipitate the final cadence, thus tying in a loop the harmonic thread that linked theme I in the exposition with Transition 1. In both D173 and D703 the 'poetic' transition is linked in with a three-key exposition, and it is to the ramifications of this structure – and the 'transition complex' associated partly with it[22] – that we now turn.

The transition complex

With the exploration of the three-key exposition in the first movements and finales of the Symphonies in B flat major, D125 (December 1814–March 1815) and D major, D200 (May–July 1815), Schubert set his transitions a series of unusual tasks (as for example in modulating from tonic to subdominant, and thence progressing to the dominant for the end of the exposition); in fulfilling these, they establish their own terms.[23] The three-key exposition was thus available as an option from early in Schubert's instrumental writing, finding later expression in such well-known examples as the String Quintet and the Ninth Symphony. Between these early and later examples it gathered an association with what may be termed the transition complex, although this was also developed in conjunction with other forms of exposition and in other ways.

Ex. 2.15a   D173 – i, bb 31–45

Ex. 2.15a   concluded

Ex. 2.15b

Again, in this regard the String Quartets, D173 and D703 share features (not surprisingly, since after D103 (extant only in incomplete form) D173 was Schubert's first completed quartet in a minor key and D703 the next quartet in this relatively rare choice of mode). In both their first movements, Transition 1 and Transition 2 present opposite types: to the rapid and lyrical Transition 1, Transition 2 offers the contrast of a more extended dramatic and developmental passage leading to the third key area. Thus Transition 2 of D173 draws powerfully on older contrapuntal prototypes (and possibly on Mozart's 'Jupiter' Symphony finale) to create a sequential design: the arrival on B flat forms a harmonic crux – at first tonicized and then characteristically taking the augmented VI chord (in an intensely concentrated texture, spread over two bars) to cadence in D minor. Transition 2 of D703 plunges into the minor at the end of theme II, setting up in the long term the relationship of Neapolitan minor to the dominant (third key area):[24] again this transition, developing intensely the motivic and harmonic ideas presented previously, is based freely on sequential design, and reaches its harmonic crux on an augmented VI as pre-cadential chord (in this case extended over first three, then four bars before releasing the cadence into G). In D173 and D703 each individual transition is all the more sharply characterized by belonging to a contrasting pair within the exposition.[25] The profound integration of the transition works in D703 in relation to the retransition, which creates a deceptive lead-back to the unconventional recapitulation (apparently preparing for the dominant minor – the dominant recapitulatory return had in fact been established as an option early in Schubert's instrumental *oeuvre*) but then leading, with a shift of the [i] – vii – i motif, into B flat major (b 195). This deceptive preparation is built on the identical bass pattern and harmonic plan to those of the cadential preparation at the end of Transition 2 in the exposition; and this resonance with the earlier passage makes the deflecting of the goal in the later instance particularly affecting.

'Resonance' can link transitions of different movements within a work to form a complex. The general harmonic colour or specific structural progression, or the melodic and rhythmic content, recurring from one movement to another, give these transitions a role as unifying agents in the work as a whole. The Piano Sonata in A major, D664 (Summer 1819),[26] is strikingly unified, both within and between movements. Its slow movement transition is clearly comparable to the equivalent point in the first movement (see Ex. 2.16a and b) and in both cases there is some ambivalence over theme II, which is handled with tonal instability. By comparison with the recapitulation it could be suggested that theme II 'proper' begins at b 25 of the first movement's exposition. (Thematic and harmonic boundaries are blurred in bb 21 ff.) While in the first movement the almost inconspicuous link (b 20) is given a high profile in the development section, transformed in apocalyptic style (bb 57 ff.), in the finale the inverted scale-figure (developed from theme I but perhaps also connecting with i – b 20 and ii – b 15) that launches the transition is immediately dramatized and extended in what is the most substantial transition passage of the sonata, and this is then followed up in the 'development' section. (Incidentally, this finale also demonstrates a subdominant recapitulation

Ex. 2.16a   D664 – i, bb 19–21

Ex. 2.16b   D664 – ii bb 14–16

in which the transition is not merely parallel.) In the finale, the F sharp minor tonality which formed such a strong subtext to theme I in the first movement, and also featured as the second key-area in the slow movement's (fluidly-constructed) sonata form, is associated with the transition and its development. (The three movements together present a harmonic complex with special emphasis on F sharp and B minors.)

In one case the transition complex within a movement links exposition, recapitulation and coda strongly together. The Piano Sonata in A minor, D784 (February 1823) was the first sonata written after the 'Wanderer' Fantasy,[27] and shows its effects. Its first-movement exposition has a high-profile transition which releases the aggression latent in theme I. This transition merges from a counterstatement (*ff*, of the original *pp* theme) starting at b. 26; the 'urge to move' is first truly felt at b. 31 where the D minor 'question' is given a D minor answer (cf bb 5–8, 30–3). But rather than leading, classically, through a logical harmonic chain, this comes to its crux with the aggressive confrontation between the two echo forms of the theme I phrase-ending, B flat – G and B natural – G sharp. The melodic presentation, intensified by repetition and tremolo in addition to the octave doubling associated with theme I, gives the hymn-like chordal style of theme II (briefly previewed as part of the transition's closing rhetoric) a strong context from which to emerge in contrast. In the recapitulation, the adjustment to the transition (cf bb 205–7, 40–1) leading to a parallel procedure is not simply carried through: the aggressive confrontation is now eliminated and the two elements – theme I octaves and theme II chords – are brought closer together in a reconciliatory passage resolving the original tension (cf bb 213–18). The coda, for the first time in the piano sonatas, is given a compensatory role other than effecting the return of the original theme in the tonic. The aggressive element apparently tamed in the recapitulation transition is now released from the same diminished seventh which there (b 215) initiated the reconciliatory passage into theme II. Here, in the coda, it gives rise to the E flat – C/E natural – C sharp juxtaposition which could, in the recapitulation, have paralleled the exposition transition. The sequence of events that should have led on to theme II now prefaces a final resolution of themes I and II (which were already heard as motivically related) culminating in the *ff* descending third in the tonic major. The coda of D784–i, uniquely, refers virtually exclusively to transition material.

Parallelism and its ramifications

In numerous cases where exact parallelism was a possibility, Schubert in fact modified the transition in the recapitulation. However, where a neatly parallel procedure is followed, this need not be regarded as constituting an artistically inferior solution. Perhaps for Schubert in these cases, as it often seems for Mozart, the perfectly worked-out exposition was best served by a minimally altered recapitulation. But in other cases, in keeping with Schubert's imaginative approach to transition, and to key-structure, the possibility of parallelism may be set up in such a way as to spring surprises. With the first movement of the String Quartet in E major, D353 (1816) the brief transition merging out of the tailpiece to theme I (bb 25–31) refers to Classical harmonic procedure (taking II of V, for the echo of the tailpiece, as its starting-point and settling on a V of V pedal to resolve into the dominant for theme II) but in a lyrical context. For the recapitulation, the process is begun as might be predicted, echoing the tailpiece in F sharp minor (II of E), but then slips to the Neapolitan-related G major for the entry of theme II. It is the easily reusable nature of this transition – and its setting up in parallel with the exposition – that makes the recapitulatory adjustment so surprising. A dramatized approach to the flat mediant would have been more obvious, and less effective. The G major tonality is not simply a relatively ephemeral colouring; it links up with the C – G sub-text that surfaces throughout the work.

A special case of parallelism is the four-key exposition of the Piano Sonata in B major, D575 (August 1817). Its first movement almost seems to be in a constant state of transition, although with some settled points. The key-scheme could be interpreted as eventually reaching the dominant after two previous failed attempts, but there is an impression, in fact, of Schubert not so much losing his way repeatedly, more finding his own way through the characteristic series of thirds.[28] (The changes of key-signature, for the first time in a piano sonata exposition, acknowledge the tonal exploration.) Each of the three transitions takes a different approach. Transition 1 (bb 8–14) dramatizes the modulation non-Classically, building up melodically a minor ninth and reinterpreting the C within G major to lead into theme II after a pause. Transition 2 (continuously worked in from b 20 onwards but gathering its main momentum from b 22/^{4}) picks up the major-minor colouring of theme II, approaching the next tonal goal (E major) through its minor, by a lyrical transformation (pre-echoes of 'Der Lindenbaum' seem to resonate here). For Transition 3, in a more architectural approach, the echo of the theme III cadence in C sharp minor (b 38) precipitates a swift series of V – I progressions on the circle of fifths with the B major harmony (reached at b 39) reinterpreted as IV of V. Clearly Schubert could have achieved the modulation from tonic to dominant earlier if he had not designed a more novel scheme. The continuity and unity of this exposition are remarkable. In the recapitulation Schubert's liking for extended parallel tracts is evident (and here validates the unusual design). One detail deserves attention. The registral treatment of parallel transitions can transform the given series of events in subtle but meaningful ways.[29] Here, for the subdominant recapitulation of theme I, Schubert transposes up; for the F major approach to theme II he transposes the RH down but the LH up; and theme II itself is transposed up in both.[30] In works involving instrumental ensemble, Schubert may alter registral relationships in reusing transition material and thereby change the relationship of instrumental parts within the ensemble.[31]

The interest in parallel key-schemes manifested in the earlier symphonies emerged strongly in another work of 1817, the Symphony in C major, D589 (October 1817–February 1818). Newbould[32] rightly connects this symphony with the Overtures 'in the Italian Style' in D major and C major, D590 and D591

(November 1817), and interprets the finale as an overture sonata form (without development section). The multiple key-areas of its exposition and recapitulation, as in D575–i, give rise to a variety of transition devices. Transition 1 takes as its starting-point, after a tonic fanfare, the vii – i transformation which was one of Schubert's 'fingerprints' (cf the Piano Quintet, D667, slow movement: Ex. 2.17a and b). Here this motif forms a chain eventually arriving on F, which takes a 'Phrygian cadence' as approach to A major for theme II: the progression is identical to the equivalent point in the Overture, D591. Transition 2 takes the pivot note G (emerging from C major) moving instantly into E flat in songlike fashion,[33] while Transition 3 works by a melodic passage setting off from v of E flat to move chromatically to v of G major. Each of these three arrival points has its parallel in the recapitulation (from initially C major to D, A flat and finally C). The transitions here belong in a context of tonal virtuosity.

Some observations on unfinished works

A number of unfinished movements break off at, or before, the point where a recapitulation (sometimes evidently a subdominant recapitulation) was due. Their transitions are thus left without their full context. Nor should it be assumed that the recapitulatory treatment of the transition in these cases can automatically be predicted. The flexibility inherent in Schubert's treatment of the transition is evident from such examples in the finished works as the bifocal close that is classically set up in an exposition but then not reused as expected in the recapitulation (Piano Sonata in D flat [E flat] major, D567 [568], June 1817, first movement);[34] the application of identical transition procedures in the recapitulation where parallelism might have been expected, thus creating an unforeseen bifocal close (Overture in C major, D591, 1817);[35] and the various small but significant adjustments and developmental extensions made to numerous transition on recapitulation. The key-schemes surrounding them are also subject to flexible treatment; some movements with three-key expositions may feature three-key recapitulations (of varying types), while others show reduction or expansion of the key-areas in the recapitulation, and occasionally a two-key exposition has a three-key recapitulation (Symphony in C minor, D417, April 1816, first movement). Schubert's 'irregular' recapitulations, beginning in various other than tonic keys, link in with these structural variants.

One of the most contextless transitions occurs in the 38-bar fragment of a first movement for piano in E minor, D769a (1823), frustratingly in view of the searching quality of the music (possibly picking up ideas fruitfully from Beethoven's Op. 90). At the point where transitional momentum has built up through a series of quite experimental pivotal progressions, it is stopped with a set of repeated chords whose dominant resolution is followed by a dominant seventh chord (b 38). Possibly, as in the unfinished first movement of the Piano Sonata in F sharp minor, D571 (July 1817), there would be a return to the tonic before once

Ex. 2.17a   D589 – iv, bb 51–3

54 *Schubert Studies*

Ex. 2.17b D667 – ii, bb 59–61

again setting up a transition to the second area. Noticeable in D769a is the intensity with which Schubertian harmonic fingerprints are piled up within a short space. In the Piano Sonata in A minor, D537 (March 1817), first movement, this kind of intensity had been successfully integrated into a fully worked-out structure:[36] in D769a it need not have precluded completion.

Among the unfinished movements it is rare to find a transitional failure. In the incomplete first movement of the Piano Sonata in C major, D613 (April 1818), the level of invention is less imaginative than usual for Schubert, and the transition is correspondingly awkward in its effect. An uncomfortable attempt at the progression later to be perfected in the String Quintet first movement is then reworked (bb 60–5) to achieve the close in the dominant. (The key-plan C – E flat – G is thus identical to that of the String Quintet exposition.) Two reasons for the awkwardness of the proceedings in D613 are, first, in Transition 1 the choice of V^7b of G (following a Neapolitan A flat chord) as launching-point for the chromatic run into E flat (crowded with too many notes compared with the economy of D 956) and, second, the harmonically clumsy approach from E flat through the same V^7b chord (now following an augmented VI on A flat) into G major, so that Transition 2 seems a disturbingly off-balance version of Transition 1. (Ex. 2.18 a and b shows the two transitions.) It is interesting to observe that the setting-up of the remote progression did not necessarily work smoothly for Schubert even after the successful experience of creating such tonally richly worked-out movements as D537–i (where, *inter alia*, Schubert's tonal conjuring enabled him to move from C to E flat within four bars).

The Piano Sonata in C major, D840 ('Reliquie'), dating from April 1825, has possibly attracted less attention than other sonatas of the period 1823–8 because it is classed as an unfinished work. As such, it has not yet attained a comparable

Ex. 2.18a   D613 – i, bb 37–41

Ex. 2.18b   D613 – i, bb 59–65

status in the Schubert 'canon' to that of the Symphony in B minor, D759, or the *Quartettsatz*, D703.³⁷ Its first movement is as powerfully constructed and expressed as that of D784, and similarly has a high-profile transition. (One reason for its prominence is that the recapitulation proper is launched at the point where the transitional passage began in the exposition.) It also marks the first appearance of the truly elliptical enharmonic transition within a sonata-form structure. After various misleading and uncertain harmonic events, effectively building up suspense, the moment of transition to B minor for theme II has 'magical' qualities (see Ex. 2.19). D840–i belongs with the finest examples of Schubert's transitional strategies. Characteristically, the 'urge to move' is manifested early in the exposition (through the vii – i transformation, to A flat at bb 12–13 ff.) and thereby plants a crucial element which is more fully composed out, its various implications realized, in the transition (where A flat is heard in a sequential and then cadential context emerging from C major, and then transformed enharmonically, from the dominant minor ninth of C to the diminished seventh over dominant pedal to cadence in B minor). An apparently wide-ranging tonal plan is tautly held together by harmonic motif, as well as its content being held together by melodic and rhythmic motif.

Drawing the threads together

Returning now to the examples with which this discussion began: the String Quintet, D956, the G major Quartet, D887, the B flat Piano Trio, D898, and the B flat Piano Sonata, D960, we can see that those mature transitions in which

Ex. 2.19   D840 – i, bb 27/⁴–56

Ex. 2.19   concluded

Schubert seems to perform a kind of miraculous tonal alchemy did not spring fully-formed into being, but were the outcome of a long creative preoccupation with transitional strategies throughout his instrumental *oeuvre*. The experience of song-writing, and the (related) interest in creating melodic and elliptical transitions within episodic instrumental movements, doubtless influenced Schubert's idea of transition in sonata-form structures.[38] The 'nostalgia for the tonic' already built in to the exposition of D173-i (see pp. 45–6 above) was absorbed into the richly-woven complex formed by transition and theme II in the G major Quartet, D887 and String Quintet, D956 first movements.[39] So the E flat theme in the exposition of D956–i repeatedly returns to C (by a miniature transition matching the original) as well as reviewing the route from G to E flat.[40] Transition 1 itself is of the most elliptical type: it is achieved in a few seconds. But its immediate repercussions extend over several minutes of music, and its long-range effects even further. An essentially melodic transition is here followed by a long passage expressing, intensely, a harmonic argument as well as presenting a melody. Theme II explores the transition's meaning and context. In D887–i, transition and theme II are interrelated (an idea already developed in D664–i: see pp. 49–50 above) to such an extent that the 'false' transitional approach has become part of the theme. (The progression, incidentally, is classically one that was connected more with retransitions, through V of VI followed by V^7 of I.) Here, multiple possibilities of transition are reviewed even more fully within the three-fold presentation of theme II, so that the alternative approach from G minor (an agent of ambivalence throughout the work) to B flat is expressed in the central part of the complex. David Beach has suggested[41] that theme II here has 'the character more of a transition than of a theme'. Perhaps in this, Schubert's transitions found their apotheosis.

Acknowledgements

I am grateful to the students who attended my Schubert seminar at the Faculty of Music, University of Oxford, 1992–3 and 1996–7, for many stimulating discussions; and to the colleagues who shared with me their thoughts on the subject of Schubert's transitions.

Notes

1. The passage builds up a dominant preparation, although tinged with considerable ambivalence (discussed further on p. 58).
2. The two bars mentioned specially, both here and with reference to the previous example from the String Quintet, are those where the music is poised to move to the new key.
3. On the question of dating this work, see John Reed, *Schubert: the Final Years* (London, 1972), pp. 260–5 and Eva Badura-Skoda, 'The Chronology of Schubert's Piano Trios', *Schubert Studies: Problems of Style and Chronology*, ed. Eva Badura-Skoda and Peter Branscombe (Cambridge, 1982), pp 277–95.
4. For a comparison with Dvořák's transitional strategies, see Susan Wollenberg, 'Celebrating Dvořák: Affinities between Schubert and Dvořák', *The Musical Times*, cxxxii (1991), pp 434–7.
5. The most recent manifestation of this tendency is Xavier Hascher, *Schubert, la forme sonate et son évolution* (Bern etc., 1996).
6. Valuable studies of individual works include those of Harold Truscott ('Schubert's D minor String Quartet', The *Music Review*, xix (1958), pp 27–36; 'Schubert's String Quartet in G major', ibid., xx (1959), 119–45); and Christoph Wolff, 'Schubert's "Der Tod und das Mädchen": analytical and explanatory notes on the song D531 and the quartet D810', *Schubert Studies*, ed. Badura-Skoda and Branscombe, pp 143–71. Perceptive studies of particular structural aspects of the instrumental works include Malcolm Boyd, 'Schubert's Short Cuts', *The Music Review*, xxix (1968), pp 12–21, and James Webster, 'Schubert's Sonata Forms and Brahms's First Maturity', *Nineteenth Century Music*, ii (1978–9), pp 18–35.
7. The point is made, *en passant*, in the historical survey by R.M. Longyear and K. Covington, 'Sources of the Three-Key Exposition', in *Journal of Musicology*, vi (1988), pp 448–70 (p. 451).
8. Reference as n. 6. See also Brian Newbould, *Schubert and the Symphony: a New Perspective* (Surbiton, 1992), p. 116, on Symphony no. 5.
9. It will be helpful to establish some terminology for the discussion here. Reference to 'parallel' procedures indicates transitions, or parts thereof, which are transposed in the recapitulation within equivalent parameters to those set up in the corresponding

passage of the exposition. Reference to 'identical' procedures indicates transitional material which is reused untransposed in the recapitulation. The crucial point is that Schubert's transitions may display varied combinations of these and other procedures (such as development or compression).
10. Op. cit., p. 10.
11. Op. cit., p. 8, from Miriam Whaples, 'On Structural Integration in Schubert's Instrumental Works', *Acta musicologica*, xl (1968), pp. 186–95, here p. 186.
12. Small roman numerals indicate notes of the scale.
13. Op. cit., p. 193.
14. The recapitulation here – typically experimentally – is in the dominant (beginning at b 160).
15. The presentation of Ex. 2.10 and some subsequent examples is in a sketch form to show the essential progression.
16. The movement-structure (lacking a central 'development' section) is basically:

Theme I: D	Theme II: A	Theme III: A
Theme I: A	Theme II: G	Theme III: D

so that considerable readjustment is required in the recapitulation.
17. This terminology derives from the classic formulation by Robert Winter, 'The Bifocal Close and the Evolution of the Viennese Classic Style', *Journal of the American Musicological Society*, xlii (1989), pp 275–337.
18. Among points of special structural interest are the tonally reversed recapitulation, which together with the three-key exposition gives a unique symmetrical key plan (g B flat d: ıı ... B flat g); and the tonal instability of theme II, whose successive phrases in B flat, then g, and then d, reflect the main key areas of the movement as a whole.
19. See Whaples, op. cit., and Martin Chusid, 'Schubert's Cyclic Compositions of 1824', *Acta musicologica*, xxxvi (1964), pp 37–45.
20. 'Transition 1' and 'Transition 2' are used here to refer to the two transitions in a three-key exposition.
21. An example of the intensity of the tonal argument is the formation of an A flat – G – A flat progression around the central arrival at G major, with A flat transformed from tonic of theme II to Neapolitan of theme III, then G transformed from tonic of theme III to leading-note of theme IV (which begins the 'development' section). This progression reflects the basic motif of the movement.
22. The idea of a structural complex, in this case formed by Neapolitan harmonic relations, is developed in Christopher Wintle, 'The "Sceptred Pall": Brahms's Progressive Harmony', with reference also to Schubert, in *Brahms 2: Biographical, Documentary and Analytical Studies*, ed. Michael Musgrave (Cambridge, 1987), pp 197–222.
23. For a sympathetic discussion of the unconventional form of these movements see Brian Newbould, *Schubert and the Symphony: a New Perspective*, pp 60 ff., 83 ff.
24. The Neapolitan minor element in Schubert is discussed by Wintle, op. cit.
25. It is noticeable that in both movements the 'development' section itself is lyrical, while the dramatic development of material occurs in Transition 2 of the exposition (and recapitulation).
26. This seems the probable date, although a later date has been suggested (Deutsch-Verzeichnis).
27. For the biographical context see Elizabeth Norman McKay, *Franz Schubert: a Biography* (Oxford, 1996), pp 148–9 and 193–4.
28. The outline is:

Theme	I	II	III	IV
Exposition:	B	G	E	F flat
Recapitulation:	E	C	A	B

29. The classic account of this phenomenon in Mozart is Esther Cavett-Dunsby, 'Mozart's "Haydn" Quartets: Composing Up and Down without Rules', *Journal of the Royal Musical Association*, cxiii (1988), pp 57–80.
30. How easily such changes can be overlooked is demonstrated in Boyd's statement (op. cit., p. 1) that 'since the exposition avoids the extreme ranges of the instrument, Schubert is able to recapitulate a fourth higher throughout'.
31. An example is the first movement of the Sonata for Violin and Piano, D384 (cf bb 28–9 and 133–4, where the starting-point for the transition has altered registrally. The idea of registral change then impinges more on theme II (bb 142 ff; cf bb 37 ff.) and on the relationship of violin and piano parts.
32. Op. cit., pp 126, 133 ff.
33. The technique familiar from the songs is aptly exemplified by Newbould in 'Der Musensohn', D764 (1822): op. cit., p. 193.
34. The implication in the exposition of a potentially bifocal close is evaded in the recapitulation by the simple device of joining theme II (without transition) straight on to theme I. However, the transition does have repercussions beyond the exposition: the retransition utilizes the almost identical progression on to V (cf D 567–i bb 137–8, 34–5) but enhanced by the diminished seventh; the recapitulation later refers to the transition idea in closing (cf D567–i, bb 215–18; D568–i, bb 234–7). On the dating of D568 see M. Chusid, 'A Suggested Redating for Schubert's Piano Sonata in E flat, Opus 122', *Schubert – Kongreß Wien 1978. Bericht*, ed. O. Brusatti (Graz, 1979), pp 37–44; and J. Reed, 'Schubert's E flat Piano Sonata: a New Date', *The Musical Times*, cxxviii (1987), pp 483–7.
35. Exposition: arrival on E with three-note chromatic descent to iii of A major for theme II; recapitulation: identical arrival on E instantly transforming to iii of C major for theme II (cf Allegro, bb 34–6, 104–5).
36. For example, in D537–i C major coloured by F major is incorporated into the opening series of events before the decisive transition to F.
37. Howard Ferguson in the Associated Board edition of the Sonatas offers a sympathetic evaluation of this sonata (see vol. ii, p. 133, col. 1). As Hinrichsen points out, Tovey valued the subtlety of D840–i (H.J. Hinrichsen, 'Die Sonatenform im Spätwerk Franz Schuberts', *Archiv für Musikwissenschaft*, xlv (1988), pp. 16–49, here p. 36, citing D.F. Tovey, 'Franz Schubert', *Essays and Lectures on Music* (London and New York, 1949), pp 103–133, here p. 126). Hinrichsen (op. cit., pp. 36–7) provides a useful comparative summary of the tonal structure of the exposition/recapitulation in D 840–i.
38. Although this point deserves exploration, it can only be mentioned briefly within the scope of this article.
39. Westrup identified this quality in theme II of D 956–i (see J.A. Westrup, *Schubert Chamber Music* (London, 1969), p. 20: 'the music reverts almost nostalgically to C major').
40. David Beach, in 'Harmony and Linear Progression in Schubert's Music', *Journal of Music Theory*, xxxviii (1994), pp 1–20, notes the dual treatment of G major in relation to the transitional approach. It could be suggested that the initial arrival on G (from a chromatic build up) is a Romantically conceived version of a potential bifocal close; Transition 1 then merges with what is to become Transition 2, by subsequently reapproaching theme II via G tonicized.
41. Op. cit., p. 7.

3 Schubert's string and piano duos in context
Elizabeth Norman McKay

Schubert composed seven string–piano duos, six for violin and one for the arpeggione. None of these duos can be included amongst his greatest masterpieces, but each has a special appeal of its own. Some are significant either for their musical content or on account of the circumstances under which they were written. All of them are related in some way to other chamber music he was writing at the time.

An understanding of why and how these duos came to be written and performed is enhanced by awareness of the Viennese musical background at that time. I begin therefore with a survey of the musical scene, and how Schubert and some of his music fitted into it. The survey covers domestic music-making and public concerts and the role of musical societies, in particular that of the prestigious and influential *Gesellschaft der Musikfreunde*, hereinafter referred to as the *Musikverein*.

PART I

The string duos in the context of the Viennese musical scene

Although Schubert described each of his first four duos for 'pianoforte and violin', in that order, as a 'sonata', this was not the title they were given by the first publishers. The first three, D384, D385, and D408, written in March/April 1816, were published together in 1836, eight years after Schubert's death, as 'Drei Sonatinen für Piano-Forte und Violine' – as sonatinas. The fourth, D574, of August 1817, appeared as a 'Duo pour Piano et Violon' in 1851. The titles 'sonatina' and 'duo' have persisted in many editions to this day. The two other pieces Schubert is known to have completed for violin and piano were products of his mature years: the Rondo in B minor, D895, dating from October 1826, published as *Rondeau brillant* in the following year, and the Fantasia in C, D934, dating from December 1827, published in 1950. Schubert composed the Sonata in A minor for arpeggione and piano in November 1824. This was not published until 1871.

The first three sonatas were written while the nineteen-year-old Schubert was employed as a reluctant assistant teacher in his father's elementary school in the Himmelpfortgrund suburb of Vienna. In April 1816, probably during the school Easter holiday period, he spent some time in the company of young friends inside the city, and with them took part in musical activities.[1] His host on these occasions was often, if not always, his friend Josef von Spaun, who played the violin, though not outstandingly well. It is possible that on these domestic musical occasions Schubert tried out his most recent compositions. However, it is more likely that he wrote the sonatas for his older brother, Ferdinand, who was a competent amateur violinist, leader of the Schubert family string quartet, and also an accomplished organist, later church choirmaster, and a composer of modest talent.

The men of Schubert's family were known in the Himmelpfortgrund both as schoolmasters and as musicians. As soon as Schubert had sufficient mastery of the violin and viola, and while he was on home leave from his boarding school in the inner city, he made music with his father (cello) and older brothers Ignaz (second violin) and Ferdinand (first violin) in the family string quartet, himself playing viola. They enjoyed a repertory that at first made only modest demands on the players, probably mostly dances and the easier movements of quartets by Haydn and Mozart, assuming, that is, that they had access to these works, and others by Schubert himself. For his brother Ferdinand in June 1816 Schubert composed the Rondo in A, D438, for violin and string orchestra.[2] It therefore seems likely that his duo sonatas for solo violin and piano composed a few weeks earlier were also for Ferdinand.

The domestic music-making in which Schubert took part in the Himmelpfortgrund in the years 1814–16 was not restricted to playing in the school-house chamber music and singing part-songs with his brothers or some of his former school friends. He also visited the family of Therese Grob, a neighbour a little younger than himself with a charming, clear high-soprano voice. By 1815 he seems to have been in love with Therese; and for her he now composed many songs, as well as the soprano solo roles in the sacred music he wrote for performance in their local Lichtental parish church. Her younger brother, Heinrich, was a gifted amateur pianist and string player. According to Heinrich's sister, it was for him as pianist that Schubert in October 1816 composed his Adagio and Rondo concertante in F, D487, for piano quartet.

In time Schubert's chamber group expanded into a larger ensemble, which rehearsed regularly in the evenings in the school-room, until the players grew too numerous for the room, and they moved into more spacious premises in the city. Here, now as a full rehearsal orchestra, it developed into an orchestral society, existing for the delectation of its members. And here many of Schubert's early orchestral works were played for the first time. Later, after several further moves, premises were found that could accommodate a small audience in addition to the players. There were several such orchestral societies in Vienna. One of them, the *Privat-Musikverein* (not to be confused with the *Gesellschaft der Musikfreunde*), of which Ferdinand was at one time musical director, may have developed from the Schuberts' rehearsal orchestra. This society sometimes gave concerts in the hall of the hotel '*Zum römischen Kaiser*'. At these concerts some of Schubert's compositions were heard for the first time.

At the other end of the social scale were the private musical salons held in houses and palaces of wealthier Viennese citizens, most of whom would have boasted the ownership of a good square piano if not a handsome Hammerflügel (grand piano). The atmosphere here was more sophisticated. Schubert referred in a diary he kept in June 1816 to one such salon which he attended. He was invited on this occasion to participate as a young performer. He writes that he played a set of Beethoven's piano variations and sang, to his own accompaniment, his settings of Goethe's 'Rastlose Liebe' and Schiller's 'Amalia'. Other works performed included a Mozart string quintet, which made a deep impression on Schubert, and piano solos played, as he described it, by 'an extraordinarily fluent pianist ... somewhat lacking in true and pure expression'.[3] Schubert is known to have attended and performed at several of the grander salon concerts later in his life, both in Vienna – those of Ignaz von Mosel, Karoline Pichler, and Charlotte, Princess Kinsky, for example – and in Salzburg, Gmunden, Graz and Steyr. Later, his appearances as performer were rarer, but he was remembered as an accompanist for singers such as Vogl and Schönstein in varied programmes of vocal and instrumental music performed by several different artists. On the other hand, Schubertiads held in the homes of friends and acquaintances usually consisted entirely of Schubert's music, certainly his Lieder, but also piano solos and duets. Only at the party that Josef von Spaun gave early in 1828 to celebrate his betrothal can we be certain that string chamber music was included, in this case the Piano Trio in E flat, D929. This was played by the musicians Schuppanzigh, Linke and Bocklet, to whom I return later. However, one of his three last string quartets, that in D minor ('Death and the Maiden'), D810, was included in a private concert on 1 February 1826 at the home of Josef Barth, another friend of Schubert's (a tenor in the court chapel choir), in the winter palace of his employer, Prince Schwarzenberg.

Many professional musicians with ambition supplemented their regular earnings by promoting their own benefit concerts. These could be grand occasions with full orchestra and held in large venues, or more modest affairs in small concert halls. The former sometimes included, between the musical items, recitations spoken by established actors, usually members of the Burg-Theater (court theatre) company, such as Heinrich Anschütz, with whom Schubert was well acquainted. Solo performers other than the benefiting artist were likely to be his friends who readily, and often on a tit-for-tat basis, gave their services. In these concerts single movements of symphonies and concertos, sometimes also of complete concertos, alternated with vocal numbers and, not surprisingly in this musical context, solo virtuoso pieces designed to show to advantage the distinctive talents of the concert-giver. One such showpiece, technically demanding for both pianist and violinist, was Schubert's Fantasia in C which, on 20 January 1828, ended the benefit concert of the young Bohemian violinist, Josef Slawjk. Schubert had been introduced to Slawjk by his Czech friend Karl Maria von Bocklet, who was the pianist in this concert.

Schubert's String Quartet in A minor, D804, received its first public performance on 14 March 1824 in the twelfth of the Schuppanzigh Quartet's winter series of subscription concerts. These chamber-music recitals, promoted by the leader of the quartet, Ignaz Schuppanzigh, like other concerts promoted by members of the *Musikverein*, and in particular by professors teaching at the *Musikverein*'s conservatoire, took place in that society's concert hall at their premises in the Tuchlauben in Vienna. In another of the same quartet's series of benefit concerts, the last of their 1827 season on 16 April, they ended with the first known public performance of Schubert's Octet, D803 (written early in 1824). The only benefit concert that Schubert gave consisting entirely of his own compositions took place on 26 March 1828, also in the concert hall of the *Musikverein*. The occasion began with the first movement of his last string quartet, in G, D887, composed in 1826; and the centre-piece was the Piano Trio in E flat. To this important concert we return later.

The *Gesellschaft der Musikfreunde des österreichischen Kaiserstaates* (Society of Friends of Music of the Austrian Empire), or *Musikverein*, founded in 1812, played a very important part in the musical life of Vienna. The programmes of its concerts, details of many of which have survived, are a clear indicator of the tastes that prevailed amongst its members, mostly Viennese music-lovers of the aristocracy and the growing middle class. Performing membership was officially open only to amateur musicians, although professionals who were teachers at its conservatoire were encouraged to take an active part in the society's activities as organizers and performers. How Schubert came to be rejected when he first applied for membershp in March 1818 while he was teaching in his father's school and strictly an amateur, and yet accepted as a performing member early in 1821, remains a mystery. By 1821 it must have been common knowledge that in the previous year two of his compositions for the theatre (*Die Zwillingsbrüder* and *Die Zauberharfe*) had been performed in the leading opera theatres of Vienna, and reviewed. It was obvious that he was no longer an amateur musician.

While some members of the *Musikverein* were non-performers, a sizable proportion of the members were elected as performers, their membership as such being dependent on their ability to contribute, to an acceptable standard, in performances at *Musikverein* concerts, which included four grand orchestral concerts given each year in the Grosser Redoutensaal (Great Hall) of the Imperial Palace. In these concerts the performance of a symphony, or movements of a symphony, was *de rigueur*. The first of only two of these concerts to include a work by Schubert during his life-time took place on 8 April 1821. The work chosen was his vocal quartet 'Das Dörfchen', D598. In the following November his Overture in E minor, D648, featured as the penultimate work in the programme. (It had opened with Beethoven's Seventh Symphony.) Only after Schubert's death were his symphonies introduced into these concerts. For performances of his chamber music, however, Schubert should have stood a better chance in the less formal *Abendunterhaltungen*, (evening entertainments) of the *Musikverein*, which were held weekly on Thursday evenings during the winter season. As far as is known, not one of his instrumental compositions was included in these programmes during his life-time. In complete contrast, his songs were frequently performed.

A study of the programme of the informal evening entertainments of the *Musikverein* from 1821, the year Schubert became a member, up to some five years after his death leads to certain conclusions about the concerts, the organization, and the music that was played. Each concert was organized by one of the committee members appointed to this task, who selected the music, chose the artists, and sometimes himself took part in concerted numbers. With very few exceptions, the concert opened with the whole, or part of, a string quartet or quintet. Those of Haydn, Mozart and Beethoven were the most played, but others by Mayseder, Spohr, Hummel and Romberg were also popular. As already mentioned, not one of Schubert's chamber works was included in these concerts while he was alive. Operatic arias and ensembles, mostly Italian, featured regularly amongst the five or so other items on the programme. The final item, with rare exceptions, was an operatic ensemble, often a finale, involving participation of as many members present as possible. Solo songs and part-songs were seldom included in early years, but they came into their own from around 1823, when Schubert's songs far outnumbered those of all other composers. Other concerted instrumental chamber works were sometimes played, apart from the opening number. Beethoven's Septet was clearly a favourite, but more usually the work performed was a duo for piano and violin or, less frequently, cello. On 11 March 1819 Beethoven's Cello Sonata in G minor was played, and a week later a violin sonata by Worzischek (Vořišék), the pianist on both occasions. After these two performances, and although piano trios occasionally featured, it is doubtful whether any other complete string–piano duo sonata was to be heard at any of the evening entertainments until 1833. In place of sonatas, the most favoured genres for duos were the rondo, with or without slow introduction, and sets of variations. By 1826 the polonaise and potpourri (a medley of popular arias and tunes) predominated. The fantasia, surprisingly, was seldom represented.

By 1824 Schubert's songs appeared quite frequently in programmes, and their popularity increased steadily until by 1827 at least one of them featured in virtually every concert. Indeed, in the sophisticated private musical scene of the *Musikverein*, as in some public concerts in Vienna and further afield in Austria and Germany, Schubert was making his mark as a composer of songs – a 'tone-poet' of notable talent. On the other hand, there appeared to be no future for his operas. After his limited success with stage-works in 1820, both his attempts at grand German opera, *Alfonso und Estrella* and *Fierrabras*, had been rejected. Throughout the last years of his life the Kärntnertor-Theater (court opera-house) and Theater an der Wien were in and out of serious financial difficulties which forced their closure sometimes for months on end. There was no market, then, nor any prospect, for the operas on which he had expended so much of his energy and his ambition. He was now looking for success for his orchestral music, both in the Redoutensaal concerts of the *Musikverein*, in the series of *Concerts spirituels*, and in the occasional *Akademien* (public concerts).

The *Concerts spirituels* were established in 1819 for the express purpose of performing music which would not otherwise have been played in Vienna. The organizers and supporters belonged to a section of the musical community to which Beethoven and Schubert also subscribed, which deplored what they perceived as declining tastes: the vulgarization or trivialization of musical culture, the rejection of serious content in favour of sentimentality, of virtuosic thrills and tasteless bombast at the expense of sensitivity. The *Concerts spirituels*, which took place in the Landhaussaal (County Hall of Lower Austria), usually included in their programmes a symphony, those of Mozart and Beethoven being particularly popular, and either a short sacred work or excerpts from a longer one, such as an oratorio by Handel.[4] Thus works, some of them from an earlier age, which would not otherwise have received performances were kept alive. Unfortunately the amateur status of most of the musicians taking part made it difficult to ensure high standards of performance, particularly when works were played through with virtually no rehearsal.[5] Early in 1829, soon after Schubert's death, there were two performances of his music in *Concerts spirituels*. The first, on 5 March, was a sacred choral work which he composed in May 1828, *Veni, sancte spiritus* (Hymnus an den heiligen Geist), D948. The second, a week later, was his 'Little' Symphony in C, No. 6, D589, which had already been performed three months earlier in a Redoutensaal concert, as is discussed later.

Some of the grander *Akademien*, especially those in aid of charities, were professional concerts which took place in the Kärntnertor-Theater. Programmes for these concerts were designed as money-spinners, to attract audiences, and the content was very varied. Sometimes each half of the programme began with an overture. Bravura concertos and concerto movements were popular, while symphonies and sacred music were not. Italian operatic scenas, ensembles and choruses could be included, along with a solo song or part-song. Both Schubert's 'Erlkönig' and 'Gesang der Geister über den Wasser' for four tenors and four basses with string orchestra were included for the first time in such a concert on 7 March 1821, Ash Wednesday. There were also instrumental solos, but these were show-pieces rather than concerted chamber music. As in the evening entertainments of the *Musikverein*, polonaises, rondos and works in variation form predominated.

To the very end of his short life, Schubert was striving to succeed as a symphonist, as is evident from the sketches of the Symphony in D, D936, on which he was working shortly before he died. While organizers of the *Akademien* showed no interest in his symphonic music, those of the amateur *Musikverein* concerts and *Concerts spirituels* were the first to accommodate one of them in their programmes, but only after his death, and for both of them the same Symphony in C No. 6 of 1817/18 was selected. It appears that there were plans for the *Musikverein* orchestra to play his 'Great' C Major Symphony, the score of which he had presented as a gift to the society at the end of 1826. Preparation of the orchestral parts was completed in the summer of 1827, and the symphony was rehearsed or played through by the *Musikverein* conservatoire orchestra soon afterwards. However, it was the 1817/18 Symphony in C (in fact designated by Schubert in his autograph manuscript as 'Grosse Sinfonie in C') which opened the society's concert on 14 December 1828, less than a month after Schubert's death.

Of particular importance to Schubert in the final years of his life was his friendship with musician colleagues: musical directors, composers, and especially some of the leading instrumentalists of his day, such as Ignaz Schuppanzigh, Josef Böhm, Josef Slawjk (violins), Franz Weiss (viola), Josef Linke (cello), Karl Maria von Bocklet (piano), Josef Lewy (horn), and Franz Lachner (pianist, musical director and composer). Some, if not all of them, invited Schubert to write music for them to play. They were ready to try out his new compositions, and no doubt offered advice. They may have recognized his genius, and undoubtedly encouraged him to compose chamber music, in particular for strings alone and for strings with piano: the String Quartet in G, the String Quintet, Piano Trios in B flat and in E flat, and the two duos he wrote for Slawjk and Bocklet. The influence of these musicians on Schubert's instrumental music, and the encouragement they gave him by performing it, were surely comparable to the influence and encouragement of the singers Johann Michael Vogl, Franz Jäger, Baron Schönstein, and Ludwig Tietze. It is likely that some of these singers, as well as the instrumentalists, helped Schubert to choose the programme for his benefit concert of March 1828; and several of them took part, in so doing adding greatly to the success of the occasion.[6]

Schubert's concert was a considerable success. The capacity audience in the hall of the *Musikverein*, made up largely of friends and admirers, was enthusiastic. The performances had gone well and, spurred on by the appreciable sum of money he made from the event, he was soon talking about another. But within six months he was seriously troubled by illness. In the course of 1828 Schubert composed some of his greatest masterpieces, very few of which he ever heard performed. He appears to have written at immense speed, and with boundless inspiration. But the creative energy he expended, together with his desperate efforts to find publishers for his music both in Vienna and abroad, left him with little time or energy to plan another benefit concert.

Probably all Schubert's early music, up to 1817, was written for performance by himself, his family and friends. Later, and certainly from 1823, it was composed for publication and professional performance by musician colleagues. Some of the music, for example, the 'Trout' Quintet (1819), the Octet, Introduction and Variations on 'Trockne Blumen' for flute and piano, and the Arpeggione Sonata (all from 1824), Rondo in B minor (1826) and Fantasia in C (1827) both for violin and piano, were composed by request or on commission. The few other compositions which do not appear to have been written for any specific occasion or performers were, however, influenced by the sounds he had come to associate with his colleagues.

PART II

The string duos in the context of Schubert's chamber music

The Sonatas (Sonatinas) for Violin and Piano in D, D384, in A minor, D385, and in G minor, D408 (1816)

The young Schubert grew familiar with an appreciable repertory of compositions for stringed instruments and orchestra when at home he played string quartets and at school (the *Stadtkonvikt*) the violin in daily rehearsals of the orchestra. Through these early experiences of his musical heritage he mastered both the classical style of, in particular, Haydn and Mozart, and the cyclical (three- or four-movement) structures of that music. In the years 1812–15 he completed his first three symphonies and also ten string quartets, the former being a particularly important part of his education, or self-education, as a composer. Although his earliest quartets were somewhat orchestral in their conception, by 1814, when in nine days between 5 and 13 September he composed the String Quartet in B flat, D112, his music had a distinct quartet quality. This quartet, written just three months before his Symphony No. 2 also in B flat, is a remarkable work, of fine musical content and, despite its dependence on his classical forebears, of considerable originality. The charm of the music is immediate, revealing his obvious delight in the subject matter and his skilful treatment and development of his material. There is no sign yet of a prodigious wealth of characteristically Schubertian harmonies and harmonic progressions, but there is plenty of evidence of the composer's concern with formal structures. The first movement, like that of the G minor Quartet, D173, written a few months later (completed on 1 April 1815), has a three-key exposition.

The concise final movement of this B flat Quartet is also in three-key exposition sonata first-movement form, but with an additional return of the first subject (A) after what appears to be the final coda. This immediately suggests a formal relationship with rondo or sonata rondo (see Figure 3.1). On this occasion Schubert seems to have been unwilling to let go of his material, to end the movement, before

| A trans- | B C | cod- | Devel- | A trans- | B' | C' | false | A – Coda |
| ition | | etta | opment | ition | | | coda | |

1–50 51–70 71–91   92–119   120–140   141–180   181–230 231–250   251–271   272–301   302–316   317–367   368–380

I———— V— iii–V————————➤ I————— IV— ii–I——————————

Exposition   Devel-   Recapitulation
                               opment

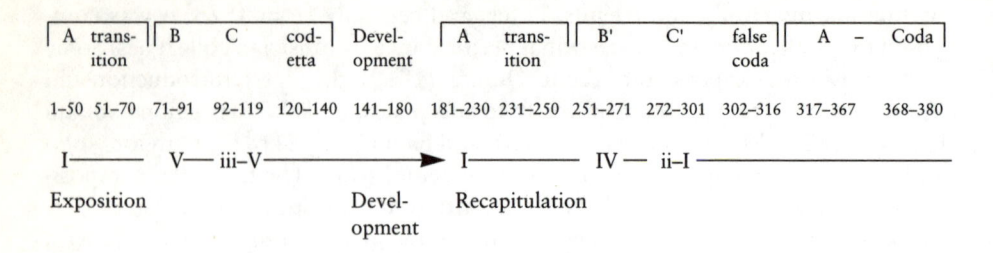

Figure 3.1   String Quartet in B flat – IV (Presto)

a final statement of his first theme. Indeed, some of the motifs on which the themes of this movement were built clearly fascinated the composer, who used them again in a more sophisticated form eleven years later in the Scherzo of his 'Great' C major Symphony.

In the finale of the B flat String Quartet Schubert was experimenting with an amalgam of sonata first-movement and rondo forms, but the result was not one to which he frequently returned. The basic hybrid form he developed was a combination of first-movement sonata form with appropriate key structure but without development, and sonata rondo without a second episode: A B A (or A') B' A, with or without coda.(the dash signifies in my argument a new key for this section.) This was the form which Schubert adopted for the slow movement of the same quartet:

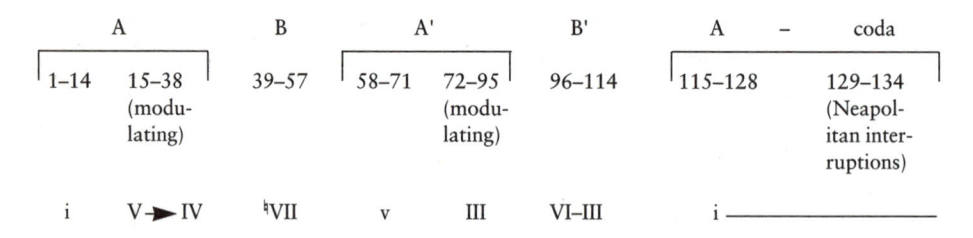

A		B	A'		B'	A –	coda
1–14	15–38	39–57	58–71	72–95	96–114	115–128	129–134
	(modu-			(modu-			(Neapol-
	lating)			lating)			itan inter-
							ruptions)
i	V➤ IV	♮VII	v	III	VI–III	i ————————	

Figure 3.2   String Quartet in B flat – II (Andante sostenuto), in G minor

After the String Quartet in G minor (April 1815) it was some fourteen months before Schubert completed his next, the Quartet in E, D353. The slow (second) movement, in A major, is in a form developed from the hybrid sonata/rondo described in Figure 3.3 below.

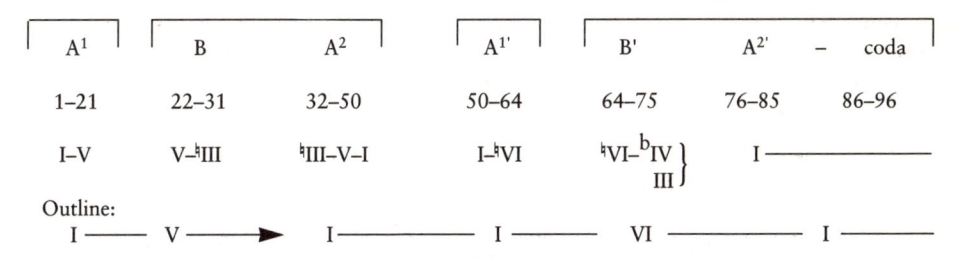

A^1	B	A^2	$A^{1'}$	B'	$A^{2'}$	–	coda
1–21	22–31	32–50	50–64	64–75	76–85		86–96
I–V	V–♮III	♮III–V–I	I–♭VI	♮VI–♭IV / III	I		

Outline:
I ——— V ——▶ I ——————— I ——— VI ——————— I ———

Figure 3.3   String Quartet in E – II (andante), in A major

A^2 is a variant, in the style of a sonata-form development, of A^1, but shortened (21 to 12 bars) by beginning at the ninth bar of A^1. However, with the outline tonal structure of I V I–I VI I, in which the second appearance of B does not appear in the tonic, the movement cannot be in sonata first-movement form (without development). Of particular interest is the move in bars 75–6 from D flat, or C sharp, major to A major, rather a glide into the tonic than a prepared modulation, and achieved by flattening the F in the viola line on the second crotchet.

The structure of the finale of this quartet, designated a 'Rondo' by the composer, looks at first sight rather similar to that of the slow movement (Figure 3.4).

A^1	trans-ition	B	A^2	$A^{1'}$	trans-ition	B'	$A^{2'}$	A^1	–	coda
1–22*	23–30	31–61	61–106	106–128*	129–136	137–166	167–214	215–237		237–262
I–V–I	I–V	V	♮III–IV	IV–I–IV in IV: I–V–I	IV–I	I	♮VI–I			
Exposition		2nd group		Recapit-ulation		2nd group in tonic		coda		

Figure 3.4   String Quartet in E – IV (Rondo: Allegro vivace)

The first unusual feature of this structure for a rondo is that the second statement of the complete rondo theme, $A^{1'}$, itself in open binary form with each part repeated (see * in Figure 3.4 above) is not in the usual obligatory tonic (E major) but in the subdominant (A major), which suggests a subdominant reprise of the first theme of the exposition in sonata form. The second is that the group of two themes constituting the first episode (B and A^2) is in two-key structure: B in the dominant (typical of a second subject); A^2, consisting of a varied statement (or development) of the main rondo theme (A) in G major on the first appearance, modulating to the subdominant, in C♯ major (as $A^{2'}$) on the second, modulating to the tonic. Clearly, Schubert intended this as a rondo movement, but there is more than a touch of sonata first-movement in its structure. (A further interpretation of this movement in sonata form, and in a manner stressing the tonic-dominant relationships, would fix the exposition in bars 1–61, the development as bars 61–106; the recapitulation beginning in the subdominant in bars 106–167; but the final bars 167–262 then become something of an anomaly.)

This examination of some movements from Schubert's early string quartets shows the important part they played in Schubert's development of the hybrid movement. In the course of this study of his string–piano duos, further diagrams in the above format show the formal and tonal structures of, in particular, the movements in hybrid form. The rondo elements of the hybrid are generally easy to recognize: recurring statements of the rondo theme, usually in the tonic, and separated by an episode or episodes. Each episode may be in two or more parts with different tonalities, and thus similar to Schubert's frequent three- or even four-part expositions in sonata first movements. On the other hand the structural elements of the sonata form in the hybrids are not always immediately obvious. A basic tenet for strict sonata first-movement form is that on the final appearance the second subject (or group of themes) should be in the tonic. The tonal relationships in Schubert's movements demand special examination.

From the same period as the String Quartet in E dates also Schubert's Rondo in A, D438, for solo violin and string orchestra, the solo part written for his brother Ferdinand. Not surprisingly, there are similarities between the character of the first violin writing in the quartet and that for the solo violinist in the Rondo. These include motivic patterns, and passages of ornate *pianissimo* sextuplets. However, there is little in either which has much in common with the violin writing in Schubert's three 'easy' sonatas for violin and piano, composed two or three months earlier.

When Schubert in March and April 1816 composed the three short sonatas, this was probably his first attempt at writing duo sonatas, or the first to survive. In March, when composing the first two, he also wrote the twelve-movement *Stabat Mater*, D383, to a German text by Klopstock, and some fifteen songs of varied content. In April, his composition of the Sonata in G minor coincided with that of the Symphony No. 4 (the 'Tragic'), D417, and more songs, probably without exception on the theme of love.[7]

Whether the three sonatas were composed for Ferdinand or no, they were probably written for reasons of diplomacy to further his own career. In April 1816 Schubert, encouraged by his teacher Salieri, applied (unsuccessfully) for the position of musical director at the Teachers' Training College in Laibach (now Ljubljana), then part of the Austro-Hungarian Empire. His aim was to escape from the unwelcome and poorly-paid drudgery of teaching the youngest children in his father's school. He may also have been motivated by the necessity to increase his income if he was to have any hope of marrying Therese Grob. In his application for the Laibach position he wrote that he had 'knowledge and skill in all branches of composition'. These sonatas for violin and piano would serve as proof of his ability to compose attractive but technically none-too-demanding chamber music suitable for performance by students.

Sonatas of any kind, like symphonies, were of very limited appeal in concerts, public or semi-public, in the Vienna of Schubert's day. Indeed, the performance of a complete sonata in the programme of a *Musikverein* evening entertainment was almost unthinkable. (In 1813 the very first public performance of a complete piano sonata by Beethoven was not even in Europe, but in Boston, USA.) The content was considered too intellectual and serious; the classical three- or four-movement structure left little room for the now preferred freer Romantic expression and fantasy, with its associated virtuoso display. In salons or concerts of chamber music, if a sonata appeared in the programme then it was frequently represented by just one movement. Thus the second movement, theme and variations, of Schubert's solo Piano Sonata in A minor, D845, played on its own, proved very popular during the composer's 1825 summer tour of Upper Austria and the Salzkammergut. With such little demand for sonatas, one might wonder why Schubert expended so much energy in composing them. He completed eighteen in all, eleven for solo piano, two for piano duet, and five for string and piano duo.

Between 1815 and 1816 Schubert experimented, even struggled, with the solo piano sonata. He left fragments of four which date from this period, but with the possible exception of the Sonata in E, D459, of August 1816, he was unable to complete any to his own satisfaction. It is therefore probable that the three little sonatas for piano and violin were his first successful attempts in the sonata genre. They are structured in classical form, showing marked influence of Mozart and Beethoven in particular. Not one of the movements in these three sonatas was designated by Schubert a 'Rondo', but the finales of the first two and the slow movement of the second are in some variant of the hybrid rondo form. The sonatas are in three or four movements as follows:

Sonata in D
1. Allegro moderato – sonata form (with very short development)
2. Andante – closed ternary (ABA)
3. Allegro vivace – hybrid: A B A B' A – coda

Sonata in A minor
1. Allegro moderato – sonata form, 3-key exposition (with very short development)
2. Andante – hybrid: A B A' B' A – coda
3. Menuetto e Trio
4. Allegro – hybrid: A B C A B' C' A – coda

Sonata in G minor
1. Allegro giusto – sonata form, 3-key exposition
2. Andante – open ternary (ABA)
3. Menuetto e Trio
4. Allegro moderato – sonata form, 3-key exposition (with very short development)

74 *Schubert Studies*

At this juncture, and as varied versions of Schubert's hybrid form appear more frequently, it is relevant to note that his predecessors were also working with this structure. Reference to the finale of Mozart's Piano Sonata in D, K576, his last, shows how Mozart experimented with the form. This movement is a rich mix of sonata and rondo structures. Written in 1789, with the expertise and daring of an established composer at the peak of his powers, the structure of his D major finale is as follows:

A^1	A^2	B	A^1	A^3	$A^{2'}$	B'	A^1	– coda
1–25	26–50	50–64	65–94	95–116	117–141	141–162	163–189	
I–V	V		I–i–V	iii–V	I			
Exposition			Development		Recapitulation			
1st group	2nd group				2nd group		1st group	– coda

Figure 3.5 Mozart: Piano Sonata in D, K576 – III (Allegretto)

This movement is in sonata form, but with reversed recapitulation, the second group $A^{2'}B'$ appearing before the first, A^1. However, A^1 is clearly of a rondo character, and its repetition at the beginning of the 'development' in the tonic enhances the overall rondo effect.

In Schubert's 'sonatinas' for violin and piano the influence of Beethoven is most obvious in striking similarities between the basic material, in particular thematic material, and that of Beethoven's sonatas for the same instruments. For example, in Schubert's Sonata in D, in each movement there are echoes of Beethoven's three-movement sonata in the same key, Op. 12 No. 1. (It is relevant that when Beethoven's three Op. 12 sonatas were published in 1799, he dedicated them to his teacher, Salieri, who was now Schubert's teacher.) As will be seen from Ex. 3.1a–h, it is likely that Beethoven and Schubert were familiar with Mozart's sonatas for the same instruments, K304 and K305.

Ex. 3.1a   Schubert D384: Beethoven Op. 12 No. 1 – first movement

Schubert's string and piano duos 75

Ex. 3.1b   Schubert D384: Beethoven Op. 12 No. 1 – first movement

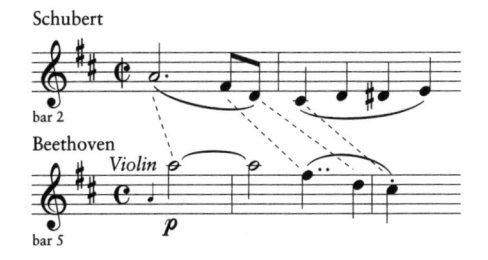

Ex. 3.1c   Schubert D384: Mozart K304 – first movement

Ex. 3.1d   Schubert D384: Mozart K304 – first movement

Ex. 3.1e   Schubert D384: Beethoven Op. 12 No. 1 – second movement

76 Schubert Studies

Ex. 3.1f   Schubert D384: Mozart K305

Ex. 3.1g   Schubert D384: Beethoven Op. 12 No. 1 – third movement

Ex. 3.1h   Schubert D384: Beethoven Op. 12 No. 1 – third movement

A short analysis of the first and last movements of Schubert's first sonatina follows. This is to stress the neatness and technical skill of this work, and serves also as a starting point for an observation as to how richly Schubert was developing his individual style and expression. The opening D major theme is a statement suitable for development in the classical style, and not strictly speaking a melody. It consists of a four-bar unison motif, which is repeated twice sequentially (see Ex. 3.2).

Ex. 3.2

Schubert repeats the passage, this time with the violin playing the theme, with canonic imitation at one bar's interval between violin and piano bass. After 28 bars of piano sequential treatment of the opening motif, a sudden *fortissimo* unison passage based on the same motif is boldly interrupted at the climax by an unprepared F major chord, ♮III (b 33), followed by a slide to a chord of E major (b 36). This chord is at once the dominant for the new key, A major, which is established in the transition leading to the second subject. The opening of this second theme is itself derived from the first three notes of the first subject. The four-bar codetta, also based on the opening motif, prepares both for a repeat of the exposition in D major, and for the development by means of a simple chromatic lift of the expected D to D sharp. The development is short, again canonic, and from b 83 with a bass line descending chromatically every two bars from C sharp to G sharp. Accented G naturals and repeated B flats hint at the minor key, but this quickly resolves into D major for the recapitulation.

The construction of this movement is straightforward. Schubert's treatment of his inter-related material, the non-lyrical themes, their development in phrases of different lengths and tonal ambiguities indicate, as in his string quartets of this period, how he was concerned with over-all structures, the architecture of the piece.

The light-hearted, playful third movement has already been described as in hybrid rondo form, A B A B' A–coda. The main statement and answer are tossed between violin and piano, and repeated in a passage of, in all, 56 bars' length. As Figure 3.6 suggests, on the two reappearances of the main theme (of 28 bars' length) there is no such repetition. This figure also shows the close relationship in the hybrid form of Schubert's first duo sonata finale between a single-episode sonata rondo and sonata first-movement form without development. But the final statement of the rondo theme in the tonic places the movement firmly in the hybrid category.

An example of Schubert's thinking, though not yet to a high degree of sophistication, is found in the second appearance of the transition in this finale where,

A	trans-ition	B	A	trans-ition	B'	A	–	coda
1–56	56–91	92–114	115–142	142–185	186–204	205–232		232–245
I	v–V	V	I	v–I				

Figure 3.6 Sonata in D – III (Allegro vivace)

having moved quickly to the dominant key, he returns to the tonic via C and E flat majors, G minor/major, through keys he reached by intervals of a rising third. This was later to become for him a typical means of modulating, particularly in development sections. (There is no indication here of Schubert's later 'aversion to the dominant' and preference for non-dominant keys, referred to by James Webster.[8])

This sonata, which Schubert in a revised autograph manuscript of the work entitled 'Sonate für Pianoforte mit Begleitung einer Violin', is a charming piece in the classical style, concentrated in content and tautly constructed, economic in length, notes and textures.

In contrast to the high spirits of the Sonata in D major, the A minor Sonata is in a more serious mood, emphasized from the start by the widely-spaced intervals between the minim notes of the opening theme of the first movement and the crotchet notes of the second melody (episode) of the slow movement.[9] Schubert's model for the opening theme seems to have been the first theme of Beethoven's Piano Sonata in E, Op.14 No.1 (composed in 1798/9) (see Ex. 3.3).

Schubert's first movement has a three-key exposition (a, C, F, recapitulating in d, F, a). The slow movement is in F major, and here the opening phrase briefly

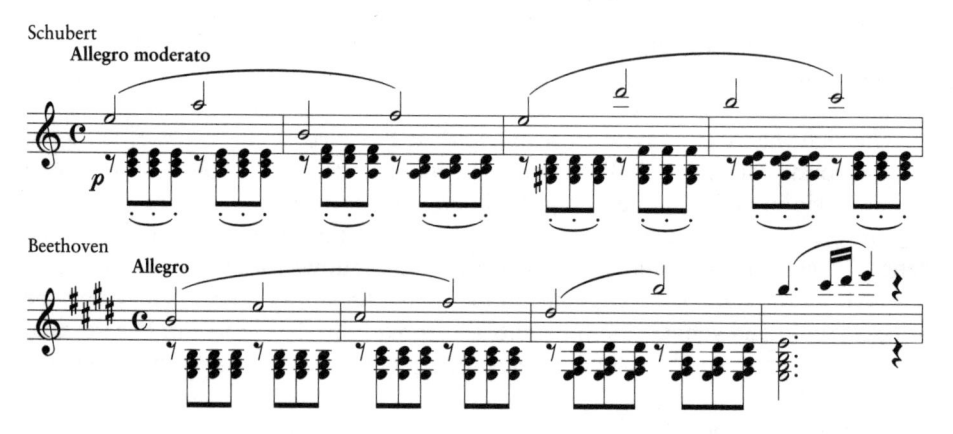

Ex. 3.3   Schubert D385: Beethoven Piano Sonata Op. 14 No. 1 – first movement

echoes that of the faster-moving last movement, *Tempo di Menuetto*, of Mozart's Sonata in F for violin and piano, K377 (see Ex. 3.4).

Ex. 3.4 Schubert D385: Mozart K377 – second movement

For such a short sonata Schubert's slow movement, in F major, a lyrical *andante*, is disproportionately long. Like the corresponding movement of the previous sonata, it is written basically in four-part string-quartet style, but unlike that movement (in ternary form) this is in a version of the hybrid form, with no second episode but a daring key structure:

A	B	A'	B'	A	–	coda
1–20*	20–40	41–60*	60–85*	86–101		101–114
I–V–I	IV…♭III	♭III	♭VI…I	I–V–I		

(*A is in open binary form, and both parts are repeated.)

Figure 3.7 Sonata in A minor – II (Andante), in F major

At the end of the first statement of the rondo section (A) Schubert used the cadential tonic note, F, pivotally as the dominant of the B flat key that follows in the episode, in the same simple way that he had modulated for the second subject in the first movment of the D major Sonata. (The move from the second A flat version of the rondo section into the key of D flat for the return of the episode is achieved in like manner.) Finely tailored modulatory passages at the end of each statement of the episode are fully integrated into the structure of that episode.

These passages are early examples of the typically Schubertian harmonic and tonal progressions which arouse in turn anticipation, surprise and ultimate satisfaction, and are a hallmark of his music.

In the finale there is again no second episode, but instead Schubert created variety by composing the one episode in two parts, the first in F major (VI) and second in D minor (iv). (These recapitulate in C major (III) and A minor (i).) This structure marks the sonata first-movement element of the hybrid rondo structure. (See Figure 3.10, p. 97.)

The Sonata in G minor begins authoritatively with an *allegro giusto*, unison-octave opening statement of the main theme. This first movement, with three-key exposition (g, B^b, E^b, recapitulating in g, E^b, B^b – g) starts in urgent mood, but relaxes in the third-key section. Material from this section serves as the principal inspiration for the development, which plays a longer and rather more important part in this sonata than had the developments in the first movements of the earlier two. The second movement in E flat, again written in string-quartet style, is in simple ternary form. There is more drama and originality in this impressive movement than in the slow movements of the previous sonatas. In the middle section, Schubert was yet more daring in his approach to tonality than he had been in the *andante* movement of the Sonata in A minor. The section begins in B flat, but moves quickly through B major/minor, G major/minor, E flat, C flat, and back to E flat, all in the space of twenty bars. The Menuetto (in B flat) is more conventionally classical, but in the Trio we are reminded that the sonata was contemporary with the Symphony No. 4, whose trio movement is in the same key (E flat), and with which there are melodic and harmonic similarities. The final movement of the sonata, in first-movement sonata form, with three-key exposition in G minor, E flat, and B flat (recapitulating in C minor, E flat and G major), effervesces with ideas and momentum. Schubert was at ease composing this sonata, remarkably self-confident, and no doubt eager to complete his fourth symphony.

In these first three early sonatas, written in the space of a few weeks, we have seen how Schubert composed in basic Classical sonata style, showing his mastery of it. In the next two sonatas he was increasingly daring, experimenting with new structures, delighting in more adventurous harmonic and tonal patterns – indeed, in developing his own personal musical language.

Sonata in A major for Violin and Piano, D574 (1817)

Allegro moderato, Scherzo-presto, Andantino, Allegro vivace

Schubert cut his teeth as a composer of sonatas on the three 1816 'sonatinas', delightful, finely constructed, youthful, optimistic, and vibrant. The Sonata in A major, composed in August 1817 for the same instruments, is a very different piece. Schubert's debt to Mozart and Beethoven is nowhere near as obvious as it had been in the early months of 1816. This is a more mature work, and one on which Schubert's musical personality is firmly stamped.

In August 1816 Schubert had left the school-house in the Himmelpfortgrund suburb and his position there as his father's assistant, and moved in with the family of his friend Franz von Schober. Here, in the inner city of Vienna, he lived rent-free with the Schobers – mother, son, and daughter – in a very comfortable home. He had his own room, presumably for the first time in his life, and the use of a good six-octave square piano. The new freedoms and comforts, the lively companionship, and the opportunity to compose music as often and for as long as he chose, resulted in an outpouring of music both cheerful and inventive. A young man, healthy, and free for the first time from restrictions formerly imposed by school and paternal authority, he was content. In March 1817 he was introduced by Schober to the great operatic baritone he had long admired, Johann Michael Vogl. The meeting had begun somewhat frostily on Vogl's side, distinctly timidly on Schubert's; but the atmosphere soon warmed. Vogl fast developed a great interest in the young composer, at first encouraging him and guiding him in his song compositions, and later helping him in his career as a composer, backing him with financial assistance. Within a few weeks of their meeting, Schubert was probably writing nothing but songs and music for solo piano. May saw the composition of some half-dozen songs, settings of picturesque poems by Goethe, Mayrhofer, and Salis-Seewis, of great charm and of a kind which suggest they were written with a carefree heart.

In composing music for solo piano, Schubert's progress and invention during this year was considerable, even if his starting point had been late in comparison with his other instrumental music. In March he completed the very promising Piano Sonata in A minor, D537. Between May and July he began the composition of four more piano sonatas: those in A flat, D557, in E minor, D566, in D flat, D567 and in F sharp minor, D571. He completed only the Sonata in D flat.[10] In August he composed both the Piano Sonata in B, D575 and 13 Variations on a Theme of Anselm Hüttenbrenner, D576. These last two works for solo piano were thus contemporaneous with the violin and piano duo Sonata in A, which was written with the benefit of Schubert's experience throughout that summer of composing sonatas and sonata movements for solo piano. During this time he had advanced his mastery of sonata structures to embrace new textures, fresh rhythmic figurations, more sophisticated tonal progressions, bold statements and elegant elaboration. Exuberance and high spirits alternate with calm and grace. Whom this sonata was written for and the circumstances of its first performance are unknown. As very little has been recorded about Schubert's activities during the year, one can only surmise that the composer may himself have played the piano part in any private performances there may have been.

The first movement, like that of Schubert's experimental and exploratory Piano Sonata in B, D575 written in the same month, has a four-key exposition of variety and invention (Figure 3.8).

i) Exposition

			2nd group			
A	transition	B	C	D		codetta
1–20	20–28	29–39	40–56	57–66		67–76
I	I–V	v–♮VII	♮VII–II–V ———————————————			

ii) Development 77–101

iii) Recapitulation

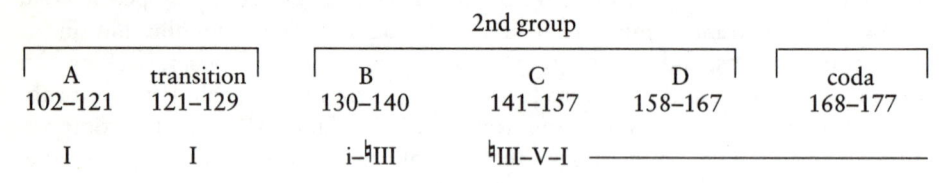

			2nd group			
A	transition	B	C	D		coda
102–121	121–129	130–140	141–157	158–167		168–177
I	I	i–♮III	♮III–V–I ———————————————			

Figure 3.8 Sonata in A major – I (Allegro moderato)

It opens with a *pianissimo* four-bar introduction for piano alone. This includes a rocking cello-like theme in the bass which becomes a counter-subject when the violin enters with a gentle, lyrical first theme. Unlike the opening themes of the early sonatas, this is a memorable, singable melody. As the first section (A) ends in a modulating transition, a new idea emerges, a gracefully falling triplet figuration which in turn leads to a melancholy, sighing violin phrase in E minor (B). This is accompanied by a contrasting lively keyboard accompaniment, of the kind Schubert was rapidly making his own (Ex 3.5).

Ex. 3.5

The pianist next introduces the third lyrical melody, in G major (C), repeated by the violin (in B major). Finally, in the regular dominant key (E major) there follows a happy, buoyant passage (D), in which confident rising arpeggio motifs are shared between the players. In the short development it is significant that, with so much material to choose from, Schubert opted to exploit its more obscure elements. The recapitulation follows a normal course, with the four sections in the appropriate keys (A, A minor, C, A). This movement is rich in Schubert's distinctive tones: the multi-keyed first-movement form, a stream of lyrical passages of melody and melodic motifs, unusual harmonic twists, and accompanying figures influenced by Schubert's obsession – or that of his age – with dance.

The slowish tempo (*allegro moderato*) and predominantly thoughtful character of the first movement may have occasioned Schubert's decision to follow it with the energetic Scherzo (in E major). This has some of Beethoven's vitality and rhythmic subtlety, but these qualities are here modified by Schubertian grace. Schubert based the opening motif of this movement on the arpeggio motifs of the fourth section of the first movement's exposition, interspersing this with ascending scales (with chromatic elements) and widely leaping crotchet passages, unexpected accentuations, and overlapping phrases such as marked many of Schubert's compositions at this time. In contrast to the dynamism of the Scherzo, the trio is delicately poised, of light texture, full of delicious twists and turns.

In the slow movement (in C major), in simple rondo form, there is quiet expressive beauty, but not without sudden and disturbing interruptions, surprising modulations (for example, from C to D flat after only eight bars), interesting rhythmic patterns, elegant accompanying figures, and some fine melodic ornamentation.

Because the autograph manuscript of this sonata is lost, the order in which Schubert originally composed the movements cannot be confirmed. If at first he placed the Scherzo immediately before the finale, then the closely related thematic material, key, tempo and triple time ($\frac{3}{4}$) would have encouraged him later to separate them with a slow movement. Both the rising A major arpeggio opening and the quasi-chromatic upward scale first heard in bars 5–7 of the finale, rather closely related to similar passages in the Trio, might have convinced him of the expediency of the re-arrangement. The finale, like that of his G minor Sonata but unlike all his other duo-sonata last movements, is in sonata first-movement form, with three-key exposition: A, C, E, recapitulating in A, F natural, A. It is again full of the exuberance and joy that abounds in much of Schubert's music of his early years, before he was struck down with syphilis towards the end of 1822. Despite the many delights of Schubert's inimitable creativity in this finale it is, for example in the development section, a little less elegant than the other movements. But it is well to remember the enormous advances he had made in the sixteen months or so since composing the Sonata in G minor, a considerably less ambitious work.

There was to be a period of seven years before Schubert returned to a duo sonata for stringed instrument and piano. In the meantime, he produced just one other chamber work for piano and strings, the five-movement Piano Quintet in A,

D667, the 'Trout' Quintet, written in 1819. Two versions of the quintet have survived, the first a simpler version suitable for amateurs, the second a more technically demanding version which was published in May 1829. The progress that Schubert had made in the three years from 1816 to 1819, the technical and imaginative fluency he had acquired, is remarkable. The little Sonata in D was a classical work of charm and competence in its limited way; the Sonata in A major brims with Schubertian originality. It shows the speed with which he was developing his musical vocabulary in all its manifestations.

Sonata in A minor for arpeggione and piano, D821 (1824)

Allegro moderato, Adagio, Allegretto

In the autumn of 1824 Schubert was commissioned to compose a piece for piano and arpeggione. After the 'Trout' Quintet, all his chamber music until now had been for string quartet: in December 1820 the *Quartettsatz*, D703, and in February/March 1824 the String Quartets in A minor, D804 and in D minor, D810.

The arpeggione was a new instrument, variously described as a *Guitarre-Violoncello*, *Bogen-Guitarre* and *Guitarre d'amour*. It was invented in 1823 by a Viennese instrument- maker, Johann Georg Staufer, and a description and illustration of the instrument appeared in the musical periodical *Cäcilia* in May 1824.[11] In the following year Diabelli published in Vienna a tutor for it.[12] This was written by Vincenz Schuster, for whom Schubert is thought to have composed his sonata, and who performed it shortly afterwards. The arpeggione was a six-stringed bowed instrument and, as the various names suggest, a cross between a cello and a guitar. In its overall appearance and the manner in which it was held between the knees, it was similar to a small cello. However, details in the shape of the body and the fretted fingerboard had more in common with the guitar. The tuning of the strings, in perfect fourths and one major third, was closer to that of the guitar than to the violin family: E A d g b e'.[13] This arrangement of the strings was designed for easier playing of arpeggio passages and of some figurations involving crossing the strings. It also points to the keys of A minor and E (major), those chosen by Schubert for his sonata, as being eminently suitable for the instrument. It soon fell out of use.

Early in 1824 Schubert suffered a recurrence of syphilitic illness. He now realised that he might not recover his health, as he had at first hoped, but was likely to suffer a gradual physical decline over at best a period of many years. In the course of 1824 he composed perhaps only six solo songs, four of them (to texts by Mayrhofer) dating from March, and maybe just a single song each in June and December (the latter with male-voice chorus). He wrote no orchestral or stage works that we know of, and only one sacred piece (*Salve Regina*), of 119 bars. In Zseliz that summer he completed dances and marches for piano, and two of his finest piano duets: the 'Grand Duo' Sonata in C, D812, and Eight Variations on an Original Theme in A flat, D813. On his return to Vienna he set to work on the Arpeggione Sonata. As it transpired, this was to be Schubert's last string–piano duo written in sonata format. It may be considered either as in two movements, the second beginning with a slow (*adagio*) introduction, or, as here, in three movements, with no break between the second and third.

In the first movement Schubert, perhaps uncertain of the arpeggione's full potential and limitations, restricted himself to a two-key exposition. As in the 'Duo' Sonata in A for violin and piano, he opens with an immediately memorable, lyrical first theme. (In the three early sonatinas his opening themes, in the tradition of much classical music, had been either rhythmic or short melodic motifs ideal for development.) However, he transforms what might have been a straightforward eight-bar theme into something more interesting. Firstly, having begun the piece on the first beat of bar 1, he prefaces the fourth bar (second half of the theme) with a three-quaver anacrusis derived from a similar pattern at the end of bar 2, thus destabilising an otherwise four-square melody. Having thus reduced the first half of the theme to 3½ bars, he extends the second to 5½ bars by lingering over a Neapolitan chord (bar 7) shortly before the cadence. When the arpeggione takes up the melody, the second half is lengthened further to nine bars, as Schubert repeats the Neapolitan chord over three bars (bars 18–20), delaying the cadence (see Ex. 3.6).

Ex. 3.6

Throughout this sonata Schubert made much of extended phrases. During the second part of the exposition he chose to stress (five times in all, between bars 49 and 67) a diminished seventh chord on F sharp with E flat in the highest voice (bars 49, 59, 61, 63, 67). In all except bar 61 the chord is rhythmically emphasized by an accent on the arpeggione's top E flat. This extension works well. Another, at the end of the development, where the content is less compelling, is not so successful. Here, through fourteen bars (112–125) he delays the resolution of a perfect cadence (in the tonic) on the first note of the recapitulation.

For the second subject of the first movement Schubert wrote in gentle dance style, to contrast with the lyricism of the opening theme. This is most obvious in bars 41, 43 etc., but is also present in the intervening bars disguised in two-hand form for the pianist, while the arpeggione plays the semiquaver figure. In March 1826 Schubert was to compose his song 'Im Frühling', a strophic setting in G major, with variations in the piano accompaniment and a temporary shift to the minor key in the last verse. In the second verse of the song is found perhaps the most memorable of all examples of Schubert's graceful 'stride bass' – to adopt a jazz term – accompaniments (see Ex. 3.7).

Ex. 3.7

(1828 version)

This kind of writing for the left hand, frequently in quiet or very soft passages, with roots in his dance music and in particular in the *Ecossaises*, is found not infrequently in his piano music in duple time. It occurs in the first movement of the violin and piano 'Duo' Sonata in A in the second E minor section of the exposition already quoted (see Ex. 3.5). In 1823 he used it throughout the third of his six *Moments Musicaux*, D780. In the Arpeggione Sonata the same pattern recurs at the opening of the development section, but now in slower, crotchet form (see Ex. 3.8).

The Arpeggione Sonata and 'Duo' Sonata in A both begin in *allegro moderato* tempo and common time. Each also starts with a solo piano introduction (though of a rather different kind). The 'stride bass' is a common feature. But despite these similarities in their first movements, the two works are fundamentally very different: the one, an early work of surprising maturity; the other a mature work written for an unsympathetic instrument, inspiring music of profundity but also of banality. There is profound depth of feeling in the song-like E major slow movement. Just 71 bars long, it opens with a three-bar piano introduction which could well be the prelude to a reflective Lied. Schubert achieves the intensity and beauty of the opening arpeggione melody, intimate and tender, by several means. The music rarely stays rooted in any key for more than two bars at a time, thus arousing tonal and harmonic expectations which are no sooner awakened than resolved or rejected. Already in the introduction, after only one bar of secure tonic major tonality Schubert introduces in the second bar a diminished seventh chord on G sharp followed, at the end of the bar, by a C natural, the flattened fifth of the supertonic (F sharp). In bars 12–15 tonal ambiguities are anchored by a piano bass descending

Ex. 3.8

scale. Bars 6–7 waver near the dominant key (B); in bars 9–10 there is a suggestion of C sharp minor, in bars 15–17 of E minor, in bar 18 briefly of C major; bars 26–29 slide into C sharp, stressed in the following bar by a Neapolitan chord, which also serves to reverse the tonality in preparation for a comfortable cadence in E major (the tonic). Indeed, the whole movement presents a continuous struggle to break from the tonic, E major tonality, to explore more distant tonal landscapes. But on every occasion the efforts end in failure, with a firm cadential close on the tonic. Just once, in bars 18–19, there is a half close in E minor.

In the brief second part of this movement (bars 34–48) there are both threat and drama. The tonality returns to E minor, a key Schubert now establishes firmly by repeating the second bar (35–36). He then moves to dominant tonality in the fourth bar (37) with sharpened A and C and a disturbing *fp* seventh chord. After further rhythmic augmentation, the music resolves in a rather abrupt, now customary, cadence in E major. These eight bars are then repeated in varied form, and with different tonal excursions, leading, via a final brief move into C major, to a more confident tonic cadence. In the final section, a coda (bars 49–71), a very slow-moving pair of lyrical phrases played by the arpeggione are accompanied by a progression of chords which move from E major through elements of minor tonality and, by way of another Neapolitan harmony, back to the tonic. Particularly remarkable is the progression in bars 61–62, where a suspended minor seventh on G resolves, through a descending semitone, to an augmented sixth on G flat, which to the listener may sound as another minor seventh. Thus Schubert has transformed the simple lyrical material of the opening bars by a series of harmonic and tonal tensions, in association with rhythmic accentuation and augmentation of phrases, into music of concentrated expression and unfailing interest.

The *allegretto* finale, in duple time, is paradoxically 477 short bars long. Despite some delightful content, it is the least acceptable of the movements. The composer's failure to avoid over-use of rhythmic and melodic motifs can arouse aggravation in the listener, even when the performers respond to every dynamic and rhythmic nuance. The movement is in modified sonata rondo form with two episodes; but after the second episode and a modulatory transition, the customary return of the rondo theme is omitted. Instead the first episode follows immediately in the tonic minor. Thus the structure is as shown in Fig. 3. 9 below.

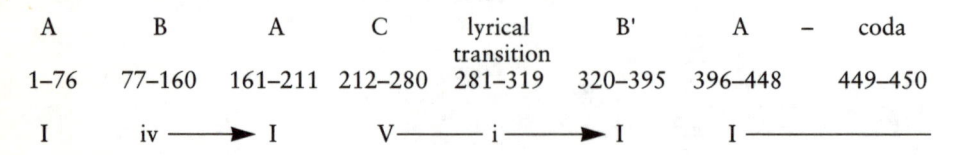

A	B	A	C	lyrical transition	B'	A	–	coda
1–76	77–160	161–211	212–280	281–319	320–395	396–448		449–450
I	iv ⟶ I		V ⟶ i ⟶ I		I			

Figure 3.9 Sonata in A minor for arpeggione and piano – III (Allegretto), in A major

The coda consists of no more than a straight cadence. In his efforts to write for the arpeggione in a manner he thought would be to the tastes of arpeggione-players and audiences, Schubert pushed the instrument further than he had in the first movement. For the arpeggione both episodes, the second (as customary) considerably longer than the first and in two parts, are indeed virtuosic.

If the first two movements of this sonata cannot be included amongst Schubert's greatest works, they are representative of the composer, full of charm, interest and, in the case of the slow movement, beauty. So far in this study I have tried to show how Schubert sometimes achieved success in his compositions, whether intuitively or by methodical structuring. In examining the weaknesses of the last movement of the Arpeggione Sonata, it is evident that Schubert failed here just where he had succeeded before. The movement begins well, and the main theme is related to the opening melody of the first movement (see Ex. 3.9).

The first episode, in D minor, is attractive and varied in content, if harmonically and tonally unadventurous. Was this perhaps on account of limitations imposed

Ex. 3.9

by the instrument for which it was written? Twice Schubert expands a four-bar phrase into six bars (93–98), and into ten in bars 141–150. He uses the same basic rhythm of the rondo theme but reverses the pairing of notes in three bars of a four-bar phrase, as in bars 106–108 (see Ex. 3.10).

Ex. 3.10

In the second episode, the first part (Ci), from bar 212, is light and lively, with a dancing lilt (see Ex. 3.11). In a gentle interlude between the two parts of this episode, in bars 236–240, Schubert's melodic line is derived from the opening of the middle section of the slow movement (bars 34–6) as Ex. 3.12 shows.

The second part of the episode (Cii), from bar 241, derived from the first part (Ci) but more urgent in character, is followed by a variant of the interlude. The second part and associated interlude are repeated in entirety. A third and final part of the episode (Ciii), bars 281–319, almost a codetta, a passage of tender expression and pathos, incorporates a gradual tonal change to the tonic minor and might therefore be considered a transition. An oddity of the finale is that it is in no way a duo for equal partners. It is a solo for arpeggione with piano accompaniment. The only time that the pianist plays anything more than an accompanying role occurs in this codetta and, perhaps significantly, this contains the most appealing moments of the movement, a passage of essentially Schubertian beauty (bars 295–319).

Ex. 3.11

Ex. 3.12

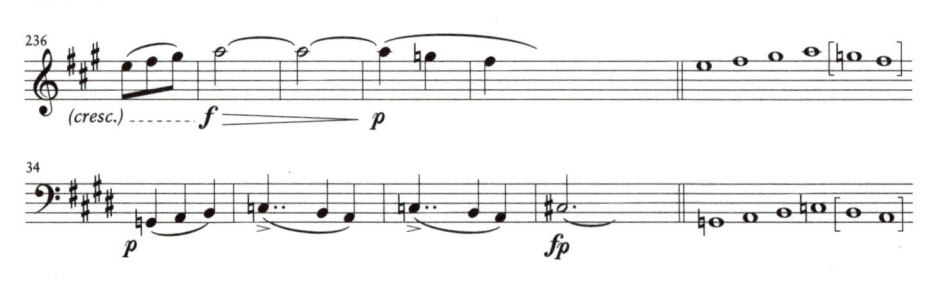

There is a rather obvious way in which Schubert might have improved this last movement and at least avoided tedium. At the end of the second episode he could have omitted the reprise of the first episode (B) and moved instead at once to the final statement of the main rondo theme. This would have created a simple five-part rondo structure: A B A C A (coda) rather than the more complex six-part modified sonata rondo structure. Maybe had he thought of this change, he would have rejected it, preferring the more elaborate structure he had first decided on. But the alteration is surely worth consideration.

As far as is known, Schubert never tried to interest any publisher in this sonata;

in any case, as the instrument soon went out of circulation, his efforts would no doubt have failed. He did, however, retain the manuscript, which passed after his death to his brother Ferdinand. One can but surmise whether Schubert ever considered transcribing it for cello or violin, the form in which it was eventually published in 1871. Since then the sonata has been taken over by cellists and violists, and more recently by clarinettists (and flautists) to enrich their repertoire. As there are no known contemporary reviews of any performances in Schubert's life-time, there is no means of knowing whether it was successful or well written for the instrument.

The Arpeggione Sonata cannot be numbered with Schubert's major compositions of this year, such as the String Quartets in A minor and in D minor, the Octet, the piano duets 'Grand Duo' and A flat Variations, but it is an interesting work which has a place in chamber music recitals. As we have seen, it is also a composition from which we can learn much about Schubert's genius, where he succeeded and where he fell below his own high standards.

Rondo in B minor – 'Rondeau brillant' – for Violin and Piano, D895 (1826)

Andante, Allegro

Almost two years were to elapse before, in October 1826, Schubert composed another string–piano duo, the Rondo in B minor. Meanwhile, in the summer of 1826 his unhealthy financial situation made it impossible for him to take the summer or early autumn holiday which had for the last three years been his custom. On 10 July he wrote to his friend Eduard von Bauernfeld:

> I cannot possibly get to Gmunden or anywhere else, for I have no money at all and altogether things go very badly with me. I do not let it worry me, and am cheerful.
> Anyhow, come to Vienna as soon as possible. Duport[14] wants an opera from me, but the libretti I have so far set do not please at all, so it would be splendid if your libretto were favourably received. Then at least there would be money, maybe fame as well![15]

Schubert's reference to Bauernfeld's libretto of *Der Graf von Gleichen*, which he had been awaiting for some time, implies that he saw the completion of this opera as a possible turning-point in his career and fortunes. This period was one of several in his life when, short of money and running up debts with landlords, innkeepers, tailors, and maybe doctors, he made considerable efforts to sell his compositions to publishers. On 12 August he wrote to both Breitkopf & Härtel and Probst in Leipzig trying to interest them in his compositions. He offered 'songs, string quartets, pianoforte sonatas, 4-handed [piano] pieces etc. etc ... I have also writen an Octet.'[16] Of the two string quartets he wrote early in 1824, only that in A minor, D804, had already been published (in September 1824 by Sauer & Leidersdorf). He was now offering the Leipzig publishers the String Quartet in D minor ('Der Tod und das Mädchen'), D810, and the recently completed (in June) String Quartet in G, D887.

For Schubert the Quartet in G was an important new composition, bringing striking developments in his compositional techniques. It can perhaps be assumed that he wrote the quartet after hearing performances, and maybe also rehearsals, of three of Beethoven's late string quartets, those written for Prince Nikolai Golitsïn. Although there is no conclusive evidence that Schubert was present at any performance of the Beethoven quartets, it is very unlikely that he would willingly have missed such important musical occasions. The first performance of Beethoven's String Quartet in E flat, Op. 127, completed in February 1825, was given on 6 March of that year by the Schuppanzigh Quartet.[17] Between Beethoven's completion of the score and the performance Anton Schindler, in the role of Beethoven's secretary, sent the members of the quartet a contract, which they duly signed and returned:

MOST EXCELLENT FELLOWS!

> Each of you is receiving herewith his part. And each of you undertakes to do his duty and, what is more, pledges himself on his word of honour to acquit himself as well as possible, to distinguish himself and to vie in excellence with the others.
> Each of you who is participating in the said undertaking must sign this paper.
>
> BEETHOVEN
Schindler secretarius
>
> Schuppanzigh,
>   Weiss,
>   Linke,
> the accursed cello of the great master
>   Holz,
> the last of all, but only when signing this paper[18]

The players were Ignaz Schuppanzigh and Karl Holz (violins), Franz Weiss (viola) and Josef Linke (cello), all of whom were well-known to Schubert as colleagues, if not friends. The same musicians also gave performances of Schubert's own chamber works on several occasions.

The premiere of Beethoven's Op. 127 was not a success. On this occasion the composer blamed last-minute changes of personnel in Schuppanzigh's quartet for an inadequate performance which gave the work no chance. Less than three weeks later, on 23 March, it was performed again, played this time by a quartet led by Joseph Michael Böhm[19] in a concert organized by Böhm for his own benefit.[20] Böhm's musicians performed the quartet to a much higher standard than had Schuppanzigh's, and Beethoven's work was now received with considerable enthusiasm. According to the composer, the same Quartet in E flat had, by 10 July, 'been splendidly performed six times by other artists and received with great applause.'[21] The quartet was published (by Schott in Leipzig) in December 1825.[22] It is very improbable that Schubert could have missed all these early performances and most likely that he heard more than one.

Schubert was on holiday with Vogl in Upper Austria and the Salzkammergut at the time of the two early, private performances, on 9 and 11 September 1825, of Beethoven's next quartet, that in A minor, Op. 132.[23] This five-movement quartet Beethoven completed in July of the same year. Again it is difficult to believe that Schubert would have missed without good reason its first public performance, by the Schuppanzigh quartet on 6 November, after his return to Vienna. In December 1825 Beethoven completed the third of his Golitsïn quartets, that in B flat, Op. 130, in six movements. This was premiered by Schuppanzigh and his colleagues on 21 March 1826.

The impact on Schubert of these quartets, and later those in C sharp minor, Op. 131 and in F, Op. 135, both completed in 1826, must have been considerable. It may also have resulted in a more than two-year delay (from early 1824 until June 1826) before he composed the third of his own trilogy of string quartets, that in G major, his last work in this genre. There can be little doubt that changes in his own string-quartet language and the evolutionary process of these changes were largely the result of his experience of Beethoven's Golitsïn quartets.

According to his autograph manuscript, Schubert composed the String Quartet in G in ten days between 20 and 30 June. It is however likely that these dates apply only to that period during which, as was now often his custom, working from sketches dating from an earlier period, he completed and wrote out the full and final quartet score. Schubert selected the first movement of this quartet as the opening number in his benefit concert at the *Musikverein* in March 1828, when it was played by Böhm, Holz, Weiss and Linke, each of whom, as we have seen, had been involved in performances of Beethoven's late string quartets. The influence of Beethoven extended beyond the G major Quartet into Schubert's later chamber music in general, and in particular to the manner in which he composed for the violin.

Four months after completing the string quartet, Schubert composed his Rondo brillant in B minor. This was a showpiece written for Karl Maria von Bocklet, his Czech piano-virtuoso friend, and for Bocklet's twenty-year-old friend Josef Slawjk, who had recently arrived in Vienna hoping to make a career for himself as a violinist. The Rondo brillant received its first performance, with Schubert in the audience, at the home of the publisher, Domenico Artaria. The date of the performance is uncertain, but it was surely around the time that Artaria published the work on 19 April 1827.[24] The musical content of the quartet and this Rondo brillant are poles apart; and yet there are two pointers to their being composed within a short period of time. Firstly, there is a fast minor-scale motif in the slow movement of the quartet which speaks the same language as the opening motif of the Rondo's slow (*andante*) introduction (see Ex. 3.13a and b). Secondly, the opening cello theme in the slow movement of the quartet may have encouraged Schubert in his transferring of the violin theme in the Rondo *andante* into a cello-like melodic bass line for the piano from bar 20 (see Ex. 3.14a and b). However, the main *allegro* section of the rondo which follows is dominated not by the string quartet quality but by Schubert's knowledge and experience of Czech music, an

Ex. 3.13a Rondo in B minor

Ex. 3.13b String Quartet in G – second movement

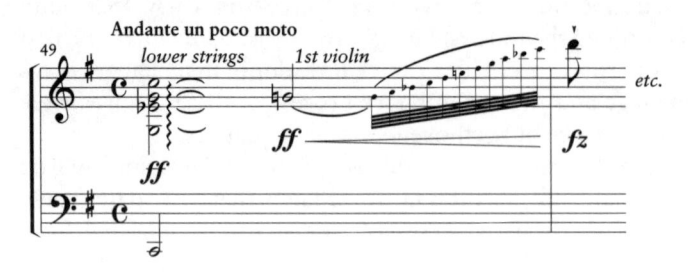

Ex. 3.14a String Quartet in G – second movement

Ex. 3.14b String Quartet in G – second movement

important part of his own musical heritage in Vienna, where many Czech musicians congregated and worked as performers and composers.

In the same October as he was composing the Rondo, Schubert was also working on his fine lyrical Piano Sonata in G, D894. His previous sonata for piano, that in D, D850, an extrovert work of great energy, dated from August 1825, when he was in Gastein. This he had dedicated to Bocklet on its publication in April 1826.

Some elements of the final Allegretto rondo movement of the G major Sonata reappear in more forceful form in the Allegro of the duo Rondo: the repeated rhythmic cell ♪♪♪♪ ♪♪ pervades both movements; the pattern of the melody in bars 57–62 of the *Rondo* is related, though inverted, to bars 8–13 of the sonata rondo movement (see Ex. 3.15).

Ex. 3.15a

Ex. 3.15b

However, in general the similarities between the two works are slight. The differences, on the other hand, are considerable. The sonata is an introverted expression of Schubert's complex inner world – both his concern with gentler sensitivities and the desperations and anger of a man tormented by mental and physical anguish. The Rondo, however, is not chamber music. It is an extrovert piece written for public or semi-public performance, calculated to exploit the musical personalities and technical prowess of the performers, Bocklet and Slawjk. After its publication, a reviewer in the *Weiner Zeitschrift für Kunst, Theater, Literatur und Mode* of 7 June 1828 described the composer of the Rondo in B minor, more renowned as a creator of songs than of instrumental music, as:

> a bold master of harmony, who gives his picture a strong, vigorous fundamental tone and within that knows how to unite his shapes and groups in such a way that they all contribute to the making of a beautiful whole. A fiery imagination animates this piece and draws the player to the depths and height of harmony, borne now by a mighty hurricane, now by gentle waves.[25]

Of the piece, the critic continued:

> Although the whole is brilliant, it is not indebted for its existence to mere figurations ... The inventive spirit has here often beaten its wings mightily enough and lifted us up with it. Both the pianoforte and the fiddle require a practical artist, who must be prepared for passages which have not established their right to be there by instant repetition, but which rather announce a new, inspired train of ideas. The player will feel attracted in an interesting way by beautiful shifts in the harmonies.[26]

As was discussed in Part I of this study, an *allegro* Rondo with or without slow introduction was one of the most popular forms of solo (or duo) performance in all Vienna's concerts. Schubert's Rondo brillant in B minor was created in this mould. It is a long work – 713 bars in total – with an elaborate structure. The *andante* slow-moving introduction, 49 bars long, is in simple ternary (ABA) form. The opening section is made up of four basic ideas: the piano's double-dotted rhythmic motif with rising bass (i); and immediately after this, a perfect cadence under a rising semitone (ii); a fast upward scale for the violin (iii); and an ornamental figure beginning and ending on C sharp, which is voiced in turn by piano and violin (iv) (see Ex. 3.16 i–iv).

Ex. 3.16 i–iv

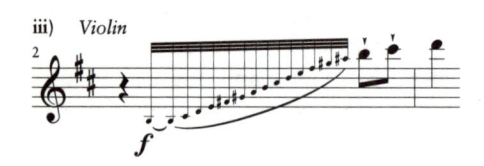

There follows a lyrical section, with violin melody and flowing piano accompaniment. The violin and piano left-hand then exchange roles, with the melody now in the bass, *quasi* cello (as already mentioned above). This begins in the tonic major, but passes through several keys, including A flat, G and E majors, before returning to B major for the reprise of the first section. The semitone motif (ii) and violin scales (iii) now fall rather than rise. In the last six bars, in the minor mode, motifs (i) and (iv) are combined with a further persistent motif, a rising tone – B to C sharp – in the upper voices. In the final appearance of this two-note motif, it takes the form of an unharmonised *pianissimo* statement by piano and violin in octaves.

Schubert's string and piano duos 97

The same two notes become the opening motif of the *allegro* Rondo which follows immediately (see Ex. 3.17a).

Ex. 3.17a

[Musical example: Violin and Pianoforte, marked Allegro, with bar 49, dynamics p and ff]

This motif (v), along with the four motifs of the opening slow introduction referred to above (i–iv), provide the inspiration for much of the Rondo.

It is perhaps interesting at this juncture to compare the opening of the Rondo with that of Beethoven's Kreutzer Sonata, Op.47, another virtuosic work. Both Schubert's Rondo and Beethoven's first movement begin with a majestic slow introduction. The final bars in each case and in a similar manner introduce the two-note motif which becomes the germ of the fast movement which follows: in Schubert's case, a rising major second (see Ex. 3.17a, above); in Beethoven's, a rising minor second, as Ex. 3.17b shows.

Ex. 3.17b

[Musical example: Violin, Adagio sostenuto to Presto, dynamics pp and sfp]

Although this is the only duo piece which Schubert entitled 'Rondo', the hybrid rondo/sonata first-movement form had long been a favourite for him. It is relevant at this juncture to take a sideways look at his sonata rondo and hybrid movements, both for duo and for solo piano, and to observe some of the ways in which he adapted the structures to different circumstances, and at different times in his life up to this point. To recapitulate, for the last movement of his first violin and piano sonatina of 1816, Schubert adopted the simple A B A B′ A–coda form with transitions (see Figure 3.6, p. 78). For the second sonatina, written in the same month, the episode was in two keys:

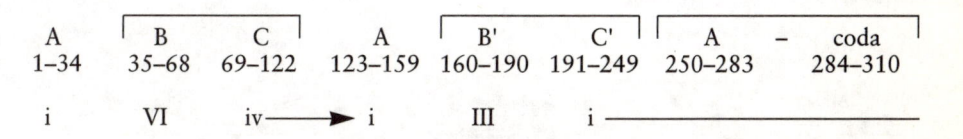

A	B	C	A	B′	C′	A	–	coda
1–34	35–68	69–122	123–159	160–190	191–249	250–283		284–310
i	VI	iv ⟶	i	III	i			

Figure 3.10   Sonata for violin and piano in A minor – IV (Allegro)

The structure of the second is clearly more complex than that of the first, but still far simpler than those of his string quartets written a year or so earlier. However, structural details of Schubert's hybrid form were always changing. Just as he extended basic sonata first-movement form by creating three- or even four-key expositions, as in the first movement of the 1817 Duo Sonata in A, and then reduced the length of the development, so he now complicated his rondos with three-key and multi-sectional rondo themes (A) and episodes (B). As his themes and episodes became more complicated and longer, so he tended to shorten them on their reappearances. An example of this is found in the finale of the solo Piano Sonata in A minor, D845, of April 1825. However, in the last movements of the Piano Sonatas in D, D850, and in G, D894, of August 1825 and October 1826, he adopted a different structure: whereas the rondo and episode sections had lengthened considerably, he now reverted to the standard rondo form, A B A C A – coda. This was also the outline structure he employed for the Rondo brillant in B minor here under discussion.

The Rondo theme A is in three short parts, while both episodes, B and C, are in four parts. A detailed plan of the movement is found in Figures 3.11a and b. As can be seen, the main development of material occurs in the two episodes, B being almost three times, and C four times, as long as the rondo section A. Melodic and rhythmic links between the slow introduction and the rondo are to be found in the opening section of the second episode. The thematic structure of the opening *andante* bars is the source of the theme of this episode, but now in G major; and the double-dotted rhythm is modified in the Allegro to a single-dotted crotchet (see Ex. 3.18).

Ex. 3.18

Schubert's string and piano duos 99

A
49–101 rondo section in 3 parts, each beginning with rising BC♯ motif (v) originating in final bars of *andante* introduction.

    a) 49–64, first theme   i
    b) 65–82, lyrical second theme   I
    c) 83–101, third theme: unresolved final cadence   I

transition¹ – based on *andante* motif (v), BC♯   V–III
102–110

B
110–269 first episode: in 4 sections, ab, a'c, each in open binary form

    a) 110–139, *pp* 'fanfare' theme   III
    b) 139–192, development of material from a):
        tonalities – v,(ii,vi),v,V, (iii), ♭I, III   v–III
    a') 192–208, shortened restatement of a), leading into: III
    c) 208–269, new lyrical theme (219–231, 239–262) derived from *andante*
        theme (13–14, 21–22), punctuated by thematic material from a (a')   III–V–III

transition² – including *allegro* version (269–276) of final bars of
269–280 *andante* (44-49)   III–i

A
280–332 restatement of rondo section (as A above)   i–I

transition³
333–345 – as transition¹ above, extended   V–III–VI

C
345–569 second episode: in 4 sections, ab, a'b'

    a) 345–413, lyrical theme, rhythm (now single dotted) derived   VI
        from *andante* opening motif (i); violin melody of 403–412
        from *andante* violin line of 18–20
    b) 413–467, development of a) *animato*,   vi–♮II
        tonalities vi, (I, ii, III,VI) ♮II
    a') 467–526, repeat of a) in ♭IV   ♭IV
    b') 527–569, repeat of b)   vi–VI

transition⁴
569–585 – varied version of transition²   VI–i

A
585–652 restatement of rondo section (as A above) extended and with   i–III–I
    3 parts in i, III, I

transition⁵
652–667 extended version of transition¹   i–I

Coda – *più mosso*   I
667–713 – bars 667–682 based on 178–191
        683–686..........208–211
        687–699..........106–109

Figure 3.11a   Rondo in B minor – Allegro

A	trans-ition[1]	B	trans-ition[2]	A	trans-ition[3]	C	trans-ition[4]	A	trans-ition[5]	coda
49–101	102–110	110–269	269–280	280–332	333–345	345–569	569–585	585–651	652–667	667–713
i–I	V–III	III	III ⟶ i	V–VI	VI	VI ⟶ i	i–I	I
b–B	F♯–D	D	D ⟶ b	F♯–G	G	G ⟶ b	b–B	B

Figure 3.11b   Rondo in B minor – Allegro: basic structure

An ornamental motif in bars 223–224 of the short lyrical passage of the first episode of the rondo comes from the violin melody in bars 13–14 of the Andante, also repeated in the piano bass of bars 21–22, as shown in Ex. 3.19.

Ex. 3.19

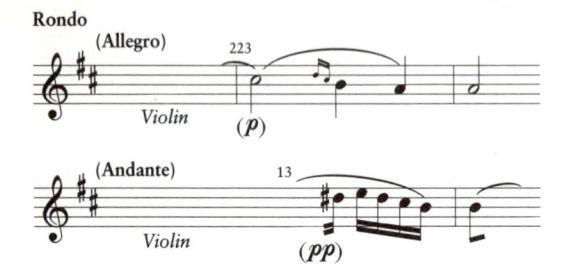

In the second episode, the *tranquillo* violin passage in bars 403–412 is a quotation from the violin passage in the introduction, bars 18–20 (Ex. 3.20).

Ex. 3.20

Also, the bridge passages, or transitions, from each episode back to the rondo theme are derived from the final bars of the introduction.

Schubert's avoidance of tonic cadences is particularly marked in this rondo, as indicated in three places in Figure 3.11a. This avoidance is interesting when considered in the context of his previous string–piano duo, the Arpeggione Sonata, in which he tended to overstate full-close cadences.

This is a full-length work, with good tunes and invigorating rhythms. The skill with which Schubert presents, develops and re-uses material is impressive. If there are no great harmonic surprises or, in the rondo, rather few moments of tenderness or Schubertian pathos, there is an abundance of tonal excursions to fascinate and keep interest alive. Indeed, the music passes through either the major or minor key, and mostly both, of every note of the chromatic scale, even if some of these modulations are of only brief duration.

The Rondo in B minor is a vigorous and exciting piece with many extremes of sound levels in close proximity. For this reason, careful observation of the composer's dynamic markings is desirable, and particularly so when performances are on modern instruments, with their considerable potential for extremes of sound levels which are seldom appropriate in music of an earlier age. This is a grand work, perhaps intended as the climax of a concert programme; and it certainly does not deserve the neglect which it has suffered.

Fantasia in C for Violin and Piano, D934 (1827)

Andante molto – Allegretto
Andantino

Tempo primo (Andante molto) – Allegro vivace – Allegretto – Presto

In December 1827, a little over a year after Schubert composed the Rondo brillant in B minor, he wrote what was to be his last, or last surviving, string–piano duo: the Fantasia in C for violin and piano. Neither his surviving autograph manuscript nor the first edition, published in 1850, includes in the title the tonality 'in C', now customarily included. The tonal structure of the work, given in Figure 3.12 below, might suggest that this 'in C' would be better omitted, although it remains in the title in this article.

The Fantasia, like the Rondo brillant was a concert piece and not a chamber work. It was again written for Slawjk and Bocklet, who played it on Sunday 20 January 1828 as the final work in a mid-day benefit concert for Slawjk in the Landhaussaal in Vienna. The Fantasia dates from the same month as Schubert's second set of Four Impromptus, D935, for solo piano, and the completion of the Piano Trio in E flat, D929, which he had begun in November. Each of these three works, like most of the piano music he was composing at this time, was written for Bocklet to perform, and shows the influence of Bocklet's pianism on Schubert's compositions for the piano. The Fantasia is written in three distinct but continuous movements, separated by a short pause or caesura. (A short pause is also written into the music before the *presto* coda of the last movement.) As the three movements incorporate seven sections in different tempi and tonalities, one must wonder whether Schubert, in planning the structure of this work, was influenced not only by the 'Fantasia' element, but also by the commanding example of Beethoven's Golitsïn string quartets and possibly the Op. 130 Quartet in particular.

It is likely that Slawjk, who commissioned the work from Schubert, was familiar with the 'Forelle' variations in the Piano Quintet which Schubert had composed for Sylvester Paumgartner in 1819, and the 'Trockne Blumen' variations for flute and piano written for Ferdinand Bogner in 1824, and that Slawjk now asked the composer to include in the Fantasia a set of variations on another of his Lieder, 'Sei mir gegrüsst'. Schubert obliged, placing the set of variations at the centre of the work, as the second, Andantino, movement. In a strikingly novel manner, he returned to the song for a single and final variation in the Allegretto section of the last movement. He also introduced into the same movement, in the tempo primo section, a shortened but still sizable portion of the opening slow introduction to the first movement. With these reprises of materials from the earlier movements, Schubert was aiming at creating unity in the fantasia, perhaps with Beethoven's innovative recent string quartets still working in his mind.

Slawjk's benefit concert was advertised in the *Weiner allgemeine Theater Zeitung* of 17 January. In a review in the same paper on 29 January,[27] the writer informed his readers that in this concert the Fantasia was not a success with the audience. It was better suited to a more sophisticated musical public. While Bocklet's performance confirmed him as a 'supreme master' of the piano, Slawjk experienced some technical difficulties with the virtuoso violin part. In *Der Sammler* of 7 February, the critic wrote that the Fantasia:

> rather outlasted the time which the average Viennese is prepared to devote to the pleasures of the intellect. The hall gradually emptied, and your correspondent confesses that he too is unable to say anything about how this composition ended.[28]

In other words, the music 'went on' too long, and many of the audience walked out before it was over. The critic of *La Revue musicale* (Paris) claimed that Schubert's Fantasia earned unanimous praise, but reserved his greatest compliments for other concerts which had been given around this time by the cellist Bernard Romberg, 'son of the celebrated composer of the same name'.[29] In July 1828 the London *Harmonicon* caught up with Slawjk's concert, describing the Fantasia as possessing 'merit far above the common order', although – and the writer may well have been the same Viennese critic who contributed to *La Revue musicale* – he claimed that Romberg's concerts were more exciting than Slawjk's.[30]

The basic structure of the Fantasia is represented in Figure 3.12, which makes clear the manner in which Schubert again bound the long, continuous (except for pause bars) fantasia together by returning to material from earlier movements in the final movement. The work opens with a slow-moving, sustained Andante molto introduction, the style of the music essentially central European, if not immediately recognizable as Czech or Bohemian. Here, in the opening eight bars,

				Bars
Movement I	– (1)	Andante molto (slow introduction) –	C major	1–36
	(2)	Allegretto (A B C A B' D)	– A minor	37–350
		PAUSE		351
Movement II	– (3)	Andantino, theme and 3 variations and coda	– A flat	352–480
		SHORT PAUSE		480
Movement III	– (1')	Tempo I°, as (1) above, curtailed and altered	– C major	481–493
	– (4)	Allegro vivace, rondo	– C major	494–639
	– (3')	Allegretto, 4th variation of Andantino theme (3)	– A flat	640–664
		PAUSE		665
		– coda Presto, based on (4)	– C major	666–701

Figure 3.12 Fantasia in C – basic structure

the major–minor dichotomy in this Fantasia, which is also a common feature in much of Schubert's music, prepares the way for the tonal ambiguities that follow, not least of these the A minor tonality of the Allegretto.

The pianist's continuous *tremolando* passages in the first seventeen bars, and subsequent fast upward scales, falling arpeggio figurations in thirds, and wide leaps for the left hand, all to be played *pianissimo* and with utmost delicacy, accompany the violin's soaring theme with atmospheric intensity. The introduction finally comes to rest with a pause on the final chord, the dominant of A minor, the tonality of the Allegretto which follows. This faster and main section of the first movement starts with a lively Czech dance-like theme, the opening motif of which, without the anacrusis, corresponds to the first four notes of the violin melody in the opening slow introduction – in C minor (see Ex. 3.21).

Ex. 3.21

As Figure 3.13 shows, the Allegretto of the first movement is in a form close to that of sonata first-movements, with three-key exposition and no development. It is also marked by the absence of a full close (cadence) at the end of the exposition and the recapitulation.

A	B	C	trans-ition	A	B'	D	trans-ition
36–83	83–131	131–159	159–181	182–219	219–263	263–335	335–351
I	I—V	V	V–i (no final cadence)	i	III…i	I…♭v	♭V–♭I (no final cadence)

Exposition: 1st group, 2nd group — Recapitulation: 1st group, 2nd group

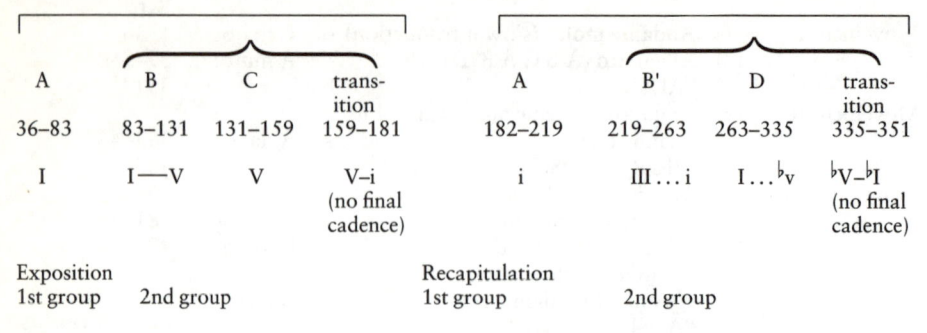

Figure 3.13   Fantasia in C – I – Allegretto, in A minor

In the first A-major section of the second group – B – Schubert adopted his favoured sequential treatment of the theme: by repetition at the interval of a falling third (A – F♯– D – b) before E major is reached. On its repeat in C major – B' – the tonal relationships are similar (C – a – F – d). Section C is an extended passage using material from section B, in which over 29 bars the dominant, E major, is firmly established. Section D, of 73 bars length, is considerably longer than C, and uses material from sections A and B, modulating widely but now at the interval of a rising fifth (a – e – b – f♯) before settling in E flat, the dominant of A flat. The predominance throughout this first movement of tonalities i, I, V and ♭V, generally associated with sonata first-movement form, is evident. A silent bar lengthened by a pause is all that separates this movement from the theme and variations second movement, in A flat, which follows.

Some critics have harshly criticised Schubert for taking his beautiful song 'Sei mir gegrüsst', written some six years earlier, and treating it in these variations in what they consider to be a vulgar manner. I would dispute this judgement. The song was published in April 1823, in the key of B flat. It was headed at the start both *langsam* and *pianissimo*: to be played in slow tempo and very softly. In the Fantasia Schubert directed that the theme, now somewhat amended, be played *andantino* and *piano*, rather faster than the song (but slower than *andante*) and softly. The theme section climaxes in the second half with a *fortissimo*; but so did each verse of the song. However, the main concern of critics is not so much the tempo or loudness but the style of variations 1–3, the centre-piece of the work. A virtuoso *tour-de-force* for first the pianist, then the violinist, and finally both together. The dynamic levels for much of these variations are, like the theme, *piano* and *pianissimo*, despite the louder climaxes. But clearly, the emphasis in performance of these variations was not meant to be obtrusive virtuosity, but rather lightness of touch, achieved only with difficulty on today's instruments, and especially on the modern piano. As far as Schubert was concerned, he wrote the Fantasia at the special request of his friends. If the performers and audience were not offended by Schubert's adaptation of his own song, maybe we, a hundred and seventy years later, should not be over-respectful in our attitudes but accept Schubert's use of his own material. His purpose was not vulgar self-plagiarism for commercial ends but, whether we like it or not, the honest and generous advertisement of the musicianship and technical facility of his friends through his music.

At the end of the variation movement, a final statement of the theme leads naturally into a gentle coda including further passages of Czech character, as the music sinks again to a brief stillness, with a pause on a quaver rest. Out of the silence there emerges an echo of the opening bars of the slow introduction to the first movement, a passage of shimmering beauty. Whereas on its initial appearance this whole section (36 bars) had remained at a gentle sound level and finally died away completely, on this reappearance in the last movement the music builds up to a *fortissimo* climax, which in turn leads directly into the *allegro vivace* of the last movement.

In this finale, a monothematic movement, Schubert reverted to the hybrid rondo sonata structure and, in this instance, one of some complexity (see Figure 3.14).

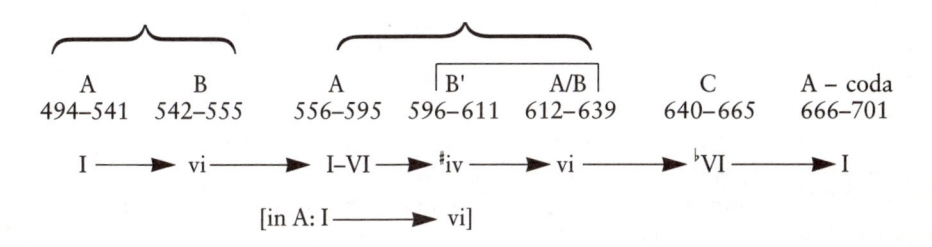

A	B	A	B'	A/B	C	A – coda
494–541	542–555	556–595	596–611	612–639	640–665	666–701
I →	vi →	I-VI →	♯iv →	vi →	♭VI →	I
		[in A: I →		vi]		

Figure 3.14   Fantasia in C – III – Allegro vivace

(Towards the end of the first appearance of the rondo theme A, in bars 526–527, 534–535, 580–581 and 588–589 there are echoes of an idea taken from the first movement of Beethoven's 'Archduke' Piano Trio, bars 76 etc.)

For the second episode, C, which is not preceded by the usual tonic statement of the rondo theme A, Schubert placed a new, fourth, variation of the 'Sei mir gegrüsst' theme of the A flat slow movement, now again in A flat but in the slightly faster *allegretto* tempo. His preparation in the final bars of the A/B section for this episode bears comparison with the similar final bars of the A minor section, B. A dominant seventh chord in the last bar of B (bar 555) resolves cadentially, as prepared, into the tonic relative major (C major) in bar 556, ready for the return of the rondo theme. A similar dominant seventh at the end of the corresponding F sharp minor section B', (in bar 611) resolves (in bar 616) not into the prepared relative major (A major) at the start of A/B, but into the unprepared key of A minor. Thus the C major/A minor tension built up in the two parts of the first movement (*andante molto* and *allegretto*) returns here before the fourth 'Sei mir gegrüsst' variation of section C.

Although the key structure of the *allegro vivace* section on paper shows some daring, there are too many long sections in C major. When tonal monotony is compounded with the predominance of repeated tonic, dominant and sub-dominant harmonies, and the over-persistent rhythmic pattern ¢ ♩♩♩|♩♩♪ 𝄾 ♩|, the result verges on the tedious, or exasperating. There is no real development of material and, with close similarities between themes and a general lack of variety, Schubert fails to maintain the excitement for which he was presumably aiming. When at its frenetic climax, in the A/B section, the momentum is abruptly stilled by the re-entry of the slow movement melody, in the role of a further and a new episode, this comes as a relief. It is an entirely fresh presentation of the song theme, elegant and gently flowing, a beautiful reminiscence, eventually subsiding onto a silent pause. But the new-found calm is shattered totally as the somewhat perfunctory *presto* coda bursts in with a *fortissimo* flag-waving finish.

Schubert's autograph manuscript of the Fantasia, a tidy first draft with later amendments, has survived and is preserved in the Wiener Stadt- und Landesbibliothek. The title page is headed in Schubert's hand 'Fantasie für Pianoforte u. Violon', and signed 'Dec. 1827. Frz. Schubertmpia'. It is clear from the manuscript that he composed the music, whether from earlier sketches or not, in a continuous fluent manner and in a short space of time. There are a fair number of alterations, many of them minor, but of particular relevance to interpreting the work in performance. Others are more fundamental.

The small amendments are usually associated with phrasing and articulation. Schubert did not always include all directive markings in this score, especially in repeated passages, and he was sometimes inconsistent. Be that as it may, within every section in which accents feature, these are not restricted entirely to one particular beat or half-beat of a bar. Nothing can be taken for granted. He was very concerned with the manner of articulating notes, and indicated how this should be done in several ways, including the use of accents, which written as > signified an accent regardless of the length of the note. He had three different ways of signifying that a note should be played non-legato. A dot over or under a note always implied a shortening of an unaccented and usually *piano* note. The short horizontal line – or ∪ on a note might sometimes be a slip of the pen when writing a dot, but sometimes seems more deliberate, implying a stronger, detached note which may or may not be on a normally unaccented beat. A short vertical line appeared most often in loud passages where it suggested notes should be detached but not too short, and stressed.[31] If these markings are carefully distinguished by performers of his music, they contribute a strong rhythmic variety to any interpretation; for both accents and articulation marks sometimes reveal elements of Schubert's phrasing which otherwise are blurred.

In another amendment to his score, Schubert deleted the violin line in the second section of the first movement, bars 109–110, 113–114, etc., so that the piano could come through more clearly (see Ex. 3.22).

Ex. 3.22

[musical example]

Of more fundamental alterations, one of the most interesting occurs in bars 3 and 4 of the Introduction, repeated in bars 7 and 8. As far as I have been able to discern from the autograph manuscript which, in its altered form, is not easy to read, the composer's original harmonic pattern for these bars was simpler than in the final version. The alterations he made created a far richer harmonic progression, of the kind that stamps much of his music with genius – see Ex. 3.23.

Ex. 3.23

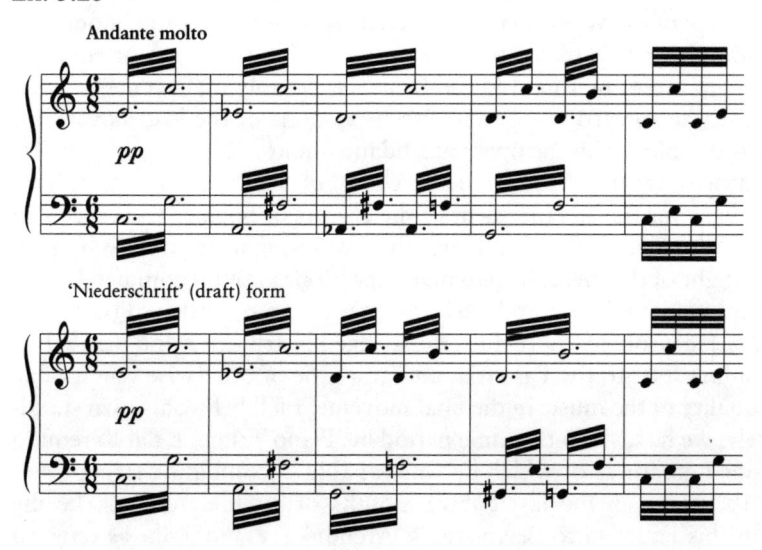

[musical example]

'Niederschrift' (draft) form

[musical example]

This particular passage is one of those in Schubert's music which calls to mind some of Wagner's harmonic jewels. With these amended harmonies at the very opening of the Fantasia, the listener is immediately prepared for, or led to expect, a Fantasia of serious personal content, if not of drama and pathos. The introduction now flows smoothly. The piano tones rustle and sway, rise and fall, while the violin sustains the slow melody of dignity and passion, expressing positive hope through the gentle off-beat octave lifts in a lyrical line otherwise dominated by conjunct intervals. This is music both noble and expressive. Unfortunately, not all that follows is of the same excellence.

The early nineteenth-century fantasia, which was now overwhelmingly replacing the sonata in popularity, had a romantic role to fulfil which the classical sonata could not. In a fantasia, an autobiographical content was permitted, if not expected. The composer, unrestricted by prescribed classical structures and philosophy, was free to express whatever he thought appropriate and, as it transpired, frequently in personal terms. In the Fantasia in C we experience in striking fashion the state of Schubert's mind in the final year of his life. He was suffering from symptoms of syphilitic illness that must have caused him alarm for his long-term future, and also from the effects of its treatment. The illness, its treatment, and Schubert's way of life, which was not always in his own best interest, had a cumulative effect on his generic cyclothymic temperament. He was now probably to some degree psychotically manic-depressive, subject to distressing mood swings. In his calmer, normal state he had hopes and plans, sensitivities to beauty and tender emotions, sublime stillness and vision. In depressions the world around him was full of darkness, his inner world one of despair and extreme anger, probably also of great fear and foreboding. In manic mood, he had wild enthusiasms, obsessions to be with people, to talk, to drink and to spend money; and he had almost unlimited energies. When manic, his creative powers were phenomenal. When depressed, composing music was impossible. Manifestations of some of these characteristics are to be found in the Fantasia, notably manic energy, even self-indulgence, in the Allegro vivace and Presto sections of the last movement, and sensitivity and sublimity in the opening Andante molto.

The Fantasia was written with some freedom of structural ideas. It was intended as a vehicle for the advancement of the careers of Bocklet and especially Slawjk, and for the financial advantages that it brought to the composer. Whatever he thought of the piece, he had no reservations about recommending it, a few weeks after its completion and performance, to the publishers Probst and Schott in Leipzig. He wrote no more duos for stringed instruments and piano. It is sad that, after a fine start to the Fantasia, and at a time of otherwise remarkable fecundity, the quality of the music in the final movement fell below his own standards. Fortunately, we have from the same period his Piano Trio in E flat to remind us of the sustained greatness of which he was capable in combining string tones with those of the piano in the last twelve months of his life. And maybe the brief allusion in this Fantasia to Beethoven's 'Archduke' Piano Trio, as referred to above, is indicative already of Schubert's preoccupation with his own piano trio.[32]

Summary

This survey of Schubert's seven string–piano duos has covered his adult life, from the age of nineteen to less than a year before his death. Of them all, the first three, written for domestic use, have been most performed. They are standard works of the amateur and student repertoire. The fourth, the Sonata in A, a very personal work and a favourite among performers, professsional and amateur, was composed for the private concert scene – domestic and salon. It embraces in its music the emotional characteristics of humanity, tenderness, warmth and sense of fun associated with the music of Schubert's earlier works, those written before he was struck down with illness and serious, though intermittent, mental anguish. After this, all the duos were composed for particular people and performances, presumably with some financial advantages to himself.

The first of these was the Arpeggione Sonata, arguably more popular today with cellists and violists than with their audiences. Certain similarities, though superficial, between the first movement and that of the violin Sonata in A might suggest that Schubert looked with some affection on the earlier sonata before he began the Arpeggione Sonata. His first task after agreeing to compose for this new instrument was to explore its technical practicalities, and the kind and style of music most suited to it. With this accomplished, and some remaining doubts as to the long-term value of the instrument, let alone how he was to write the sonata, he had to ignite some creative fuse before inspiration would flow. The Sonata in A for violin and piano could have been that fuse. Once he had begun the Arpeggione Sonata, he produced a work which inspires affection in many, of charm and spirit, somewhat flawed (especially in the over-long final movement), but surely unique in its kind and character.

The last two duos, the Rondo brillant in B minor and Fantasia in C are not chamber works. They are of a totally different nature – less intimate, altogether longer and more complicated in structure. Schubert had recently experienced the late string quartets of Beethoven, and recognized the momentous importance of the novel construction and content of these chamber works. Both the Rondo and Fantasia are essentially Schubertian, but they belong to those of his compositions which are least understood and excite least admiration and affection. To place them in context: they were written for performance in public or semi-public venues, for concerts of mixed musical fare. As such they, along with compositions of Paganini also for stringed instrument (violin) and piano, are some of the first concert pieces of this kind to have survived and remained in print.

An examination of the structure of each of the duos in turn has shown how Schubert, reared on classical forms, composed his first duos in rather conventional structures. Yet he soon began to experiment, as he already had in his string quartets, with new ways of expressing the romantic ideas and ideals which were increasingly influencing and permeating his thinking. He moved away from the multi-movement format of his first four duos to the freer structures of the Arpeggione Sonata, Rondo brillant in B minor and Fantasia, with interconnected sections and movements, and more complex tonal and harmonic structures.

In the period of writing his string-piano duos, 1816–27, Schubert developed from a young composer of the late classical period into a mature composer of increasingly romantic persuasion. Knowing this, and being aware of both the musical culture in which he was working and the fact that he was frequently ill and depressed, we can arrive at a better understanding of these duos.

Acknowledgements

I am deeply indebted to Dr Nicholas Marston (St Peter's College, Oxford) who helped me greatly in the analytical sections of this paper, and made various other illuminatory suggestions. Any remaining errors are mine. My thanks are also due to Dr Suzannah Clark (Merton College, Oxford) who also read the paper, and contributed some useful comments, and to Dr Otto Biba, Archivdirektor of the Gesellschaft der Musikfreunde in Vienna, and Dr Otto Brusatti, Bibliotheksrat of the Wiener Stadt- und Landesbibliothek.

Sources

Details of the works studied in this chapter may be found in O E Deutsch's *Franz Schubert. Thematisches Verzeichnis seiner Werke*, Kassel, 1978–97.

On publication, each of the duos with violin was designated for 'pianoforte and violin', in that order. Only the Arpeggione Sonata, not published until 1871, appeared for '*arpeggione* or violoncello and pianoforte'.

Notes and references

1. O E Deutsch, *Schubert: A Documentary Biography* (London, 1946) (hereinafter referred to as *Documents*), 54–5, 58–9.
2. The Violin Concerto in D, D345, which also dates from 1816 and has survived in full score written in Ferdinand's hand, was almost certainly the work not of Schubert but of Ferdinand; and this despite Ferdinand's claim in the manuscript that it was written by Franz 'für seinen Bruder Ferdinand'. *Schubert durch die Brille*, journal of the International Franz Schubert Institute [*Brille*], 5 (1990), 57–9.
3. *Documents*, 60.
4. With similar concern for great music of an earlier age, Baron Gottfried van Sweiten (1733–1803) in the latter part of the eighteenth century championed the music of J.S. Bach and Handel in Vienna.
5. The following are examples of the content of *Concerts spirituels*: 1 March, 1827 – Beethoven's Overture to *Die Weihe des Hauses*, Mozart's Symphony in C, Overture and Chorus from Handel's *Israel in Egypt*; two weeks later – overture to Abbé Vogler's opera *Samori*, Trio in E minor and Chorus from Mozart's oratorio *Davidde penitente*, Beethoven's Ninth Symphony.

6. Schuppannzigh was sick. His place was taken by Böhm.
7. The songs of this period do not rank amongst his finest. Perhaps surprisingly, none of those dating from the first six months of 1816 was published during his life-time (and most not until long after his death), and this despite the publication of some twenty songs of late 1814–15.
8. James Webster, 'Schubert's Sonata Form ...', *19th-Century Music*, July 1978, ii, I, p. 22 etc.
9. Other music of this period in which Schubert used similar thematic patterns with wide intervals includes the introduction to Laura's aria, no.17, in *Die Freunde von Salamanka*, D326, and the vocal melody of his song 'Der Herbstabend', D405.
10. Probably in 1826 he revised and transposed it into E flat, D568. Other sonata movements of the summer of 1817 which have survived in manuscript but separated from their manuscript sources may complete some of the other fragmentary sonatas.
11. *Caecilia. Eine Zeitschrift für die musikalische Welt* (Mainz: B. Schotts Söhne) May 1824.
12. 'Anleitung zur Erlernung des von Herrn Georg Staufer neu erfundenen Guitarre-Violoncell. Verfasst von Vinc. Schuster. Mit einer genauen Abbildung des Instrumentes.'
13.
14. Louis Antoine Duport, acting for the management of the Court Opera Theatre.
15. *Documents*, 538–9.
16. *Documents*, 546–7.
17. *The Letters of Beethoven*, ed. E. Anderson, London 1961, iii, 1177n.
18. ibid, iii, 1182–3.
19. ibid, iii, 1187.
20. ibid, iii, 1214.
21. ibid.
22. The *Leipzig allgemeine muskalische Zeitung* gave notice on 26 March 1818 that Schuppanzigh's quartet had again played Op. 127 in one of their subscription concerts in the hall of the *Musikverein* on 24 January.
23. 'Beethoven', *The New Grove*, J. Kerman, A Tyson, London (Papermac) 1983, 81.
24. *Documents*, 599.
25. ibid, 781.
26. ibid, 781–2.
27. *Franz Schubert. Dokumente 1817–1830*, ed. T.G. Waidelich, Tutzing 1993, i, 394 (entry no.573).
28. ibid, 401 (no. 586).
29. ibid, 467 (no. 674).
30. ibid, 424 (no. 623).
31. See Chapter 1 in this volume.
32. For a more comprehensive view, detailed analysis and thorough evaluation of Schubert's Fantasia in C, the reader is referred to the recent article by Patrick McCreless, 'A Candidate for the Canon? A New Look at Schubert's Fantasie in C major for Violin and Piano', in *19th-Century Music* XX/3 (Spring 1997), 205–30.

4 'Am Meer' reconsidered: strophic, binary, or ternary?
Edward T Cone

Although Schubert has sometimes been excoriated for his treatment – or mistreatment – of Heine in *Schwanengesang*, notably by Stein,[1] he has also been bravely defended, recently by Richard Kramer.[2] Kramer takes issue with Stein's 'provocative, sometimes exasperating study' (p. 138). Nevertheless, he concedes, 'The rhetoric of irony ... does not easily translate into music. One might even suggest that irony is a quality of thought that music is incapable of expressing. It is at any rate a quality foreign to Schubert's profound, pathetic naïveté.' As a result, 'Heine's poem is no longer his own' even though 'The conceptual vision in Schubert's Heine cycle is breathtaking' (p. 139).

Kramer is certainly right that Schubert's poems are no longer Heine's. As I once wrote, '... a composer cannot "set" a poem directly ...; what he uses is one reading of the poem. ... And to say that he "sets" even this reading is less accurate than to say that he appropriates it: he makes it his own by turning it into music'.[3] With regard to the Heine songs, I cautioned that 'Schubert's protagonist is not Heine's – nor, if I am right, should one expect him to be. The texts of the songs, we must remember, are now Schubert's.' But what I called Schubert's 'apparent insensitivity' to the poet's mordancy' in 'Am Meer' does not preclude the expression of the composer's gentler form of irony. 'Perhaps', as I suggested, 'the sentimental ending of the song ... is the composer's way of indicating that, whatever the poetic persona may feel, the vocal protagonist is subconsciously still in love with the "unglücksel'ge Weib"' (pp 39–40). I should now like to return to this song, examining it in detail, and interpreting its conclusion within the wider context of the composer's concept of the whole.

Since one cannot properly discuss the expressive values of a composition without due attention to its formal and technical aspects, those must be my first concern. Here Stein leads us in a fruitful direction when he points out that the design of the song can be considered as 'a slightly varied strophic form, each musical strophe incorporating two of the poem's stanzas, so that there is just one musical

Ex. 4.1　Am Meer

Ex 4.1 continued

Ex 4.1 concluded

repetition.' But when he continues, 'This scheme alone negates the main effect of the poem',[4] he reveals his insufficient comprehension of the possibilities of the strophic pattern. Let us consider what some of those might be.

I

It is often noted in discussions about strophic song that variation in the performance of the successive stanzas can not only obviate monotony but also modify the musical sense so that it corresponds more closely to the progress of the poetry. Thus a singer may 'darken' her tone to mark a tragic turn of events, or a pianist may 'bring out' a detail of programmatic significance. (I well remember my delight long ago when Bruno Walter – accompanying Lotte Lehmann? Elizabeth Schumann? – emphasized the horn fifths concealed in the piano texture of the final song of *Die schöne Müllerin* in order to reflect the third stanza's words, 'Wenn ein Jagdhorn schallt'.) Composers themselves sometimes make such modifications explicit, and may even go so far as to treat subsequent stanzas as thoroughgoing variations of the first – especially in the accompaniment. That is what Beethoven did in the opening song of *An die ferne Geliebte*. Schubert carried the process one step further when he changed the mode of the final stanza of 'Im Frühling'. Such alterations, however, are still interpretative, so to speak, rather than structural. The music exhibits certain mutations of detail under the influence of the poetry, but the fundamental strophic principle remains supreme.

The poetic influence can be less obvious yet more profound when the words of the successive stanzas affect one's perception of the musical form, sometimes even when the musical surface displays no apparent irregularities. Often the shifting phraseology of the verbal text can induce fresh construals of the overall musical design. A case in point is 'Morgengruss' from *Die schöne Müllerin*. The reiterated six-line pattern of the poem's four stanzas accommodates a shift in their grammatical and rhetorical structure. The principal division in the first stanza occurs between lines five and six, when the initial greeting and questions yield to the protagonist's stated intention: 'So muss ich wieder gehen.' But each of the remaining three stanzas consists of two three-line sections. The second stanza contrasts the watchful lover with the awakening beloved; the third asks two questions; and the fourth turns from the beloved herself to the image of the singing lark and the love it symbolizes. The musical surface of the four stanzas, identical except for variants of rhythmic detail, reflects the strophic pattern of the poem. At the same time, the musical structure is flexible enough to permit a reading that shifts under the influence of the verbal articulations.

Figure 4.1 correlates the verbal and musical aspects of the strophe. *A*, *B*, and *C* represent the musical subdivisions. The prelude and coda are omitted in this outline, but the dash between *A* and *B* stands for a bar of instrumental interlude. The corresponding punctuation between *B* and *C* is the notated fermata. The second line refers to the number of bars in each section; the third, to the verses of the

'Am Meer' reconsidered   117

poetic stanza. (Note that the five bars of C are basically two, repeated wholly and then partially – as is the corresponding poetic verse.) Finally, the last line shows the fundamental harmonic structure: a move from tonic to dominant, an elaboration of the dominant, and a return to the tonic.

	A	B	C
bars:	6	4	5 = 2+2+1
verses:	1–3	4–5	6 (with repetitions)
	IV	V	I

Figure 4.1

The two major points of division – the interlude after *A* and the fermata at the end of *B* – enable one to realize a musical distinction between two ways of articulating the poetry. The words of the first stanza suggest the musical reading *(AB)C*, in which section *B* is heard as extending the dominant close of section *A*. In contrast, the remaining stanzas imply *A(BC)*, with *B* serving as a development before the reprise of the tonic and its thematic material. In performance, then, their fermatas would be understated in comparison with that of the first stanza. Perhaps further distinctions might be made by means of rhythmic inflections that contrast the fairly loose connection of the final line in the second stanza, 'ihr blauen Morgensterne', with the periodic sentence structure that grammatically binds the last line of the concluding stanza, 'die Liebe Leid und Sorgen', to what precedes it. There is an opportunity, moreover, to establish the finality of that stanza. Section *C*, based on a single line and its repetitions, consists melodically of three subphrases: a reiterated vocal descent from mediant to tonic, imitated by the piano and followed by a concluding elaboration of the mediant in the voice. By making that mediant the goal of the section (and thus of the entire strophe), the performers can obviate a sense of finality (Ex. 4.2a). In contrast, they can achieve closure the last time around by emphasizing the descent to the tonic, in both voice and piano (Ex. 4.2b).

It is possible, then, for a single musical structure, under the influence of the words, to call for more than one interpretation. The poetry, as it were, coaxes a

Ex. 4.2a

Ex 4.2b

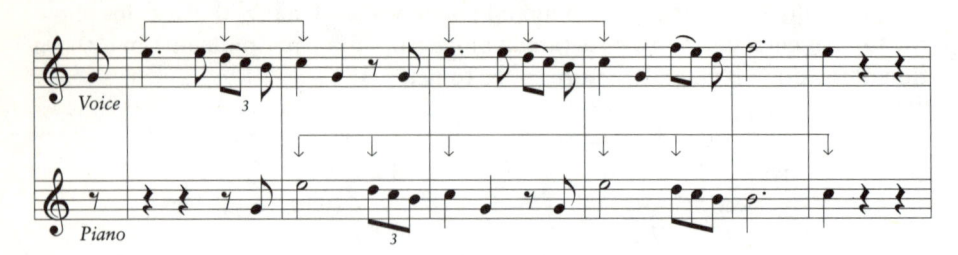

diversity of meanings from the musical text. The influence can also work in the other direction, but in that case the effect is almost the opposite: the music can suggest or confirm a unity of meaning underlying the superficial diversity of the poetic strophes. Thus in another song from *Die schöne Müllerin*, 'Die Liebe Farbe', the use of the same wistfully sad melody for all three stanzas gives the lie to the empty bravado of the second, with its 'Wohl auf zum fröhlichen Jagen!' And that stanza's pathetic major–minor setting of 'Mein Schatz hat's Jagen so gern', identical with that of the earlier 'Mein Schatz hat's Grün so gern', ensures that 'Jagen', like 'Grün', is associated with the protagonist's longing for death – even before he refers to his own 'Wild' as 'der Tod'. The final stanza, returning to 'Grün', confirms the connection.

When the influence of poetic and musical texts on each other is mutual, a new unitary structure may emerge that is no longer effectively strophic. Something like that happens in 'An die Musik'. That its two stanzas create an indissoluble whole is signalled by the differences between the piano interlude and the coda. True, they are almost identical, elaborating a simple cadential progression (I–IV–I–ii^6–V^7–I) under a melody which is basically a descending major scale that omits the third degree – in what may be a typically Schubertian gesture. (Compare the bass line that opens the Andante of the Unfinished Symphony.) The steady succession of quavers is individualized by the recurring motif of an *appoggiatura* or suspension. But whereas the interlude abandons that motif just as it reaches the tonic, in preparation for the commencement of the second stanza (Ex. 4.3a), the coda delays the tonic resolution by one more application of the motif (Ex. 4.3b). The

Ex 4.3

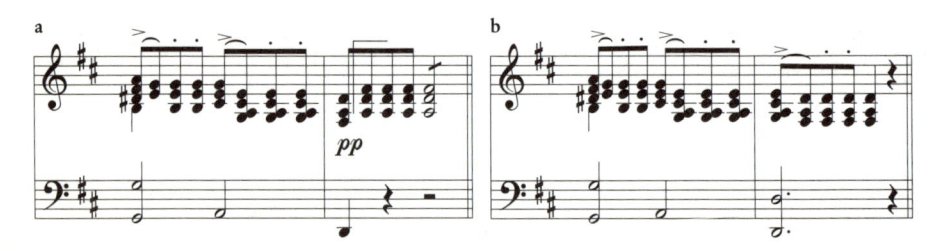

distinction is exactly appropriate: the simple tonic that concludes the interlude could not effect the necessary discharge of momentum needed at the end, nor could the concluding measure of the coda have been used to introduce the second stanza without a break. We are thus encouraged to hear the song as a unit – as *AA'* rather than simply as *AA* – almost like a huge period. Can the second stanza in that case sustain the role of consequent to the first stanza's antecedent? By a happy coincidence of words and music it can. Its final return to the opening words 'du holde Kunst' underlines a musical reference to the opening motif. (Compare Exs 4.4a and 4.4c.) The coalescence of verbal and musical themes at that point imparts a sense of resolution more satisfying than that of the merely musical reprise at the end of the first stanza (Ex. 4.4b). That this effect was deliberate on Schubert's part is suggested by a comparison of the schemes of repetition he adopted. The musical phrase does not accommodate the repetition of an entire line. The first strophe accordingly repeats the end of the line, omitting the first two words (Ex. 4.4b); the second strophe, omitting its final word instead, repeats the apostrophe to 'du holde Kunst' (Ex. 4.4c), affecting the correspondence with the opening of the song. (Was it just luck that the word divisions here made the original scheme of repetition unavailable to the text of the second stanza? Not entirely: there was at least one other possibility that would have more closely paralleled the first text-setting. See Ex. 4.4d.)

Ex. 4.4a

Du hol - de Kunst, in

Ex. 4.4b

hast mich in ei - ne bess - re Welt ent - rückt, in ei - ne bess - re Welt ent - rückt!

Ex. 4.4c

du hol - de Kunst, ich dan - ke dir da - für, du hol - de Kunst, ich dan - ke dir!

Ex. 4.4d

du Kunst, ich dan - ke dir— da - für!

II

From 'An die Musik' we can at last return to 'Am Meer' as an example of the mutual influence between words and music in a quasi-strophic setting. In 'An die Musik' two strophes approximated the pattern of a period. In 'Am Meer' a huge period can be analysed as almost strictly bistrophic. That is because Heine's four stanzas are set as two pairs, almost identical except for their endings: a half-cadence for the first pair and a full cadence for the second. In Schenker's terms, the song exemplifies the technique of interruption: I–V | I–V–I.

First, however, comes the famous introductory motif. That has been convincingly placed in musical and historical perspective by Joseph Kerman,[5] who also appreciatively discusses its expressive potential. Praising the motif's 'unforgettable, enigmatic solemnity, which seems to plumb infinite marine and spiritual depths', he claims that 'from the Romantic point of view it suggests everything – everything in the world that is inward, sentient, and arcane' (p. 52). That may be an extreme description but I do not find it an exaggeration. What is excessive, however, is Kerman's insistence on what he calls the introduction's independence: 'It does not signal ahead to a later event in the song.... It simply recurs' (p. 52). This, as we shall see, is not quite the case. Nevertheless, the introduction does stand in a certain isolation; that is a source of its uncanny effect. But by the time it returns as a coda, it is charged with a meaning derived from the song itself, both music and text.

Even at the outset the isolation is not complete. Whether one accepts the ordering of the Heine songs proposed by Harry Goldschmidt[6] or whether one wishes to preserve the traditional succession, the opening of 'Am Meer' can be heard as arising from a reinterpretation of the final sonority of the preceding song. In the first instance, that is the A flat major triad of 'Das Fischermädchen', which is transformed into an augmented sixth by inversion and by the addition of an F sharp. The resolution to C major accordingly introduces a change of key. In the more familiar case, the diminished seventh of 'Die Stadt' is altered by the substitution of A flat for A natural. This time the resolution changes mode but not key. I myself feel the latter connection to be the more mysteriously evocative, throwing new light on the unresolved conclusion of 'Die Stadt'.

Looking ahead, one realizes that the introduction has at least a registral connection with what follows. It prepares for the mellifluous piano sound that characterizes the accompaniment of the first stanza. That sound, a favourite of Schubert's, is produced by a right-hand melody in octaves, assigned to the warmest range of the piano and further coloured by intervals within the octave – predominantly thirds and sixths. Examples abound in the composer's piano works: the openings of the Sonatas in B flat and G, the development of the first movement of the unfinished Sonata in C ('Reliquie'), the second *Moment Musical*. In accompaniments, it is found in the introduction and coda of 'Das Wirtshaus' (from *Winterreise*), at the phrase that concludes each strophe of 'Des Baches Wiegenlied' (from *Die schöne Müllerin*), and in Mignon's song 'So lasst mich scheinen' (D877 No. 3). Is it a coincidence that all of the songs are about death, but at the same time solace? In the present instance the music seems to depict the dying day, whose sunset still offers solace by illuminating sea and shore – a metaphor, perhaps, for the lingering sweetness of a love affair that is now dying. But there is also the possibility of a more direct musical symbolism. Voice and piano present two parallel melodies of equal weight. The piano melody is doubled at the lower octave, and the vocal line is doubled by the inner part of the piano's right hand. What might the unusual strictness of that parallel motion (violated only at the half-cadence) suggest about the relations between the two implied characters of the poem? On the one hand, propinquity, as the thoughts of both follow the same path. On the other hand, distance: parallels, after all, never meet. Perhaps Schubert was reading two meanings into Heine's word 'alleine'. The lovers, sitting alone – i.e. just the two of them – are physically close to each other and separated from the rest of the world. At the same time each, individually, is emotionally alone. (Compare Schubert's somewhat similar use of parallelism in 'Sei mir gegrüsst'. There the lovers are together in spirit, apart in actuality.) It may be the second meaning of 'alleine' that underlies the repetition – in the piano only – of the last measure of the stanza.

In the next section of the song the calm sea gives way to a stormy one, and the picture of the two quiet lovers yields to that of the restless gull. A single gull may be strange from a naturalistic point of view; but it is symbolically important here, as the second half of the stanza suggests. There the woman is weeping – because of a vision of her lover's flight 'hin und wieder'. The identification of gull and lover will be reinforced in the second strophe; but what is already obvious is the replacement of the single couple, alone but together, by two utterly lonely individuals, the gull and the weeping woman. The music reflects the shift simply but vividly. The rising storm is depicted by piano tremolos, above which the vocal line, now a quasi-recitative instead of a lyrical cantilena like the opening, indeed flies back and forth. C major has given way to C minor, which quickly modulates to D minor before returning to the tonic for the second half-stanza. Now, as the poetry focuses on the weeping woman, the mood of the first stanza returns; but here voice and piano are independent of each other, both melodically and rhythmically. The unity of togetherness-in-loneliness has been broken. And so, when, as before, the piano marks the end of the stanza by repeating the last measure, it is a mere echo, ***ppp***, an octave below.

That measure is the half-cadence that marks the end of the first musical strophe and prepares for the repetition of the musical material. The second strophe, consisting of the second pair of stanzas, parallels the first. Their correspondence can be outlined as follows:

    A (4 lines): Focus on the two lovers together;
    B (2 lines): Storm;
    C (2 lines): Focus on one lover alone.

Whereas the first strophe ends with the woman weeping, as if alone, the second begins by bringing the two once more together by the man's acknowledgement of her tears and by his tender, if sentimental, reaction. The music accordingly returns to the glow of the opening theme, suggesting a moment of renewed affection; but it is followed, as before, by the tremolo-accompanied recitative. Now the association of this passage with the protagonist's own life confirms our earlier interpretation of the image of the restless gull. This time, in the final section, it is the protagonist who is alone. His bitter memory of the tears recalls the corresponding music, now altered so as to achieve a perfect cadence and to permit a return of the introductory chords.

The binary division of the music, in accordance with its quasi-strophic period, thus neatly groups the poetic stanzas in pairs – too neatly according to Stein, for whom the pattern 'negates the main effect of the poem'.[7] He had a point, as we shall see. But he failed to realize that the musical form permits a more subtle interpretation. The suggestion of that possibility came to me from an unlikely source: Beethoven's Bagatelle, Op. 126, No. 4. That piano piece is more literally bistrophic than the song – an unusual design for an instrumental work. Nevertheless, as I wrote in an essay on the Bagatelles, 'The piece ... does not consist of the mere strophic repetition of a two-part form, *AB – AB,* ... but is to be construed more organically: *A – (B as Trio) – A – (B as Coda)*'.[8] I found a clue to that reinterpretation of the form in the bars added between the reprises of the two contrasting sections. In the present instance, the clue is provided less by the music than by the poetry. The musical alterations in the second strophe, embracing the approach to the final cadence and its attainment, mostly conform to the requirements of the overall binary periodic pattern; but, as Stein understood, the dramatic structure of the poem is at odds with that simple parallelism. The story requires a grouping of the stanzas that honours the time-sequence of the narrative: a contrast of past (the first three stanzas) with present (the last one). That grouping implies a different reading of the musical form as well – an alternative that Stein failed to entertain. Instead of one huge period, *ABC* (half-cadence) – *ABC'* (full cadence), one can hear a three-part song-form whose central section, *BC*, returns, suitably modified, to constitute a coda: *A(BC)A – (BC')*.

The word 'coda' may well be misleading. Here (as indeed in the Beethoven Bagatelle as well) what I have so designated plays an important structural role in the composition. Harmonically (through its ii^6–V^7–I cadence) and melodically (through its 3–2–1 descent) it finishes the fundamental progression. But that is often the case with so-called 'codas': they are codas only with reference to a conventional formal design, occurring as they do after the apparent completion of that design. That is the case here; and in this respect the 'coda' beautifully corresponds to the words it sets. After the first three stanzas of the poem, which present a picture complete in itself, the final stanza may at first seem to produce a true verbal coda – an afterthought. But what we get is an afterthought in a temporal sense only. Rhetorically, that stanza conveys the whole point of the poem. Both musically and poetically the 'coda' is the tail that wags the dog.

To be sure, the new reading does not accept analysis in terms of an orthodox Schenkerian interruption. In its sub-division I–V–I | V–I the first dominant now behaves like a neighbouring harmony. From a purely musical point of view that analysis may well seem less cogent; but the song is not pure music any more than it is pure poetry. In the first reading the music, by suggesting correspondence between the two halves of the poem, modified our interpretation of its content. In the new reading the influence moves in the opposite direction: the poetic narrative, separating past from present, reshapes the music.

Is it necessary to choose between the two? One can imagine a performance embodying the one or the other. More interesting, however, would be a performance making use of both analyses and enabling the listener to comprehend the song as a structure that is not a fixed, quasi-spatial entity but one that forms and re-forms itself as it progresses in time. Here again there are precedents in the instrumental works of Beethoven: for example, the finale of the Eighth Symphony, which converts an apparent coda into a new development and recapitulation; or the first movement of the Quartet Op. 132, which transforms an inceptive sonata-allegro into a unique design that Roger Sessions once aptly dubbed a 'three-stanza form'.

In the present instance the medium is not purely musical; the interpretation of its formal organization must recognize poetic and dramatic elements as well. A prime point of musical ambiguity is the central half-cadence. Is it the focus of an interruption, or is it the herald of a reprise? A performance that articulates the ensuing stanza as a return rather than as a new beginning (e.g., by dwelling on its cadence at 'fortgetrunken') encourages the listener to hear it as the reprise of the three-part song-form – and as the end of the story. But the fourth stanza recommences the action – musically, by recalling the storm; verbally, by referring to more recent events. That association emphasizes what turns out to be a crucial function of the stanza: to relate past and present. For the stanza explains the significance of the narrated incident in the light of what has happened since, revealing the unanticipated effect of the tears. At the same time, its music encourages a reinterpretation of the formal design by uncovering an alternative to the song-form. As a result its final cadence can appropriately fulfil and answer the mid-cadence, which is thus retroactively transformed into the half-cadence of an interruption.

The approach to the final cadence contains an important detail that remains to be examined – a striking alteration that is not required by the obligatory change of half to full cadence. When the poet refers to 'das unglücksel'ge Weib', the composer heightens both the melodic and the harmonic tension. (Compare this line with its earlier version, 'Aus deinen Augen, liebevoll', Ex. 4.5). The vocal climax on F and its accompanying A flat clash against the chordal C–G; and that fifth is left emptily ringing as the voice rests after 'Weib'. Schubert's 'unglücksel'ge Weib' is not Heine's woman, who seems to have caused more misfortune than she suffered. Nor is Schubert's protagonist the same as Heine's: his attitude is one of sorrowful regret rather than of anger. Still, the unusual musical treatment of 'Weib' darkens the succeeding bar as well, so that the dissonances once pathetically associated with the falling tears now sound harsher when ironically applied to their poisonous effect. Those tears, Schubert's protagonist no doubt feels, must have been as bitter for the one who shed them as they have since become for himself.

Ex. 4.5

The final perfect cadence is succeeded by the real coda: the return of the enigmatic chords of the introduction. We are now in a position to appreciate their relation to the song as a whole, both musically and dramatically. At the outset the augmented sixth and its resolution can at most suggest a key. Harmonically less explicit and therefore less stable than the music of the stanza that follows, they offer a range of possibilities – like a wide but incompletely defined landscape within which a specific scene is to take shape. That occurs, verbally and musically, when the first words symbolically associate the image of the sea with the C major of the opening phrase, actualizing the tonal potential of the introduction. In the song, as opposed to the poem alone, the memory of that sea, glowing 'in letzten Abendscheine', pervades the narrative; for the music never moves far from the tonic. (Even the short sections of harmonic contrast begin in the tonic minor and modulate – only briefly – to D minor, which is soon revealed as the supertonic of C major.) But the sea, too, is symbolic. Its meaning is confirmed by the musical association of the stormy waters with the protagonist's own vicissitudes. Key and sea coalesce in what I fear must be identified by that hackneyed phrase 'the sea of life'.

Thus, when the introductory chords at last return, they do so within a context that has established their tonality. They can also now be heard to refer motivically to the body of the song. Most obviously, they can be connected with the two measures of accompaniment that punctuate the close of each of the odd stanzas. Echoing V^7–I cadences, those brief piano interludes recall the texture and the register of the introduction and look forward to the postlude.

More subtly, that postlude harks back to the minor–major mixture of the turbulent sections, and of the echoed half-cadence ($I^6_4 - i^6_4 - V$) at the midpoint of the song. Closer at hand is the A flat–G motif of the 'unglücksel'ge Weib'. The augmented sixth and its resolution enhance that detail, colouring it in a way that also suggests the chromaticism of the poisonous tears, but without their acerbity. And this time the chord of resolution is no longer the empty fifth left sounding by the 'Weib'; that has now been replaced by a full triad.

Here, especially, we realize the difference between Heine's poem and Schubert's: Heine's concluding tone of bitter resentment has given way to Schubert's mood of calm acceptance. We feel that the poisonous tears are at last absorbed, and with them both love and anger – because that is what happens in the music. The postlude receives and assimilates all that has occurred, whether musically or dramatically. The chord-succession is not like that of the perfect cadence that preceded it, for its dissonance is not so much resolved as dissolved. The augmented sixth melts into the Cs that envelop it.

These harmonic and thematic connections between song and postlude at last explain, retroactively, the meaning – one meaning – of the mysterious introduction. But we might now equally say that the introduction proleptically announced the role of the postlude. Both statements are partial. For introduction and postlude should be understood as one and the same: an introduction-postlude – the manifestation, as it were, of a permanent environment subsisting, not before and after, but outside the time of the song that it surrounds. In that sense the motif is not repeated; it is always there, even when we cannot hear it. In an odd way, the two-chord succession is itself emblematic of that status. Its impassive Cs, elements of permanence, frame the inner moving voices in chordal space, just as the introduction-postlude horizontally frames the tonal structure and temporal flow of the song.

The C major of the introduction-postlude, then, is not precisely the same as the C major of the song proper. That one is 'the C major of this life', a key of actuality, with its tonics, supertonics, and dominants. This one is an all-encompassing tonality of possibilities. The key of the song actualizes one of those possibilities, the specific C major of 'Am Meer'; but the introduction-postlude, surrounding the song, embeds the key in a kind of transcendental tonality from which everything arises and into which everything ultimately sinks. Our little life is rounded, not with a sleep, but with a chord.

Thus, although Kerman's characterization of the introductory motif as a 'prototype for those "unconsummated symbols" that Suzanne Langer has urged us to find in music' (Kerman, pp 52–3; Langer[9]) is apposite, it no longer applies by the time the motif returns in the coda. The entire song has 'consummated' the symbol.

References

1. Stein, Jack M. (1971), *Poem and Music in the German Lied from Gluck to Hugo Wolf*, Cambridge (MA): Harvard University Press, pp 80–91.
2. Kramer, Richard (1994), *Distant Cycles*, Chicago and London: University of Chicago Press, pp 125–47.
3. Cone, Edward T. (1974), *The Composer's Voice*, Berkeley, Los Angeles and London: University of California Press, p. 19.
4. Stein, op. cit., p. 87.
5. Kerman, Joseph (1986), 'A Romantic Detail in Schubert's *Schwanengesang*' in Frisch, Walter (ed.), *Schubert, Critical and Analytical Studies*, Lincoln (NB) and London: University of Nebraska Press.
6. Goldschmidt, Harry (1974), 'Welches war die ursprüngliche Reihenfolge in Schubert's Heine-Liedern', *Deutsches Jahrbuch der Musikwissenschaft für 1972*, pp 52–62.
7. Stein, op. cit., p. 87.
8. Cone, Edward T. (1977), 'Beethoven's Experiments in Composition: The Late Bagatelles' in Tyson, Alan (ed.), *Beethoven Studies 2*, London, Oxford and New York: Oxford University Press, p. 97.
9. Langer, Suzanne (1948), *Philosophy in a New Key*, New York: Mentor Books, p. 195.

5 Schubert's 'Great' C major Symphony: the autograph revisited
Brian Newbould

Several strands of experience come together in the making of this essay, among them a forty-year devotion to the 'Great'; a recognition that it represents a *ne plus ultra* of a particular kind of symphonic aspiration – driven by an obsession with motion – that was one of the prime fixations of the Classical period; an appreciation of its harmonic riches, for all that it is bedded down on pillars of strong, fresh-as-air diatonicism; the expectation that, as it is in some respects a sequel to the sketched but abandoned Seventh Symphony (in E, D729), its autograph would yield special interest to one who had attempted to make a performing version of that earlier sketch; and an absorption in the very stuff of symphonic thinking that holds and leads the ear and inevitably invites a musician to explore its note-for-note construction. More immediately, there was the urge to look for new insights which might illuminate some of the topical issues that have surfaced in a quarter of a century which has seen an unprecedented proliferation of performances and recordings of Schubert's symphonies, including many motivated by a quest for authenticity in performance. A fresh source study, in the course of which existing accounts of the autograph would be reviewed, might in some way enable one to come closer to the soul of the work, while at the same time stimulating further analytical reflection on the piece. As preparation, the music would be committed to memory, and held in the mind as, above all, an expressive document addressed to the ear.[1]

From the 1970s onwards the Ninth Symphony has been an important focus of Schubert scholarship. This trend was initiated before the late-twentieth-century absorption in questions of authentic performance reached as far as the 'Great', and before the reception history of long-in-the-tooth masterpieces became a discipline of its own. The re-dating of the symphony was one concern,[2] and revisions made to the autograph have been another. Other topics that have become or continued to be live issues are time-signatures, tempi and tempo relationships and dynamic markings, not to mention the accuracy of published editions. The aim here is to present some fresh thinking on all these fronts, in a way which might interest conductors and players as well as listeners.

One has only to open Schubert's autograph score to the first page, and two specific issues are already confronted. The time-signature is indeed *alla breve* (₵) rather than the common time (C) that appears in most published editions; and the very first bars of music are themselves enough to challenge a solution proposed in the 1980s to the vexed question as to when the composer's hairpin marking denotes an accent and when a *diminuendo*.

The observation that Schubert began his 'Great' with an *alla breve* sign was widely hailed as a discovery of the 1980s, brought in on the tide of late-twentieth-century authenticism. In truth, this was a rediscovery, not a discovery. An ageing score issued by Peters of Leipzig and edited by F A Roitzsch accurately transcribed the *alla breve* symbol.[3] The import of this indication for modern performance becomes clear when, a few pages further into the score, it is noted that there is no trace of an *accelerando* from the introductory Andante into the Allegro ma non troppo. Evidently Schubert had in mind a smooth transition into the Allegro without gear-change: the pulse would remain the same, with the crotchet becoming a minim in the 'new tempo'. It takes considerable courage – in fact a steely resolve in the face of old habits and prejudices – to implement this conclusion. It is one thing for a conductor to write a supporting note pointing to the inevitability of this conclusion, but another to hold one's nerve enough to see it through on the rostrum. A recording which honours the finding and applies it literally is yet to be made. Of course, players and listeners cling to familiar perceptions of familiar music, and to hear the Andante move at a flowing pace and the Allegro at a steady, measured tread is the kind of shock to entrenched sensibilities that may only cease to disturb after repeated hearings.[4]

One further aspect of the autograph tends to support the above analysis of the tempo requirements for the first movement. Schubert originally marked the second section *allegro vivace*, and later changed this to *allegro ma non troppo*. It may well have been as an attempt to establish the proper relationship with the foregoing Andante that this was done. Musical analysis strengthens the bond of tempo further, in that all three sections of the Allegro (exposition, development and recapitulation) make extensive use of the Andante theme, and especially its second bar. This does not, of course, clinch the matter, but does at least tend to enhance the validity of the one-tempo interpretation.

There is no evidence that Schubert conceived the reprise of the Andante theme at the end of the movement as being in the same tempo as the beginning of the movement. (The reprise is part of a coda marked *Più moto*, and there is no slower tempo marked when the theme returns, although the *ben marcato* injunction may suggest a slight broadening.)

The consistency of tempo from Andante to Allegro does not, therefore, make possible a final hearing of the Andante theme in the tempo at which it was first heard. But it does mean that, if the conductor opts for a broadening at the *ben marcato* reprise, a less extreme adjustment is needed than is the case when the Andante is taken at the traditional slower pace.

It has been opined by Stefano Mollo that 'Schubert differentiated quite clearly between accents ... and *decrescendo* markings'. This extraordinary claim, which has the appearance of resolving generations of musicological doubt, wins the blessing of Claudio Abbado, for whose recording of the symphonies Mollo conducted his researches. The problem is so well-known as to hardly need articulating here. Suffice it to say that the traditional distinction between a short hairpin for an accent (>) and a long one for a *decrescendo* (>) is not observed by Schubert, who casually varies the length of the sign without apparent regard for distinctions of meaning. But now Mollo pronounces that when the hairpin is written by Schubert 'over the notes concerned' it denotes an accent, and when 'below the staff', a *decrescendo*.[5] It sounds a seductively neat solution. Unfortunately for Mollo, the first page of the autograph of the 'Great' is reproduced in the booklet a few pages before his statement. It shows what, according to Mollo, would be a *decrescendo* in each of the first six bars of the symphony; but Abbado's performance wisely observes no *decrescendo*. More serious challenges to Mollo's dictum abound in other autographs. At bar 256 in the first movement of the Fifth Symphony, for example, the hairpin on an offbeat chord appears in some instruments above the note and in others below the stave. At bars 272 and 274 in the same movement, where two parallel two-bar passages follow each other (one a re-scoring of the other), the hairpin is written the first time below the cello/bass note, the second time above. In the first movement of the B minor Symphony (the 'Unfinished'), the famous long-held horn note that heralds the second subject has its hairpin below the stave in the exposition and above the note in the recapitulation. Perhaps Mollo sees this as a varied recapitulation! A few bars later, when the second subject fades to a bar's silence, the shock *ffz* chord that follows has simultaneous upper and lower hairpins arbitrarily scattered among the instruments.

It would appear that Mollo's strictures have never been substantiated by writings from him in the musicological press. Nor has another claim by Mollo made in the same booklet and specifically endorsed by Abbado in an accompanying note – that changes made to the autograph scores of the symphonies were made by Brahms – ever been properly exposed to the critical light of musicological day in the appropriate academic media. Brahms, who edited the symphonies for the first complete edition issued by Breitkopf und Härtel, was a sensitive and conscientious musician who would never have tampered with the works of a composer he so admired.[6] There is no reason to doubt that the changes were made by Schubert himself, or at least made on his instruction. One may, for instance, easily put down to the composer's own good judgement the decision to delete four bars originally placed between the present bars 112 and 113 of the Scherzo, reinstated with bizarre results in Abbado's recording of the work.

My own study of the autograph was carried out in the light of four particular earlier studies by other scholars. Maurice Brown's was the first of the four.[7]

Brown's purpose is to show that the 'Great' is 'a magnificent summary and epilogue to' Schubert's earlier *oeuvre*. He is little concerned with the autograph score itself. John Reed's study is an account of the autograph seen as an '1825 sketch revised and updated'. That is a tenable view of the autograph as long as the use of the word 'sketch' does not imply that there was ever any intention to abandon the work. Of course, every work begins as a sketch in that it cannot all be written on paper in an instant.[8] Reed's essay wears well, and there will be little with which the following pages take issue. L Michael Griffel attempts to learn about Schubert's working methods from this autograph, and does so up to a point.[9] Within the symphonies alone, Schubert in fact had two distinct working methods, one for the symphonies composed directly into score (D2B, Nos 1–6, 7 and 9) and another for those first sketched in a two-stave particell (D615, D708A, No. 8 and 'No. 10'). The autograph of the 'Tenth' develops sketching methods largely of its own, and little that can be extrapolated from the 'Great' helps in understanding them.[10] Finally, Robert Winter makes extensive reference to the 'Great' in a pioneering essay with much wider concerns, giving attention primarily to paper type and use, and the implications for dating that arise therefrom.[11]

A resumé of the history of Schubert's symphonic sketching habits has been offered elsewhere.[12] The *modus operandi* evident from the autograph of the 'Great' resembles closely that practised in the unfinished Seventh Symphony in E, D729, which in turn builds on the experience of other symphonies composed directly into full score (Nos 1 to 6). A leading instrumental line would be plotted, on full-size orchestral paper, for several bars or even a few pages ahead, after which Schubert would either go back over the passage to add bars here and there in other instruments – perhaps only a snatch of the bass line or a bar or two of new texture for all the instruments involved in it – or fill out the orchestral texture once and for all. In the case of the Seventh Symphony, once the first 110 bars had been set down, the former method prevailed for the remainder of the work, the pages being empty but for a leading line and fragmentary indications in other parts now and then. This was to be the method in the 'Great'. The size of the structural blocks to be plotted with one take of the pen, as it were, varied from a few bars to several pages.

In the first movement, for example, variation in ink colour makes clear that the four bars 456–459 were first written in flute and basso (cello and bass) parts only. At bar 326 (Ex. 5.1) one can see that the harmonic and melodic skeleton took shape before the rhythmic and textural fleshing-out. The first two bars of Ex. 5.1 were at first left blank while in the next four bars only the slow-moving clarinet parts, the thematic fragments in bassoon, violas and cello/bass, and the flute response were etched in. The repeated notes in the clarinets (326–327) and violins (327/8 onwards) were added at a later stage. It is not possible to tell how much later that later stage was reached, but one could imagine that it came sometimes moments later, and sometimes not until the composer's next working session. In the finale Schubert tended to work in much longer spans, as one can readily believe from the nature of the material.

Ex. 5.1

On occasions the cello/bass line was in place before any upper part was added. This is perfectly in line with Schubert's strongly harmonic as well as melodic thinking. Again, ink colour clearly shows that in those famous passages where the trombones have a prominent melodic role, such as bars 199ff (Plate 1) and 304ff, the trombone line was a first-comer in the score.

A page of the Seventh Symphony (first movement) is given for purposes of comparison (Plate 2). It should be borne in mind, however, that this is not a wholly typical page, since roughly one-third of the Seventh Symphony was left as a single instrumental line only. Reed implies that the relationship between the two symphonies was close – that is, that the gap between first sketching and ultimate filling-out was sometimes a long one: 'What he had to show as a result of the work done at Gmunden and Gastein in the summer of 1825 must have looked very like the existing manuscript of the E major Symphony...'[13] He could well be right, but we can only guess: the circumstances of composition – first inspiration on the Gmunden-Gastein trip, continued work at home in Vienna, some evident later revisions, and orchestral parts copied by the summer of 1827 – lend credence to the supposition.

Brown is duly sceptical of attempts to read too much into variations of ink colour. 'As the quill drained of its ink the writing grew fainter; redipped, the colour of the ink regained its original depth. It does not follow, therefore, that a page containing parts in a faint brown ink and others in a dark brown ink was written at different times.'[14] This is not strictly true, since while Schubert redipped his quill, time obviously elapsed. This is not merely a pedantic point: one may still determine by ink colour the order in which certain actions were taken, and for some purposes this is enough and the length of time between actions is not critical. Even so, Brown's caution is salutary, and Griffel's rather categorical conclusions (some years after Brown) seem in that light incautious: 'He ... would use one shade of ink in setting down the melodies and a different shade for scoring the other voices. Schubert edited and revised his symphonies a great deal; in this regard, too, the use of a different color of ink for each stage of revision provides graphic evidence of Schubert's procedure.'[15] For one thing, this presents a picture of Schubert with a palette of colours from which he makes deliberate selections – a scenario quite removed from Brown's more realistic view. But the statement that Schubert edited and revised his symphonies a great deal needs qualification too. The autographs of the first six symphonies are remarkably free of corrections and revisions. Griffel implies that his views are based on a study of all the symphonies in autograph: 'The following commentary is based on the results of my examination of the autograph scores of the Schubert symphonies during the summer of 1970.'[16] The distinct impression is given by the essay, however, that it draws on a knowledge of only the 'Unfinished' and 'Great'. Indeed, since he goes on to say that 'the Fifth Symphony's autograph is in the Deutsche Staatsbibliothek in East Berlin', when in fact it had been securely confined in Cracow (Poland) since the Second World War, one has to question whether he had seen that one at all. He pronounces that 'it was Schubert's normal practice first to sketch a work in piano score': this was a commonly held opinion at the time, but a study of the autograph scores of the early symphonies points in the contrary direction.[17] The 'Unfinished' was, of course, first sketched in piano score, but there is no evidence that any of the finished symphonies, of which there are seven, was first thus sketched. To be fair, Griffel seems to contradict himself later, saying that the method used in the E major Symphony (No. 7, D729) 'had always been the composer's procedure in writing symphonies'.[18] But perhaps he meant by that that the Seventh first existed as a piano sketch, although there is no evidence to support that view and a certain amount to contradict it. Reed, incidentally, helpfully points out that the G major String Quartet was worked upon in the same way as the Seventh Symphony and the 'Great'.[19] The autograph does indeed compare interestingly with that of these two symphonies. Reed also ascribes the same method to the Fantasy in F minor for piano duet, although there is an important difference, for Schubert in that instance was not composing by stages into one score, gradually filling in the gaps previously left bare: he abandoned that sketch, with its gaps, and took fresh paper to write out a finished version.

To return to the opening of the 'Great', one sign that a scholar is human is his susceptibility to wild aberration. Brown spilt much ink explaining that Schubert first wrote his opening eight-bar theme as a six-bar one, just as it sounds to the ear on its return at the end of the movement, but then added in two bars by inserting extra barlines and squeezing in the notes required. He went on to hypothesize as to the compositional cogitations that lay behind the change.[20] Alas, there is absolutely no sign of any change in the autograph! Astonishingly, Griffel accepts Brown's observations on this matter.[21] Could it be that Brown, working within the short opening hours of the Gesellschaft der Musikfreunde where the autograph is kept, worked fast, made inadequate notes and, perhaps not writing up his research until some time later, somehow took hold of the idea that the shape of the final reprise had some precedent earlier in the movement and imagined he had found it on page 1? Or did he go to the library wondering if by any chance an amended opening might conceal the origin of the reprise version – and in a daydream became convinced that it was so? There may be a lesson here for all who milk manuscripts hard in meagre library opening hours and become susceptible to lapses of organisation or imagination.

An insight into aspects of Schubert's orchestral thinking is provided by a short passage in the Andante 'introduction'. Ex. 5.2b shows this passage in its completed form, which evidently came into being in two stages, the second being penned in blacker ink than the brownish ink used for the first stage. Ex. 5.2a shows the first stage. The initial chords are carried by the strings. An overlapping 'answer' is given to the woodwind, supported by the bass trombone – a mix favoured at places in both the 'Unfinished' and the 'Great'. A bass trombone is more versatile than a (valveless) horn for providing bass lines to the woodwind choir, since the horn could offer only a severely limited choice of notes so low in its harmonic series. When he wrote the woodwind chords Schubert had presumably already decided that the brass would be present to add weight to the string

134 *Schubert Studies*

Ex. 5.2a

Ex. 5.2b

chords: he would have left the clarinet and bassoon staves empty on the first beat of bar 36 because the notes selected for the lower woodwind would have to be worked out in conjunction with the choice of notes for the brass. Schubert wrote in no rests until the notes were all in place: all the rests appear in the blacker ink. Other points of interest here are that the strings are placed at the top of the page, as is usual in Schubert's orchestral scores; that 'frame dynamics' suffice (the *ff* in the first violins standing for *ff* in all instruments); and that accidentals are readily omitted where they are obvious to the composer (all woodwind in bar 38, second violins in bar 37).

The fact that Schubert changed his Allegro vivace to Allegro ma non troppo, not commented upon by Brown, has already been noted. The changes he made at a late stage to the contour of the first Allegro theme have been extensively covered, and a musical justification offered.[22] A particularly significant change is made soon after the commencement of the second group of the Allegro. Ex. 5.3 shows the passage as it appears after Schubert had revised it. From the *fortissimo* at bar 162, Schubert originally entered only the first violins and basso in his score, in the way in which he would have done it in the Seventh Symphony sketch, as Reed rightly points out.[23] What is of special interest here, though, is that the two bars preceding the *ff* took the place of a single bar originally intended. Ex. 5.4 shows the original single bar, followed by the final two-bar version. The revision does

Ex. 5.3

Ex. 5.4

not confer any indispensable melodic advantage. What Schubert was achieving by this change was, above all, to honour the pattern of bar-groupings he had already established: from the beginning of the Allegro the music had unfolded in four- and occasionally two-bar groups. An odd bar standing on its own (the original bar 160) was disturbing; and it was to maintain the metrical *status quo* that Schubert inserted the extra bar. The issue of bar-groupings is of immense importance for the symphony as a whole, as will be seen later.

In the coda of the first movement, some way before the final reprise of the Andante theme, Schubert inserted a lengthy extra passage, evidently after the movement had been finished. The way in which, in paper-and-ink terms, this was managed has been accurately detailed by Reed: Schubert deleted an existing page, tore out one sheet, and added three extra sheets (recognisably of a heavier paper type), since the added passage was clearly much longer than the rejected one.[24] Of the musical aspects and purpose, Reed notes that the deleted page shows that the original passage touched on F sharp minor, as does the revised version (modulation is too strong a word, since F sharp minor is merely touched in passing); that the revision strengthens the climax; and that 'those "heavenly lengths" were very much a part of Schubert's conscious intention'.

We may go beyond that and point to this added passage as a crowning example of something Schubert had learned from Beethoven. In the first movement of his Second Symphony, Beethoven recapitulated his material in the tonic key, in the usual way. A conventional recapitulation such as this is the longest span in a sonata-form movement which is confined to the home key. To compensate for this, when Beethoven added a coda (in the Second Symphony) he included an 'excursion' – a passage the purpose of which is to imply adventurous tonal digression followed by a climactic re-approach to the tonic. The fact that Beethoven completely loses sight of the thematic material of the movement here, writing music that simply comprises pure harmony and orchestral sonority, underlines the purpose of using digression from the key as a specific means of generating excitement and building an impressive final climax. Schubert knew and adored this work; and he adopted the 'excursion' himself in the finale of his Third Symphony.[25] Now, in the first movement of the 'Great', he saw fit to carry this principle to new lengths. The harmonic implications are far-reaching: Schubert sets off on one harmonic circuit, returns home, then sets off in the same manner once more, reaching new harmonic regions not touched the first time, and extending the close to a thrilling threefold cadence which in its triple format echoes the cadences at the end of exposition and recapitulation (bars 228–240, 546–558).

Reed's statement that the second limb of this double excursion reiterates the first, 'with some extra emphasis on the concluding cadence', ignores the harmonic variation towards its close, which is of some importance.

Ex. 5.5 is a harmonic reduction of the whole passage, showing the varied second-time ending as 'second time bars' written below the 'first time bars' to facilitate comparison (Schubert did not use repeat marks but wrote out afresh those 14 bars which are identical). It will be seen that the revision enables Schubert to introduce (at the asterisk) a chord which is one of his personal imprints and which has a recurring, almost thematic, function in the 'Great' C major.[26] Another climactic excursion, of slightly different type, occurs in the finale.

Ex. 5.5a

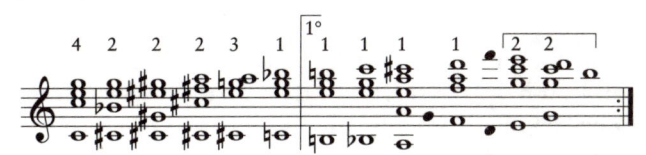

Ex. 5.5b

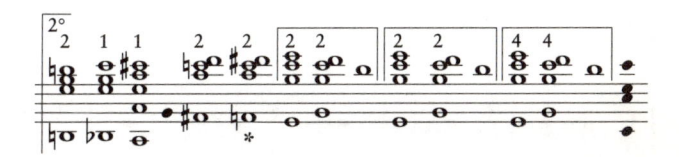

The oboe tune at the eighth bar of the slow movement was originally written in the clarinet part. Griffel assumes that it was Schubert's intention that the clarinet should double the oboe.[27] This would have been the potently expressive doubling favoured at the 13th bar of the 'Unfinished'; but it cannot be assumed that the composer did not first intend the slow movement theme of the 'Great' to be played by the clarinet *alone*. When, sixteen bars further on, he changed Ex. 5.6a to Ex. 5.6b, Schubert had presumably recognised the weakness of the last bar – although he allowed later references to that superseded bar to stand, as at bar 32 (Ex. 5.7), where the context purges it of its weakness. His second thoughts also give the line a smoother, more cantabile quality that better sets it off from the choppier first theme. There is no reason to suppose that Brahms or anyone else other than Schubert made this alteration.

Ex. 5.6a

Ex. 5.6b

Ex. 5.7

Much later in the movement come two other small but significant changes. The first involves that wonderful lead-in to the reprise of the first theme, where, for Tovey, the horns 'toll like a bell haunted by a human soul'.[28] For a time the horns seem suspended in limbo and uninclined to move, until the strings force the issue, pulling them down to the dominant of the now targeted home key (Ex. 5.8). The

Ex. 5.8

seesawing between lower and upper strings, like the pianist's right hand completing a chord whose foundation was laid by the left hand, may have been triggered by the memory of a passage in the first movement (development) of Beethoven's Fifth, where it is strings and wind that alternate in a similar way. Be that as it may, Schubert seems originally to have planned that the lower strings would sustain the chords for two bars, upper strings adding their voices to the lower ones in each second bar. The more aerated texture that he eventually decided on permits him to reserve that fuller texture until the four-bar cadence-approach, where the warming of the hairpin crescendo is set into greater relief and the homeward modulation has more articulative force.

The second instance comes at the dramatic climax where a *fff* diminished seventh is followed by a Tchaikovskyan silence. After the silence Schubert originally had Ex. 5.9 a rather than the ultimate 5.9b. The revised choice more literally echoes the *fff* spread of the chord, letting the one tiny but decisive change of harmony (F sharp to F natural) show up all the more. The turn to the Neapolitan key (B flat) which this change of harmony induces, with a lyrical tenor-register cello line to lead the way, is of course as dramatic in its quietude as the diminished seventh was in its force.

Ex. 5.9a

Ex. 5.9b

One notable revision in the Scherzo was well-documented by Griffel.[29] From bar 84, Schubert originally had seven bars of music before what is now bar 105. Having continued past this point, possibly to the end of the movement, he went back, deleted those seven bars, and replaced them with 21 – the present 84–104 inclusive. Thus one of the most sublime inspirations in the movement was apparently an afterthought. A new flute melody in C flat, which could be regarded as a variant of an earlier idea (Ex. 5.10), is hoisted bodily by a semitone so that it appears in C major. The simultaneous change of timbre from solo flute to first violins doubled by oboe is a master-stroke, pleasurably maximising that sense of turning a corner to be instantly confronted by a new vista.

Ex. 5.10

[musical notation: m. 89, with V I V I harmonic labels]

[musical notation: m. 33, with V I V I harmonic labels]

If one is asked what are the typical characteristics of a trio section in a minuet or scherzo of the Classical period, one might reply 'rustic', or 'courtly', or 'dance-like', or 'thinner/lighter in texture than the minuet/scherzo', or 'self-effacing', or 'tending not to upstage the minuet/scherzo'. On further reflection one might add, 'sometimes humorous or quirky' (Haydn Quartet in C, Op. 54, No. 2, or Symphony No. 101 in D; Beethoven Rasumovsky Quartet in E minor, Op. 59, No. 2), 'sometimes contrapuntal' (Mozart Wind Serenade in C minor, K388; Beethoven Fifth Symphony), or 'like a tune-and-accompaniment serenade with a dash of virtuosity thrown in' (Haydn Quartet in G, Op. 76, No. 1; Mozart Quartet in D minor, K421, or String Quintet in D, K593). But one may well not come up with a categorisation into which the Trio of the 'Great' will fit. With its full-throated songfulness, its rhythmic energy, its expansive form, and its predominantly heavy scoring, it is clearly not the least original part of this symphony. It flops, however, if taken at a pace other than that of the Scherzo itself: it demands to sail in on the pulse which drove the Scherzo. Brown thought there were no grounds in the score for a *meno mosso* here, this being seemingly an instinctive stance on his part.[30] If arguments are required to back up instinct, it could be pointed out that the contrast afforded by the Trio's distinctive gait, quite different from that of the Scherzo, is lost if the referential link – the sameness of tempo – is removed; and that Schubert did specify a slower pace for a trio when he wanted it – as in the Sixth Symphony.

Barlines in music of Classical times are the tip of a metric iceberg. Just as one may divide up the printed bars, if the bar contains an even number of beats, with imaginary dotted barlines, so one may group the printed bars into sets of 'larger bars' – usually two or four to the set. Indeed, conductors often write in markers in their scores at every fourth bar, to provide the eye with guidance additional to that which is the purpose of the printed barlines. Occasionally the existence of these alternative scales of division into bars, or 'metric levels' as Cooper and Meyer[31] called them, left the composer pondering which was the best level to choose as the basis of the actual barring. If Beethoven or Mendelssohn sometimes preferred $\frac{6}{8}$ time to $\frac{3}{4}$ for a scherzo, however, halving the number of barlines thereby (and of course taking advantage of the fact that if notated in $\frac{3}{4}$ the piece would have comprised dual bar groupings from beginning to end), one cannot assume that a scherzo Beethoven chose to notate in ¾ does not also move in regular two-bar blocks. The grounds for preferring one 'level' to another are complex and the decision may involve instinct as much as analysis.

Schubert was as liable as Haydn or Mozart or Beethoven to invent ideas that run counter to the expectation of regular two- or four-bar blocks. He would write phrases of three or seven bars, usually reverting eventually to patterns based on blocks of two or four. The five-bar phrase, such as is found in the finale of the A minor String Quartet or the second theme of the Rondo in A for piano duet, becomes a unifying characteristic across the movements of the Seventh Symphony.[32] The 'Great', however, rediscovers the natural force of the two-bar, and more especially the four-bar, unit: in fact the assertiveness with which it champions this norm is in large part responsible for the dynamic momentum that powers the work.

It was seen in the first movement that at one point Schubert went back on himself to replace a single bar with two bars (see Ex. 5.4 above). Significantly, the effect of that change was to make the entire Allegro ma non troppo – development and all – fall into two-bar blocks. Removing the only one-bar obstacle to that unbroken pattern was surely Schubert's ulterior if subconscious motive for making the change. Incidentally, when Schubert wrote in a 'spare' bar's rest at the end of the first movement, this was merely because the last chord falls on the 'downbar', which must be completed by a rest in the 'up-bar'. For the same reason – to fill out the rests in an implied larger bar just as one would in a literal bar – Schubert added *three* bars' rest at the end of his Sixth Symphony.[33]

Four-bar groupings predominate in the Scherzo of the 'Great'. It is noteworthy that in the penultimate four-bar block of the first section of the Scherzo Schubert originally marked the strings (at least, first and second violins and cello/bass) to play all four bars with one bow. He replaced this hasty, intuitive solution (reflecting the musical reality) with the more practical expedient of two bars to a bow; but he left the previous four-bar block to be played in one bow by the cellos and basses – a significant curiosity which happily finds its way into some printed editions. Already before this (bars 33–36, 37–40) Schubert's sense of long-breathed lines not confined by barlines is demonstrated when repeated dominants in the horn part are slurred in fours, with accent and staccato marks under the slur (Ex. 5.11). While the Scherzo sometimes deviates from its four-bar conformity, the Trio does so only once: indeed, in its march-like tread it has its eyes forward so determinedly that its long lyrical paragraphs can be thought of in eight-bar groups for most of the time.

Ex. 5.11

With these metrical precedents as its context, the finale soon becomes subject to the same spacious urges. Evident enough to the listener, it is also apparent to the reader of the autograph. The bars of 2/4 are so short and all is so flowingly written that the actual bars quickly become incidental to the fleet onward momentum. At the recapitulation the handwriting is so racy – resembling that in the confidently-sketched Seventh Symphony – that one can easily imagine the passing bars being, for the composer, merely passing beats. Eventually, as far as the progress of the sketching is concerned, one senses that the four-bar block has become the obligatory element and Schubert is plotting and notating events with 'nodes' at every fourth bar rather than at every barline.

Two familar landmarks in this finale are the fourfold note-repetition which initiates the second subject (Ex. 5.12) and the powerful 'resolution' of this to the tonic as climax of the coda (Ex. 5.13). But already, before the second subject, this fourfold repetition has surreptitiously asserted itself (Ex. 5.14), and the habit of chords enduring for four bars at a time becomes entrenched – the process even going beyond that to the extent that one chord can last for 24 bars, with changes merely of texture at each fourth bar. After the first four notes of the second subject, Schubert placed the next four bars under a single slur for the bassoons, before

Ex. 5.12

Ex. 5.13

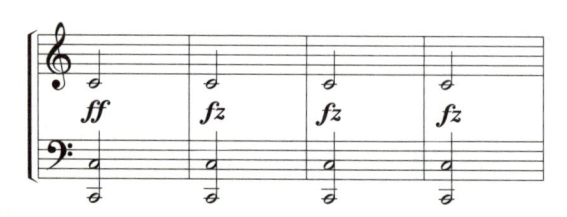

Ex. 5.14

opting for the more practical 2+2. But a four-bar slur won the day at 289–292, while at the wonderfully atmospheric *decrescendo* – accompanied by held Cs – at the end of the recapitulation there is even a scattering of eight-bar slurs.

The role of four-bar groupings in the finale has already received attention elsewhere.[34] Roy Howat has made an illuminating notational comparison between the second subject and the Impromptu in C minor, D899, No. 1 showing how, in different contexts, Schubert fixes his barlines on one metrical scale or another.[35] Ex. 5.15 shows the cumbersome effect that would have resulted if Schubert had chosen to make the 'larger bar' the actual bar in the finale of the 'Great'.

Ex. 5.15

In the light of this metrical discussion, one of the most fascinating revelations of the autograph score is the fact that Schubert had at first contemplated a quite different second subject from the one we know. Thus, those first four minims of our familar second subject – the acorn from which an oak tree has grown by the end of the coda – might never have seen the light of day, despite their being latent within the transition at bars 113–116. It is astonishing to think that the subsequent course of the movement might have been quite different had Schubert stayed with his first thoughts. Those passages which take their cue from the four repeated notes – the lead into the recapitulation and the coda among them – would never have come about. And the four-bar grouping would presumably not have assumed such dominance in the closing stages of the movement.

As Schubert's original second subject has never appeared in print with total accuracy, it is given as Ex. 5.16. Strangely, neither Brown nor Reed quoted this theme. Brown, moreover, actually went out of his way to deny that there was any previously-intended second subject at all.[36] Griffel quoted the theme but omitted the two semiquavers in the sixth bar, and the slur on the following two quavers. The *Revisionsbericht* accompanying the Breitkopf und Härtel first complete edition likewise omits the slur. This sixth bar might be seen as a distant echo of a

Ex. 5.16

germ present in the first movement, at bar 93 (with five reappearances later in the movement) (Ex. 5.17). Furthermore, it seems to have been retained as an incidental (but delectable) feature of the *new* second subject (Ex. 5.18).

Ex. 5.17

Ex. 5.18

This original second subject has been variously categorised as a 'fugue-subject' (Tovey[37]), and a 'so-called *fugato* theme' which at least 'suggests some canonic imitation' (Reed[38]), while Griffel offers in turn 'fugato', 'canonic writing' and 'fugal writing'.[39] In point of fact it is not possible to say that Schubert would have treated this theme fugally, and certainly a canonic continuation would be highly unlikely. It is clear that if the treatment were to be in any way fugal, it would be only in a limited sense. In the first place, Schubert himself begins the continuation, and it is a self-repetition in the flutes, not a fugal answer. Secondly, the presence of the second flute in thirds below the first implies a harmonic texture not characteristic of the opening stages of a fugue, or a fugato for that matter. What would be possible, even if the flutes' repeat is fully harmonized, is a 'fugal' answer itself fully harmonized. The result would be roughly analogous to the second subject in the finale of Elgar's Second Symphony. Beyond that 'answer', there would probably be no fugal follow-up at all. Just as interesting as what that original second subject might have been is what it was not: it was not an idea that could have generated the same kind of movement as its replacement.

Could it be that the imputations of fugue which infect the literature of the second half of the twentieth century stem from Tovey? Tovey quoted Schubert's deleted second subject, but so inaccurately that it is hard to believe that the divergencies from the truth are transcription errors. He even changes the flutes' repetition of the theme to a fugal answer beginning G, B, A.[40] (See Ex. 5.19.) One can

Ex. 5.19

only guess that he had at some time seen the *Revisionsbericht*, carried the deleted theme in his head or scribbled it down without looking too closely, and later imagined how it might continue. Then, with the passing of time, he perhaps came to believe that his imagined fugal continuation was actually Schubert's. So what Tovey dismisses as a 'schoolmasterly little fugue' was actually Tovey's, not Schubert's! Once the seed was sown, it could easily have germinated in other minds and proved too hardy to dislodge.

Griffel seems to believe that Schubert had written a piano sketch, and that 'when he came back to the sketch of the second theme, he changed his mind about it'. He reworked the piano sketch, 'then returned to sketch the new theme in the score'.[41] It would be logical to suppose, then, that when he scrapped his first thought he also abandoned the several hundred bars of music he had composed from there to the end of the movement in the piano sketch. The more likely scenario, since there are so many indications that Schubert was composing directly into score as he had done in the Seventh Symphony, is that he had at this point composed only the first group and transition, and was confronting the task of inventing a second subject for the first time. If he *had* begun with a piano sketch he would probably have resolved his problem with the second subject at that stage – and long before he had constructed an entire finale in that sketch on the basis of the old one. The coda of the finale is free of revisions, yet not without interest in the autograph. The approach from recapitulation to coda is a variant of that from exposition to development. There, in the long *decrescendo* on the current tonic (G, the dominant of C), the bass moves down to the low tonic, and the upper harmony dies away leaving uncovered the low G, which then falls by a tone, twice, to E flat, where Schubert recalls the last eight-bar strain of his second subject but proceeds to shape it into something resembling the 'joy' theme of Beethoven's Ninth Symphony. Now, at the end of the recapitulation, the current tonic is of course C, and the bass falls by a tone, then a semitone to A natural. It is an evocative incident, far removed from yet perhaps spawned by the previous symphony (the 'Unfinished'), where an unaccompanied descent in the cellos and basses early in the development of the first movement leads to a new and unpredictable harmonic area. It is also, surely, the source of Schumann's linkage at the same point (recapitulation-to-coda) in the first movement of his Symphony No. 2, also in C major (Ex. 5.20). Schumann's advocacy of Schubert's 'Great' is well known.

Ex. 5.20

If Schubert had followed the model passage as at the end of the exposition, his bass would have descended to A flat. The relaxation embodied in an A flat major chord, which finds a home within itself for the tonic C, is a far cry from the energy implicit in the upward-pointing major chord on A, which pushes the tonic C up by a semitone. Here begins the 84-bar climax-preparation which has as its goal the four repeated notes of the second subject, now on the tonic and in weighty bare octaves – after which what follows is simply reaffirmation, celebrating the fact that the goal has been attained. These 84 bars are a marvel of musical engineering. To carp that Schubert merely takes a 20-bar span and lets it be heard four times at different pitch-levels is to miss the subtleties that even a cursory examination can reveal.

The whole passage is built of four-bar blocks, essentially with a change of chord at every fourth bar. In each 20-bar span, the first four-bar model serves three times, and the second twice (but with an extension in the fourth span). The first model (Ex. 5.21) combines two elements from the first theme (Ex. 5.22). The second model (Ex. 5.23) entails three elements from the second group (Ex. 5.24),

Ex. 5.21

Ex. 5.22

Ex. 5.23

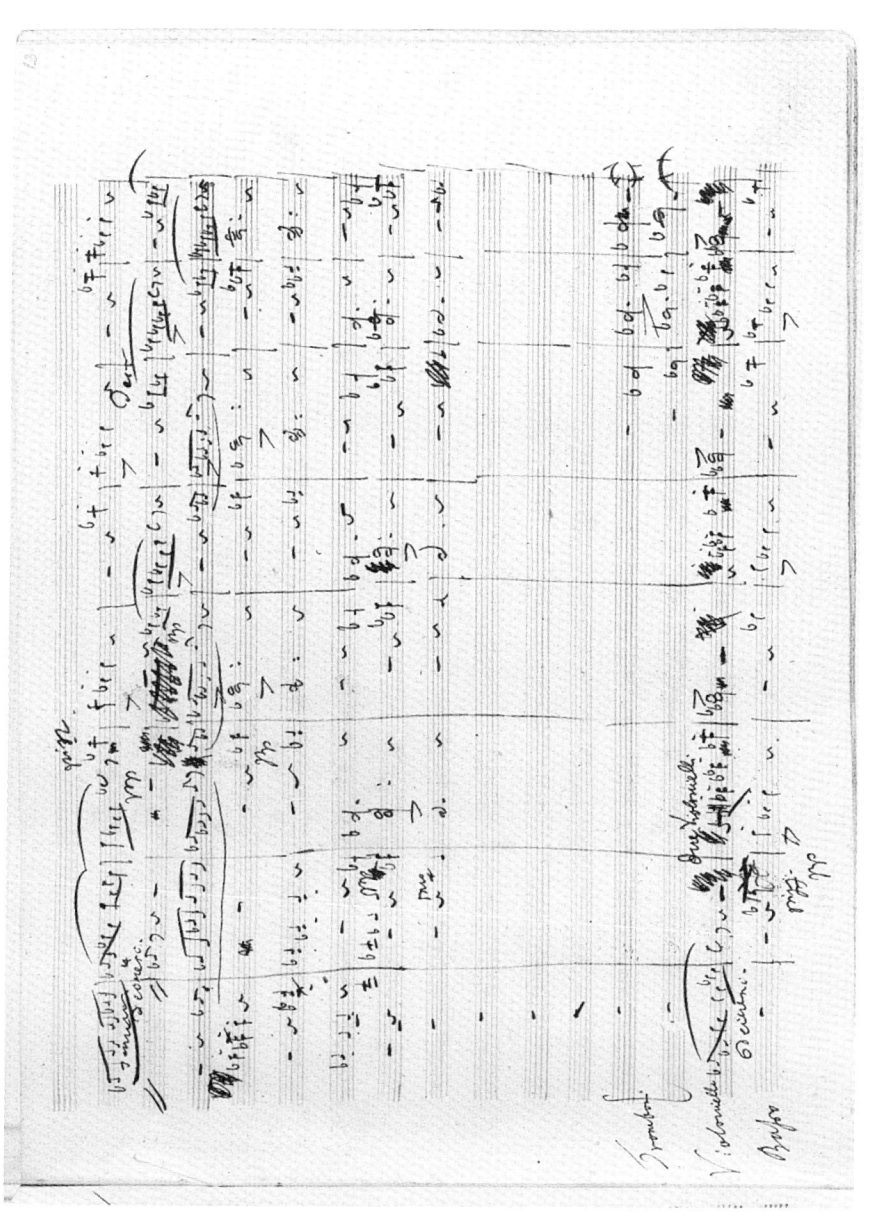

1 Symphony No. 9, folio 13r (autograph score).

2 Symphony in E, folio 57.

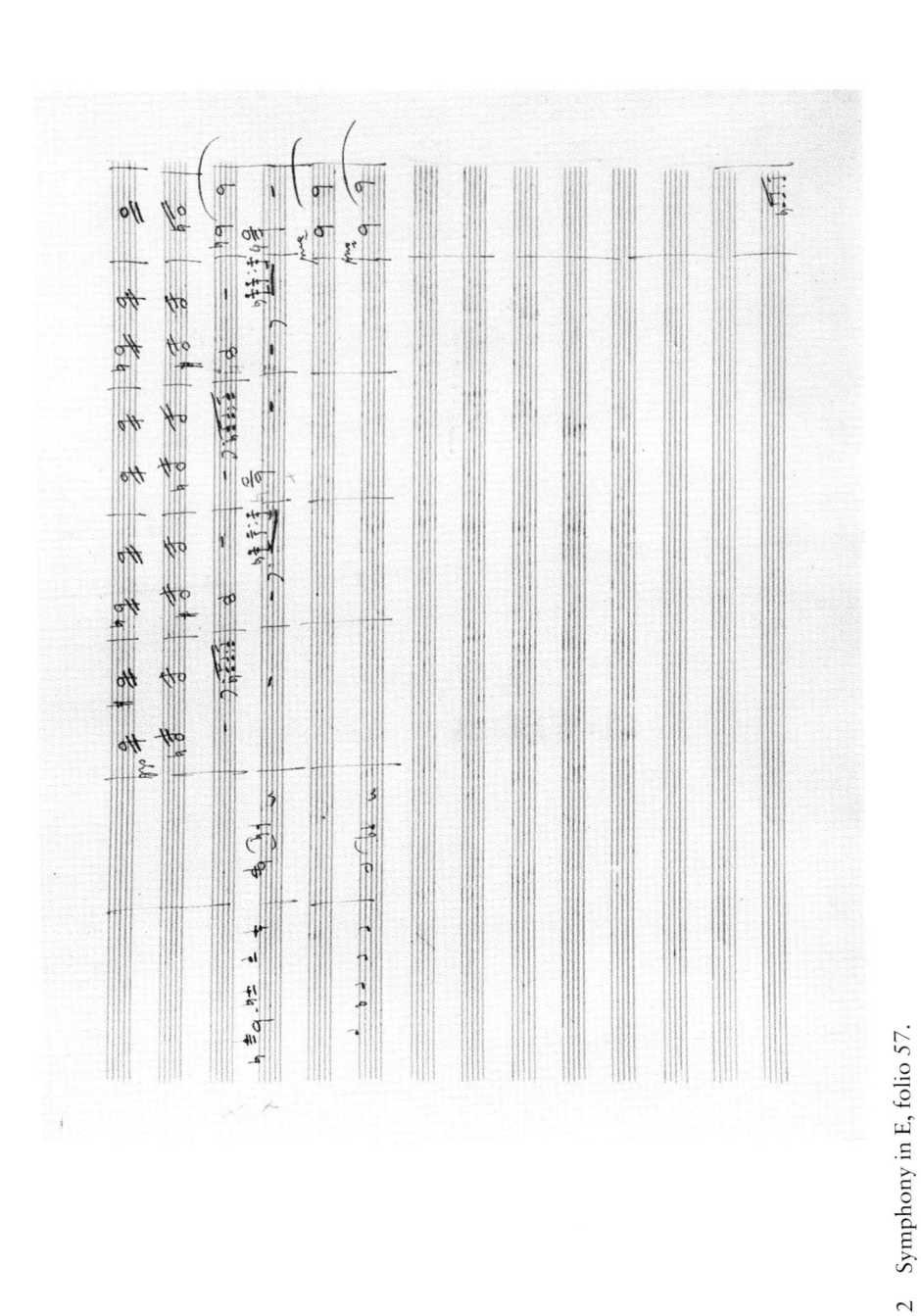

3 Symphony No. 9, folio 130v (autograph score).

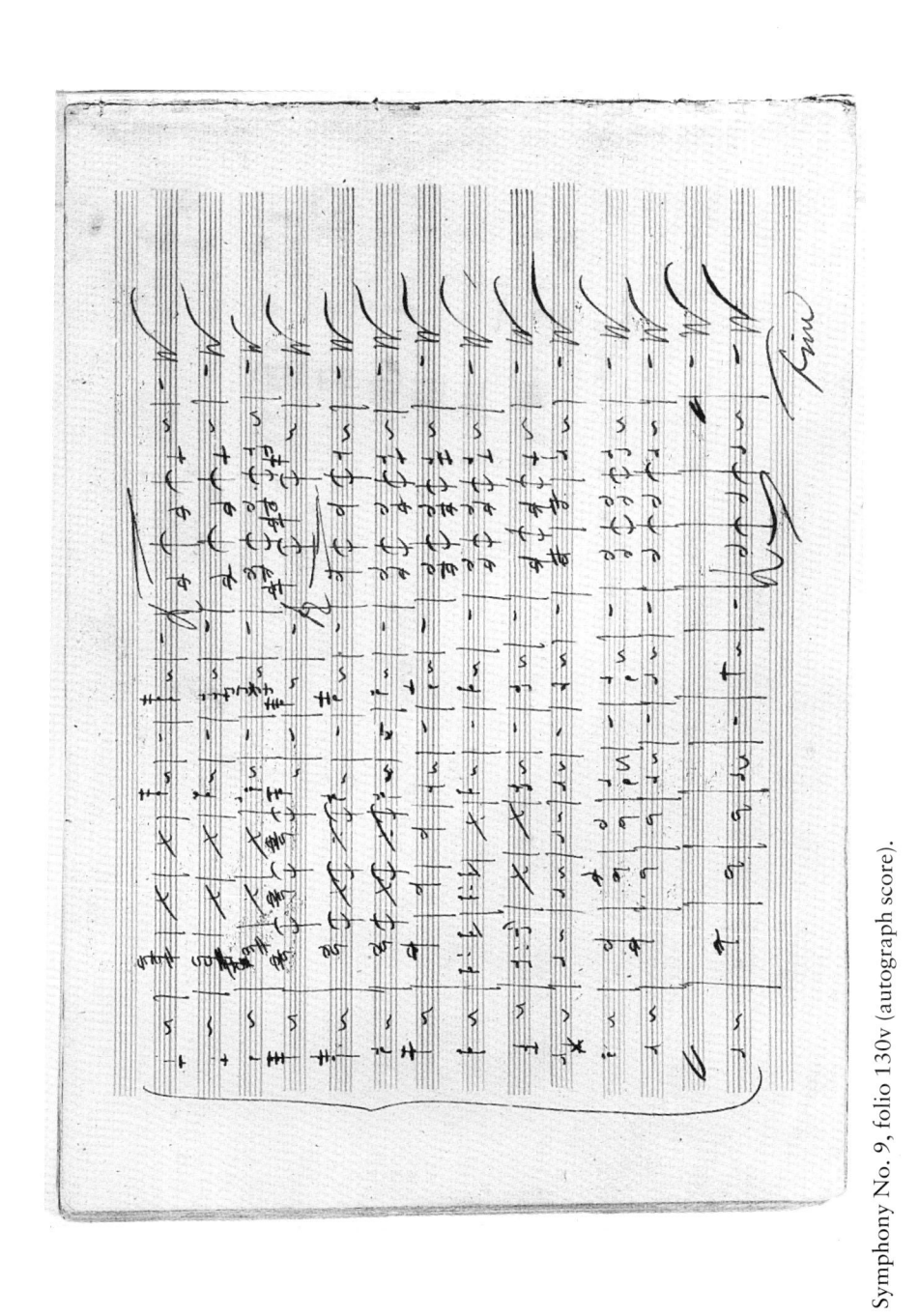

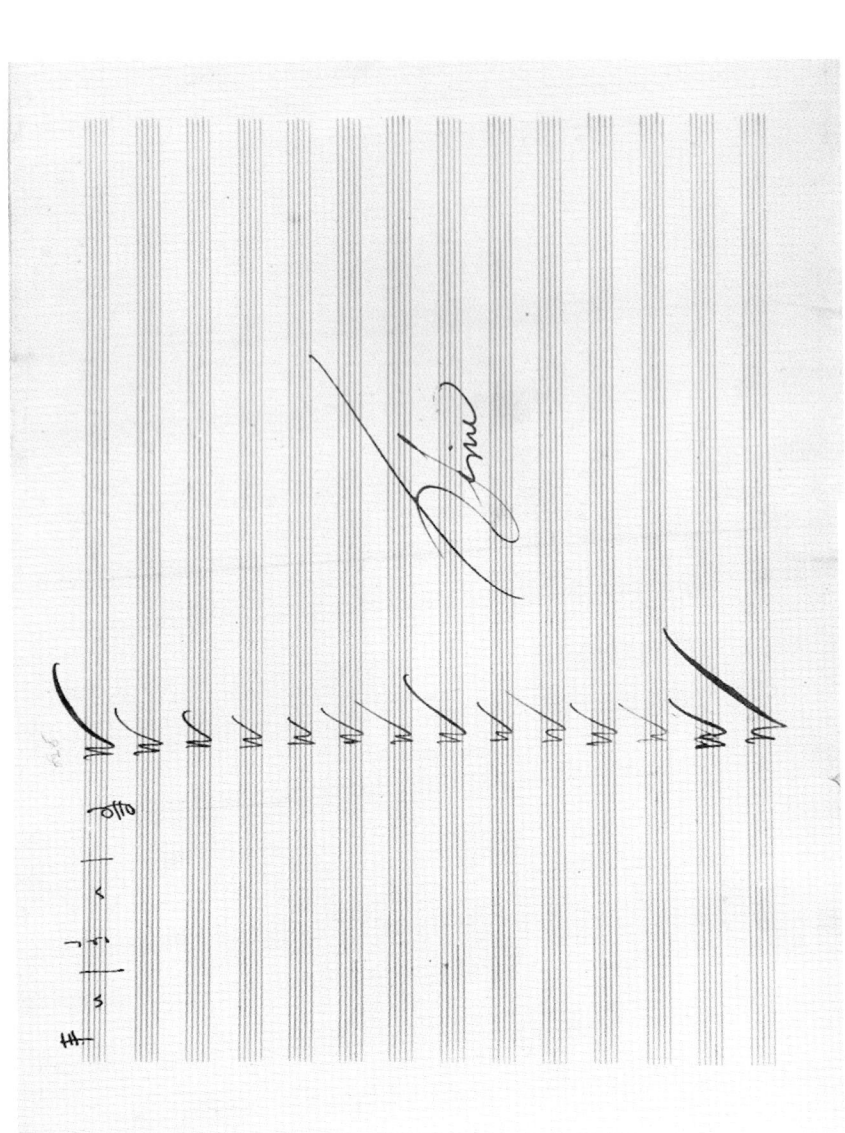

4 Symphony in E, final page of last movement (sketch).

Karoline Unger
(Carola Ungher, Lenaus Braut, später verehelichte Sabatier)
Lithographie von Ferdinand v. Lütgendorf (1823)
K. k. Hofbibliothek, Wien

5   Engraving of Caroline Unger from O.E. Deutsch, *Franz Schubert, Sein Leben in Bildern* (München and Leipzig, 1913).

6   Portrait of Nikolaus Lenau from Nikolaus Lenau, *Sämtliche Werke Briefe* (Stuggart, 1959).

7 'Zur Unsinniade–5ᵗᵉʳ Gesang, 31 December 1817.' Watercolour by Carl Friederich Zimmermann.

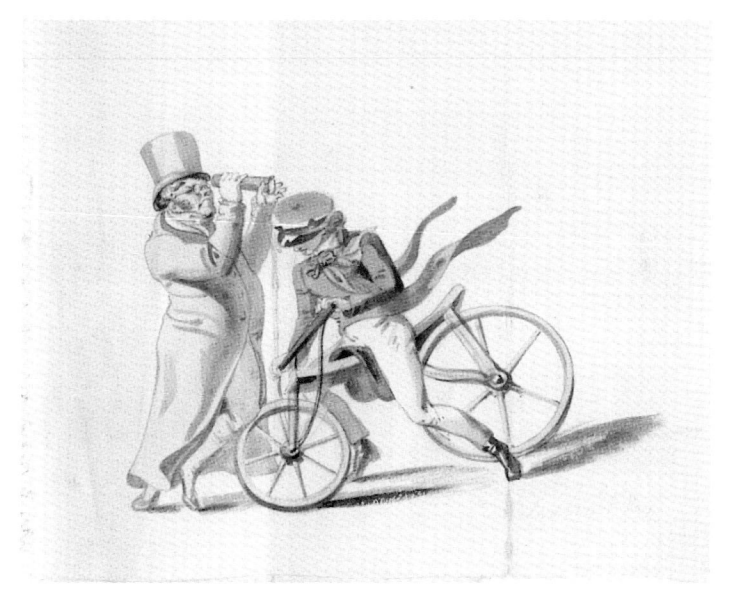

8 'Schubert and the Kaleidoscope, Kupelwieser and the Draisine.' Watercolour by Leopold Kupelwieser, 'Unsinnsgesellschaft' newsletter dated 16 July 1818.

9   Watercolour portrait of Schubert by Wilhelm August-Rieder (1825) from O.E. Deutsch, *Schubert: A Documentary Biography* (London, 1946).

10 Anonymous portrait of Schubert aged about 18 years from *Heritage of Music – The Romantic Era* (Oxford, 1989).

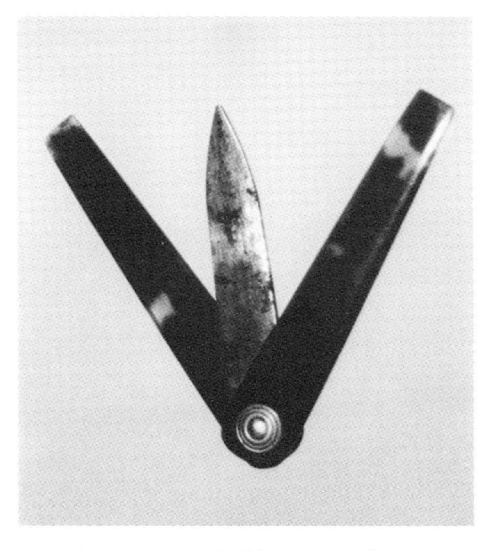

11 A lancet used for bleeding in the nineteenth century. Photograph by Peter Gilroy Bevan.

Ex. 5.24

the third of which is now assigned to the double basses alone. The only important thematic ingredient not present is the four repeated notes which head the second subject: but they are to be the destination, so for the time being are present only by implication – in the bass of Ex. 5.21, for example.

Ex. 5.25

In Ex. 5.25, by re-drawing the barlines at the 'superior metric level' (four bars of Schubert's in one of ours), we can gain a more comprehensive bird's-eye-view of the structure. The following table extracts the salient statistics to aid comparison of the four spans.

Table 5.1

Span	Duration (bars)	Dynamic	Scoring	Harmony	Pitch level
1	20	*ppp*			
2	20	*pp*	changed, esp from *fp*	developed in first 3 bars	semitone higher
3	20	*p*	more ww doubling	same	tone higher
4	24	*mf*	trbnes added; cb change	further revision/ extension	begins tone up/ends 4th up

It emerges from this analysis that the only spans of this loosely sequential structure that are near to being identical are spans 2 and 3, although the pitch-relationship with its predecessor is different in each span's case. The harmony of span 4 is at first identical with that of span 2, but with the conspicuous addition of trombones at this late stage in the *crescendo*, until its fourth bar, where Schubert moves to a dominant seventh of B flat (the inner extension to the span which makes it 24 bars long instead of 20). This change is necessary if span 4 is to be the last, since a repetition of span 2 here would lead to A major, not the targeted C major. What, then, does a V^7 of B flat achieve, if C major is the goal? It is, by an inspired *double entendre*, a chromatic chord within C – in Schubert's personal harmonic vocabulary at least: it is that chord which has by now become an almost thematic component in the 'Great' – the German sixth on the subdominant. Specifically, Schubert is reactivating the climax of the second subject itself, both harmonically and melodically, as will be seen if Ex. 5.26 is compared with bars 4 and 5 of span 4 in Ex. 5.25.

This climax-preparation is, then, a feat of thematic integration of a high order, and it is hard to resist the thought that it conditioned Schubert's thinking on the way to the ultimate thematic integration he evolved in the last movement of his sketched 'Tenth' Symphony (D936a), where the two principal themes of the

Ex. 5.26

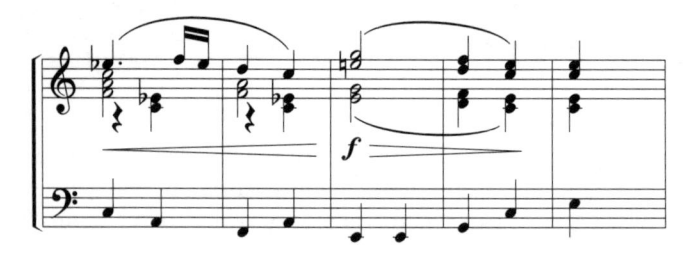

movement are simultaneously combined. Another important aspect of the passage, corroborated by fresh study of the autograph, lies in the dynamic markings. The four spans are marked, in succession, **ppp** – **pp** – **p** – **mf**. The fact that **mp** was not a marking in Schubert's palette, of which this is a neat reminder, gives us pause to reflect that – in a passage like this where there is a regular grading of dynamic levels – the execution of dynamics requires an adjustment to compensate for the lack of **mp**. In other words, it should be assumed that the dynamic step from **pp** to **p** is equal to the step from **p** to **mf**. Recognition of this fact is an imperative of historically-informed performance.

The 'excursion', a feature of codas which was exemplified in the first movement of the 'Great', reaches new lengths in this 84-bar example. Earlier examples tended to be somewhat shorn of thematic references, exposing their harmonic/tonal *raison d'être*. But the present epoch-making example is uniquely rich in thematic allusion. From this point, the finale quickly reaches its conclusion. The four repeated minim Cs, one of the supreme points of climax and resolution in the symphonic literature, were originally conceived as crotchets with intervening rests. Schubert then opted for the solidity of minims (strengthening the reference to the second subject), as well as the stentorian sonority of low bassoons, horns and strings, with no pitch sounding above middle C. Throughout this coda, the notation in Schubert's autograph appears to underline the dominance of the 'superior metric level' by using the standard 'ditto' marks in the second, third and fourth bars, with fresh note-indications in the first bar of a group (Ex. 5.27). Soon

Ex. 5.27

there comes a threefold cadence (bars 1093–1104) which mirrors the threefold cadences at the end of the exposition and recapitulation of the first movement (228–240, 546–558). The last note of the symphony has generated much debate: does Schubert's hairpin denote an accent or a *decrescendo*? An imaginative response to the autograph at this point, coupled with due consideration of some musical factors, tends to lead to one and the same conclusion. Schubert, saving labour by writing 'frame dynamics' in the usual way, places hairpins above the first violin, below the first flute, and below the basso line (Plate 3). (According to his own strictures, Mollo would have to interpret this as meaning both an accent and a *decrescendo*; but he dodges the issue in his commentary and Abbado opts for an accent.)

Klaus Tennstedt performed a decrescendo on this last chord, claiming that nowhere in music except at the last chord of the 'Great' is there both an accent and *sforzando*.[42] In truth there are plenty of instances where Schubert combines hairpin and *fz*, in contexts where, every time, an accent is clearly intended. Numerous examples occur in the 'Great'. At I.190 and 192 the combined hairpin and *fz* is evidently for an accent, as is seen from comparison with the foregoing four bars where analogous incidents carry only the *fz* marking. Later in the same movement the double marking appears several times in the passages 240–243 (exposition) and 558–561 (recapitulation), but for one crotchet in the exposition version he writes a *fz* only and for the same crotchet in the recapitulation version a hairpin only. In these instances a *decrescendo* would be meaningless. In II.67–68 the general cast of the context leaves no doubt: the double symbol in the woodwind implies an accent only.

Nicholas Toller's plea that Schubert seems to have retaken his pen to complete the (large) accent sign, and this fact argues against it being taken as an accent, is an appealing one.[43] But if Schubert had already written a long hairpin at the top of the page, and his pen (or his aim) let him down with the second one, might it not be natural to take the time (as there were no notes left to compose) to make things tidy by supplying the missing stroke? In any case, it was characteristic of Schubert at the end of a symphony to indulge in extravagant flourishes; witness the final double-bar in Plate 3. Even if a symphony was unfinished, he still enjoyed a larger-than-life double-bar, as in the Seventh Symphony (Plate 4). So perhaps some allowance for exuberant self-satisfaction should be made at the end of a 2623-bar symphony that was finished.

Although the evidence already rather points in favour of an accent, two musical points seem to add fuel to the argument. The rhythm of the final note may be construed as a thematic rhythm, present and repeated without interruption for example from bar 889 to bar 916, where there is no possibility of a *decrescendo* (indeed the last statement is marked *crescendo*). And if Schubert had really wanted a *decrescendo*, he would surely have written a longer note, almost certainly a full bar (which here means a full four bars) with a pause on it. A *decrescendo* takes more time to accomplish properly. Listen to the final *decrescendo* in Nikolaus Harnoncourt's recording: the lengthening of the note well beyond the duration specified by Schubert tells its own story. The finale of the 'Great' was surely destined to end as affirmatively as it began.

Notes and references

1. The author acknowledges with gratitude the award of a research grant from the British Academy for study in Vienna, and the co-operation of Dr Otto Biba, Archivdirektor at the Gesellschaft der Musikfreunde.
2. Brian Newbould, *Schubert and the Symphony: a New Perspective* (Toccata Press, 1992), pp 210–12.
3. Symphonie (C dur) Franz Schubert, Partitur rediviert von F.A.Roitzsch (Edition Peters, 1871).

4. The author himself brought the two tempi into exact alignment in a performance with the Hull Philharmonic Orchestra in the City Hall, Hull, on 22 February 1997. A fine recording which comes close to doing so was made by Sir Charles Mackerras with the Orchestra of the Age of Enlightenment in 1988 (Virgin Classics, reissued on the Veritas label).
5. In the booklet issued with the recordings of the Schubert symphonies by Abbado with the Chamber Orchestra of Europe (Deutsche Grammophon), p. 10.
6. Professor Robert Pascall, editor for the New Brahms Edition, has not identified any marks in the autograph of the 'Great' as emanating from Brahms, and believes that Brahms's purpose in the Schubert *Gesamtausgabe* was editorial, not compositional.
7. 'The Genesis of the "Great" C major Symphony', in *Essays on Schubert* (London, 1966), pp 29–58.
8. 'How the "Great" C major was written', in *Music & Letters* (LVI/1975), pp 18–25.
9. 'A Reappraisal of Schubert's Methods of Composition', *Musical Quarterly* (LXIII/2, April 1977), pp 186–210.
10. See Brian Newbould, 'A Working Sketch by Schubert (D936a)', in *Current Musicology* (No. 43, 1987), pp 22–32.
11. 'Paper Studies and the Future of Schubert Research', in E Badura-Skoda and P Branscombe (Eds), *Schubert Studies: Problems of Style and Chronology* (London, 1982), pp 209–75.
12. *Schubert and the Symphony*, Chapter XIV (pp 247–57).
13. Op.cit., pp 21–2.
14. Op.cit., p. 31.
15. Op.cit., p. 190.
16. Op.cit., p. 189 (n.).
17. Op.cit., pp 250–51.
18. Op.cit., p. 200 (n.).
19. Op.cit., p. 19.
20. Op.cit., pp 32–3.
21. Op.cit., p. 201.
22. Op.cit., pp 225–6.
23. Op.cit., p. 21.
24. Op.cit., p. 23.
25. These matters are amplified in Newbould, Op.cit., p. 84, and Brian Newbould, *Schubert: the Music and the Man* (London & California, 1997), pp 83 and 382.
26. The chord is a German sixth on the subdominant. Its use elsewhere in the 'Great' and elsewhere in Schubert's work is discussed in Brian Newbould, *Schubert and the Symphony – a New Perspective* (London, 1992), pp 245–6.
27. Op.cit., p. 203.
28. D F Tovey, *Essays in Musical Analysis*, Vol. 1, Symphonies 1 (London, 1935), p. 208.
29. Op.cit., pp 204–7.
30. Op.cit., pp 43–4.
31. Grosvenor W Cooper and Leonard B Meyer, *The Rhythmic Structure of Music* (Chicago, 1960), p. 2.
32. *Schubert and the Symphony*, pp 177–8.
33. See Brian Newbould, *Schubert: the Music and the Man*, p. 88.
34. *Schubert and the Symphony*, pp 238–9; *Schubert: the Music and the Man*, pp 383–5.
35. See Ex. 7.1 on page 168.

36. Op.cit., p. 46n.
37. Tovey, Op.cit., p. 211.
38. Reed, Op.cit., pp 21, 24.
39. Op.cit., p. 208.
40. Op.cit., pp 210–11.
41. Op.cit., p. 208.
42. In an interview in *Ovation*, December 1982.
43. Nicholas Toller, 'Gesture and Expressive Purpose in Schubert's Instrumental Music of 1822–28' (unpublished thesis, University of Hull, 1988).

6 'Biding his time' – Schubert among the Bohemians in the mid-nineteenth century
Jan Smaczny

Schubert's influence on the composers of the so-called Czech national revival has always been considered axiomatic, a self-evident state of affairs to which spice, if not a great deal of substance, has been added owing to the origins of the composer's parents in north Moravia and Austrian Silesia. Even without the possibility of a common ethnicity, the assumption has been that Schubert's muse was close to the soul of the Czechs, that he was a musical, if not an actual, cousin. Nearly all the literature on Dvořák, for example, makes reference to Schubert's impact on his music. While these various perceived resemblances and affinities between the music of the two composers have been accrued as demonstrations of a clear link,[1] Dvořák himself appears to add weight to the connection in his own writings.

In an article entitled 'Franz Schubert',[2] written three years in advance of the centenary of the composer's birth, Dvořák wrote extensively and with considerable insight about Schubert's style, standing and posthumous influence. The title of the present essay is, in fact, derived from a sentence in the article in which Dvořák states, with evident feeling: 'While a pianist or singer may find immediate recognition, a composer, especially if he has so original a message to deliver as Schubert, has to bide his time'. In this substantial piece, Dvořák reveals a knowledge of songs such as 'Erlkönig', D328, 'Der Doppelgänger', from *Schwanengesang*, D957/13 and 'Der Leiermann' from *Winterreise*, D911/24, a broad range of piano and orchestral music, choral music, the String Quartets in A minor, D804, and D minor, D810, and the C major String Quintet, D956. As a composer of chamber music, Dvořák placed Schubert above Mendelssohn, and as a composer of symphonies he put him on a par with Beethoven, above Schumann, and 'far above' Mendelssohn. Amid these ringing endorsements of his genius, Dvořák states in categorical terms his debt to Schubert: 'Dr Riemann asserts with justice that in their use of harmony both Schumann and Liszt are descendants of

Schubert; Brahms, too, whose enthusiasm for Schubert is well-known, has perhaps felt his influence; and as for myself, I cordially acknowledge my great obligations to him'. As a further earnest of Dvořák's interest in Schubert his allusion to the Schubert *Gesamtausgabe* amounts to a recommendation that would have warmed the heart of any publisher:

> Fortunately the works of the great masters have at last been made accessible in complete editions; the Schubert collection is just being completed by Breitkopf and Härtel. It contains many gems unknown to the public, or even to the profession; and it now behoves artists and conductors to select from this embarrassing wealth what most deserves revival.

These fulsome assertions might seem to leave little room to question Schubert's signal presence in Dvořák's creative life. But when we look beyond the public statement which the article on Schubert constitutes, the picture that emerges is by no means unequivocal. In a surviving correspondence with Eusebius Mandyczewski amounting to seventeen items (twelve letters, three messages written on Dvořák's visiting card, and two postcards),[3] much of it occasioned by Dvořák's succeeding Brahms, after the latter's death in 1897, as a composer member of the Austrian State Commission for Awarding Artistic Grants, there is no mention of Schubert at all, even though the composer must have been aware of Mandyczewski's activities as editor of the complete edition. With Dvořák's clear admission of his debt to Schubert in his New York article referred to above, it is perhaps strange, even given a general avoidance of small talk in business letters, that he did not mention the composer once. Although Schubert does not figure in these letters, some suggestive evidence regarding early influences on Dvořák, much of which challenges the conventional wisdom relating to Schubert, emerges.

Here, we must turn to what remains, from many points of view, one of the most perceptive discussions of Dvořák's style, Gerald Abraham's essay 'Dvořák's Musical Personality', first published in Viktor Fischl's symposium commemorating the centenary of Dvořák's birth, *Antonín Dvořák: His Achievement*,[4] and undoubtedly a major source of wisdom where influences on the composer are concerned. With reference to Dvořák's first serious attempts at composition, Abraham wrote as follows: 'And so, as one would expect, his [Dvořák's] earliest compositions – the A minor Quintet [B7] of 1861 and the A major Quartet of 1862 [B8] – were (we are told) written under the influence of Mozart, Beethoven and Schubert', and later, with ringing confidence: 'Beethoven and Schubert formed an important part of the corpus of music from which Dvořák naturally acquired the beginnings of his own idiom, but they also served at first – and from time to time in later years – as his conscious models'.[5]

We might wonder who exactly told Gerald Abraham that Dvořák's first two extant chamber works were written under the influence of Schubert; it certainly was not Dvořák. Returning to Dvořák's correspondence with Mandyczewski, we find, in a letter dated 7 January 1898, the composer providing a list of early and later works (Mandyczewski needed it in order to assemble a catalogue of Dvořák's compositions as an appendix to František Krejčí's essay on the composer, 'Antonín

Dvořák', in *Musikbuch aus Österreich*, no. 2, 1905). In the same letter, Dvořák described influences on his earlier works, writing about his Quartet in A major as follows: 'The quartet [is] in the style of Mendelssohn and Beethoven and also Mozart...'.[6] In the next sentence he also wrote about his B flat major Symphony (No. 2, B12) as 'displaying Schumann's influence'. In the case of his very first chamber work, the Quintet in A minor, where commentators have seen clear evidence of the presence of the initial motif of Schubert's A minor Quartet, D804, in the design of the first theme of the opening Allegro ma non troppo,[7] the composer makes no reference to Schubert, despite describing Schubert's own A minor Quartet in his New York article on the composer as the one which was, in his opinion, 'the most fascinating'.[8] Nor do we find any confirmation that Schubert was a major feature of Dvořák's formative early days in Prague when the composer was speaking directly about this period. In an interview printed in the *Sunday Times* (London) of 10 May 1885 Dvořák spoke about his time at the Prague Organ School as follows: 'I was chosen with some of the best pupils to sing in the choir. Now it was that I first heard of Mozart, Beethoven, and Mendelssohn as instrumental composers; previously, indeed, I had hardly known that the two last-named had existed'.[9] Strange, indeed, that a composer who 'cordially acknowledged' his debt to Schubert, should not mention him as featuring in his experience at this time. Spurred on by Dvořák's admission of 1894, commentators have come to see the impact of Schubert on these works as a given feature of the composer's early style, a fundamental building block present from the beginning, in Gerald Abraham's words: 'part of the corpus of music from which Dvořák naturally acquired the beginnings of his own idiom'.

But Dvořák's failure to mention Schubert in this context to Mandyczewski when reflecting on his early works and, incidentally, an absence of any mention of Schubert at all in any of his correspondence, should lead us to question the safety of judgements such as Abraham's. (In Dvořák's collected surviving letters dispatched there are five references to Liszt, four to Mendelssohn, five to Mozart, three to Schumann and six to Wagner; Beethoven, with eight citations, is most frequently mentioned, once referred to as 'Papa Beethoven';[10] Bach, Handel and Haydn merit only two references each.)[11] Even when prompted in connection with Schubert, Dvořák seems strangely unresponsive. On 18 January 1880, the German violinist and leader of the Quartetto Fiorentino, Jean Becker, wrote to Dvořák with news of an enormously successful performance of his Quartet in E flat major, Op. 51, B92 he had given with his quartet in Halle that day.[12] In the second paragraph of the letter he asked the composer if he would write a concertpiece for piano and violin for himself and his daughter which they would play the following summer, adding the suggestion that it be modelled on Schubert's B minor Rondo (presumably the Rondo brillant, D895), 'though somewhat shorter'.[13] Not only does Dvořák not seemed to have replied, no such work modelled on Schubert was forthcoming; although Dvořák produced his F major Violin Sonata, Op. 57 [B106] the following March, it was not dedicated to Becker and the only compositional affinities it seems to have are with Brahms.

The disjunction between the evidence of the letters and Dvořák's article of 1894 requires a brief gloss. There is a perceptible qualitative difference between Dvořák's public statements and his correspondence. The former tended to reflect an idealized image of life and art. For example, in the extensive advice attributed to Dvořák in newspaper articles in New York regarding the founding of a native style, Dvořák frequently recommended recourse to the repertoire of 'negro melodies', just as he claimed he had advised English composers to turn to the 'fine melodies of Ireland and Scotland' for inspiration.[14] The seemingly unchallengeable good sense of this begins to look a little threadbare when Dvořák's own reliance on and use of folksong in his own music is so minimal: hardly more than a couple of quotations in the totality of his vast output and barely a hint of specific 'negro melodies' in his own symphony 'From the New World'. Dvořák's letters, on the other hand, have a relaxed and workaday frankness that promotes confidence in them as a more realistic record of his feelings and doings.

However well versed in Schubert's music Dvořák appeared to be in 1894,[15] questions concerning the extent of his knowledge of it during his formative years in the late 1850s, 1860s and 1870s inevitably arise; indeed, how much of Schubert's music was known to the Czechs in these crucial years? Examining the concert life to which Dvořák, Smetana and their contemporaries had access reveals the extent to which Schubert was part of their musical world. The 1860s in particular saw dramatic developments in the musical life of Prague with the opening of the Provisional Theatre on 18 November 1862 for the performance of plays and opera exclusively in Czech. Beyond this fillip to the operatic repertoire, the Theatre was also used occasionally for concerts, providing a venue for touring artists in particular. In the twenty-five year period between 1850 and 1875, there was a perceptible quickening of the pulse of concert life in Prague. Schubert, however, was by no means a major feature in programmes.[16] During this time the most frequent items by him to appear were songs. Although isolated numbers from the three song cycles ('Der Neugierige', 'Ungeduld', 'Die böse Farbe' and 'Der Müller und der Bach' from *Die schöne Müllerin*; 'Der Lindenbaum' and 'Die Post' from *Winterreise*; 'Liebesbotschaft', 'Aufenthalt' and 'Am Meer' from *Schwanengesang*) were performed, none of the cycles was given complete in this period; no songs emerge as particular favourites, although 'Gretchen am Spinnrade', D118, 'Die Forelle', D550, 'Der Pilgrim', D794, 'Der blinde Knabe', D833, 'Der Hirt auf dem Felsen', D956, were all given; an arrangement for military band of 'Der Wanderer', D489, had an isolated performance, as did one of 'Die junge Nonne', D828, by Gounod, for voice, piano, harmonium and cello. Curiously enough, although 'Erlkönig' appears to have been given at least three times, two of the performances were of Liszt's piano transcription, S558/4.

The piano music played was also a fairly miscellaneous selection including a couple of the 'Moments Musicaux', D780, the Sonata in G major, D984 (described as Fantasie in G major), the Impromptu in A flat, D935/2, various unspecified items, two performances of Liszt's orchestral version of the 'Wanderer' Fantasia (D760, S366) and orchestrations of the F minor Fantasy for piano duet (D940, arr. Rudorff), the fifth of the six Grandes Marches (D819/5, arr. Liszt S363/2) and the 'Grand Duo' (D812, arr. Joachim). The Octet, D803, and C major String Quintet seem only to have been given once each in this period, while the quartets in D minor and A minor were played twice and once respectively; there was also a performance by the Quartetto Fiorentino of some variations (?D810/2). The Piano Trio in B flat major, D898, was played once and the Trio in E flat major, D929, twice. Orchestral music was scarcer still, the only symphonies being the 'Great' C major, D944, played three times (1859, 1864 and 1869),[17] and the 'Unfinished', D759, given in 1867, one year after its first publication. To this can be added the overtures to *Fierabras*, D796, *Alfonso und Estrella*, D732, and an unspecified overture (?D591) played as a prelude to a performance of *Othello* in the Provisional Theatre on 23 April 1870. A few choruses were performed, including 'Hymne an den Unendlichen', D232, 'Nachtgesang im Walde', D913, 'Ständchen', D920, 'Gott im Ungewitter', D985, and 'Gott der Weltschöpfer', D986, as well as the Kyrie, Gloria and Benedictus of the Mass in E flat major, D950 on 8 December 1866, as with the 'Unfinished' Symphony, a year after its publication. Rounding out the picture were single performances of an arrangement by Reményi for violin and piano of the Divertissement à l'hongroise, D818, a transcription for violin and piano of the 'Romance' from the incidental music to *Rosamunde*, D797, and two performances of an *Hommage à Schubert* for two violins (?accompaniment) by the Belgian violinist Hubert Léonard.

With each work placed end to end, the list seems not unreasonable a representation of Schubert in a period when much of his music was unavailable. Viewed, however, against the background of the twenty-five year timescale with few repeats for many of the items, it does not suggest a general admiration for, or knowledge of, Schubert in Prague at this time. In Dvořák's case, the exposure would have been further curtailed since he only came to Prague in the autumn of 1857. Furthermore, throughout the 1860s he was on the whole too poor to attend public concerts and was also much occupied by his duties as a viola player in the Provisional Theatre orchestra (November 1862 to July 1871).[18] What experience of Schubert Dvořák was likely to have had in these circumstances was probably through his own performing activities. A notable event must have been the concert on 12 December 1869 in the concert hall on Žofín Island (in the Vltava near the Provisional, now National, Theatre) in which Smetana conducted the Provisional Theatre orchestra (presumably including Dvořák) in a performance of an unspecified symphony in C major assumed to be the 'Great' C major. Given the rarity of the event and the composer's later enthusiasm for Schubert, it seems remarkable that he failed to mention it as one of the signal events of his early years in Prague; his involvement as part of the orchestral personnel in Gounod's *Roméo et Juliette* that evening in the Provisional Theatre (again conducted by Smetana) could hardly have expunged the memory of such an important occasion. While he seemed to have no desire to recall this particular musical encounter in later life, an event he did remember, in his *Sunday Times* interview, was a rehearsal at the Prague Conservatoire of Beethoven's Ninth Symphony, conducted by Spohr, into which Dvořák, in his own words: '...contrived somehow to slip'.[19] Other non-Czech composers mentioned, or referred to by reference to their works, in this interview, in what seems a fairly comprehensive account of this time, were Cherubini, Haydn, Mozart, Mendelssohn, Wallace, Weber, Bellini, Rossini, Onslow, Wagner and Brahms – no hint of Schubert whatsoever. Nor was Dvořák in a financial position to buy scores. For this he relied on his better-heeled friend Karel Bendl; and yet, the only ones he detailed in his interview were '... Beethoven's Septet and the quartets of Onslow'.[20]

Beethoven, Mendelssohn and Schumann, in terms of frequency in concert performance and availability of scores, as his letter to Mandyczewski cited above indicates, were very much part of Dvořák's musical universe in these crucial early days when he was laying the foundations of his style. Schubert, on the other hand, was virtually unknown to him at this formative stage. For Dvořák, Schubert bided his time rather too long. But for two other Czech composers the experience of Schubert was both more direct and, in terms of influence, a good deal easier to pinpoint. Unlike Dvořák, whose exposure to Schubert at this stage might well be described as accidental, Smetana was involved in the planning of concerts which included Schubert's music. Well before his conducting of the 'Great' C major Symphony in 1869, he had, as a pianist, been close to Schubert's music, both performing and arranging it. In an early attempt to establish himself as a piano virtuoso, Smetana gave a concert in Eger (now Cheb) on 7 August 1847 which included Liszt's transcription of 'Ständchen', D889, S558/9, and in a concert on 7 January 1848 in Prague he took the piano part in the Kalkbrenner Septet Op. 32, Beethoven's piano and wind Quintet Op. 16, and Schubert's E flat major Piano Trio, D929.[21] During his time teaching music in Göteborg in Sweden (1856–61), Smetana arranged numerous chamber concerts including trios, in which he took part as pianist, and quartets by Schubert; among the works given by his pupils during a concert on 24 April 1860, was an improvisation for piano on Schubert's 'Die Post', D911/13. According to a fellow Czech musician, Josef Čapek, working in Göteborg: 'Schubert was a musician after Smetana's own heart'.[22] In 1857 Smetana also transcribed 'Der Neugierige' and 'Trockne Blumen' (not extant) from *Die schöne Müllerin* (795/6 and 18). Earlier in Prague he had accompanied one or possibly more songs by Schubert in a concert on 26 February 1855, which had also included the first performance of his *Triumph-Sinfonie*, and on 3 December the same year he had taken the piano part in Schumann's Piano Quintet, Op. 44 in a concert which included Schubert's String Quintet in C major. After his final return to Prague from Göteborg, Smetana gave a concert on 18 January 1862 which included a transcription of 'Ungeduld' (D795/7, not extant) and accompanied singers in 'Der Neugierige' and 'Gretchen am Spinnrade'.

Not only was Smetana involved in performing Schubert's music, there is clear evidence of influence, notably in the impact which Schubert's E flat Major Piano Trio had on Smetana's own G minor Piano Trio, Op. 15. The opening theme of the finale of Smetana's Trio (composed in 1855, although the finale is based in part on an earlier Piano Sonata in G minor of 1846) has close affinities in both outline and the cimbalom-like manner of delivery with the second theme of the finale of Schubert's E flat major Trio (see Ex. 6.1 and 6.2). In addition to this

Ex. 6.1   Smetana: Trio in G minor, Op. 15

Ex. 6.2   Schubert: Trio in E flat major, D929

resemblance, its haunted, galloping nature recalls the pounding rhythms of the outer movements of Schubert's D minor String Quartet, D810. Whether Smetana intended an explicit connection with Schubert's 'Death and the Maiden' Quartet in a work which was written as a tribute to his recently deceased daughter, Bedřiška, must remain a matter of speculation, but it is fascinating to note that in material and manner both works seem to have such strong connections.

The other Czech composer who seems to qualify as a genuine Schubertian by dint of performance and influence was Zdeněk Fibich. Though far less well-known today than Smetana or Dvořák, he represented a distinctive strand in the development of Czech music. Described by one critic as the 'Son' in a 'Holy Trinity of Czech music' (in which Smetana, naturally enough, was the 'Father' and Dvořák, rather less obviously, the 'Holy Spirit'[23]), he was seen as a figure of great substance by the Czech musicological establishment well into the twentieth century. Like Smetana, and unlike Dvořák, Fibich's first language was German and much of his early education was in that language. He studied for two years in Leipzig (1865–7) with Moscheles and E.F. Richter. Many of his musical and intellectual affinities showed an orientation towards German culture, and though he often resorted to subject-matter from Czech history and mythology in his symphonic poems and operas, his musical voice was noticeably less nationally inflected than that of either Smetana or Dvořák. His early song settings, all of them to German texts and some seventeen to verse also used by Schubert, have close affinities with the available Lieder of Schubert and Schumann. The Schubert manner is not only present in the German settings, but was also apparent when Fibich began to set Czech verse in 1871. Not only is the melodic outline and phraseology of his Čelakovský setting 'Tak mne kouzlem ondy jala' Schubertian, he also adopts a favourite modulatory device from the older composer of using a solo repeated bass note of a chord as the third of a triad in a new major key (in this case D major to B flat major).

Fibich also performed Schubert songs, accompanying a singer in excerpts from *Die schöne Müllerin* at a concert on 16 February 1873. Even more persuasive evidence of his admiration for Schubert is to be found in his library where Schubert's scores abounded, including chamber music (a volume of duos, trios, quartets, quintets and the Octet arranged for piano four hands), piano sonatas and other keyboard works for four hands, a vocal score of *Die Zwillingsbrüder*, D647; the 'Great' C major Symphony in score, *Lazarus*, D689, piano solo compositions, choruses, duos for violin and piano, and a number of overtures arranged for piano.[24]

In Fibich's instrumental works the influence of Schubert is to be heard most plainly in his Quintet in D major, Op. 42, for violin, clarinet, horn, cello and piano. It is often possible to discern the presence of Schumann in the background of even late works by Fibich, the finale of this quintet and that of the Second Symphony in E flat major, Op. 38 (1893), for example; the Scherzo of the Quintet, however, is surely an attempt to capture the Schubert manner. Although most of the Quintet was written in 1893, the Scherzo is based on a much earlier Piano Sonata, in D minor, written in 1871 when the twenty-one year old Fibich had still to formulate many aspects of his style. Here is more than just an echo of the Schubert manner: the scherzo of the 'Great' C major Symphony, that of the F minor Fantasy for piano duet, perhaps most of all the Allegro vivace of the Octet are called to mind (see Ex. 6.3). It is clear that Schubert entered Fibich's style at a formative point in his development.

While Smetana and Fibich stand out as convincing Schubertians in the middle years of the century, Dvořák remains a much more problematic case; as we have seen, his contact with Schubert until quite late in his career appears to have been minimal and also to have carried no truly lasting impact. In his recent study of Schubert, Brian Newbould speaks about a Schubertian usage of the diminished seventh: '...which the Bohemian composers inherited from Schubert'.[25] The notion of inheritance is an interesting one and certainly deserves consideration against a slightly broader background. While assessing the concert life of Prague, or what certain composers might have had in their libraries, can help establish the potential for influence, a less direct route should not be ruled out. For all his

162 *Schubert Studies*

Ex. 6.3   Fibich: Quintet in D major, Op. 42

Ex. 6.3   concluded

originality, Schubert was as much a product of his day as any composer; the musical and cultural pressures brought to bear on such Czech contemporaries as Tomášek (1774–1850) and Voříšek (1791–1825) were certainly comparable to those affecting Schubert. Parallel aspects of style and direct influence surely played their part in helping formulate style in both Vienna and Prague; indeed, Tomášek's *Eclogues* are described by Newbould as '... the true precursors of both Schubert's piano pieces and those of the later Romantic age'.[26] The long-lived Tomášek with a string of pupils who were to provide the personnel for Prague's musical establishments, might well be considered part of the phylogeny by which aspects of style common to Schubert's musical world might have been inherited by Dvořák's. Where testimony and concert statistics fail to provide support for Abraham's statement that Schubert was: '... part of the corpus of music from which Dvořák naturally acquired the beginnings of his own idiom',[27] the possibility of a stylistic inheritance via the continuum of musical life in Prague should not be ignored.

Notes and references

1. Susan Wollenberg explores some of these in 'Celebrating Dvořák; affinities between Schubert and Dvořák', *Musical Times*, cxxxii, no. 1783 (September, 1991), pp 434–7.
2. Antonín Dvořák (in co-operation with Henry T. Finck), 'Franz Schubert', *The Century Illustrated Monthly Magazine*, xlviii (1894); reprinted in John Clapham, *Antonín Dvořák, Musician and Craftsman* (London, 1966), pp 296–305. All quotations in this paragraph are taken from this article.

3. All these communications are printed in Milan Kuna ed., *Antonín Dvořák: korespondence a dokumenty* [*Antonín Dvořák: correspondence and documents*], vol. 4 of correspondence sent (Prague, 1995).
4. Gerald Abraham, 'Dvorak's Musical Personality' in Viktor Fischl ed., *Antonín Dvořák: His Achievement*, (London, 1942), pp 192–240. Reprinted in Gerald Abraham, *Slavonic and Romantic Music* (London, 1968), pp 40–69.
5. Abraham/Fischl op. cit., pp 198–9.
6. Milan Kuna op. cit., p. 112.
7. See David Beveridge, 'Romantic ideas in a classical frame: the sonata forms of Dvořák', PhD diss. University of California at Santa Barbara, 1980, pp 34–6, and Hartmut Schick, *Studien zu Dvořák's Streichquartetten*, Neue Heidelberger Studien zur Musikwissenschaft (Laaber-Verlag, 1990), p. 16.
8. Antonín Dvořák, 'Franz Schubert', op. cit.
9. Interview by Paul Pry, part of a series entitled *Enthusiasts Interviewed*, *Sunday Times*, 10 May 1885 (London), p. 6; reprinted in David Beveridge, *Rethinking Dvořák: Views from Five Countries* (Oxford, 1996), pp 281–8.
10. Milan Kuna ed., *Antonín Dvořák: korespondence a dokumenty*, vol. 2 of correspondence sent (Prague, 1988), p. 148.
11. Figures from Milan Kuna ed., *Antonín Dvořák: korespondence a dokumenty*, vols. 1–4 of correspondence sent (Prague, 1987, 1988, 1989 and 1995).
12. Milan Kuna ed., *Antonín Dvořák: korespondence a dokumenty*, vol. 5, documents received (Prague, 1996), pp 222–3.
13. Milan Kuna ibid.
14. See 'The real value of negro melodies', *New York Herald*, 21 May 1893, reprinted in John C. Tibbets ed., *Dvořák in America*, 1892–1895 (Portland, 1993), pp 355–8.
15. We can assume that Dvořák's knowledge of Schubert was reasonable some three to four years before this owing to the testimony of his pupil Josef Suk. On more than one occasion Suk spoke of Dvořák's knowledge and love of Schubert, notably in an address given beside the composer's grave in the cemetery of Vyšehrad on 30 April 1935 (published Prague, 1936, see p. 11). Suk, however, was only acquainted with Dvořák in the early 1890s when he began to study with him.
16. I must record here my gratitude to Karl Stapleton whose extensive research on the concert life of Prague in this period was invaluable in achieving a conspectus of performances of Schubert's music at this time.
17. The first performance was in an arrangement for six pianos given by pupils of J. Jiránek's 'Piano Institute'; the arrangement and performance of works for large numbers of piano players was not uncommon in this period.
18. Even if Dvořák had been able to afford concert-going, which his own testimony suggests he could not, his performing activities would have prevented him from attending at least fifteen of the concerts which featured Schubert's music including almost certainly the ones which included the movements from the Mass in E flat major (8 December 1866) and the Prague premiere of the 'Unfinished' Symphony (8 December 1867).
19. See note 9 above: Beveridge op. cit., p. 285.
20. Ibid., p. 286.
21. Altogether Smetana performed the E flat major Trio six times and the Trio in B flat major twice; see Frantisek Bartos ed., *Bedrich Smetana, Komorní skladby*, Complete Edition (Prague, 1977), p. XIII
22. Taken from Zdeněk Nejedlý, *Bedřich Smetana*, (Prague, 1924), p. 55 and reprinted in Vojtěch Kyas, 'Franz Schubert ve světlé nových pohledu', *Hudební věda*, 1981/3, p. 259. Kyas examines a number of parallels between Schubert and Smetana in this article, as he does also in 'Paralely v harmonické struktuře skladeb B. Smetany a F.

Schubert; k metodě kvantitativních harmonických analýz', *Hudební věda*, 1974, no. 4, pp 313–29.
23. William Ritter, *Národní listy* (Prague, 8 April 1896); reprinted A. Rektorys, *Zdeněk Fibich: sborník dokumentů a studií*, (Prague, 1951–2) i, pp 189–90.
24. Details in A. Rektorys, op. cit., p. 341.
25. Brian Newbould, *Schubert: the Music and the Man* (London, 1997), p. 396.
26. Newbould, ibid., p. 341.
27. Abraham, op. cit., p. 199.

7 Architecture as drama in late Schubert
Roy Howat

If scholarship has long abandoned the old notion of Schubert the somnambulantly-inspired bumpkin, performing habits have made patchier progress in throwing off that moth-eaten old garment. Programme notes, for the most part, have ceased to append the word 'rambling' to the late sonatas, yet performances of the utmost respectability still often indulge the leisurely at the expense of rhythmic, dramatic and architectural vitality – as if the incandescent rhythms of the 'Great' C major Symphony, for instance, had nothing to tell us about the late piano works. Some of this can also be attributed to the persisting 'Poor Schubert, how he suffered' school of interpretation, in part a *Lilac Time* hangover.

To blend expressivity, overall coherence, and the music's essential dance in Schubert can sometimes, however, be very elusive, for if soggy rhythm or tempo makes his music sag, mere 'playing in time' can leave structural problems unsolved, never mind expressive ones. To understand why, and suggest solutions, we need to observe his rhythmic thinking, especially in his late works, the products of a decade in which he moved from his youthful Haydnesque idiom to a new scale of massive architectural sophistication. A central focus here is provided by the late piano sonatas in C minor and A major, D958 and D959, in which we can observe Schubert's innate and visible sense of musical geometry, and his skill at turning this into drama.

Before we settle on the piano sonatas, some apt illustration of Schubert's architectonic skill comes from the finale of the 'Great' C major Symphony of 1825, D944. One of the perennial delights of this movement is the unfailing surprise of its E flat recapitulation, following 76 bars of decoy dominant preparation on G, including four brief C major touch-downs in second inversion that virtually make our tongues hang out for a full C major resolution. Surprises continue, for a chain of apparently anarchic modulations eventually establishes F major as the next clear tonality (bar 670), only to subvert it 32 bars later by E major, as another decoy dominant preparation for the second subject's return. Just as we have abandoned hope of hearing C major again, the second subject sideslips into it as effortlessly as if to say 'Was something the matter?' As a final surprise, the coda's string of even bolder modulations begins with the bass sliding down from C to A (bars 969–73), in the same way as it earlier slid down from G to E flat to begin the development section.

Yet under the surface all is logically prepared. Cadential surprise number one, the E flat recapitulation, arrives via a middle-voice G – F – E flat progression that simply repeats the bass line by which the exposition had earlier moved into the development. Cadential surprise number two, the sideslip to C major for the second subject, is of course the delayed resolution of the long G dominant pedal, while in turn the coda's surprise start on an A major chord is the delayed resolution of the E major half-close before the second subject return. This logic continues in the coda's chromatic rising sequence of four times twenty bars, in which, as Brian Newbould has observed, the first three blocks each make us expect a cadential resolution which is frustrated by the start of the next block.[1] One may add that the frustrated cadences would have been respectively to the movement's three main secondary keys of E flat, F and G. It is as if the music says in each case, 'no, not this time', to emphasise the now unstoppable momentum towards the final C major arrival and peroration.

Another element of geometry binds those progressions together, in the form of intervallic symmetry around the tonic, something that can also be observed in many of Schubert's earlier scores.[2] This shows itself immediately through the E flat – A symmetry around the home key of C, defined by the matched transitions to the development section and the coda. F major, the recapitulation's second established key, likewise mirrors the G major of the exposition's second subject; and the twofold large-scale emphasis of E flat, to launch both the development and the recapitulation, outreaches the context of the finale, balancing the A tonality of the symphony's second movement and the trio of its Scherzo.[3]

An essential part of the drama lies in the way in which that underlying balance quietly earths each surprise, giving it simple retrospective logic. A further element of drama in this finale is its sheer velocity, especially relative to its notation in very short bars ($\frac{2}{4}$, *allegro vivace*). The violinist Hugh Bean has recalled playing this under the shimmering baton of Wilhelm Furtwängler, at a very fast lick which concentrated so much on long musical lines that 'the barlines vanished'.[4] As it happens, Furtwängler was not the first to make the barlines vanish, for Schubert literally did this when he 'recycled' a moment of that movement in the first of his Impromptus, D899, as shown in Ex. 7.1.

Two such different notations, for momentarily the same music at the same sounding tempo, naturally reflect their different contexts. If choice of metre here is largely dictated by the slower accompanying articulation in the Impromptu, it is also affected by many varied phrase lengths in the symphony finale which would disrupt the $\frac{4}{4}$ metre of Ex. 7.1b. Ex. 7.2 shows one case, a small but dramatic compression across exposition and recapitulation that introduces a sudden ternary element (triple groups of paired bars); in the notation of Example 7.1b this would

168 *Schubert Studies*

Ex. 7.1a   'Great' C major Symphony, Finale (Allegro vivace), in piano reduction

Ex. 7.1b   Impromptu in C minor, D899 No. 1 (Allegro molto moderato)

Ex. 7.2   'Great' C major Symphony, finale (piano reduction)

entail a more visible change of metre from $\frac{4}{4}$ to $\frac{3}{2}$. The point becomes clear that larger bar grouping can be musically equivalent to metre within the bar; it just depends on the metric scale employed for the piece's notation. For example, performances of the 'Great' C major finale tend by necessity to be conducted a beat to a bar, in a mixture of two, four and six, depending on the bar groupings.[5]

As we thus observe metre on more than one scale, new layers of rhythmic and formal organization can become apparent. A telling illustration comes from the Menuetto of the C minor Piano Sonata, D958 (Ex. 7.3). The piece's opening section of 12 bars at first appears divisible in various ways: 4+4+4, with a mirrored rhythmic structure across bars 1–4 and 5–8; or 4+3+2+3, giving more priority to the *f* articulation at bar 8 and to the cadential and melodic relationship of bars 8–9. This ambiguity, plus the mirrored patterns, lend the movement a suggestion of riddle. Schubert solves the riddle for us in the somewhat disguised reprise from bar 28, by adding silent bars that define three 4-bar phrases around them.

Meanwhile, the central portion (bars 13–27) starts with a mirrored 3-bar rhythmic pattern (itself partly mirroring that of bars 1–4). One can feasibly read through to bar 27 as 3+3+3+3+3 bars, but the *fz* and double cadence of bars 24–7 more clearly mark out 2+2+2 bars across bars 22–7.[6] On a larger metric scale, bars 22–7 thus form an effective hemiola (a ternary grouping of paired bars) against the preceding 3-bar groups.

The whole Menuetto (without the Trio) now comes into rhythmic focus as a sequence of three times four bars, three times three bars, three times two bars, and finally three times five bars (taking into account the silent bar at the start of the Trio). Schubert's peculiar notation of pushing this last silent bar into the Trio has a simple practical purpose, for it allows bar 41 on the first time repeat to link back to bar 12 by a sequence of 5+4+3 bars (counting from bar 33).

The visibility of this highly geometric musical thinking matches its audible dramatic effect, progressively compressing the music's articulation before ending with a geometrically compensating expansion. In dramatic terms, however, the reprise's apparent expansion actually packs the compressive effect even tighter by the impact of the sudden silent bars. Similarly the relative hemiola of bars 22–7 introduces a simultaneous augmentation working across the grain of the larger-scale compressive tendency. Small wonder if this movement has the feeling of a riddle about it.

That example illustrates the dramatic possibilities when a sequence of 4-bar groups is cut into by a 3-bar group (a similar relationship to that seen in Ex. 7.2). A more dramatic case, on a larger scale, occurs in the same sonata's finale, a movement whose main subject establishes a strong opening pattern of 8-bar groups. Ex. 7.4 shows the second part of the movement's development section, as it gradually tightens the dramatic tension on the way to the movement's principal climax. Schubert achieves this by combining chains of modulations with progressive subversion of metric regularity. Regular 8+8-bar groups in bars 309–24 are first disrupted by the incursion of 6-bar groups at bars 333–8 and 347–52. This produces a compression (to 14-bar 'sentences' after the preceding 16-bar ones) and also

Ex. 7.3   Sonata in C minor, D958

Ex. 7.3 concluded

[musical notation]

introduces a ternary element, with each 14-bar 'sentence' ending in a triple group of paired bars.

The decisive turning point is the accented interrupted cadence at bar 356, suddenly kicking the music into 3-bar groups from bar 353 onwards. The enormous impact of this (if played effectively) is fortified by another level of rhythmic compression, for the new 3-bar groups relate by diminution to the 6-bar groups (grouped in triple pairs) preceding them.

To make all this clearer to the eye, Ex. 7.5 rebars this entire passage to a larger metric scale (in the manner of Ex. 7.1b). (Original bar numbers are retained for reference; large arabic numbers, like simplified time signatures, show the number of original bars in each new 'large bar'; double bars mark changes in the new larger metre; and broken barlines within the larger bars show the consistent pairing of original bars up to bar 352, emphasizing the shock at bar 356.)

172 *Schubert Studies*

Ex 7.4 Sonata in C minor, D958, finale

Ex 7.4   concluded

174 Schubert Studies

Ex. 7.5

Ex. 7.5   concluded

Following their launch from bar 353, (original) 3-bar groups form a continuous pattern to and over the movement's (and arguably the sonata's) main climax. Only when the crisis has broken, at bar 413, does Schubert relent, letting the articulation relax (and us with it) back into 4-bar regularity. Ex. 7.6 shows this, again rebarred like Ex. 7.5 for visual clarity. In the process Schubert's galloping horse has a final rebellious kick in store for us, before it submits to the reins of the recapitulation. Bars 413–16 convey the first clear return to 4-bar grouping; as another clear 4-bar group follows we naturally relax – only to be taken by surprise again with the *subito forte* D flat minor of bar 421.

Schubert's surefootedness in this last case is best appreciated by imagining how much weaker the effect would be, had he not broken the 3-bar run just before: intensity would have remained too high to allow the new gesture optimum impact. His ploy is reminiscent in some ways of the first movement of Mozart's Piano Concerto in G, K453, which surprises us three times with the same interrupted cadence (opening tutti, solo exposition and recapitulation), strategically relocated on the second and third occasions to catch us off guard each time. One suspects that Schubert savoured Mozart's prank with glee – a word I use deliberately, for all the dark etching in Schubert's C minor finale is mixed with a strange glee and storytelling humour, in the manner of the melodrama genre to which Schubert was no stranger.

A level of rhythmic architecture in this climactic passage still lies concealed. To uncover it we have to move a metric level higher again, and observe how the long sequence of 3-bar groups itself falls into larger 'macro-groups'. This is easily followed from Ex. 7.5 and 7.6: the total of twenty 'large bars' of $\frac{18}{8}$ time (original bars 353–412), falls into larger 'macro-groups' of 5+5+4+6. This sequence follows a shape already familiar from the sonata's Menuetto, starting with a repeated pattern (the 5s), compressing it (the 4), and then making a compensating expansion (the 6) for the final group. Another level of expansion sets in at the third macro-group (the 4), from which point the 'large bars' themselves are consistently grouped in pairs. The final macro-group of 6 'large bars' frames and focuses the movement's climactic crisis, bringing it to its culmination in an emphatic ternary sequence (three pairs of 'large bars', original bars 395–412). As Ex. 7.7 shows, this overall structure is an exact augmentation (double compound) of the original 3-bar phrases that comprise it.

The movement, in fact, is permeated by hidden augmentations and diminutions, as can be seen briefly by two other examples. One is the entire development section (bars 243–428), made up as often with Schubert of two opposed parts (almost like two independent songs within the structure), respectively lyrical and stormy. If the latter overwhelms the former in dramatic terms, that is an essential part of the sonata's story, reflected exactly by numbers, for out of the entire development section's 186 bars, 62 form the lyrical first part, and 124 the stormy second part, a simple ratio of 1:2. This might be less remarkable were it not for the density of rhythmic structure already seen within the latter section. The second example is the progressive compaction of the movement's opening

Ex. 7.6

Ex. 7.6 concluded

Ex. 7.7 Sonata in C minor, finale

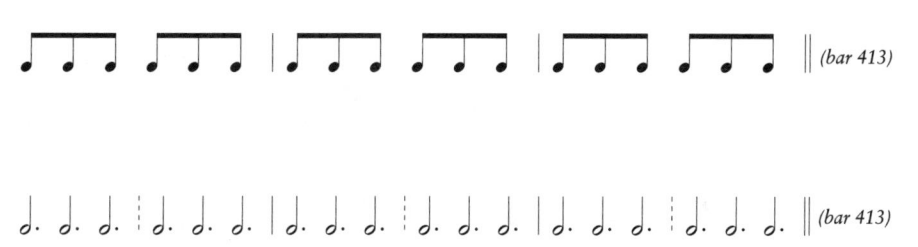

(bar 413)

(bar 413)

material at each subsequent return: the material is structured in such a way that the recapitulation can take a short cut after 24 bars (bar 453, relative to bars 25 and 67), while the coda can undercut this again by taking its short cut in the twelfth bar (bar 672, relative to bars 12 and 28). A slight looseness of terminology here betrays another dramatic coup, for the latter short cut, with its *sforzando* twist to A flat, more exactly intrudes after 11½ bars, just undercutting a halfway relationship in a way that perfectly matches the music's galloping urgency.

Probably the most sophisticated case here of layered rhythmic structure appears in the A major Sonata, D959, a work that displays a near-palindromic relationship between its joyful opening and the dark, brooding end of its tragic second movement (Ex. 7.8). Apart from the obvious drama of the symbolic reversal, this also lets Schubert draw the whole sonata together at its close: as Ex. 7.8 again shows, the finale's last bars not only quote and transform the Andantino's ending, but also make a more extended near-palindrome with the sonata's opening (8 bars

Ex. 7.8a Sonata in A, D959: 2nd movement

180 Schubert Studies

Ex. 7.8b   Sonata in A, D959: 1st movement, opening

Ex. 7.8c   Sonata in A, D959: end of finale

in each case, discounting the final tied-over bar of the finale). Such devices are already known in Schubert, including not only a passage of vertical mirror image in his *Wanderer* Fantasy, but also the horizontal equivalent, a literal palindrome in *Die Zauberharfe* (both traced and described elsewhere by Brian Newbould).[7] Schubert's only liberty with strict palindrome in the example from *Die Zauberharfe* is that he very occasionally maintains the original rhythm or order of notes within a single beat, doubtless to make the palindrome clearer and more musically coherent to the ear. The A major Sonata adds another dimension to this, for the brackets X, Y and Z in Ex. 7.8 show how Schubert goes beyond mere palindrome, to resolve at the same time the three constituent motives of the sonata's opening. For example, the opening downward dominant arpeggio (Y) is answered not just by the same thing in reverse but by a transposition that cadentially resolves it. (In the process the answering figure also links to the end of the first movement.) Similarly the first movement's vital E – F progression (element Z), moving beyond the dominant, is resolved by the finale's answering F – E, leading *through* the dominant back to the tonic. (That F – E in turn also resolves one of the finale's major musical arguments, as at bars 95–104, 119–20 and 298–316.)

A curious source variant betrays how the first movement of this sonata also embeds an important layering of metre. Despite the movement's C time signature, its frequent running triplet passages have a natural tempo akin to the opening *alla breve* of the earlier D major Sonata, D850, and this is doubtless why Schubert's preparatory draft for D959 indicates ¢.[8] His change to C for the fair copy was presumably dictated by the broader character of the main subjects, as well as by the development section and the coda. (The two main subjects, with their shared rising diatonic bass, are so closely related that their first two-and-three-quarter bars can be played together.)

Two levels of rhythmic energy are really at play here, and in practice each needs its own tempo, in order to set off the broader main subjects (bars 1–6, 16–21, 55–81 and 117–22) against the incursions of the more *alla breve* material (essentially the Y and Z elements from Ex. 7.8) with its running triplets and chromatic rising bass – always from E and increasingly dramatic at each appearance (from bars 7, 28 and 82, with a final exposition echo at bar 123). Not only does this suggest that the movement's basic C tempo is near the borderline with ¢, it also implies that some layering of tempo, far from distorting the piece, is of the architectural and dramatic essence. In practice, judicious tempo layering here is less intrusive or even discernible to listeners than the sagging or cramping that results from imposing a uniform basic tempo throughout.[9]

This metrical duality runs in counterpoint with another structural layering in the movement's exposition. As already seen in Ex. 7.8, the first subject statement fills six bars, and indeed the whole first subject group (bars 1–27) largely follows triple groups of paired bars (2+2+2), broken only by one 3-bar extension in bars 13–15. The passage thus has a clear metrical flavour, essentially triple groupings of $\frac{4}{2}$ or $\frac{8}{4}$. From bar 28 the modulating transition section makes a contrast, now characterised by 4- or 8-bar groups (bars 28–35 and 39–54), with just one exceptional 3-bar extension at bars 36–8. Bar 55 brings the second subject, this time with the new metrical flavour of 5-bar groups, in this case essentially 4-bar phrases with a single-bar extension at the end. This allows them to yield gradually to 4-bar groups in a rather pleasing dovetailed symmetry of 5+5+4+5+4+4. The different rhythmic character of each main subject group is therefore well defined.

By the end of the second subject group at bars 78–81, it is easy to imagine the imminence of the double bar. Instead the texture is suddenly disrupted by a much more turbulent and extended development of element Z from Ex. 7.8, *subito f* and with initial 3-bar groups (Ex. 7.9). The impact of this rhythmic device, already familiar from the C minor Sonata, is heightened here by an inverse hemiola effect that makes the first nine bars (bars 82–90) sound more like $\frac{3}{2}$ metre. The steady build-up from there to the sudden climactic silence thirty bars later is also carefully articulated. An initial 'stretched' sequence of 3+3+3+4 bars (including the inverse hemiola effect) culminates in a sudden minor mode cadence; an augmented triple group (2+2+2) then leads to an emphasised repeat of the cadence, the hands now reversing voices. From there the music goes in 4-bar momentum to and over the silent bar-and-a-half (the silent full bar completes a group of four), until calm is restored with the second subject's return at bar 117.

In textbook terms this odd structure has no business in a sonata form, and even here would have no place were it not the outcome of two earlier anticipations at bars 7–8 and 28. It also grows out of another piece of threefold structural momentum. Alert readers may have observed a pleasing geometry hidden in the proportions of the preceding sections. The first subject group, consisting of four 6-bar groups plus one 3-bar extension, is neatly reciprocated twice: first by a transition section comprising six 4-bar groups plus one 3-bar extension, and then by a second subject group comprising six 4-bar groups plus three single-bar extensions. This ensures that first subject, transition and second subject groups each make up the rather curious total of 27 bars, forming a larger ternary structure of 81 bars. Given the role of the number three in this structure (3 times 3 to the power 3), it seems humorously ironic that it manages to unroll without a single true 3-bar phrase – until its completion, when it is immediately followed by an exact imitation in miniature, 3 times 3 bars (bars 82–90). As if to sum this up by mediation, the movement's coda (distinctly set off by a preceding silent bar) comprises 27 bars, clearly divided 9+9+9.

Returning to the exposition on a larger scale again, Fig. 7.1 maps the whole exposition, showing how bar 82 (that is, the completion of 81 bars) separates a diatonically regular, symmetrical, self-contained 'classical' exposition from its disruptive, irregular and tonally unstable adjunct. The tripartite symmetry of the stable portion is underlined by its halfway division at its dynamic apex, the *ff* accented chord at the upper octave halfway through bar 41.[10]

Architecture as drama in late Schubert 183

Ex. 7.9 Sonata in A, D959: 1st movement

Ex. 7.9 concluded

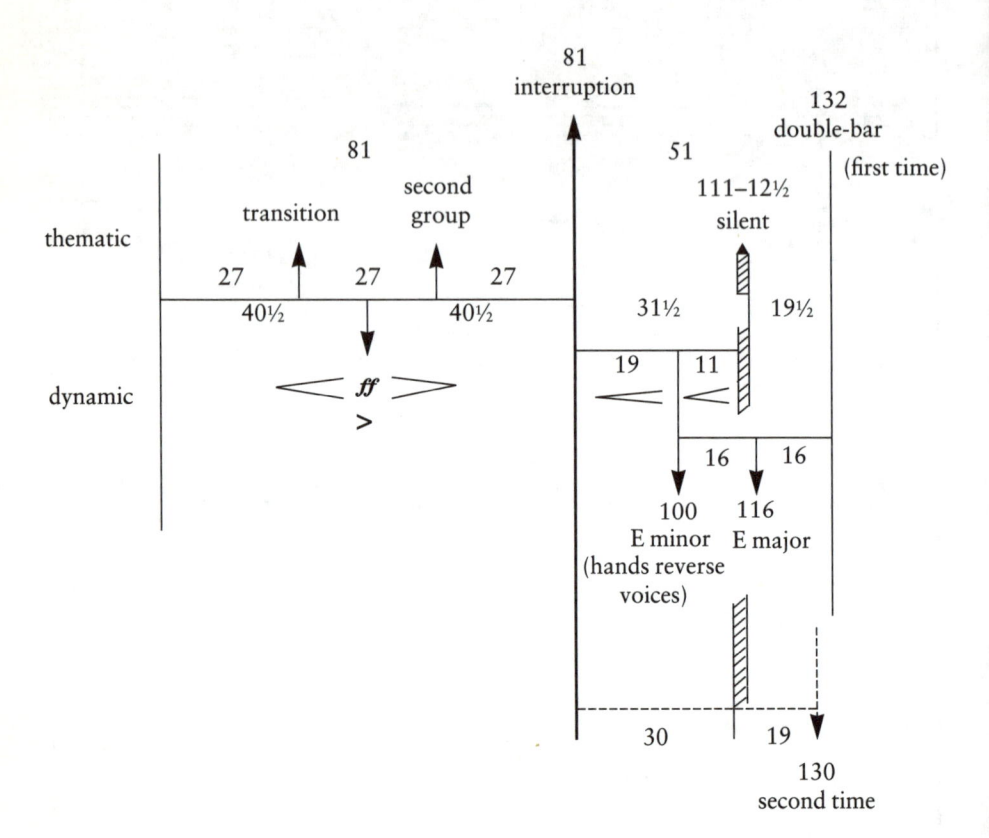

Figure 7.1 Sonata in A, D959, first movement exposition

A more unusual geometry dominates the later portion, playing an equivalent role to the ratio 2:1 already seen in the finale of the C minor Sonata. The exposition's total length is 132 first time, and 130 second time (counting over its closing cadence). A division of these after 81 bars in each case falls within two-thirds of a bar of golden section, a ratio well-known in painting, architecture and botany, approximating to 0·618...[11] (132 divided in this way yields 81·58..., and 130 yields 80·34...) The inherent (though slight) approximation of this, relative to the whole numbers by which we count bars, might make a conclusion seem hasty, were it not for supporting detail. The second part of this main division in turn has its golden section fall within the climactic silent bar-and-a-half (bars 112–13) for both first and second times, and again the 31 bars up to the silence are divided by golden section (19·159... to be precise) at bar 101, the minor-mode cadence where the two hands reverse voices. No other simple ratio can account for this geometric unanimity. In sum, the structurally normal or stable part of the exposition, up to bar 81, is visibly dominated by symmetry, and the later more unstable adjunct by golden section. Finally, the second subject's return at bar 117 restores symmetry along with tonal and musical stability, dividing the last 32 bars 16:16. It can be added that – besides Schubert's documented interest in geometrical and mirrored structures – golden section structures, using the associated Fibonacci numbers, are reliably documented in works by Haydn and Beethoven.[12]

In at least one respect this whole extract can be read as a double-layered exposition in a sort of augmentation with itself, the larger 'first subject' consisting of regularity and diatonic stability against a 'second subject' of irregularity, instability and disruption. The 'second subject' then similarly divides itself into two contrasted portions around the bar-and-a-half of silence. This relates to another thread of counterpoint seen already, since the eruption at bar 82 is the third and crucial emergence of a figure that had already rumbled more quietly at bars 8 and 28. In those terms the 'double exposition' of Fig. 7.1 can be seen as the largest scale of realisation of a constantly exploited tension between the movement's opposed opening elements, seen in Ex. 7.8 as motive X versus motives Y and Z.

More of this structural logic comes from the development section, which in fact is hardly a development section at all (we have already had at least one of those in the exposition), but more a set of variations on the second subject's tail (the decorated form heard in bars 121–2). This theme, somewhat in the character of a Russian dance (note the Borodin-like progression in its third and fourth bars), at first maintains exclusively 5-bar groups, distinct again from those of the second subject in that these are true 5-bar phrases, with no hint of 4+1 as was the case with the second subject. Fig. 7.2 maps this section's three-part layout, the first part in major mode, the second part in minor mode with freer extensions, and the third part a dominant preparation for the recapitulation.

Fig. 7.2 links directly to Fig. 7.1: the change from major to minor in Fig. 7.2 marks exactly the same sequence of 30:19 bars as the end of the exposition for the second time in Fig. 7.1 (golden section), while the subsequent return to tonic stability with the dominant pedal marks a near-symmetry of 19:18 bars, following the same musical logic as the 16:16 division at the end of the exposition in Fig. 7.1.[13]

186   Schubert Studies

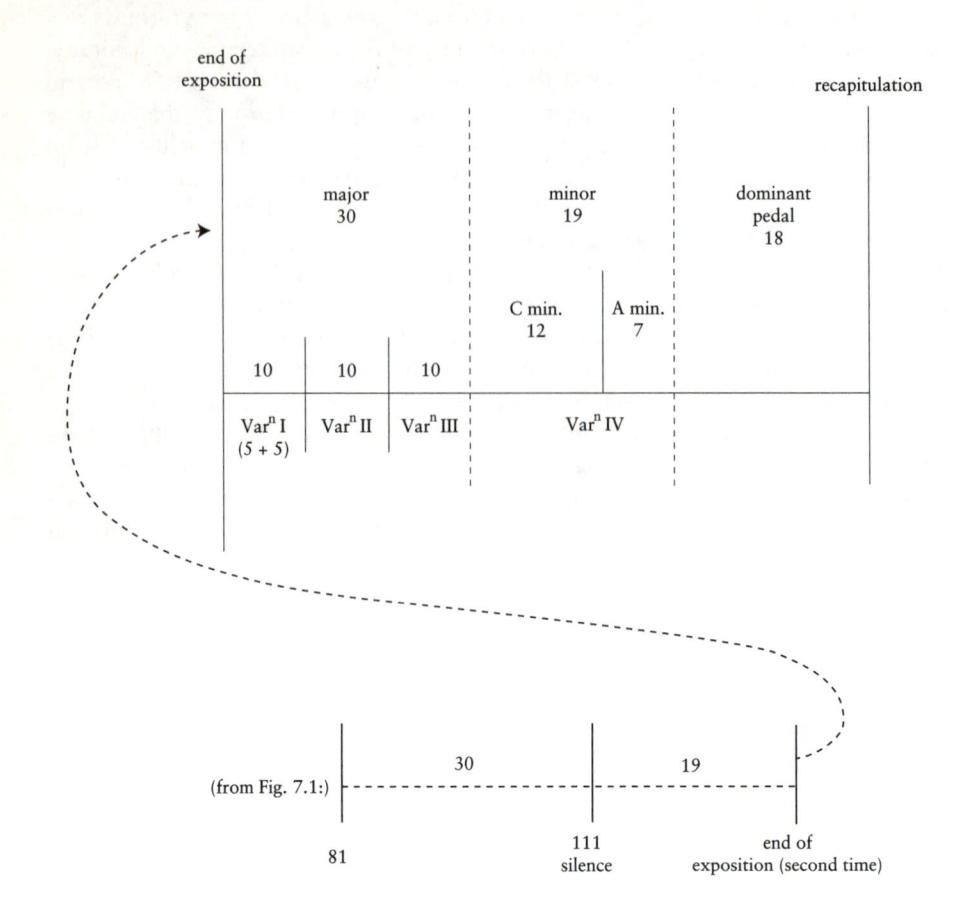

```
                end of                                                    
              exposition                                      recapitulation

                    │          major       │    minor       │   dominant
                    │           30         │     19         │    pedal
                    │                      │                │     18
                    │              ┌───────┼────────┐       │
                    │              │ C min.│ A min. │       │
                    │              │  12   │   7    │       │
                    │   10  │  10  │  10   │        │       │
                    │───────┼──────┼───────┤        │       │
                    │ Varⁿ I│Varⁿ II│Varⁿ III│ Varⁿ IV│       │
                    │ (5+5) │      │       │        │       │
```

                    │   30   │   19   │
    (from Fig. 7.1:)│─ ─ ─ ─ ─ ─ ─ ─ ─ ─ ─ ─ ─ ─ ─ ┼ ─ ─ ─ ─ ─ ─ ─ ─ ─ ┤
                    │   │   │
                             81   111   end of
                                                       silence   exposition (second time)

Figure 7.2   Sonata in A, D959, 1st movement 'development' section

(The small irregularity is explicable in terms of smaller-scale structure, notably the momentum of paired bars called for in the development's last 18 bars.) The two-bar shortening of the exposition on its repeat (as seen in Fig. 7.1) thus has visible structural logic, linking directly to Fig. 7.2. Since bar 82 onwards is itself more of a development section, its double linking to both what precedes it (the first portion of Fig. 7.1) and what follows it (Fig. 7.2) is as apt musically as it is geometrically.

To sum up this sometimes contentious topic, golden section does not visibly figure elsewhere in Schubert's late sonatas (it occasionally appears approximately or casually, but not in ways that suggest structural importance), suggesting that its presence here is more than just a vaguely pervasive intuitive factor.[14] Its role, I would argue, is simply akin to that of the 2:1 ratio in the finale of the C minor

Sonata, one of many interesting ratios well known to curious and educated artists of the time. In this regard Brian Newbould has drawn attention to the thorough education Schubert received at home (the brightest one of the class in his father's school) and then at choir school, and to the documented interest of Schubert's father in embedding hidden numbers in a play of words – the very sort of thing Schubert *père et maître d'école* is most likely to have passed on to a bright offspring who all too quickly soaked up the basic education offered to his schoolmates.[15]

It is not the purpose here to pursue the arguable æsthetics and philosophy of all these structures; it is interesting enough in performance merely to know they are there, however they came about. Those interested in further implications might peruse with interest Jacques Chailley's 1975 study of *Winterreise*, in the course of which Chailley found himself being unexpectedly and increasingly persuaded of Schubert's probable involvement in Freemasonry.[16] One part of Chailley's evidence, involving symbolism and structures based on the number three, has obvious links to the multiple plays on the number 3 seen above, not only in the first movement of D959, but also in D958, most notably the finale's development section divided exactly a third of the way through. Among many other less obvious examples of ternary play that can be added, the 81-bar opening structure of D959 is immediately followed by the third incursion of the movement's third distinct motive (element Z from Ex. 7.8). After all that it seems almost weak to add that Chailley's arguments also touch on Mozartian use of triple-element key signatures: we need only look at the key signature of three of the movements in D958, as well as all four movements of D959 (the only one of Schubert's last five sonatas with the same key signature for all movements).

The many links across Schubert's last three sonatas sometimes tempt a view of them, again on a structurally augmented level, as a sort of macro-sonata. Naturally three large works in the same genre, all composed together, will inevitably share ideas and motives, such as the virtual identity between the first movement second subject of the C minor Sonata and the opening of the B flat Sonata (a motive almost ubiquitous in less obvious form through the three sonatas). A more dramatic link is the powerful role in each sonata of C sharp minor, the more interesting here for being diatonically unrelated to any of the sonatas' home keys. In the light of Jacques Chailley's questions, one could add that a macro-sonata view yields twelve movements, a total redolent of *Winterreise*. On a practical level, it shows an interesting large-scale symmetry across the three sonatas in terms of their relative weighting: if the emotional and dramatic crux of the C minor Sonata is in its finale, and that of the A major more centrally in its Andantino, the B-flat Sonata answers this with its weight mainly in the first movement.

The larger-scale view has a more ubiquitous role in performance, where a clear grasp of large-scale shape and coherence balances our attention to smaller detail. As part of this balance, musical evidence suggests that an unqualified *allegro* indication in Schubert often means a faster tempo than in Haydn or Mozart, at least relative to the barline and to a time signature such as ₵. In the light of the tempo layering seen here, as well as of the varying levels at which he employs barlines, we can often usefully read Schubert's tempo indications as more descriptive of the sounding effect than prescriptive in terms of metre and barlines.[17]

Naturally our constant guide has to be musical sense, allied to source evidence. For example, Schubert's draft of the C minor Sonata shows a cautionary *moderato* appended to the opening *allegro* indication, a timely warning for the passage around the recapitulation, as well as for the second subject and its variations.[18] In this case it may have been the urgency of the development section, with its hints of hemiolas, that prompted Schubert to drop the *moderato* from his fair copy. On the other side, Schubert's draft of the B flat Sonata, D960, omits the 'molto' from the opening *moderato* indication, and even *moderato* here has to be read as a qualification of the understood default 'allegro' of classical usage.[19] This brings it very near the opening tempo heading in the draft of the C minor Sonata, and indeed the same crotchet pulse can work excellently for both movements: the mention of *allegro* in D958 merely reflects the extra perceived velocity provided by its running semiquavers (as well as by the quavers in the second subject of D958, relative to the steady crotchets of the same theme at the start of D960). Attention to this in the B flat Sonata – ever-associated by retrospection, it seems, with Schubert's deathbed – can help rouse it from long slumber, restoring its intrinsic dance and making it something much more than the familiar introspective rumination. Schubert's own phrase breaks, articulation and rests speak for themselves here if we pay attention to them, with our right foot as well as our fingers.

All in all, the damaging image of Schubert the rambling (or even ruminating) café tunesmith needs to be left far behind: 'heavenly length' can look after itself while we can look to the phenomenal energy coiled inside this music. We might also be wary of an oft-repeated half-truth to the effect that Schubert's music 'expresses suffering'. Literally to do that would be depressing: more to the point, it touches suffering, along with intense joy and every feeling known to human hearts, to an extent that few composers have approached. In touching its releases, and the energy and rhythm of this music lift our hearts to dance, just as its singing lines calm the mind. To play it soggily is like saying 'no thanks, we'd rather stay sad'. Schubert's artistic courage, I think, deserves a worthier response.

Notes and references

1. Brian Newbould, *Schubert: the Music and the Man* (London, Gollancz, 1997), p. 384. Thanks are expressed to Professor Newbould for many helpful comments, as well as the invaluable background of all his Schubert research and publications.
2. Examples can be seen in the first movement development sections of the piano sonatas in B and D, D575 and D850.
3. The first movement shows analogous balance through the second subject's irregular added keys of E and A flat minors, again symmetrically surrounding C.
4. Conversation with the present writer. This can be heard in Furtwängler's 1951

recording of the symphony (Deutsche Grammophon CD 447 439–2), in which the finale lasts 11'38"; another Furtwängler concert recording from 1942 (Music & Arts CD-826) clips more than a minute off that timing, in probably the fastest finale of the symphony on record.

5. Brian Newbould also draws repeated attention to such 'larger bars' relative to the finales of the Sixth and Ninth Symphonies and the Scherzo of the String Quintet (*Schubert: the Music and the Man*, pp 88, 362 and 400–1). A parallel case is the Scherzo of Fauré's A major Violin Sonata of 1875–6, notated in very fast 3/8 bars to avoid notational congestion across frequent alternations of *de facto* 2/4 and 3/8 groups. In Fauré's Thirteenth Nocturne, composed almost half a century later in 1921, large 2/4 and 3/8 sections alternate in much the same way as they would if Ex. 7.2 here were to be rebarred in the manner of Ex. 7.1b (but keeping its original note values).

6. The $f\!f$ at bar 21 allows another alternative articulation as bar 8 did, but the pattern from bar 22 onwards sounds retrospectively stronger, especially if bar 22 is well marked as it needs to be in performance.

7. See Newbould, *Schubert: the Music and the Man*, pp 198 and 401, also the same author's 'A Schubert palindrome', *19th Century Music*, XV/3 (Spring 1992), pp 207–14.

8. Facsimile in *Franz Schubert: Drei große Klaviersonaten für das Pianoforte, Frühe Fassungen, Begleitender Text und Kommentar von Ernst Hilmar*, Tutzing, Hans Schneider, 1987, vol. II, p. 1. The edition of D850 published in Schubert's lifetime conversely reads **C**, though that may be a misprint. For more complete details of Schubert sonata sources see the complete edition edited by Howard Ferguson (London, Associated Board, 1979, 3 vols). A microfilm of the autograph fair copy of the last three sonatas, D958–960, is in the Library of Congress, Washington; prints from this microfilm are in the Pendlebury Music Library, Cambridge.

9. This is probably why Schubert does not indicate such fluctuations, as it might risk exaggeration and musical fragmentation. He usually indicates tempo layering carefully when it has to be audible as such, for example between scherzos and trios, or in rondo episodes or dance movements. Notably, such implicit terracing of tempo usually affects first movements of late works, notably the A minor Piano Sonata D845, and the first movement of the Great C major Symphony where Schubert's three indicated tempo layers – *andante, allegro ma non troppo*, and *più moto* – arguably tell only the part of the story that the audience has to hear as such. For more discussion of those two movements in this respect see Roy Howat, 'What do we perform?', in John Rink, ed., *The practice of performance; studies in musical interpretation*, (Cambridge, CUP, 1995), pp 14–16.

10. Numbers in Fig. 7.1 necessarily indicate bars completed, so that 81, for example, coincides with the beginning of bar 82, and 40½ with the centre of bar 41.

11. Golden section – documented in Euclid's *Elements* as 'extreme and mean ratio' – is the division that cuts a fixed length in such a way that the shorter portion bears the same ratio to the longer portion as the longer portion bears to the whole length. Its exact value is irrational, its decimal places continuing indefinitely; it approximates to 0·618034 of the length measured.

12. Regarding golden section structures in Haydn and Beethoven see John Rutter, *The sonata principle*, Open University Course A241 (Elements of music), (Milton Keynes, Open University Press, 1975). The overall proportions of Fig. 7.1 here are also charted in Roy Howat, *Debussy in proportion* (Cambridge, CUP, 1983), pp 187–9.

13. Bars are left unnumbered in Fig. 7.2, since different editions have different numbers resulting from different ways of counting first and second time bars.

14. Those who bring healthy scepticism to the overfished waters of golden section surveys have sometimes argued that it would only be 'intuitive', or in any case that

aesthetic arguments about it are overdone, with no proven human capacity for sensing or preferring it. With no wish to become too embroiled here, it can be briefly pointed out that the two arguments are mutually exclusive. In Schubert's draft of D959 the first movement exposition does not yet have the exact proportions of Fig. 7.1, so the movement was not composed *a priori* to any such proportional template.

15. See in particular Newbould, *Schubert: the Music and the Man*, p. 401.
16. Jacques Chailley, *Le voyage d'hiver de Schubert* (Paris, Leduc, 1975); see especially pp 9–10, 36 and 49–50. Chailley observes that Schubert would have had to be covert about any Masonic involvement in Metternich's politically repressed Vienna. One of the works Chailley finds especially suggestive of Freemasonry is *Die Zauberharfe*, the work with the literal palindrome.
17. See the silent bars between the main subjects in the first movement of the E major Symphony, D729, which sag (along with much of the movement) if taken at normal classical tempo. A better known case is the G flat Impromptu, D899 no.3, whose *andante* heading, with its curious ¢¢ signature, can sensibly apply only to the melody, resulting in quite nimble quavers if the piece is to avoid sounding *adagio*. This key signature, for all its ambiguity, must mean two-in-the-bar; otherwise Schubert could simply have indicated $\frac{2}{4}$ or else written it in ₵ (as the posthumous first publisher inflicted on the hapless piece).
18. Facsimile in *Franz Schubert: Drei große Klaviersonaten*, op. cit., vol. I, p. 1.
19. Facsimile in *Franz Schubert: Drei große Klaviersonaten*, op. cit., vol. III, p. 1.

8 Schubert's piano sonatas: thoughts about interpretation and performance
András Schiff

Franz Schubert's piano sonatas are unquestionably among the most sublime works ever written for the instrument. It is quite astonishing how much nonsense has been said and written about them – hence their relative unfamiliarity and neglect. They have generally been accused of being too long, lacking in formal coherence, being un-pianistic and therefore ineffective in public performance. Such clichés tend to persist: people like repeating them even if they do not know the works in question. A musical work's survival depends largely on the frequency and quality of its performances. Beethoven's magnificent sonatas soon found their way into the central repertoire after his death, since virtually all the major pianists – from Czerny to Liszt – were playing them.[1]

Schubert's shorter works for piano – the Impromptus, *Moments musicaux*, dances – were regularly played, and Liszt's transcriptions of several songs and of the *Wanderer* Fantasy have brought these works to a wider public. (To perform these works today, however, is questionable. I find them contrary to Schubert's spirit and simplicity.) Artur Schnabel and Eduard Erdmann were probably the only two prominent pianists before World War II who tried to champion the sonatas. Sergei Rachmaninov – who adored Schubert – supposedly said in the 1930s that he only knew one Schubert sonata, the B flat major. Through the continued efforts of Wilhelm Kempff, Rudolf Serkin, Alfred Brendel and others, much has been done to set the record straight, but the sonatas have still not received universal public recognition.

One of the main problems is that these works do not form a logical cycle like the Beethoven sonatas. Our master completed eleven works, while he left several others unfinished. In one case, D840, two finished movements are followed by fragments, in another, D571, none of the movements is completed. In further cases, D625/505, musicologists have suggested that certain movements belong together, yet nobody seems to be sure of the validity of such suggestions. This means that we performers must conduct our own research in order to resolve the major musicological dilemmas that confront us.

There have been various attempts by a number of musicians to finish the fragments. Some of these are better than others. It is a matter of taste if one decides to play them or not. It certainly takes courage (or is it arrogance?) to touch the work of such genius, but is our intervention really necessary? Is it not much more mysterious to see how Schubert struggled with the form in his youth, than to find 'the solution' of the recapitulation? Is there anything more to be said after the Andante of D840 or that of the B minor 'Unfinished' Symphony?

Two fragments are especially touching: the first movements of D571 and D625. Both are interrupted at the recapitulation and die away in mid-air with the softest whisper. I am quite convinced that it is correct to play them like this: another note by someone else would be quite superfluous. D625's last movement has only a few bars missing, and they are quite easy to reconstruct from Schubert's sketches of the soprano line.

Sketches and fragments: in the visual arts nobody would dare to add to Michelangelo's unfinished *Prisoners* or *Pietà*. In music, people just can't leave them alone. They should.

The sonatas were composed between 1815 and 1828. Apart from the songs, the piano sonata is the only genre in which Schubert's development as a composer can be followed, from his early youth, through his maturity, until his death. Just like Beethoven's, Schubert's works also fall into three periods – early, middle and late. But, unlike Beethoven, he only needed three or four years between style-phases. Schubert, like Mozart, lived faster. To understand and appreciate the last sonatas, one must also know the early ones. After all, the late works did not grow out of nowhere; they are rather the result of an evolution. Even the very first sonata, in E major, D157 is well worth playing: the first movement's second subject is so unmistakeably Schubertian, and the second movement, with its melancholic Siciliano, is a masterpiece (the first varied reprise is particularly beautiful). The Menuetto's Trio is a forerunner of the Trio of the great D major Sonata.

The F minor, D624 contains the trills – both mysterious and demonic – which are so prominent in the B flat Sonata, D960. The middle movement of the A minor, D537 reappears in a completely new form as the Finale of the great A major, D959. The A minor, D537, E flat major, D568, and B major, D575, are all wonderful works that are almost never played. On the other hand almost every pianist plays the so-called 'little' A major, D664.

Schubert wasn't a virtuoso pianist like Beethoven, Chopin and Liszt. He was not interested in bravura; he doesn't try to impress, to overwhelm. He is much more introverted than the others. Only very occasionally does he try to step out of his nature, as in the *Wanderer* Fantasy, a magnificent, though rather uncharacteristic work. Yet he must have been a marvellous pianist, otherwise he couldn't have written for the piano so beautifully. In one of his letters, he writes how pleased he was when people praised his playing, that he could sing on the piano, and that he strongly disliked the banging usually favoured at the time by other virtuosos (what would the poor man say about some of today's pianists?). According to witnesses Schubert didn't have the technique to play 'Erlkönig' or the *Wanderer Fantasy* and stopped in the middle of the latter saying 'Let the devil play the stuff!'[2] But he must have had the ability to play *legato* and *cantabile*, and to produce an endless range of colours, these being very much a part of piano technique. Only some very primitive piano aficionados believe that a virtuoso's main assets are speed, strength and accuracy.

Schubert had a wonderful ear and this is constantly demonstrated in his writing for piano. His hearing and his exquisite taste enable him to write transparently and economically. His scores are never crowded; even the chordal passages never lose control. Let's compare the opening of the G major Sonata, D894, with that of Beethoven's G major Concerto, Op. 58. (see Ex. 8.1) Both use the same tonic chord with the third, B, at the top, but Beethoven has eight voices marked *piano dolce*, while Schubert – who clearly had Beethoven's work in mind – only needs five voices marked *pianissimo*. Beethoven's sonority is fuller, Schubert's transparent and lucid. It is the performer's duty to realise this and it is one of the crucial musical and technical problems of interpretation. The pianist must voice each chord, making careful judgements of the right balance. In a chord of five voices – the first chord of D894 – we have two Gs (tonic), two Bs (third) and only one D (fifth). None of these can be played with the same touch or volume; the player

Ex. 8.1a   Schubert's G major Sonata, D894

Ex. 8.1b   Beethoven's G major Concerto, Op. 58

must experiment for quite a long time to find the ideal voicing. The same is true for the opening of D960, and indeed for all of Schubert's chords. How often one hears pianists who neglect this, and the result is carelessness and noise. Tonal quality is a *sine qua non* with this composer.

His scores are full of markings of *pp* and *ppp*, and nobody before him – not even Beethoven – discovered these softest and more distant ranges of the dynamic scale. Certain instruments of the period – such as the Graf fortepiano – have pedals that enable the player to produce them. On a modern instrument it is much more difficult to play softly, but it can be done if the piano is responsive and if it is sympathetically voiced. Many pianists use the soft pedal much too often whenever they want to achieve extreme softness. This is wrong: the modern piano's soft pedal produces a nasal tone quality that is unpleasant to listen to. Furthermore, a real *pianissimo* must be achieved through the player's imagination and realization (technique!), and not by the mere use of a mechanical device.

What is the right instrument for this music? Some would say 'the Graf fortepiano because this is what Schubert knew and possessed'. While it's most interesting and informative to hear a Graf, it would be dogmatic and narrow-minded to restrict us to the use of it. Great music is often influenced or even inspired by particular instruments, but it transcends them and their limitations. If we want to hear Schubert sonatas in larger concert halls and not just in small rooms or in recordings, then we must accept the use of modern pianos. Today the choice of the Steinway is taken for granted, and in all concert halls of the world the pianist is automatically presented with one. Yet it is not always the right choice. A Steinway is expected to play everything well, from William Byrd to Boulez. A Graf of 1825 will be ideal for Schubert but quite wrong for Beethoven's early sonatas or Chopin's works. The attraction of early pianos is that they play the works of a certain composer or period particularly well, but *only* that. I am convinced that Schubert is one of the few composers whose music sounds alien when it's played on a Steinway. This is because of its Austrian-Viennese flavour. German is the official language in Austria but the Viennese accent is unmistakably different from the 'Hochdeutsch' spoken in parts of Germany. Similarly, Schubert's sonatas (and other works) played on a good Bösendorfer sound to me idiomatic, because of the lighter texture and the singing tone. On a Steinway they sound to me like a good translation. It is unfortunate that so many people automatically associate the tone of a piano with the Steinway sound, regardless of the composer whose music they are listening to. They do not have the patience or tolerance to try something else and they're full of prejudice. Every time I play Schubert on my own Bösendorfer I am in seventh heaven, but some people will always say what a pity it is that I didn't play on a Steinway. Schnabel's recordings of Beethoven and Schubert were not done on a Steinway, but on a Bechstein. It's the most beautiful sound I've ever heard. Cortot preferred to use a Pleyel – to produce unheard-of colours. And let's not forget that it is Fischer's, Cortot's and Schnabel's tone that we so admire and *not* the pianos they played on. The same pianos under lesser hands will sound quite ordinary. In the case of the Graf one would like to hear it played by a great artist like Schnabel. Without the right player it is just an instrument, nothing more.

It is most rewarding to study Schubert's autographs and sketches, and luckily several facsimile editions are available. His handwriting is often difficult to decipher, his accents (>) not easy to distinguish from his *decrescendi* (>). It is often left to the performer's instinct and musicality to come to the right decision. The use of a good edition is a must and the Henle edition is probably the best one that is presently available – although the New Complete Edition of Bärenreiter is in preparation. There are also several very bad editions with countless errors and these must be carefully avoided.[3]

Sometimes even the Henle Edition cannot be absolutely reliable. Let me give two examples. One of Schubert's most popular and best-known works is the last of the three final sonatas, that in B flat, D960. It begins with a vast opening movement marked *molto moderato*. This could mean quite a number of things, the composer indicating a calm, moderate four-in-a-bar tempo. There's absolutely no instruction that would suggest extreme slowness, i.e. *largo*, *lento*, *adagio* or *grave* (all these are used by Schubert elsewhere). In recent years – since Sviatoslav Richter's celebrated performances – it has become the standard to play this movement at an excruciatingly slow speed. Those who don't follow this new 'tradition' are usually subjected to severe criticism. Richter – being a truly great artist who is meticulous about following the text – must have his reasons. The main criterion of a correct tempo in music is that it enables the performer to execute even the smallest note-values without haste. Opening the score of this sonata (Henle Edition), let's have a look at bar 19:

Ex. 8.2

So one would have to find a tempo in which this bar can be played comfortably, hence Richter's slow pace.

By good chance I recently had an opportunity to see the manuscript of the last three sonatas – kept in a private collection – and immediately looked for this passage. To my amazement I read the following:

Ex. 8.3

Reading this one thinks of a trill – unmeasured – just like the one in bar 8. The notation in the Henle edition forces the player to think in demisemiquaver units, which is clearly not what Schubert wanted here. Why did the editors see fit to change Schubert's notation? The decisive rhythmic patterns in this movement are those of semiquavers and triplets, and it is their motion that decides the tempo, not the speed of the trill. Therefore sanity should return and pianists should stop trying to achieve the goal of unsurpassed slowness. After all, Artur Schnabel's recording – after many years – is still the most beautiful one there is, and his tempo, at least for me, is just right.

Another discovery I made when studying these manuscripts occurs in the C minor Sonata, D958, in its final movement. In this most terrifying *danse macabre* a new episode appears in the remote key of B major (bar 243). All editions print the following:

Ex. 8.4

which is exactly repeated in bars 275–8. To my ears this has never sounded right. I always questioned the sixth quaver of the upper voice in bar 249 and 277. The harmony is a B major tonic chord and the melody circumscribes it, starting with a beautiful appoggiatura (A sharp) and later on the third quaver barely touching the C sharp as a passing note. But why should it come back to C sharp on the last quaver, when all the other notes are those of a B major triad? It is difficult to say with certainty whether Schubert wrote a C sharp or a D sharp but I would dare to consider the latter. He was writing at such a speed towards the end that it's often difficult to see if a small note is between the lines or on the line.

Ex. 8.5

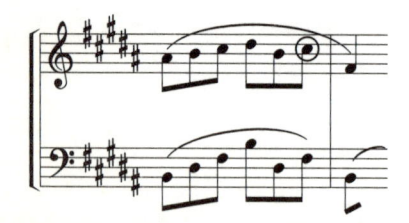

The question of repeats in a crucial one. Every single one should be observed and not simply out of pedantry. In Haydn's and Mozart's sonatas the exposition is almost always repeated and we frequently find second-half repeats. Beethoven's 'Appassionata' Sonata has no repeats at all in the first movement, and in the finale only the development section and recapitulation are repeated, while the exposition is heard only once. Schubert always repeats the first movement's exposition, but only does so twice with the second half (D537/I, D664/I) when there is still a coda to come. In the last two sonatas, D959 and D960, the opening movement contains some strikingly original and important bars of new music in the first ending (*prima volta*). Indeed, the famous trill in bar 8 of D960, suddenly appears like an erupting volcano, while otherwise it's so quietly distant. Omitting these bars is like the amputation of a limb. To sum up, let's assume that the composer knew precisely what was to be repeated and that it is not the performer's choice or right to know better. We must trust the composer and the work and play it accordingly, or not play it at all. Schubert's sonatas are not a second too long – it is only certain people's patience that is too short. (In *da capo* sections of minuets and scherzos one should not repeat any more, because we've already heard both parts twice. Some 'experts' of the authentic movement clearly disagree with this and play all the repeats. There is supposedly a reference to this practice in Daniel Gottlob Türk's *Clavierschule*. Even so, why shouldn't one follow one's musical instincts when the proportions are wrong?)[4]

In Schubert's music melody, harmony and rhythm co-exist in perfect equilibrium. As the other two are so obvious, let's consider rhythm first. Schubert's loose treatment of sonata form and his 'heavenly length' present considerable difficulties to the performer. The work is likely to fall into bits and pieces and lose coherence. The main element that helps us to avoid this is rhythm. In all of the pieces there exists a rhythmic pattern upon which the whole movement is based. It must be recognized by the performer – which is not an easy task since it doesn't always appear at the beginning of the work. Thus in the first movement of the A major Sonata, D664, it is in bar 21 that the rhythm makes its first appearance. However

Ex. 8.6

it's clear that it's going to feature prominently throughout the rest of the movement, often combined with triplet motion. It is one of Schubert's favourite rhythms derived from the second movement of Beethoven's Seventh Symphony. Schubert uses it in countless works, e.g. 'Wandrers Nachtlied', *Wanderer* Fantasy, Impromptu, D935, No. 3, the second movement of the A minor String Quartet, also in 'Der Tod und das Mädchen' – both the song and the string quartet. The pulse shown in Ex. 8.8 – if the first and third beats are slightly more stressed than

Ex. 8.7

Ex. 8.8

the others – immediately gives us the right character. This opening movement of D664 is one of those pieces that often sound sentimental and cheap because the pianist concentrates only on the beautiful melodies while totally neglecting the rhythmic aspects. The C major ('Reliquie') Sonata, D840, is another good example. Here in the first movement we have to wait until bar 29 to hear the following rhythm:

Ex. 8.9

With its unusual syncopation and the following repeated quavers it becomes a knocking fate-motive. Even when it's played *pianissimo* it sounds sinister and threatening. Between bars 53 and 71 Schubert unfolds one of his most beautiful endless melodies under which this motive carries on with its manic *ostinato*. These, combined with the most unpredictable harmonies at the cadences, result in a magical experience, uniquely Schubertian.

Another aspect of rhythm must be mentioned: the problem of notation and realization when triplet figurations are combined with dotted rhythms. It has been suggested by scholars that the semiquaver or demisemiquaver notes of the dotted figures should coincide with the ultimate notes of the triplet. This is certainly convincing in the last movement of J S Bach's Fifth Brandenburg Concerto.

Ex. 8.10

[musical example]

Later on one should be more careful. Even in the second movement of Mozart's C major Concerto, K467, it is certainly wrong to even out the difference. With Schubert there are several examples for both cases. In the second movement of the Sonata in E flat major, D568, bars 43–61 are an obvious case where the binary and ternary notations must coincide, otherwise the music would be disturbed by nervous accents that would be out of place.

Ex. 8.11

[musical example]

A similar treatment is intended in the first movement of the Sonata in E minor, bar 33 (see Ex. 8.12).

Ex. 8.12

[musical example]

In the first movement of the B major, D575, bars 78–9 show us that Schubert wanted the different rhythms to be kept distinct, exactly as notated.

Ex. 8.13a

On the other hand bars 81–8 again return to conformity (see Ex. 8.13b)

Ex. 8.13b

It is a more delicate matter to decide which cases belong to the second category, and this is very much a question of personal taste and preference. In certain cases the music benefits from the conflict that results from the clashing of rhythms. To me even the *minore* third variations of the B flat major Impromptu, D935, No. 3, belongs to this group (see Ex. 8.14).

Ex. 8.14

The first movement of the B flat major Piano Trio would lose much of its vitality if one didn't deliberately play the dotted rhythms sharply against the triplets (see Ex. 8.15).

Ex. 8.15

In the piano sonatas it seems to me that towards the end we find an increasing number of examples that belong to the second category. In the last movement of D960, bars 185–208 etc. must be differentiated, and the dotted rhythm must remain the same as it was in bar 168 etc., but the character changes and because of the triplet accompaniment and the *pp* marking it all sounds very gentle (see Ex. 8.16).

Ex. 8.16

In the coda of the last movement of the A major, D959, bars 349 etc., a clash of rhythms is desirable (Ex. 8.17a). Also the dotted rhythm in the bass must correspond with bars 13 and 15 (Ex. 8.17b).

However, good rhythm and vital pulse are not mechanical or calculated. Each dotting can be slightly sharpened or softened according to the music's requirements. These are tiny nuances that are beyond the limits of musical notation.

Schubert is one of the great composers of dance music. He was quite a miserable dancer but he enjoyed playing the piano at balls, fancy dress events and merry

Ex. 8.17a

Ex. 8.17b

gatherings of his circle of friends. The popular dances – polka, *ecossaise*, *galopp*, *valse*, *ländler* – have found their way into his most profound works and into the piano sonatas. The G major, D894, is impregnated with dance throughout. One could call it a 'Dance Sonata' instead of the misleading 'Fantasy Sonata' that has been its nickname ever since the first edition. In the first movement stillness and timelessness gradually gain momentum and the music turns into a wonderful lilting waltz (bar 27 etc.) even though the metre is $\frac{12}{8}$. The third movement is rather sinister – an ironically smiling Menuetto gives place to a B major Trio which makes one believe in heaven where the angels are dancing. And the finale is a huge sequence of polkas or ecossaises – a kind of dance scene, totally irresistible. To bring out the special character of these the performer must first recognize them, be familiar with them and finally play them in a way that will convey their spirit to the listener. The listener must be tempted to jump up and join the dance. Luckily the tradition of Viennese dances is still alive, and one can see them being danced at the annual celebrations in Vienna. As to the musical realization, let's be grateful that we can still hear the Vienna Philharmonic Orchestra play Johann Strauss. Imagine if we had to learn the 'authentic' performances of a Viennese waltz from books! Jokes apart – in dance music the steps and beats are not absolutely equal: one cannot dance to the beat of a metronome.

As a melodist, Schubert is in a class of his own. Endless melodies seem to burst out of his creative genius. Someone who has spent most of his life writing for the human voice will always think vocally, even when the music is purely instrumental. The trouble with many instrumentalists – pianists and string players alike – is that they don't breathe naturally. Wind and brass players don't have this problem; they – like singers – must follow their natural need of respiration. Singing is the most natural and ancient form of music-making, as Schubert well knew. His melodies fall into beautifully natural phrases that are always singable and it's obvious when one has to breathe. Breathing takes a little time and so it is understandable that at such moments the music reacts to the slight loss of time. The claim of certain musicians that this interrupts the flow of the music is absurd and unmusical.

Schubert's treatment of harmony is miraculous, and he is the greatest master of modulations. Alfred Brendel has compared him to a sleep-walker who goes from one tonality to the next in permanent motion. These excursions are so full of surprises that they can never be taken for granted. Even if one knows his music well one is always surprised by the direction and outcome of his modulations. He obviously cannot get enough of them, hence the 'heavenly length' of his development sections, like that of the first movement of the E flat major Piano Trio, or the first and last movements of the last sonatas.

The performer only has to follow Schubert on his journeys and recognize its various stations. How often one hears performances of this music where the player doesn't understand the harmonic movement. The result is like being driven through the countryside at high speed without having time to enjoy the view. In Schubert's modulations each new tonality or change of key must be interpreted with a subtle change of colour. This music is by no means black and white. To do justice to it one must possess an enormous range of dynamics and a palette of colours worthy of a great painter. Frans Hals – supposedly – could paint over thirty different nuances of black, so a pianist must also have that many different pianissimos.

Silence is the beginning and end of music. Schubert knew this and his sonatas are full of rests and longer pauses (*fermatas*), such as the one in bar 9 of the first movement of D960.

Ex. 8.18

There is always somebody in the audience who seizes this opportunity; I am eagerly waiting for the first time in my life when nobody will cough at this point. The rest is crucial; it represents silence after the mysterious murmuring of the bass trill and one careless cough totally spoils the magic of it. We might just as well stand up and go home. Do coughers ever think of this? Rests are there to be observed and one often hears pianists who pedal through them. It's a great mistake because it confuses the meaning of the music. The last movement of the C minor Sonata, D958,

Ex. 8.19

can easily sound like this:

Ex. 8.20

because of careless pedalling and lack of articulation. The galloping manic character is totally lost. Similarly, the final Rondo of D959 (Ex. 8.21)

Ex. 8.21

changes its meaning if the rests are not observed. For Schubert this is very important because eleven years earlier in the second movement of the A minor Sonata, D537, the same theme was notated thus (Ex. 8.22).

Ex. 8.22

[musical score: Allegretto quasi Andantino, ligato, p, staccato]

Let's look at the first eight bars of the second movement of the D major Sonata, D850 (Ex. 8.23).

Ex. 8.23

[musical score: Con moto, ligato, p, cresc., f>p>]

We have countless instructions here: accents, *crescendo* and *diminuendo*, slurs and dots to vary the articulation and the word 'ligato' to contradict them. Schubert indicates here a long melodic line with declamation. He seems to be obsessed with accents; the whole movement is crowded with the various signs of >, *fz* and *fp*. All these have different meanings according to the musical content. One should never take accents literally. An accent with *piano* is not the same as one with *forte*. The sign of > can often mean a stress or slight emphasis on a certain note or harmony, suggesting agogics. It is almost – but luckily not quite – impossible to play these eight bars simply and naturally while observing all the markings of the composer.

Schubert's music is a poetic language. It is closely related to poetry, with its rhetoric, punctuations, exclamations, questions and quotations. His musical verses are inspired by the great German poets and the interpreter must be familiar with these.

The rise and fall of German is very different from that of English or French. Schubert's songs are the best advisers for us when we are not exactly sure about the phrasing or character of a certain part of a piano sonata. Thus the D major Sonata is so full of references to *Die schöne Müllerin*, the C minor refers both to 'Der Atlas' and 'Erlkönig', and the B flat major's opening reminds me of the vast horizon of 'Am Meer'. Even the most astonishing, elusive passage – the middle section of the second movement of the A major, D959 – is easier to understand if one thinks of it as a melodrama, above which the text of a Schiller *ballade* can be recited. Schubert's own versions of 'Die Bürgschaft' or 'Der Taucher' show us why. Even so, this passage in the A major Sonata represents a terrifying scene, like an Apocalypse or the Last Judgement. It has no precedent in Schubert's music and its modernity is incredible even today. This is one of his many faces and it shows us that the greatest masters cannot be put into a closed category – they have an enormous variety of characters and 'faces'.

Schubert was one of the first masters to close the distance between the drawing room and nature. The D major Sonata was composed in Bad Gastein in 1825 under the spell of the magical countryside of mountains, brooks and forests. In the *un poco più lento* section of the last movement we even get a sample of Austrian yodelling and the second movement's variations are pure birdsong.

Works like the *Wanderer* Fantasy, the A minor Sonata, D784, or the 'Reliquie' Sonata, D840, are orchestrally conceived. Liszt orchestrated the *Wanderer* Fantasy and Joachim made a symphonic version of the Grand Duo for piano duet. However, it is much more satisfying to play these in the original and the pianist must bring out all the orchestral colours from the instrument. Schumann, who first recognised the Schubert sonatas, warned that musicians with little fantasy and imagination should stay far away from them. How right he was!

Beethoven's works for piano are full of instructions for the use of pedals, both the sustaining pedal and the *una corda* one. He revolutionized the use of pedal with incredible effects, requiring the player to pedal through long phrases. It is most curious that Schubert – who idolized Beethoven – very seldom uses the word 'pedal'. In all the sonatas there are only three or four places, such as the second movement of D960 or the coda of the first movement of D959. This doesn't mean that in all the other works one should refrain from the use of the pedal – on the contrary, one must use it continuously but sparingly, with sensitivity and control. Harmonies in figurations must ring together with the bass, and the overtones must help the melody to sing and sustain. After all many of these works are songs without words.

Ornaments are richly represented in Schubert's sonatas and they are all written out. In general, trills begin on the upper auxiliary note and they end with a *Nachslag*, but there are several exceptions. Appoggiaturas or *Vorschläge* can start on the beat but they often sound more convincing when they're played before it. It is no use nailing down the rules – we have to examine each case melodically, harmonically and rhythmically and let our musical instinct decide. Ornaments are there to make the music more agreeable and pleasing and not to confuse it or make it sound crowded. One very seldom hears them beautifully executed because the player cannot distinguish between the main notes and the embellishments. This is also a musical technical point. In a cathedral the function of the pillars and that of the stained glass windows is obvious. In music the various elements also carry an architectural function. One must take time for the ornaments, they should not be played mechanically. There must be a great variety of trills in a pianist's vocabulary, trills of different speed and character.

One can learn a lot about these things from listening to great singers, like Dietrich Fischer-Dieskau or Peter Schreier. It is a pity that most solo pianists don't have any experience in working with singers. The sonatas cannot be understood without the intimate knowledge of the songs. In Schubert's songs the pianist is *not* an accompanist but a creative partner to the singer. It is unfortunate that the public and most critics fail to recognise this in spite of the wonders performed in this field by Fischer, Cortot, Britten, Richter and others. These artists have demonstrated what a difference it makes when the piano part is played by a great pianist and musician – and not just by a good accompanist.

Simplicity is one of Schubert's greatest virtues, and the performance must reflect this. One must be extremely expressive and colourful but the music must flow naturally and be left alone. It is a bad sign when the performer's wilfulness becomes too obvious. *Rubato* must be carefully applied but an overdose of it could easily make the music sound sentimental. Schubert's world is never sentimental or too sweet; it only seems so in the horrible operetta *Dreimäderlhaus* by Berthé, and in tasteless bad performances.

Schubert's life may have been short in years, but not in the quality and quantity of his works. It's useless to contemplate what he could have written had he lived longer. Instead we should be eternally grateful for what he so generously gave us. It is good to see the ever-growing popularity of his creations, and he will even survive the celebrations of his 200th birthday. Let us hope that more and more people realise that Schubert was not just the greatest *Lieder* composer, but a creator of piano sonatas second to none.

Notes

1. Even so, it's curious to consider why certain Beethoven sonatas are more popular than others: maybe because of their nicknames?
2. *Memoirs of his Friends*, p. 194.
3. Howard Ferguson's edition for the Associated Board has gained wide acceptance (Ed.).
4. See also Max Rudolf, 'Inner Repeats in the Da Capo of Classical Minuets and Scherzos', in *Journal of the Conductors' Guild* (vol.III/4, Fall 1982), pp145–50. (Ed.)

9 Schubert and the Ungers: a preliminary study
Peter Branscombe

The name of Caroline Unger will be familiar to those with an interest in the history of opera in the second quarter of the nineteenth century. Additionally, Schubertians may recall that, at the very start of her professional career, Caroline Unger was coached by Schubert for a role at the Vienna Court Opera. She was his only professional student of singing, so far as is known. Her father, Carl Unger, is an interesting, and indeed important, figure in his own right. A facet of their careers which is almost entirely unknown, even to Viennese musicologists, is that they were both talented song-writers. This chapter will do no more than introduce this aspect of their talents – a detailed study of the topic will follow in due course.

First, a biographical outline.[1] (Johann) Carl Unger was born at Rissdorf, Zips, in Hungary [now Spiš, Slovak Republic] on 13 April 1771, the son of a schoolmaster. He was educated by the Piarists at Pudlein, and then at Kaschau, specializing in the Classics, until illness and hardship in the family led him to abandon his philosophical studies and, at seventeen, become a Piarist and a teacher. The favourable impression he made on his superiors led to their recommending him to the Bishop of Neutra [Nitra], who supported him in his desire to study theology. However, he turned to law, and in 1796 he was appointed a teacher at the famous Theresian Academy in Vienna for the sons of gentlemen. Three years later he accepted an appointment as private tutor to the son of Baron Forgács, living with the family on their Moravian estate in summer, and in Vienna in the winter; in 1810 he became financial adviser to Baron Hackelberg-Landau, and continued in this post until 1836 – by when he had long been a welcome guest in high Viennese social circles. He died in Vienna in 1836.

He was a prolific writer, his works ranging from moral and allegorical tales, travel books and topographies (particularly of his native Hungary) to works on Roman history, education, preservation of foodstuffs for men and animals, a biography of the French soprano Joséphine Mainville-Fodor, and many contributions to almanacs and periodicals – as well as a volume of poems, to which we shall return.

Carl Unger's connections with Schubert are only sparsely documented. Josef Hüttenbrenner informed Ferdinand Luib that it was Unger who introduced Schubert to Count Johann Karl Esterházy, to whose daughters the young composer was for two summers engaged as music teacher at the family estate of Zseliz in Hungary.[2] Unger appears in Schubert documents in several connections: he is one of the signatories of a reference for Schubert for the post of music director at Laibach in 1816;[3] in a letter of 27 June 1820 he told Count Esterházy that Schubert had earned honour with the performances of *Die Zwillingsbrüder* (*Dok*, 98); on 20 August 1820 he wrote to Esterházy again, this time praising Schubert's music for *Die Zauberharfe* (*Dok*, 109); and he is also mentioned in connection with Anselm Hüttenbrenner's setting for vocal quartet of his poem 'Der Abend' (*Dok*, 124, 157, 224, 343), and with the 'Wiener Schwank' mocking the German opera ensemble in 1824 (*Dok*, 263).

In January 1818 Schubert set Unger's 'Die Geselligkeit' for SATB with piano accompaniment (D609), and in or before April 1821 he set 'Die Nachtigall' as a male-voice quartet (D724). Anselm Hüttenbrenner also set one of Unger's poems, 'Der Abend', likewise for four mixed voices; it was performed at one of the *Abendunterhaltungen* of the Gesellschaft der Musikfreunde on 19 November 1818, with Unger's daughter as first soprano; the bass, 'Nestroi', was the later celebrated actor and dramatist, Johann Nestroy. Neither of these poems is included in the charming little volume, *Gedichte / von / J. Carl Unger. / [Vignette] / Wien / 1797*.[4] However, despite the fact that after the age of 26 Unger published no further collection of verses, there is no reason to suspect that he did not continue to write poetry for the pleasure of himself and friends, as well as publishing occasional poems in the almanacs and periodicals to which he contributed.

Of greater interest, at least in the present context, is a manuscript music book that reveals Carl Unger to have been a talented amateur composer. The cover of this volume, which is preserved in a British private collection, reads: *Joh. Carl Unger's Lieder*; a later hand has added in pencil: 'Lieder del padre di Caroline' and the number '21'. The title page of the volume reads: *J. Carl Ungers / Lieder. / Nach geahmt / oder / Von ihm selbst gedichtet und / in Musick gesetzt.*

The words of 'Die Geselligkeit' and 'Die Nachtigall', the only Unger poems that Schubert is known to have set to music, may well have been copied by the composer from Unger's own manuscript songbook; Hüttenbrenner's setting is likewise of a song that also occurs in Unger's song album.

In the case of 'Die Nachtigall' there are small verbal changes of the kind familiar from many of Schubert's vocal settings: Unger's 'entzückenden Lohn' becomes 'beglückenden', 'bald [gleitet]' becomes 'sanft', '[aus] sanfterer [Brust]' becomes 'schwellender', 'So Freundinn! ertönte dein himmlisches Lied / Als Cynthia traulich die Finsterniß schied' becomes 'So Freunde, verhallte manch' himmlisches Lied / Wenn Cynthias Feuer [...]', and 'Es wehte mir Frieden mit' becomes 'Es wehte mit Frieden uns', 'Laute' becomes 'Töne'; the changes tend to make the tone less personal.

'Lebenslust' (entitled 'Die Geselligkeit' in the Unger album) is in Schubert's setting identical (apart from the variant spelling 'traulichen' for Unger's 'traulichten') as far as the end of the first strophe ('Wer Lebenslust fühlet [...] Ist Seelengenuß'); but Schubert does not set the remaining three strophes of Unger's poem (and song), relying on verbal repetitions to produce the length he desires.

Carl Unger met his wife, Anna Karvinski von Karvin, in the house of her kinsman Baron Forgács. Their only daughter Caroline[5] was born at Stuhlweissenburg [Székesfehérvár, Hungary] on 28 October 1803,[6] and it is thanks to the respect accorded to her parents, and her own prodigious talent, that she had such a good start in life: a godmother was Caroline Pichler, the well-connected hostess and writer, while her singing teachers and advisers included Josef Mozatti, Aloisia Lange, Salieri, and Johann Michael Vogl. Caroline Unger is named as the solo singer in the second concert of the Gesellschaft der Musikfreunde,[7] which was held on 26 March 1818; she sang a psalm by Abbé Stadler. Thereafter she was a frequent soloist, singing arias and sharing with some of the most famous singers of the day duets, trios and larger ensembles from popular operas by Rossini and others. Indeed, few if any singers are as often named in the programmes up until 15 April 1819 (after which date there is a gap in the records of the concerts until December 1820). She is named in the programme of the concert of 7 December 1820 as one of a list of members who had evidently taken, and not returned, concert tickets. She sang a 'Bolleros Espagnol' by Blangini at the concert on 21 December 1820, but that seems to have been the last occasion on which she took part.[8] Schubert's first appearance in the programmes was five weeks later, on 25 January 1821, with 'Erlkönig'.

Following these early successes at the Society's evening concerts, she was invited to sing at the Court Opera, where she soon established a reputation in the German and Italian repertory, and sang alongside some of the greatest artists of the day. Perhaps her most obvious claim to fame is that she took the contralto part in the first performance of Beethoven's 'Choral' Symphony (the concert also included selected numbers from the *Missa solemnis*) on 7 May 1824. She had been acquainted with Beethoven since 1822, assuming Emily Anderson's identification of the 'two women singers' who visited the composer at Baden on 8 September 1822 to be correct: 'as they absolutely insisted on being allowed to kiss my hands', he tells his brother Johan, 'and as they were decidedly pretty I preferred to offer them my mouth to kiss [...]'.[9]

In the spring of 1825 Caroline Unger accepted Barbaja's invitation to sing at Naples, and she enjoyed a series of triumphs in many of the great Italian houses; it is from this time that she began, in order to encourage correct pronunciation of her name, to call herself Ungher (she was not always consistent in this regard). She was in Paris between 1833 and 1834, and in the following eight years was much in demand in German and Italian houses, as well as in Vienna. In 1841 she married the French writer François Sabatier, and two years later retired from the stage. She travelled widely and corresponded extensively, on occasion with several members of the circle who had been close to Schubert. She died at 'La Concezione', the house at Florence in which she had for many years lived in retirement with her husband, on 23 March 1877.

She must have come into contact with Schubert on the occasion of the Ash Wednesday concert at the Kärntnertor-Theater on 7 March 1821, at which she sang and three of Schubert's works were performed (*Dok*, 116–17). Her closest link with him, already alluded to, came at the time when she was preparing the role of Dorabella ('Isabella') for performance in *Mädchentreue*, the then current German title of *Così fan tutte*, at the Kärntnertor-Theater in 1821. Schubert, hoping for an appointment as repetiteur at the Court Opera, was entrusted with preparing the role with her. The expenditure book of the Kärntnertor-Theater records: '*Supernumerary remuneration.* / Schubert Franz / Composer / as per receipt of 9 Apr 821 for studying the role of D[emoise]lle Unger in the opera "Mädchentreue" / 13 April 1821 / [...] / fl 50 kr–.'(*Dok*, 123–4). She later became a greatly admired interpreter of Schubert's Lieder, and in a fascinating letter,[10] dated only '24 March', and lacking the name and address of the recipient, she somewhat peremptorily requests that the 'Verehrter Herr' whom she addresses should send her at the Albergo d'Italia, Venice, 'by return of post [...] *as soon as possible*', a list of the opus numbers of all published Schubert songs, including the *Nachlass*. She includes a lengthy list of the songs that she already owns, no fewer than 76 opus numbers, plus several further parts of published sets, *Schwanengesang*, and six other individual songs. 'I wish to complete ['*completiren*'] my collection', she writes. She specifically mentions that she lacks *Winterreise*. Her signature contains a correction of the spelling of her maiden name, the 'h' being added to the original 'Unger'.

Though the connection may be no more than a coincidence, this is the appropriate place to introduce a recently published letter to Caroline Unger from Mozart's younger surviving son, Franz Xavier Wolfgang (known as 'Wolfgang Amadeus'). The letter,[11] written in Vienna on Boxing Day 1842, is addressed "A Madame Madame / Caroline Ungher-Sabathier / Chanteuse de la Cour de sa / Majesté L'Empereur d'Autriche, et / de celle de son Altesse Imp le Grand / Duc de Toscane / à / *Florence* / en Toscane."; it is stamped "GRENZE" at the head, and "12 / GENNAIO / 1843" following the address. What seems to link it with the letter previously discussed is the subject-matter – though one cannot suppress the thought that such a good friend as Mozart seems to have been would not be likely to delay his response to a letter demanding immediate attention, by the nine months that separate 24 March from Boxing Day. Nevertheless, it is in the context of her request for the complete collection of Schubert's Lieder that he writes (perhaps the recipient of the previous letter had failed to respond, or to respond adequately):

My honoured friend,

Immediately on receipt of your kind, friendly letter my first concern was to deal with your commission as well and as swiftly as possible, and I thus have the pleasure to be able to inform you that already yesterday I have been able to hand over the complete collection of the Schubert songs to Dr. Jeitteles,[12] who will kindly forward them to you. In consequence of your so very kind permission I was also so bold as to dispatch to you on this same occasion the copy of the score of my Festival Chorus intended for H.R. Highness the Grand Duke [...].

The extensive collection of Caroline Unger's letters that is preserved in the Handschriftensammlung of the Wiener Stadt- und Landesbibliothek, which I have so far had the opportunity to peruse only superficially, contains much interesting material; unfortunately, few of the letters are dated (other than with day and month), and many contain no indication of the identity of the recipient. Perhaps the most interesting item in the collection is not a letter at all, but a folded sheet of paper[13] containing a number of brief verses, drawings and other jottings with the names (signatures?) of their authors. These include: "Das Ding wird immer schlimmer — / Ich geh nun auf mein — *Stube* / F. Schubert".[14] The temptation to claim this as a hitherto unknown Schubert autograph has to be tempered by the fact that several of the other names, including that of Caroline's husband François Sabatier, could not have been entered in Schubert's lifetime. On the other hand, it is likely that the sheet as originally used was folded with Schubert's verse as the first entry on the first of the four pages, which is stamped in the top left corner, within a simple decorative frame, "FAR BENE / LASCIAR DIRE". Not all the material has yet been fully deciphered, the ink of some of the entries having come through on to the other side of the paper. The names represented are: [p1] François Sabatier, Caroline Sabatier Ungher, Tichatschekin,[15] Maschantiers [?], Schober, Tichatschek; [p2] F. Schubert, anon.; [p3] contains scurrilous unidentified verse and prose; [p4] contains a distinctly amateurish sketch of a fat Franciscan friar, "Daguerrotyppirt von Caroline Sabatier Ungher", and a drawing of what looks like a pig (the likeness is admitted) but is actually meant to be a bear.

For the literary historian probably the most interesting event in Caroline Unger's life is her love-affair with the Austro-Hungarian aristocrat and poet Nikolaus Lenau (1802–50), one of the most important figures in Romantic literature. The details have to be reconstructed from circumstantial evidence, as their (evidently passionate) correspondence has not survived: after the relationship cooled to friendship, Lenau insisted on having his letters returned to him, and he seems to have destroyed hers. From comments in his letters to Sophie Löwenthal,[16] the married woman he adored for a decade (and whom he must have hurt through his frank avowal of his unfaithfulness), we gain a vivid impression of the impact the singer made on him with her art and her personality. Since Lenau was a good enough musician to have been praised in public print for his "powerfully fantastic" violin playing,[17] we need not hesitate to take seriously his judgment of Caroline Unger's singing, even if he was falling increasingly under her spell.[18] The earliest of the letters to Sophie about Unger was written in Vienna on 25 June 1839; its third paragraph begins:

> Graf Christalnigg visited me yesterday and invited me to Penzing for luncheon. I dined with Fräulein Unger and Graf Heissenstamm, the dramatic poet. Before the meal, accompanied by Heissenstamm, Unger sang the 'Wanderer' and 'Gretchen' by Schubert, overwhelmingly beautifully. Truly, tragic blood courses in the veins of this woman. In her performance she loosed upon my heart a singing thunder of passion; at once I recognized that I was heading for a storm, I fought and wrestled against the power of her tones, because I do not like to show myself so moved in the presence of strangers, in vain; I was quite shattered, and could not conceal it. When she had finished singing, I was seized by anger against the victorious woman, and I withdrew to the window; however she followed me and modestly showed me her shaking hand, and how she herself had trembled during the storm; that reconciled me, for I saw what I should have thought at once, that it was something stronger than she and I that had passed through her heart and mine, and in the presence of which we both stood there equally bowed once all was quiet again. We sat down to table. Unger was very friendly and talkative. 'I request that my Lenau sit next to me', she said, and thus I became her neighbour; but the singing had ruined my appetite and turned me in on myself, with the result that I was unable to give the appropriate devouring esteem to the excellent dishes, nor the proper attention and involvement to the table-talk of my neighbour. After the meal there was skittles. Unger excelled as prima donna here too; with a robust throw she toppled between five and seven skittles. (*Briefe* IV, 327)

A few days later Lenau wrote to Sophie again (this time in one of the intimate journal-like entries not intended for Sophie's husband and circle to read), indicating a growing infatuation with the singer:

> 30 June 1839. [...] The last few days have passed very turbulently for me. The playing and singing of Unger made the highest tragic effect on me. Since old Devrient[19] air from that region has not been wafted my way in the theatre; yesterday in *Belisario*[20] a mighty storm overcame me from those parts. She is an artist of the first magnitude. In social intercourse too she is very kind, and especially friendly towards me. I was with her yesterday after the theatre, today I'm eating with her at midday. You should get to know her. (*Briefe* IV, 175)

Sophie Löwenthal was again the recipient of a letter written in Vienna on 5 July 1839 that gives renewed evidence of the poet's overwhelming absorption in the singer:

> [...] The past week was a period of stormy agitation for me. Karoline Unger is a wondrous woman. Only at the coffin of my mother have I sobbed as I did on that evening when I heard the famous artist in *Belisario*. It wasn't the piece itself, the precise role, the tragic quality of which seized me; the singer went far beyond any individual detail, and I heard in her passionate lamentations, in her cry of despair the whole tragic fate of humankind ring out, the whole world of happiness break asunder, and the heart of mankind torn apart. A nameless, immense pain seized me, of which I still feel a mysterious shiver pass through my innermost being. It was plainly to be heard that Fate is serious about suffering, that this is no mere well-intentioned decision of our heart's upbringing. I was much with Karoline, she felt herself related to me as one storm-cloud is to the other. After the performance of *Belisario* I went to her, as I often do, and told her that she had made the greatest tragic impact on me; she was pleased, and told me a few days later that my rapture in that opera was her greatest triumph in Vienna, despite

her pleasure at the storm of applause after her last performance. She left for Dresden yesterday. I rejoice in her friendship, for she is, as I told her, one of the most exalted natures that we have to venerate here on earth. She is usually lively and cheerful in society, often childlike and flirtatious; at such times her soul is obviously recovering from the great exertions, and Nature is beneficently seeking to bring her life back on to an even keel. But then sometimes the grave voice of her soul suddenly comes forth, and what she said to me on the nature of tragedy, for instance, and her understanding of it, showed me her thinking on an unusually high plane. She is at home in the loneliest and wildest regions of passion and is familiar with the countenance of pain in all its aspects. I could wish that, as she has planned, she might in a few years turn to German drama; then it would be a joy to write a tragedy especially for her. – [...] The divine has never appeared to me in life without its following of sorrow. In you this has gleamed silently for five years, has warmed me beneficently; but there was much pain and grief bound up with it, and your uncertain health worries me continuously. In Karoline a sacred storm has pierced my soul; but a deep lament attaches to the great joy. (*Briefe* IV, 328–30)

The brief letter of 11 July contains the stark statement:

Karoline loves me and wishes to become mine. She sees it as her mission to conciliate my life and bring happiness to it. My feeling for you remains eternal and unshaken, but Karoline's devotion has taken powerful hold on me. It is up to you to be humane to my divided heart. Karoline loves me beyond measure. She has written to me. If I reject her, I make her wretched and myself too, for she is worthy of my love. If you withdraw your heart from me, you kill me; if you are unhappy, I shall die. The knot is tied. I wish I were already dead! (*Briefe* IV, 331)

The letters to Sophie continue to rave and storm about Lenau's love for Caroline; the next letter (16 July 1839; IV, 332) was actually written in the lodgings of another friend from the Schubert circle, Moritz von Schwind. The long letter from Linz of 22 August reports that Caroline and Lenau have decided not to marry, at least for the time being: he is aware of his own financial insufficiencies; and was unwilling to allow her to cancel her operatic obligations, which extend for the coming nineteen months. Nonetheless, her devotion to the poet is conveyed in one charming detail, as he tells Sophie: 'Karoline, as she entered the room, knelt and laid at my feet the two wreaths that had been presented to her at her final performance in Dresden, one from Tieck,[21] the other from Schröder.'[22] (*Briefe* IV, 337–38)

References to Caroline Unger in Lenau's letters grow cooler and less frequent after the summer of 1839; a cryptic comment in the short letter to Sophie (Hallstatt, 28 August 1839) touches on what was presumably the decisive period of the affair between Lenau and Caroline: 'Karoline has invited me on an expedition in the Salzkammergut, and we are now held fast in Hallstatt by the rain. Tomorrow, if it's any better, we shall proceed' (IV, 339). By the time the only known surviving letter from poet to singer was written, probably in February 1840, the relationship was over; this short note reads: 'Here is the song [*Lied*] you requested, may it still find favour with you!' (*Briefe* IV, 356); with it Lenau sent her the lengthy (but not outstandingly fine) poem 'Im Frühling', which begins: 'Die warme Luft, der Sonnenstrahl / Erquickt mein Herz, erfüllt das Tal [...]' ('The warm air, the sunbeam / Refreshes my heart, fills the valley [...]').

The last letter to Sophie in which Caroline Unger figures prominently (again one of the journal-like private missives) was written on 9 May 1840, in the evening:

> The opera[23] was good; Ungher excellent; my pleasure significant, I even let myself be persuaded by Schönstein to go to her after the theatre. He soon withdrew, and I remained with her alone. Despite that, everything remains as it was before. The barriers are immovable; she knows that very well, and is nevertheless happy when she sees me. But now I am tired. The theatre full of people and heat. But now a word to you, my dear, sweet heart! You can imagine that one final hope was attaching to this evening, and that it was expressed when we were alone. I let her find me as I am every day, apart from my pleasure at the beautiful evening. I believe I have established from henceforth our relationship as a genuine and resignation-filled friendship. But that I am her friend she deserves by reason of her truly rare goodness of heart. Not a trace of anger or injured pride. My soul is as peaceful and certain in this regard as you could wish it to be [...] (*Briefe* IV, 183)

At peace his soul may have been, but he was plagued by the thought that Caroline still held the evidence of what he called his 'documented stupidities'; in the letter of 15 July 1840, written to Sophie's husband Max Löwenthal, he tells how he had hastened from Stuttgart to Ischl in order to demand from Caroline the return of all his letters. 'I arrived here in the evening of the 13th after a very rapid journey and by the morning of the 14th I had all my letters in the bag [...]. Of course I gave her hers in return, which she said she intended to burn [...]' (*Briefe* IV, 389–90). From his letters to his intimate friends it is clear that Caroline had indeed burnt her letters to Lenau, while he postponed the burning of his to her.

A further indication of the esteem in which Caroline Unger was held both during and after her international career as a singer is the number of interesting contemporaries with whom she was in touch. As we have seen, she corresponded with Mozart's younger son Wolfgang Amadeus. His letter to her of 26 December 1842 (just a few days, as it happens, before Schober wrote his dedicatory poem for her songbook; see below) makes clear how highly Unger was by then regarded as friend, organizer of musical events, and as intercessor with the great on behalf of lesser or more modest individuals.

The Goethe-Museum Düsseldorf owns an autograph album (*Stammbuch*) of Caroline Unger, which contains 54 entries by many of the artistic luminaries of the first half of the nineteenth century, including: Amalia, Duchess of Saxony, the actor Heinrich Anschütz, the poet Bettina von Arnim, Peter Cornelius, Goethe, Grillparzer, Lenau, Meyerbeer, Frederick William IV of Prussia, the actress Julie Rettich, the poet Rückert, the philosopher Schelling, Franz von Schober, Tieck, Varnhagen von Ense, and several further prominent representatives of royal families.[24]

An album entry by Caroline Unger survives in the University Library of Lund; the sheet, detached from its album, gives no indication of the identity of the friend for whom it was written, but the tone of the eight lines of verse, as well as the fact that the sheet has the black edge familiar from such occasions, makes it clear that it was an expression of sympathy at a bereavement. The poem, signed and dated

'Wien am 12. März 1822. Caroline Unger m.p.' is in praise of friendship, which was born in heaven but is of succour to mortals on earth.[25]

Like her father, Caroline Unger too can be revealed as a song-composer of more than amateur talent. Two manuscript volumes of her songs are preserved in a British private collection, one of which served as printer's copy for a volume that was privately printed for the family.[26] In marked contrast to the lavish leather binding and tooling of the original manuscript volume,[27] the more extensive manuscript copy, bound in faded violet boards,[28] that served as the model for the printed edition is at best serviceable, workaday. The printed edition is headed: *Lieder / Mélodies et Stornelli / de Caroline Ungher-Sabatier, / publiés et offerts à ses amis / par / F.S.U. / Lithogr. Anstalt / von / C.G. Röder Leipzig. / En dehors du commerce*. Inside the front cover there is a handwritten inscription in brown ink: 'Au Conservatoire de Vienne au [altered from the crossed-out word 'du'] nom d'une de ses anciennes éleves, Caroline Unger, offert respectueusement par l'editeur François Sabatier Ungher'. This copy lacks pages 113–20. The 46 songs vary in length and ambitiousness from miniatures with a mere twelve bars to the 23-page-long ballade 'Allons Beppo', of 379 bars; this poem, anonymous in the manuscript books, is here identified as the work of Caroline's husband. The poets represented include such well-known names as Rellstab, Platen, Rückert, Uhland, Göthe (sic), Lamartine, Geibel, Heine, Georges Sand and Petöffy; from the Schubert circle there are Franz von Schober and Moritz Hartmann; four of the texts are starred as being anonymous. Eleven of the settings are of French texts, two of Italian; the rest are German, though with the inclusion of outstandingly good French translations ('La traduction des poésies allemandes est de François Sabatier').

Perhaps the most important single page in Caroline Unger's beautifully bound and decorated manuscript songbook is the one containing the dedicatory poem, particularly as it is not included in the printed edition. Hitherto quite unknown, this poem alludes touchingly to Schubert, without actually naming him, and proudly claims the poet's share in gathering together the late, great composer's scattered songs:

Den 6ten Januar 1843

> Es geitzt der Künstler nicht mit seinen Werken
> Die, reich gewährt, der Muse Gunst ihm beut.
> Gleich dem Orangenbaum, der ohnvermerken
> Ein Blütchen da, eins dortenhin zerstreut;
> Den süßen Schmuck, die duft'ge Lust der Seelen,
> Er mißt ihn nicht, – wie könnt'er ihn auch zählen!
>
> Doch deine Lieder sollen nimmer sterben,
> Laß deine Freunde, laß die ganze Welt
> Die tiefe Regung deines Herzens erben,
> Die, sie ersinnend, deine Brust geschwellt.
> Daß sich die holden Kinder nicht verlieren
> Laß sie vereinigt diese Blätter zieren[.]

> Einst stand ich jenem großen Geist zur Seite,
> Der uns durch deine Kunst so oft gewährt;
> Manch' Lied trieb schon vergessen in der Weite,
> Das sammelnd mein Bemüh'n zurückgeführt.
> Nicht weil'ich stets beglückt an deiner Schwelle:
> Vertrete denn dies Buch des Freundes Stelle.
>
> Schober mpia

The 6th of January 1843

> The artist does not boast about his works
> which, richly granted, the Muse's favour offers him.
> Like the orange-tree which, unnoticed,
> scatters a blossom here, one there;
> the sweet adornment, the delicate joy of souls
> he does not measure, – how could he count them!
>
> But thy songs shall never die,
> let thy friends, let the whole world
> inherit the deep stirrings of thy heart,
> which, in creating them, swelled thy breast.
> So that these precious children do not get lost,
> let them adorn these pages as it unites them[.]
>
> Once I stood at the side of that great spirit
> who so often rewarded us through thine art;
> many a song fluttered forgotten in the distance
> that my collecting care brought back.
> I shall not always linger joyously at thy threshold:
> may this book then take the friend's place.
>
> Schober m[anu] p[ropr]ia

Notes and references

1. Information about Carl Unger is scarce; the most useful source is the article 'Unger, Johann Karl' in C. von Wurzbach, *Biographisches Lexikon des Kaiserthums Oesterreich* (Vienna, 1856–91), 49 (1884), 61–3; bibliographical details have mainly been derived from the holdings of the Stadt- und Landesbibliothek, Vienna.
2. O.E. Deutsch, *Schubert. Die Erinnerungen seiner Freunde* (Leipzig, 1957), pp 87, 91; p. 116 (Schönstein).
3. O.E. Deutsch, *Schubert. Die Dokumente seines Lebens* (Kassel, etc., 1964), p. 40; henceforth referred to in brackets in the text as *Dok.*
4. A second title-page to the same volume reads: *J. Carl Unger's Gedichte* / [...] / *Wien,* / *für Christoph Peter Rehm,* / *mit Albertischen Schriften,* / *MDCCXCVII.*
5. C. von Wurzbach, 'Unger-Sabatier, Karoline', *Biographisches Lexikon*, 49 (1884), 66–70; *Trionfi melodrammatici di Carolina Ungher in Vienna 1839*, Coi tipi della vedova di A. Strauss; F.J. Fétis, *Biographie universelle des musiciens,* 2nd edn., VIII (Paris, 1865), 285; ibid., *Supplément et complément*, ed. A. Pougin, II (Paris, 1880), 594; *MGG*; *The New Grove Dictionary of Opera*. See also the old but informative article by Otto Hartwig, 'François Sabatier und Caroline Sabatier-Unger', *Deutsche Rundschau*, vol. 91 (April–June 1897), pp 227–43.
6. Fétis and some other sources give the year as 1805.

7. Compilation of the 'Programme der [Abend-] Unterhaltungen', Archiv der Gesellschaft der Musikfreunde, *H 24989* (formerly VI 26394).
8. Once she had an engagement at the Court Opera, she lost her eligibility to perform at the Society's concerts; see *Dok*, 176.
9. *The Letters of Beethoven, collected, translated and edited [...] by* Emily Anderson (London, 1961), II, 967.
10. In the collection of her correspondence preserved in the Handschriftensammlung of the Stadt- and Landesbibliothek, Vienna; here shelf mark *I.N. 55164*.
11. 'Ein ungedruckter Brief Franz Xaver Wolfgang Mozarts an Caroline Ungher-Sabatier, Wien, 26. Dezember 1842', ed. Rudolph Angermüller, *Mitteilungen der Internationalen Stiftung Mozarteum*, 43rd year, No. 3–4 (1995), 86–92. Despite the address in French, the letter is written in German.
12. A misreading of Mozart's handwriting is presumably the cause for Angermüller's printing of the name as 'Seitteles'; Ignaz Jeitteles was a well-known merchant, lawyer and man of letters in Vienna at this period.
13. Shelf mark *I.N. 5374*.
14. 'The thing is getting ever worse – / I'm going off to my – room' (the expected rhyme is with 'Zimmer').
15. Presumably the wife of the tenor Joseph Tichatschek, later famous as a Wagner singer, who sang at the memorial service for Schubert on 23 December 1818: *Dok*, 569.
16. References to Lenau's letters are to Eduard Castle's edition, *Nikolaus Lenau. Sämtliche Werke und Briefe in 6 Bänden* (Leipzig, 1910–23); most of the quotations from the letters are taken from vol IV: *Briefe/Zweiter Teil*, 1912; later quotations are identified in the text as e.g. (*Briefe*, IV, 327).
17. Quoted in the letter to Emilie von Reinbek of 16 January 1839; *Briefe*, IV, 324.
18. And even if one might, with the benefit of hindsight, question the musical discernment of someone who preferred Zumsteeg's lieder to Schubert's; see Lenau's letter to Nanette Wolf, [Wien, Herbst 1830], *Briefe* III, 57.
19. The great actor Ludwig Devrient (1784–1832), especially admired in the tragic roles of Shakespeare and Schiller.
20. Opera by Cammarano and Donizetti, first performed at Venice on 4 February 1836, with Unger as Antonina; the Vienna première was on 17 June 1836.
21. The poet and dramatist, Ludwig Tieck.
22. Wilhelmine Schröder-Devrient, the greatest German dramatic soprano of the era.
23. The Romani/Donizetti *Lucrezia Borgia*; its first performance in Vienna had taken place exactly a year earlier, and had been a triumph for Unger.
24. I wish to express my thanks to Gerrit Waidelich for bringing this item to my attention.
25. My thanks for this item too go to Gerrit Waidelich.
26. There is an imperfect copy in the Archiv der Gesellschaft der Musikfreunde, Vienna; shelf mark *H 24989* (formerly VI 26394); my thanks to Elizabeth Norman McKay for locating this copy.
27. Entitled in gold lettering on the dark green leather front cover (size *c*33.2 × *c*25 cm): 'C. U. S. / ALBUM / Musical'; gold lettering in a red shield on the spine reads: 'Caroline / Unger-Sabatier / Album Musical'.
28. The front cover is labelled: 'LIEDER /COMPONIRT / VON / CAROLINE UNGHER-SABATIER'; size *c*.33.5 × *c*.23.7 cm. This is clearly a working copy, with numerous markings in black ink, red crayon and pencil, and with erratic pagination and numbering of the songs.

10 Schubert's relationship with women: an historical account
Rita Steblin

In 1841 Wilhelm von Chézy (1806–65), the poet-journalist son of Helmina von Chézy (for whose play *Rosamunde* Schubert wrote incidental music, D797), published the following recollection of the composer:

> Schubert adored women and wine. Unfortunately this taste had caused him to stray into wrong paths from which he could no longer find his way back alive.[1]

In 1863 Chézy published a second version that altered the earlier direct reference to 'women and wine' into the more nebulous 'pleasures of life' as follows:

> Unfortunately Schubert, with his liking for the pleasures of life, had strayed into those wrong paths which generally admit of no return, at least of no healthy one.[2]

This change was perhaps indicative of a general effort on the part of Schubert's ageing friends (concerned with their own posthumous reputations) to preserve a more respectable image of the composer, now that his growing fame was heightening the public's interest in biographical matters. Anselm Hüttenbrenner (1794–1868), for example, who in 1858 admitted that his memory was failing, reported the following:

> From the time I got to know Schubert [c. 1816] he did not have even a suspicion of a love affair. Towards the fair sex he was boorish and, consequently, anything but gallant. [...] Nevertheless, according to his own account, before he knew me he had cast his eye in the direction of a teacher's [silk factory owner's] daughter [...] The girl [Therese Grob] could not marry Schubert because he was too young at that time and without money or position. Then, against her inclination, she is said to have submitted to her father's [mother's] wishes and married someone else [Johann Bergmann] who was able to provide for her. – From that time [1820], when he saw his dearest one lost for ever, he had a dominating aversion for the daughters of Eve. – That is all I know about Schubert's love-affairs.[3]

Perhaps Hüttenbrenner knew more about Schubert than he was willing to make public. After all, he kept quiet the fact that he possessed the autograph of the as yet unknown 'Unfinished' Symphony.

Josef von Spaun (1788–1865) in particular took offence at what he considered to be the inclusion of information detrimental to the composer's posthumous image. Shortly before his death Spaun criticized Kreißle von Hellborn's 1865 biography of Schubert as follows:

> Many similar things that are included could actually give rise to a false estimate of Schubert, as, for example, the assertion that at the time when he was eaten up with love for the young Countess Esterházy he was secretly interested in someone else on the side. I ask, what is the point of such gossip? I am absolutely convinced that, during the time [c. 1824–1828] of his affection for his pupil, the young Countess, an affection which, though hopeless owing to the circumstances, was deep and heart-felt, Schubert had no relations of the kind indicated with any other girl; but even in the quite inconceivable event of the above assertion being true, was it really necessary, in describing the artist's life, to make it known to the world?[4]

In hindsight one can now say that such efforts on the part of conservative friends to whitewash the composer have unfortunately resulted in a colourless personality and much recent puzzlement as to the real character of this great genius.

At the same time as these carefully-worded recollections were being formulated for posterity, a quite different image of the composer and his sensual lifestyle (devoted to wine, women and song) began to circulate in the popular press. This image may not have been so far removed from the truth. After all, on 28 November 1822 Schubert wrote down the following verse in Albert Schellmann's album:

> Who loves not wine, maidens and song,
> Remains a fool his whole life long.[5]

In 1864 Franz von Suppé composed the one-act operetta *Franz Schubert*, based on motives from Schubert's music (the overture, for example, begins with a persiflage of 'Erlkönig'). This operetta, hugely successful, has as its central point Schubert's love for Caroline Esterházy. According to the textbook by Hans Max (pseudonym for Johann von Paümann)[6] the composer had fled to the romantic surroundings of the Höldrich's mill (in the Vienna woods) to pine for his beloved. As the character 'Mayrhofer' recounts: 'since [Schubert] has left the aristocratic house in Hungary he can no longer bear it in Vienna. An irresistible longing has driven him into this isolation.'[7] Mayrhofer, Vogl and various others arrive and try to entice Schubert back to the city, with, for example, the offer of an organist's position, a contract to write dance music, and the like. Much wine flows over the table, accompanied by such lines in Viennese dialect as: 'A Wein-G'sellschaft, no, da is mein Franzl nit weit' [When there's wine for company, my Franz is not far away].[8] All sing together a drinking song to 'Wein, Weib und Gesang' whereby Schubert takes the pretty miller's daughter Marie by the hand – and later attempts to kiss her. Inspired both by the landscape and a subplot involving the wooing of Marie by the miller's apprentice (together with an evil hunter as rival) Schubert sets the song cycle *Die schöne Müllerin*. But he is unable to complete the song

'Ungeduld' until a letter arrives from Hungary, written in Caroline's hand, in which she invites him to come for a visit – her carriage has been sent for him – and the overjoyed Schubert sings the missing line: 'Dein ist mein Herz, und soll es ewig bleiben'.

By 1879, when the libretto of Suppé's operetta was published, the tale of Schubert and the pretty miller maid from the Höldrichsmühle had entered popular myth.[9] The librettist Paümann became concerned when the Wiener Männergesangverein was about to dedicate a plaque at the mill to the memory of Schubert. He wrote a letter, published in a Viennese newspaper in 1879,[10] explaining that the tale of the miller's daughter was pure fabrication and not based on any anecdote from Schubert's life. But he also wrote that this did not mean that Schubert had never visited the Höldrichsmühle or that he had never composed any Lieder there. In any case, by the early twentieth century so many anecdotes had surfaced supposedly documenting Schubert's presence at the mill – including one whereby he had fathered an illegitimate son with Frau Höldrich (an account confirmed by the son!) – that the attempt to distinguish between 'fiction and truth' had become hopeless.[11]

According to Paümann, his original intention had been to base the libretto on true events from Schubert's life. He started with Heinrich Kreißle's 1861 biographical sketch but found little material with dramatic potential. The following two passages, the only ones dealing with Schubert's relationship with women, no doubt inspired him to make Caroline central to his story line:

> [Schubert's Fantasy in F Minor] was dedicated to the young countess Esterházy, his only pupil, whose talent brought him much joy and to whom he also felt a personal attraction.[12]
>
> Schubert was certainly not indifferent towards the female sex but the carnal propensities were by no means as evident in his case as they usually are in men of such lively fantasy. Nothing is known of lasting love affairs and he appears to have been ardently in love during his stay in Zseliz only with a highly-placed lady, to whom the F minor Fantasy is dedicated.[13]

Paümann then approached one of Schubert's friends, Josef Doppler, for further tips and ended up – by pure chance – at the Höldrichsmühle. In all the controversy about the miller maid, however, there was no questioning of the basic premise of Suppé's operetta: that Schubert loved women and wine.

Kreißle's expanded Schubert biography (1865) included new information from material gathered in the late 1850s by Ferdinand Luib and from interviews Kreißle conducted himself with Schubert's surviving family and friends. Concerning Schubert's love life, Kreißle thanks Carl von Schönstein, the aristocratic friend of the Esterházy family, for supplying him with the following information:

> Schubert often made himself merry at the expense of any friends who fell in love, but he himself was by no means immune from this passion. He too had to undergo – certainly not to his detriment – battles of the heart. To be sure nothing is known of any lasting love affair, and he never seems to have thought seriously about matrimony; but he certainly coquetted with love, and was no stranger to the deeper and truer affections. Soon after his entry into the Esterházy house [1818] he started up a love affair with a

maid-servant. This subsequently gave way to a more poetic flame which sprang up [1824] in his heart for the younger daughter of the house, Countess Caroline. This flame continued to burn until his death. Caroline had the greatest regard for him and for his genius, but she did not return his love and perhaps had no idea of the degree to which it actually existed. But surely that this love was present must have been clear to her from a remark of Schubert's. Once, namely, when she reproached him in fun for having not yet dedicated any composition to her, he replied 'What is the point? Everything is dedicated to you anyway.'[14]

Kreißle comments further that a passage from one of Schubert's letters dated Zseliz 1824, in which the composer speaks of the 'misery of reality' and 'defrauded hopes', is probably associated with 'this heart affair which we have just hinted at'. In the corresponding footnote Kreißle links Schubert's experience at Zseliz with the following verses from Eduard von Bauernfeld's poem 'Jugendfreunde', published in 1858:[15]

> Bauernfeld hints at this passion in the following verses à la Heine, whose purport by the way has little in common with the information from Baron von Schönstein:
>
>> Schubert was in love, a pupil
>> It was, one of the young countesses;
>> But he gave himself to someone else, someone very different,
>> In order to forget the other.
>
> The 'other' is said to have been Therese Grob, the singer in the Lichtental choir, who in 1814 sang the soprano solo part in the F major Mass.[16]

This was the passage that had so offended Spaun. And yet this pithy statement by the talented dramatist Bauernfeld, Schubert's close friend in later years, is the clue to understanding the truth about the composer's relationship with women. Kreißle then summarizes the composer's character as follows:

> He revelled in the sentimental infatuations of his friends; but he himself was no stranger to erotic feelings. We have already mentioned one affair of the heart, and there may have been possibly others; but they were all of a fleeting nature, and far from resulting in any lasting relationship. With regard to attachments of this kind, Schubert (so von Schober told me) was exceedingly reserved, even to his most intimate friends.[17]

Reinforced with Kreißle's revelations about Schubert's erotic feelings and fleeting affairs (and the knowledge that Schubert died unmarried), the popular press now churned out great amounts of fiction about the hapless lover Schubert.

Otto Erich Deutsch on 'Schubert and Women'

In the meantime the 24-year-old Otto Erich Deutsch, later to become the greatest of Schubert scholars, had entered the fray with an article in 1907 on the composer's 'heart-ache'.[18] The young Deutsch tried to counter not only the inordinate attention still being paid to Caroline Esterházy as the 'immortal beloved', but also the idea that Schubert's fleeting affairs with superficial women were somehow important. He wrote as follows:

> I have now made the remarkable discovery that among these sixty or so ladies of grace created by writers on Schubert, the one woman who has been most neglected is just that woman who alone was the most significant in the master's life.[19]

By this 'one woman' Deutsch meant Therese Grob. He hoped that as a result of his biographical research, writers on Schubert 'would put the immortal beloved, in spite of her ancestry, to rest and allow to rise again, in works of pictorial art and poetry that are supposed to honour the master, the modest girl from Lichtental with whom Schubert was truly head over heels in love'.[20] Deutsch had recently discovered two independent, reliable accounts by two friends of Schubert's youth, Anton Holzapfel and Anselm Hüttenbrenner, 'that tell us of the decisive influence this girl had on Schubert's life'.[21] Through a comparison of these two accounts Deutsch felt that the riddle of Schubert's love life had finally been solved.

In championing 'the modest girl from Lichtental' as Schubert's one true love, Deutsch was confirming Kreißle's note explaining that the 'other' in Bauernfeld's encoded verse referred to Therese Grob. But Deutsch was seemingly unwilling to accept that the remainder of Bauernfeld's riddle might also have been true. He maintained that 'what Bauernfeld has related about Schubert's love pangs is not to be taken quite seriously'.[22] Deutsch summarized the rest of Schubert's love life as follows:

> Schubert's deeply wounded heart remained after Therese's marriage consistent in its quiet resignation for as long as it beat. There can be no more talk that he had a deeper affection for any of the women with whom he came in contact during the rest of his life; at best he became friends with one of them. It is even less believable that Schubert's heart was affected by one of the nameless flirtations, one of which in 1823, with its evil consequences, threatened his life.[23]

By 'evil consequences' Deutsch was referring here in discreet terms to Schubert's having acquired a venereal disease. But such dark historical facts seem not to have made their way into the romantic fiction of the early twentieth century. Schubert's love life was instead recast to fit the current Zeitgeist (and the desire to relive the Biedermeier era as 'the good old days').

In 1910 Deutsch reiterated his stance on Therese Grob in a lecture on 'Schubert and Women' and wrote as follows concerning Schubert's inherent attitude towards the female sex:

> If we inquire about Schubert's relationship with women in general, then we soon recognize with confidence that he had – what his compositions moreover attest a thousand times – a very erotic nature: but [he was] not a lover who boldly grabbed, rather an awkward, almost shy fellow. Perhaps he approached women in a too subdued way in order to be able to win from them compensation for the happiness that life had otherwise so scantily measured out to him. If, according to Kreißle, Schubert's carnal propensities did not keep pace perhaps with his fantasy, he was nevertheless very susceptible to female lures.[24]

As far as the fleeting acquaintances were concerned, Deutsch believed that it was Schubert's 'discretion in matters of love that had occasioned so much trouble for his biographers'[25] – causing them to invent women and ignore his one true love,

Therese Grob. About Caroline Esterházy Deutsch wrote here that she was merely a harmless teenager ('ein harmloser Backfisch') and should not be given the same importance as Therese.

The flood of fiction on Schubert and his pursuit of women reached a highpoint in 1912 with Hans Rudolf Bartsch's novel *Schwammerl* (which eventually sold at least 200,000 copies). Bartsch invented the tale of the three daughters of the glassmaker Tschöll – Hederl, Haiderl and Hannerl – who lived in the so-called 'Dreimäderlhaus' on the Mölker-Bastei (next to the Beethoven Pasqualatihaus). Schubert, having through Tschöll's influence lost Therese Grob, is in love with each one of the three sisters in turn, but they all chose to marry other, lesser men. After experiencing these disappointments, the composer finds peace and strength in nature and in his creative activities. In a review of this book Deutsch praised the author for giving a generally accurate account of Schubert's character:

> The historian Bartsch of course knows the true Schubert in detail; he has on the other hand enhanced him according to his own poetic necessity. The Tschöll sisters, who are only modelled after the Fröhlich sisters in their being three in number, are of course freely invented. But even here as elsewhere in his invention Bartsch comes closest to the truth. He has depicted old Vienna and the Schubert circle with wonderful refinement.[26]

Bartsch's novel served loosely as the basis for Heinrich Berté's highly popular Singspiel *Das Dreimäderlhaus* (1916), pieced together from Schubert's instrumental music and again featuring the Lied 'Ungeduld'.[27] In this Singspiel, Schubert, who is portrayed here as shy and awkward, is in love with Hannerl, the youngest of the three Tschöll sisters, but is too reserved to declare his feelings and so loses her to Schober. The success of this work – no doubt influenced by the need for light entertainment during wartime – inspired many spin-off products and a whole industry of kitsch objects centred on the *Dreimäderlhaus*. In April 1925, Deutsch, alarmed by the 'infectious danger of the Dreimäderl bacteria' and its uncontrolled proliferation (the house on the Mölker-Bastei was now being promoted as a historic Schubert site), published an article about the 'curse' of this house on Schubert biography.[28] He still praised Bartsch for having in 1912 portrayed the historical Schubert 'in more accurate terms than many biographers', but calls the introduction of the Tschöll family a 'dangerous experiment', that in Berté's Singspiel had degenerated to 'completely untruthful representations of the life and ways of the master and his standard circle of friends'. In a letter to a Viennese newspaper in November 1925 Deutsch again refuted a press report that Schubert had lived in this house. He decried the legend of the Tschöll family, now found in three operettas and a film, as a trivialization of Schubert and stated that 'he could provide evidence' that the composer had nothing to do with the 'hero' of the *Dreimäderlhaus*.[29]

Thereafter, Deutsch published just a few minor articles on the subject of Schubert and women. In an article from December 1925 he suggests that the composer's arrangement of Wenzeslaus Matiegka's guitar piece 'Notturno in G', with variations on the text 'Mädchen, o schlummre noch nicht', was written as a serenade for Therese Grob.[30] In the anniversary year 1928, when Deutsch brought out at least forty-four books and articles on the composer, only one touches on the subject of women. In this he gives illustrated thumbnail sketches of four women with whom Schubert had had repeated contact: Jeannette Cuny de Pierron, Kathi Fröhlich, Marie Esterházy and Therese Hönig.[31] His last article on the subject, written in 1929, presents the new facts, based on research he conducted personally in Zseliz, that the maid-servant with whom Schubert had had an affair in 1818 was named Pepi Pöckelhofer, and that she later advanced to lady's-maid ('Jungfer') and in 1826 married the valet Josef Rößler.[32]

Deutsch apparently had grown tired of this topic (perhaps the overkill in the media on sexual matters contributed to his lack of interest) and his research moved in other directions. But, the Zeitgeist also played a role. After the frivolity of Austrian society in the 1920s, darker matters – of economic and racial import – came to the fore. Schubert was now being misused for political purposes[33] and Deutsch, a Protestant of Jewish heritage, was forced in 1938 to flee for his life.

After a lifetime of research on Schubert, Deutsch maintained in both the English (1946) and German (1964) editions of the *Documentary Biography* the exact same view (albeit somewhat more cautiously worded) of Schubert's relationship with women that he had first proclaimed in 1907 – that the composer's only real passion was Therese Grob:

> If Hüttenbrenner's recollections of 1858 (Vienna City Library), doubtless wrong in some details, are correct in this respect, Schubert was unable ever to forget Therese Grob, and finally renounced marriage on her account. The reason why she did not become his wife seems to have lain in his hopeless material circumstances at that time.[34]

With the knowledge of Deutsch's position on this subject, it becomes understandable why he slips into the *Documents* certain comments that seem to belittle Schubert's relationships with other women. For example, his explanatory note to a discussion of *Die schöne Müllerin* reads: 'Schubert, of course, was not inspired by any maid, or any mill, but simply by Müller's poems'.[35] Deutsch is referring here to the earlier controversy about Schubert's presence at the Höldrich's mill. And, in a comment on Schubert's 1824 visit to Zseliz, he writes as follows:

> Countess Caroline too was now grown up, being almost twenty years of age; but she remained so much a child that her mother sent her to play with her hoop when she was thirty. She was particularly attached to Zseliz, and is said to have once declared that 'If it is not quite as beautiful in heaven as at Zseliz, I do not wish to go to heaven at all.' Between her and Schubert a kind of friendship had developed which may have seemed to the lonely young man to resemble love. As for his more realistic friendship with the chambermaid Pepi Pöckelhofer, it was probably not renewed during this visit.[36]

Thus the 'childlike' Caroline is made to appear unworthy of Schubert's love, and the chambermaid Pepi is kept at a distance, in spite of the fact that she appears to have delivered a message from Schubert to his father in August 1824.[37] In a comment on the following diary entry made by Bauernfeld in April 1825 – 'I am still in love with Clotilde, as Moritz [von Schwind] is with his Nettel. Schubert sniggers at us both, but is not quite heart-whole himself' – Deutsch writes:

Schubert's heartbreak may or may not have been on account of Caroline Esterházy, to whom Bauernfeld's verse [in the poem quoted above] certainly referred later on. 'Quite another' in its third line seems to be a disparaging reference to the chambermaid Pepi.[38]

It is Deutsch, not Bauernfeld, who disparages Pepi. She may even have had nothing to do with the 'quite another' kind of woman the poet was referring to, as will be discussed later. Heinrich Hoffmann von Fallersleben made the following diary entry about a visit to a new-wine inn in Grinzing in August 1827: 'Schubert with his girl we espied from our seat; he came to join us and did not show himself again' – to which Deutsch comments:

> We find Schubert without his friends and with a girl, whom the writer takes to be 'his' girl, but who was probably a casual acquaintance. He was plainly embarrassed.'[39]

The general impression is that it was Deutsch who was embarrassed when Schubert was caught with 'fleeting acquaintances'. Deutsch may have felt that it was his duty to protect the composer's reputation and hence keep all women, except for Therese Grob, away from the composer.

Therese Grob

What do we know about Therese? In spite of Deutsch's early enthusiasm about the importance of this 'Jugendliebe' in the composer's life, the *Documentary Biography* actually contains very little new information about her – beyond what was already published in Kreißle's biography of 1865. Deutsch gives her correct dates (1798–1875) and those of her brother Heinrich (1800–55) and reports that she died childless, whereby her collection of Schubert autographs passed on to her brother's children and their descendants.[40] The following is therefore an attempt to provide background material not readily available in the standard reference works on Schubert. An article by Otto Maag that appeared in a Basle newspaper on the centenary of the composer's death[41] gives detailed genealogical material about Therese's family, based on the research of Franz Köhler.[42] Johann Heinrich Grob (1731–91), Therese's grandfather, was a Protestant from Chur, Switzerland, who came c. 1770 to Vienna and founded a silk factory in a house which he owned on Badgasse, near the Lichtental church. His third wife, Christina Mitz from Preßburg, Hungary, was the mother of Therese's father Heinrich (1776–1804). The latter's two surviving children, Therese and Heinrich (junior), were only six and four years old respectively at their father's death in 1804. Heinrich's wife, Therese (neé Männer, 1770–1826), continued to direct the flourishing silk factory after her husband's early death. In 1803, shortly before his death, Heinrich stood as godfather at the birth of the later painter Heinrich Schwemminger (1803–84), brother of Carl Schubert's future wife, Therese Schwemminger. Therese Grob's mother in turn stood as godmother at the births of the first six of Ferdinand Schubert's twenty-eight children and to Heinrich Hollpein (1814–88), Schubert's oldest brother Ignaz's future step-son, who later painted the well-known oil portrait of Therese Grob in middle-age. Ignaz's wife was Wilhelmine Grob (1784–1856), the widow of the coin engraver Leopold Hollpein (1785–1836) and the daughter of Therese Grob's grandfather's half-brother Bartholomäus Grob (1760–1815). The latter also ran a successful silk-manufacturing business in Lichtental, married four times and fathered at least seventeen children. His oldest child was Wilhelmine, Therese's aunt – and in 1836 Ignaz Schubert's wife. These details reveal how closely intertwined these families were, a fact which must have made Schubert's failure to marry Therese all the more painful.

Concerning Schubert's courtship of Therese, the particulars are given in the already mentioned memoirs by Anton Holzapfel and Anselm Hüttenbrenner.[43] Schubert's school-friend Holzapfel, who had tried to dissuade the composer from his 'passion' for Therese in a long letter dated at the beginning of 1815, remembered that 'on the occasion of a musical celebration for Therese's name-day [15 October] in about 1811 or 1812, I too spent an evening with this [Grob] family.'[44] Since Schubert would still have been in residence at the Convict school until the autumn of 1813, perhaps Holzapfel erred in citing the year. Kreißle writes that 'Schubert came to this house after leaving the Convict, attracted doubtless by the lovely voice of the youthful Therese (then about fifteen years old).'[45] This would place the beginning of their friendship in the autumn of 1813, a time that agrees with the three-year span for the courtship that Hüttenbrenner gives in the following direct quote from Schubert:

> I loved someone very dearly and she loved me too. She was a schoolmaster's [silk-factory owner's] daughter, somewhat younger than myself and in a Mass, which I composed, she sang the soprano solos most beautifully and with deep feeling. She was not exactly pretty and her face had pock-marks; but she had a heart, a heart of gold. For three years she hoped I would marry her; but I could not find a position which would have provided for us both. She then bowed to her parents' [mother's] wishes and married someone else, which hurt me very much. I still love her and there has been no one else since who has appealed to me as much or more than she. She was just not meant for me.[46]

Three years of courtship brings us to the autumn of 1816 and the 8 September date of the entry in Schubert's diary that has puzzled so many of his biographers. This final entry in his one surviving diary – blank pages ensue – begins as follows:

> Man resembles a ball, to be played with by chance and passion.
> This sentence seems extraordinarily true to me [...]
> Happy he who finds a true man-friend. Happier still he who finds a true friend in his wife.
> To a free man matrimony is a terrifying thought in these days: he exchanges it either for melancholy or for crude sensuality. Monarchs of to-day, you see this and are silent. Or do you not see it? If so, O God, shroud our senses and feelings in numbness; yet take back the veil again one day without lasting harm.
> Man bears misfortune without complaint, but feels it the more keenly. – Wherefore did God give us compassion?[47]

On the day preceding this entry, 7 September 1816, Schubert had been notified by the Civic Guard in Vienna that his application, made in April 1816 for the post of music master in Laibach, had been unsuccessful. Schubert, aware of his talents and declaring in his application letter that he was the most suitable among all the supplicants for this post, reacted to this bad news by writing down in his diary his most private thoughts about the unfairness of fate. His declaration that 'to a free man matrimony is a terrifying thought in these days' refers to the repressive marriage-consent law that had been passed in early 1815 by Metternich's regime.[48] This law made it impossible for a man of Schubert's class, for a 'school assistant' as the composer was listed in official documents, to marry without proving to the government and church authorities that he had sufficient income to support a family. Schubert's three brothers, Ferdinand, Carl and Ignaz, who married in 1816, 1823 and 1836 respectively, were all able to meet the requirements of this law.[49] Schubert, who had courted Therese for three years, now saw his hopes of marriage dashed. He cried out against the 'Monarchs of to-day' and saw only two possibilities ahead of him: to substitute for matrimony either melancholy (no wife and no sexual relations) or crude sensuality (relations with women outside of marriage). Schubert, 'certainly not indifferent towards the female sex', was thus forced to follow the latter course, through which he was then infected by a disastrous disease. Herein lies the essence of the tragedy of his short life.

In November 1816, when it must have been clear to both of them that they could not marry, Schubert presented Therese with a collection of songs now known as the *Therese Grob Liederalbum*. It was probably this collection that Kreißle was referring to in the following passage when he gave Therese credit in 1865 for providing him with information about her relationship with Schubert:

> Therese, to whom I am indebted for these details, lives still at Vienna, hale and hearty, for more than twenty years the widow of Herr Bergmann. The family of Grob are said to possess compositions of Schubert unknown to the public, but I have never been able to get a sight of them.[50]

Therese, who clearly knew more than she was willing to tell, apparently revealed nothing of an intimate nature – this was, after all, the era when private matters were kept hidden from public scrutiny – and one gathers that she refused to show Kreißle these Lieder. This collection remained hidden in the possession of Grob family descendants until 1908 when Rudolf Maria Enzersdorfer announced its existence, publishing the titles of the seventeen songs in a Viennese newspaper.[51] Deutsch was able to determine, on the basis of these titles alone, that three of the Lieder were as yet unknown: 'Am ersten Maimorgen', D344, 'Mailied', D503, and 'Klage', Anhang I, 28.[52] However, his concluding wish – 'hopefully we will soon be delighted by a worthy publication of these pieces' – remained unfulfilled as the family refused to allow these Lieder to be published.

It was not until 1967, when Pater Reinhard Van Hoorickx brought out a private printing,[53] that these works could first be studied. The subsequent long article in 1968 by Maurice J. E. Brown was, in my opinion, an insufficient attempt to discuss these works.[54] That Brown was unwilling to go deeper into the personal background of this collection, perhaps because of an unromantic bias against the idea that Schubert was in love, seems apparent from his following dry opening statement: 'There is little evidence of any reliable kind to support the idea that [Schubert] was in love with [Therese] at this period [1816], but it seems likely.' However, Brown makes several significant observations in the course of his discussion. He describes the second piece in the collection, 'Klage' ('Nimmer länger trag' ich dieser Leiden Last'), with its alteration in the word-order of the first line (from 'Nimmer trag' ich länger dieser Leiden Last') as being 'the only one of the seventeen songs not in Schubert's hand but copied by an obviously unpractised writer, possibly by Therese herself.'[55] He also notes that the fifth song in the collection is set on the same text ('Nimmer trag' ich länger') and is again entitled 'Klage'. This second 'Klage' is a fair copy of Schubert's Lied 'Der Leidende', D432, composed in May 1816, and re-used later in the B flat major entr'acte in *Rosamunde*, D797. Unfortunately, Brown draws no conclusion from these observations.

In 1972 Walther Dürr described the physical make-up of the Therese Grob Liederalbum in connection with the Neue Schubert-Ausgabe.[56] The songbook opens with a title page containing the words 'Lieder (Manuscripte) von Franz Schubert, welche ich einzig u allein besitze' [Lieder (Manuscripts) by Franz Schubert which I only and alone possess]. Dürr concludes that this wording signifies Therese as the original owner of this collection, rather than Heinrich Grob [!], as had been sometimes argued. Following is a group of three Lieder which were most likely added later at the time the album was bound. No. 2 of this group is the 'Klage' not in Schubert's hand. The remaining group of fourteen Lieder – the original corpus of the album – was written out by Schubert as a fast but clean *Reinschrift*. The second of these pieces is the 'Klage' which Schubert had originally entitled 'Der Leidende'. If the first of these two settings on this text of lament ('No longer can I bear the burden of this suffering') is really by Therese then what we have here is a joint attempt by Schubert and the young talented singer at composing the same text. A romantic idea, to be sure, but this was the romantic era after all. Schubert's later re-use of the melody in *Rosamunde* may have been a cypher-like reference to this earlier love. The whole collection thus awaits an in-depth study, in particular an examination of the texts chosen and their possible autobiographical (and perhaps cyclical) significance.

Other women

What was Schubert's relationship with women after he realized that marriage to Therese was hopeless? By the summer of 1818, according to Schönstein's account, Schubert had begun an affair with Pepi Pöckelhofer, a maid-servant at Zseliz. Since it was no secret that Schubert by 1823 was seriously ill with a venereal disease, generally believed to be syphilis, there are those who, wishing to reduce Schubert's contact with women to this one affair, have put the blame for Schubert's catching this disease on her. This seems untenable, considering the time lag involved.

There must have been other women, nameless 'fleeting affairs' of which even his closest friends, as Schober intimated, were unaware. We have already encountered Hoffmann von Fallersleben's report of 'Schubert with his girl' at a Grinzing new-wine inn in August 1827. And Franz Lachner published the following anecdote about Schubert later taking as a 'sweetheart' one of his former pupils, name unknown, from the ABC school where he had once taught:

> Once, when with a group of friends, Schubert told of a sweetheart, who left him for the reason that she wanted to avenge herself for the beatings he had given her in the ABC class when he was a schoolteacher. He added: 'It is quite true; whenever I was composing, this little gang annoyed me so much that the ideas always went out of my head. Naturally I gave them a good hiding then. – And now I have to suffer for it!'[57]

Who is the mysterious woman, her gaze fixed on Schubert, whose face is partly covered by Kunigunde Vogl's hand in Schwind's sepia drawing from 1868 entitled 'A Schubert Evening at Josef von Spaun's'?[58] And who was Schober referring to when he wrote Bauernfeld the following on 6 February 1869?

> There is a sort of love-story of Schubert's which I believe not a soul knows, as I am the only one in the secret and I have told it to nobody; I would willingly have passed it on to you and left you to decide how much of it was suitable for publication and in what way, but of course it is too late now.[59]

On the other hand, some of Schubert's casual lady-friends are known by name. Thus, Schwind writes the following about the singer Katharina von Lászny née Buchwieser (*c.* 1789–1828) in a letter to Schober dated 14 February 1825:

> [Schubert's] 'Diana in Anger' and the 'Night Piece' have appeared and are dedicated to Frau von Láscny, Fräulein Buchwieser that was. What a woman! If she were not nearly twice as old as I and unhappily always ill, I should have to leave Vienna, for it would be more than I can stand. Schubert has known her a long time, but I met her only recently. She is pleased with my things and with myself, more than anybody else except you; I had quite a shock the first time, the way she spoke to me and went on with me, as though there were nothing about me she didn't know. Immediately afterwards she was taken ill again and spat blood, so that I have not seen her for a long time; but we are to eat there to-morrow. So now I know what a person looks like who is in ill repute all over the city, and what she does.[60]

Although Schubert dedicated two opus numbers (Op. 36, containing the above-mentioned songs, and Op. 54, the *Divertissement à l' hongroise* for piano duet) to this remarkable woman, she remains an elusive, little-known figure in spite of Deutsch's tantalizing hints about her correspondence with E. T. A. Hoffmann and her love affairs with two princes during the Vienna Congress. She died on 3 July 1828, just a few months before Schubert. Here is a woman in need of in-depth research.

And what do we really know of Gusti Grünwedel? Schober's memoirs of Schubert, told to Ludwig August Frankl in June 1868, contain the following account:

> Schober persuaded him [Schubert] he ought to marry Gusti Grünwedel, a very charming girl of good family (she later married a painter and went to Italy), who seemed very well

disposed towards him. Schubert was in love with her, but he was 'painfully modest'; he was firmly convinced no woman could love him. At Schober's words he jumped up, rushed out without his hat, flushed with anger. The friends looked at one another in dismay. After half an hour he came quietly back and later related how, beside himself, he had run round St. Peter's Church, telling himself again and again that no happiness was granted to him on earth.

Schubert then let himself go to pieces; he frequented the city outskirts and roamed around in taverns, at the same time admittedly composing his most beautiful songs in them, just as he did in the hospital too (the 'Müllerlieder', according to [Heinrich Josef] Hölzel), where he found himself as the result of excessively indulgent sensual living and its consequences.[61]

Gusti Grünwedel's presence at two private dances at the Schober family home in February 1827 is recorded in the diaries of the brothers Franz and Fritz von Hartmann. The former, for example, writes on 10 February: 'The loveliest dancer was a certain Fräulein Grünwedel, with whom indeed [Josef von] Spaun was altogether enchanted.'[62] Deutsch's comment here about this woman is merely: 'Of Fräulein Grünwedel nothing is known.' Here is another woman in need of in-depth research. Schober's report about Schubert roaming about the city outskirts is corroborated by Hoffmann von Fallersleben's observation about the composer and 'his girl' in Grinzing in August 1827. (Perhaps Schubert became reinfected with syphilis as a consequence of this renewed bout of 'excessively indulgent sensual living'.)

The *Unsinnsgesellschaft*

A very important inside look at the activities of Schubert and his circle of friends is now made possible through my discovery in early 1994 of pictorial and literary records belonging to a Viennese group of intellectuals known as the *Unsinnsgesellschaft* (Nonsense Society).[63] According to the memoirs of the Burgtheater actor Heinrich Anschütz, Schubert was 'one of the most active members'[64] of this club, as were also Anschütz's two brothers, Eduard and Gustav. This group of about thirty men, mostly painters, writers and actors, met on Thursdays in the years 1817–18 at 'The Red Rooster' inn in Vienna's third district – at the same inn where Beethoven threw a plate of scrambled eggs at the waiter – for an evening of fun and satire. According to my analysis of this secretive handwritten material, Schubert's code name was 'Ritter Juan [Don Giovanni] de la Cimbala' or, during the five-month period in 1818 when he was at the Hungarian estate of the Esterházy's, 'Ritter Zimbal'. These assigned names reflected the members' professional and personal characteristics: 'Ritter Juan' made fun of Schubert's pursuit of women, while 'Cimbala' or 'Zimbal' represented his musical vocation.

Schubert's name does not appear on the key of twenty-two original club members which is attached to the first newsletter dated 17 April 1817 and which included the two Anschütz brothers under the code names 'Schnautze, Redacteur'

(Eduard) and 'Sebastian Haarpuder' (Gustav) and three Kupelwieser brothers under the names 'Blasius Leks' (Josef), 'Chrisostomus Schmecks' (Johann) and 'Damian Klex' (Leopold). However, his presence, including evidence of composing activity specifically for the *Unsinnsgesellschaft*, is clearly evident by the autumn of 1817. Schubert's male quartet 'Das Dörfchen', D598, for example, appears to have been written as a private joke for the club member Ferdinand Dörflinger (code name: 'Elise Gagarnadl von Antifi'), who married in September 1817, shortly before the birth of his first child.[65] Typical of the kind of off-colour material included in the weekly newsletters is the following contribution, dated 17 April 1817, by Dörflinger:

> Lost: A young lady has noticed that she lost her virginity completely six weeks ago under the ruins of the city moat and she requests that the <u>redfaced</u> finder make no evil use thereof.
>
> *Elise von Antifi*[66]

Schubert is also clearly recognizable as the short man with curly sideburns and glasses in the last of five group scenes painted to record the society's New Year's Eve party in 1817. (See Plate 7.) He stands in the centre of the picture next to two young women in beautiful Biedermeier dress, most likely the sisters Babette and Therese Kunz with whom he concertized in early 1818. The composer is depicted in normal dress, as are the two women, in contrast to the other club members who wear elaborate costumes.[67] The accompanying text (long elegiac distichs written by Josef Kupelwieser, the later librettist of Schubert's opera *Fierrabras*) describes this last scene as taking place after 4:00 a.m. and mentions how the ladies present were offered a drink of wine by 'Aaron Bleistift', code name for the Jewish painter Carl Friedrich Zimmermann (who also painted this picture). According to my interpretation of this scene, Schubert brought these two women to the final activities of the *Unsinnsgesellschaft* party – including a staged duel – perhaps after the three had attended a soirée elsewhere.

Concerning the Kunz sisters, Deutsch includes several documents that establish their close working relationship with Schubert in late 1817 and throughout 1818: four-hand piano arrangements of his two Italian overtures, D592 and 597, one of which he performed in a public concert on 12 March 1818 with Anselm Hüttenbrenner and the two Kunz sisters; a letter written a few days later to Hüttenbrenner in which Schubert requests that they 'visit the Kunz people together'; a letter written from Zseliz on 3 August 1818 in which Schubert wishes that a Lied of his be sung at a concert planned by the Kunz's in November 1818.[68] In his commentary to the first of these documents, Deutsch writes as follows: 'The two ladies named Kunz, doubtless sisters, twice recur in these documents later, but Viennese musical history has otherwise ignored them'. What Deutsch actually meant here is that no one had troubled to inquire into the role these two women may have played in Viennese musical life. It must be admitted that research on women from the Biedermeier era is exceedingly difficult. Women are usually recorded in official documents either under their father's name or under their husband's name. If a woman marries and her husband's name is unknown, she can literally disappear. This fact, combined with a lack of interest in pursuing this research angle on the part of earlier scholars, has resulted in our current ignorance and the oft-met comment: 'nothing is known.'

Spurred on by the newly-discovered picture of Schubert and the two women at the New Year's Eve party, I tried to find out what information was lurking in Viennese archives on the Kunz sisters: my research resulted in enough material to fill a small monograph.[69] Most interesting was the hitherto unknown fact that Therese and Babette, born respectively in 1789 and 1794 to the Hungarian aristocrat Johann Alois von Gulasch (c.1758–96), had founded a music school in 1812 together with their stepfather Michael Kunz, in which the two sisters were to teach a total of six girls and their stepfather six boys. Michael Kunz (1776–1833), an employee of the Hofkammer and member of the Gesellschaft der Musikfreunde, also sold musical instruments, including an exotic hybrid piano with strings and organ pipes, advertised in a Viennese newspaper in March 1818. The documents paint a vivid picture of the harsh conditions of life in Biedermeier Vienna, including the difficulty in obtaining permission to marry. They also show what a small world Vienna was: in 1824 Schubert's composer-friend Franz Lachner dedicated his Op. 1 to Babette and his Op. 3 to Michael Kunz; in 1832 Kunz lost out in his bid to become director of the Hofkammer Archive to Franz Grillparzer. Concerning the fate of the two sisters, the older of the two, Therese, married a tax official named Poszinsky and disappeared from the musical scene, while her younger sister Babette, who pursued a successful career as teacher and performer, with glowing press accounts, died at the young age of 33 on 13 November 1827.

To return to the *Unsinnsgesellschaft*, the coded references to Schubert intensify throughout the year 1818. A watercolour picture attached to the newsletter dated 16 July 1818 and painted by Schubert's close friend Leopold Kupelwieser caricatures the composer as a portly, authoritative schoolmaster and the artist himself as a schoolboy trying out the newly-invented draisine, forerunner of the bicycle (See Plate 8.) Schubert's characteristic features – curly hair, snub nose, protruding chin and of course the glasses – are clearly recognizable in the teacher, who carries the habitual disciplining stick (Spanish rod) and who is examining another new invention, the kaleidoscope. The accompanying explanation, with its bold play on recent political events, reads as follows:

> The latest example of contemporary history proves just how dangerous the new discovery of landslides is in Paris. But even the seemingly harmless inventions of the kaleidoscope and the draisine have their danger, as the accompanying picture illustrates. The stout gentleman is absorbed in the contemplation of the kaleidoscope's wonderful play of colours – the dark glass makes him even more nearsighted than usual. He is about to be knocked to the ground by a passionate draisine rider, who likewise has his eye fixed only on his machine. Let this be a warning for others. There is already supposed to be a police order in the works on the strength of which every blockhead is strictly forbidden, on account of the danger, from using both new inventions.[70]

Among the numerous later references to the kaleidoscope, all of which appear to be allusions to Schubert, is the following account written by Gustav Anschütz for the newsletter dated 10 September 1818:

> The undersigned has the honour of faithfully informing the venerated public that he has for sale a kind of kaleidoscope (also known as looking-through-tube) with the unique property that one can use it to see through all kinds of clothing. The great benefit of this optical device should be apparent to everybody since it discloses some items that are at present carefully kept hidden. Especially for young men who like to go walking on the Graben [...][71]

The Graben, a Viennese street-square, was traditionally associated with prostitutes, the notorious 'Graben nymphs'. The same newsletter contains the following report which may refer to the member of the *Unsinnsgesellschaft* named 'Ritter' (Chevalier in French), that is, Schubert:

> *The Curious Observer* has reported – that in the dilemma in which *Madame Round-Bottom* has felt herself placed as the ardent *Chevalier Touchetout*, who casually undertook some physical-anatomical investigations with her, and his hand, to the misfortune of the lady and the great astonishment of the *Chevalier*, instead of the assumed natural curves pulled out some socks – there is nothing further to report than that these socks were without end.[72]

A poem entitled 'Impromptu' in the newsletter dated 12 February 1818, mentioning 'Ritter Cimbal's' bad painting, had featured a sock, whereas the newsletter from 5 November 1818 associates 'Ritter Zimbal' with disciplining the bottoms of Hungarian soldiers. In September 1818, the same month as the report on 'Chevalier Touchetout' (with its play on the German word 'Tasten', which means not only 'to touch' but also piano keys), Schubert wrote out his variations, D624, on the French song entitled 'Le bon Chevalier' ('Der treue Ritter'). Was Schubert's choice of this song a tribute to his role in the *Unsinnsgesellschaft*? What is the significance of his later dedication of this work (Op. 10) to Beethoven?

It is clear that Schubert, while away in Hungary, must have written letters to his friends in the Nonsense Society informing them of his activities. Indeed, his correspondence with his brother Ferdinand distinguishes between *Liederfreunde* and *Stadtfreunde*, indicating separate groups of friends in Vienna.[73] In a newsletter dated 13 August 1818, Eduard Anschütz includes the following ironic report about the activities of the Spanish 'painter' *Juan de la Cimbala*, meaning Schubert:

> According to reports from Spain, the inquisition has arrested the famous painter Juan de la Cimbala because, owing to his own admission, he has been occupied with black magic in addition to his usual duties. Nevertheless, we hope that he will get out of this alive, in that already before his arrest he had severely burnt himself.[74]

As I explain in my forthcoming book *Die Unsinnsgesellschaft*, the 'black magic' here has a double meaning. By September 1817 Schubert had apparently written the music for a dramatic production entitled 'Feuergeist' [Fire Spirit] on a text by Josef Kupelwieser, staged by the *Unsinnsgesellschaft*. The picture accompanying a performance of this work on the first birthday party of the club on 18 April 1818 (described as a ' "Schub"-filled event') portrays an astonishing correlation with a scene in Schubert's melodrama *Die Zauberharfe*, D644, thought to have been written within two weeks in the summer of 1820. Brian Newbould's recent discovery of the secretive 19-bar palindrome in music associated with the fire spirit Sutur in *Die Zauberharfe* and his comment about this amazing 'product of intellectual manipulations, the willful reversal of values, as in the "black mass" ',[75] fits in with what must have been Schubert's composition of such 'black magic' for the *Unsinnsgesellschaft* production of *Feuergeist*. The other meaning of 'burnt' perhaps refers to the romancing activities of this 'Don Giovanni' – who, having hinted at his affair with the maid-servant in correspondence from Zseliz, was in effect 'playing with fire'. If this interpretation is correct, then here is evidence that Schubert had already had affairs with women before his trip to Zseliz. As barely touched on here, this new pictorial and literary material will provide the impetus for a fresh re-examination of Schubert's character and compositions in the light of his involvement with this particular group of friends.

Coded references to Schubert are also made in at least two of the dramas written for the newsletters. In the children's ballet *Insanius auf Erden* (Insanius being the club's god) dated 15 October 1818, Schubert appears as the ABC school teacher named 'Hymen Halbgott' together with Insanius, a '¾ Gott'. 'Hymen' is of course a play on Don Giovanni and his conquest of females. 'Halbgott' may have been inspired by Schubert's comment, found in several of his letters from Zseliz: 'I live and compose like a god.'[76] In another long verse drama, written by Eduard Anschütz in the late autumn of 1818, Schubert appears as a 'Genius', a tiny creature that flies out of a drawer [Schublade] to the sound of music and is subsequently metamorphosed into a stick with an important speaking role. This stick ('Stock'), in 'Kannevas' [kann er was] fashion, will have nothing to do with untalented people ('stockgemeine Leute'). In the course of the drama, this genie-stick ironically warns the main character against succumbing to the enticements of a shapely prostitute.

This new material is so encoded that it will take years of careful analysis to interpret correctly. Particularly problematic is the role of Schober, who is perhaps hiding under the code name of 'Quanti Verdradi' – described as a womanizer – and/or 'Eustachius Krummbein', a possible play on Schober's somewhat crooked legs. It may be that Schober had a falling out with the group leaders, as evidenced by the numerous stories about the stupid travels of a blockhead with the Swedish-sounding name 'Ulf Dalkensohn' or of the many battles fought between Captain 'Blaser' [Josef Kupelwieser] and an evil 'Turk'. He may also be featured along with Schubert in the long tale entitled *Die Fee Musa oder die verwandelten Jünglinge* [The Fairy Musa, or the Transformed Youths]. Here two artists from the realm of the virtuous 'Musa' have been enticed by the rival 'Aqualina' into the sensuous, watery regions of a swamp and refuse to be rescued by their draisine-riding friends from the *Unsinnsgesellschaft*. (The draisine was habitually associated with the moral Leopold Kupelwieser.) The swamp with its transfigured friends – a quacking frog and a handsome carp – could perhaps indicate the realm of prostitutes that Josef Kenner was referring to in his later report on Schober's immoral influence on Schubert.[77]

Caroline Esterházy

The first widely-circulated accounts of Schubert's love life – by Kreißle and Suppé – began with Caroline Esterházy; my article will now close with her. The fact that in the early twentieth century she was misdeemed unworthy of Schubert's love is perhaps attributable to the fall of the Austrian monarchy and the accompanying contempt for those of aristocratic birth. This disparaging disregard of her importance is not supported by the facts. Already in a letter of August 1824 to Schwind, Schubert had written of 'the certain attractive star' in Zseliz. According to Schönstein this was a poetic, ideal love whose flame continued to burn until Schubert's death. Bauernfeld, who in his poem 'Jugendfreunde' described how Schubert had immersed himself in both real and ideal love, elaborated in prose as follows:

> He was, in fact, head over ears in love with one of his pupils, a young Countess Esterházy, to whom he also dedicated one of his most beautiful piano pieces, the Fantasy in F minor for pianoforte duet. In addition to his lessons there, he also visited the Count's home, from time to time, under the aegis of his patron, the singer Vogl. [...] On such occasions Schubert was quite content to take a back seat, to remain quietly by the side of his adored pupil, and to thrust love's arrow ever deeper into his heart. [...] Countess Caroline may be looked upon as his visible, beneficent muse, as the Leonore of this musical Tasso.[78]

Schwind fixed Caroline's portrait as the muse above 'Schubert at the piano' in his sepia drawing of the Schubertiade at Spaun's.[79] And even Schober commented that Schubert 'was in love with a Princess Esterházy, his pupil'. Bauernfeld's diary entry for February 1828, published recently for the first time, provides further corroborative evidence:

> Schubert appears seriously in love with the Countess E. This pleases me about him. He's giving her lessons.[80]

As Bauernfeld declares here – intimated also by Schönstein – Schubert continued to give lessons to the Esterházy family in Vienna during the winter months. My attempt to reconstruct Caroline's music library from her autographed prints, including copies of Mozart symphonies in four-hand arrangements and Beethoven's Piano Sonata, Op. 111, reveals her progressive development under Schubert's teaching and bears additional witness to the glowing reports about her musical talent.[81]

Concerning Caroline's character and her failed marriage to Carl Crenneville in 1844, my discovery of 48 letters written by Crenneville family members in the years 1844–61 allows the intimate details to be told for the first time.[82] Carl had a disagreeable, domineering personality and married Caroline – who in many ways comes across as an early feminist – for her money and position. He refused to live in Zseliz as promised and left her to live with his exotic plants in St Pölten in Lower Austria. The couple were officially separated, with no sign that the marriage was ever annulled.[83] (The early letters mention Caroline's possible pregnancy.) The repeated complaint by the society-climbing Crennevilles that Caroline and her mother Rosine were 'common' may explain why Schubert, who generally avoided the upper aristocracy, remained so attached to this family.

When Bauernfeld wrote in his diary that he was pleased Schubert was in love with Caroline, perhaps this was a sign that by early 1828 the composer had recovered from letting himself go to pieces in the summer of 1827, roaming around the outskirts of Vienna as Schober reported. Schubert now embarked on an incredible spurt of composition that lasted until his death. The major works of this last year include the Piano Trio in E flat (autograph score in Caroline's possession), the Violin Fantasy in C (citing his love song 'Sei mir gegrüßt'), the Fantasy in F minor (dedicated to Caroline), the String Quintet in C (with the passionate 'autobiographical' F minor section in the slow movement) and the Mass in E flat (with the powerful, emotional outbursts pleading for forgiveness of sin). Schubert's choice of F minor for the work dedicated to Caroline was influenced by the theory of key characteristics: Johann Jakob Wagner's 1823 article in the Leipzig *Allgemeine musikalische Zeitung* associated this key with hopeless love and the 'Sorrows of Young Werther'.[84] Knowing now what kind of encoded material Schubert's friends wrote for the *Unsinnsgesellschaft* newsletters, I believe that it is quite possible that the keys of these major works were chosen using a system of letter cyphers based on the initials of Schubert's and Caroline's names: F S (Franz Schubert) = f Es (F minor, E flat major) and C Es (Caroline Esterházy) = C major, E flat major (the common sound beginning their last names being Es, German for E flat).[85] Thus these last works truly would have been dedicated to Caroline, corresponding with Schubert's reported reply to her when she reproached him in fun for having not yet dedicated any composition to her: 'What is the point? Everything is dedicated to you anyway.'

Every age apparently has a need to remake the great men of the past to conform to conditions of the present. The mere fact that Schubert could now be considered a homosexual, in the face of so much evidence to the contrary, is very revealing of the current Zeitgeist. But fiction, as in the case of the Höldrichsmühle, the Dreimäderlhaus and now peacock's tales, should never be confused with history.

Acknowledgements

I should like to thank the Österreichische Nationalbank, Jubiläumsprojekt No. 5923, and especially my project director Dr Gerhard Stradner for the financial and moral support that enabled me to write this article.

Notes and references

1. Wilhelm von Chézy, *Deutsche Pandora*, Stuttgart 1841, vol. 4, p. 183: 'Schubert verehrte Mädchen und Wein, doch hatte leider diese Neigung sich in falsche Richtungen verirrt, aus denen er lebend nicht mehr sich zurechtfand.' I wish to thank Gerrit Waidelich for informing me in a letter dated 22 January 1995 of this passage. He has now published this excerpt in: *Rosamunde. Drama in fünf Akten von Helmina von Chézy. Musik von Franz Schubert*, ed. Till Gerrit Waidelich, Tutzing, 1996, p. 53.
2. See Otto Erich Deutsch, *Schubert: Memoirs by His Friends*, trans. Rosamond Ley and John Nowell, London 1958 (henceforth *Memoirs*), p. 261. For the German original see Wilhelm von Chézy, *Erinnerungen aus meinem Leben*, Schaffhausen 1863, vol. 2, p. 292, reprinted in Otto Erich Deutsch, *Schubert: Die Erinnerungen seiner Freunde*, (Leipzig) Wiesbaden (1957) 1983 (henceforth *Erinnerungen*), p. 299. (The original German of the less readily available publications only will be given here in the footnotes.)
3. *Memoirs*, p. 70; *Erinnerungen*, p. 82. My editorial additions are indicated by square brackets.
4. *Memoirs*, p. 362; *Erinnerungen*, p. 417. Just prior to this passage Spaun defends Schubert from the charge of being an intemperate drinker.
5. Otto Erich Deutsch, *Schubert: A Documentary Biography*, trans. Eric Blom, London 1946 (henceforth *Documentary Biography*), p. 246; idem, *Schubert. Die Dokumente seines Lebens*, Kassel 1964 (henceforth *Dokumente*), p. 172.
6. Hans Max [Johann von Paümann], *Franz Schubert. Original-Singspiel in 1 Akt. Musik mit Benützung Schubert'scher Motive von Franz von Suppé*, Vienna [1879].
7. Ibid., p. 5: 'Seit er das gräfliche Haus in Ungarn verlassen hat, duldet's ihn auch nicht mehr in Wien. Eine unwiderstehliche Sehnsucht trieb ihn in diese Einsamkeit.'
8. Ibid., p. 6.
9. See Otto Erich Deutsch, 'Das Urbild der "Schönen Müllerin" (Dichtung und Wahrheit)', *52. Jahresbericht des Schubertbundes*, Vienna 1915, pp 27–43, also as a special reprint, pp 1–19, esp. p. 9, n. 1.
10. Published in the 'Lokalanzeiger' of the *Presse*, Vienna, 8 August 1879. Deutsch gives the original letter in his article 'Das Urbild der "Schönen Müllerin"', pp 8–11.
11. These anecdotes are given in Deutsch's article 'Das Urbild der "Schönen Müllerin"', pp 18–19. Deutsch was as little successful in 1915 as Paümann had been in 1879 to convince the public that the tale of Schubert and the maid from the Höldrichsmühle was fiction. (Viennese newspapers in 1996 still report the account of Schubert at the Höldrichsmühle as if it were a true story.)
12. Heinrich Kreißle von Hellborn, *Franz Schubert. Eine biografische Skizze*, Vienna 1861, p. 23: '[Schuberts Fantasie in F-Moll] wurde von ihm der jungen Gräfin Esterházy, seiner einzigen Schülerin, deren Talent ihm viele Freude machte und zu welcher ihn auch persönliche Neigung hinzog, gewidmet.'
13. Ibid., p. 75, n.: 'Schubert war gegen das weibliche Geschlecht gewiß nicht gleichgiltig; die sinnlichen Neigungen traten aber bei ihm bei weitem nicht in dem Grade hervor – als dies sonst bei Menschen von so lebhafter Fantasie der Fall zu sein pflegt. Ueber dauernde Liebschaften ist nichts bekannt geworden, und nur für eine hochgestellte Dame, welcher die F-Moll Fantasie gewidmet ist, scheint er während seines Aufenthaltes in Zeléz ernstlich geglüht zu haben.'
14. Heinrich Kreißle von Hellborn, *The Life of Franz Schubert*, trans. Arthur Duke Coleridge, 2 vols, London 1869, (henceforth Kreißle, *The Life*), vol. 1, pp 142–3, translation revised (based on *Memoirs*, p. 100). For the original German (the Coleridge translation often contains errors) see Kreißle, *Franz Schubert*, Vienna 1865, pp 139–40.

15. See [Eduard von Bauernfeld], *Ein Buch von uns Wienern in lustig-gemüthlichen Reimlein von Rusticocampius*, Leipzig 1858, p. 34.
16. Kreißle, *The Life*, vol. 1, p. 144, translation revised. See the original German, pp 140–41.
17. Kreißle, *The Life*, vol. 2, pp 166–7, translation revised. See the original German, p. 480.
18. Otto Erich Deutsch, 'Schuberts Herzeleid,' *Bühne und Welt*, Berlin 9 (15 June 1907): 227–31.
19. Ibid., p. 227: 'ich [bin] nun zu der merkwürdigen Entdeckung gekommen, daß unter diesen sechzig Huldinnen von den Schubert-Literaten gerade die eine Frau am meisten vernachlässigt wurde, die für des Meisters Leben allein von allen entscheidend war.'
20. Ibid.: 'es ist zu erhoffen, daß die Schuberts Manen opfernden Künstler künftighin so weit auf die Ergebnisse der biographischen Forschung Rücksicht nehmen werden, daß sie die unsterbliche Geliebte trotz ihrer Ahnen begraben und in den Werken der bildenden Kunst und der Poesie, die den Meister verherrlichen sollen, die bescheidene Lichtentalerin wieder auferstehen lassen, in die Schubert wahrhaftig sterblich verliebt war.'
21. Ibid., p. 228: 'Und doch besitzen wir zwei voneinander ganz unabhängige, durchaus verläßliche, aber noch wenig beachtete Berichte zweier Jugendfreunde des Meisters, die uns von dem entscheidenden Einfluß dieses Mädchens auf Schuberts Leben erzählen.' These accounts are found in *Memoirs*, pp 59–61, 70, 182, and *Erinnerungen*, pp 69–71, 82, 209.
22. 'Schuberts Herzeleid', p. 227: 'Was also etwa Bauernfeld über Schuberts Liebesschmerzen erzählt, ist nicht ganz ernst zu nehmen.'
23. Ibid., p. 231: 'Schuberts schwer verwundetes Herz blieb nach Theresens Vermählung in seiner stillen Resignation konsequent, so lange es noch schlug. Von einer tieferen Herzensneigung kann bei all den Frauen, mit denen er in seinem weiteren Leben zusammenkam, nicht mehr die Rede sein; im besten Falle schloß er Freundschaft mit einer. Noch weniger dürfen wir glauben, daß Schuberts Herz bei einer der namenlosen Liebeleien affiziert wurde, deren eine im Jahre 1823 mit ihren bösen Folgen sein Leben bedrohte.'
24. Otto Erich Deutsch, 'Schubert und die Frauen', *Jahrbuch des Schubertbundes* 47 (1910): 81–89; separate publication, Vienna 1910, pp 1–8, especially p. 3: 'Wenn wir nun nach dem Verhältnis Schuberts zu den Frauen im allgemeinen fragen, so erkennen wir bald mit Sicherheit, daß er – was ohnehin seine Werke tausendmal bezeugen – eine stark erotische Natur war, aber kein keck zugreifender Liebhaber, sondern ein unbeholfener, fast schüchterner Patron. Er kam den Frauen vielleicht allzu zart entgegen, um von ihnen Ersatz für das Glück gewinnen zu können, das ihm sonst im Leben so spärlich bemessen war. Wenn Schuberts Sinnlichkeit, wie Kreißle meint, vielleicht nicht mit seiner Phantasie Schritt hielt, so war er doch für Frauenreize sehr empfindlich.'
25. Ibid., p. 5: '[...] seine Diskretion in Liebessachen, die so viel Unheil für seine Biographen heraufbeschworen hat.'
26. [Otto Erich Deutsch], review: '*Schwammerl. Ein Schubert-Roman von R. H. [sic] Bartsch*,' *Die Zeit*, Vienna, 1 October 1912, p. 3: 'Der Historiker Bartsch kennt freilich den wirklichen Schubert genau; aber er hat ihn nach seiner dichterischen Notwendigkeit gesteigert. Die Schwestern Tschöll, die nur in ihrer Dreizahl an die Fröhlichschen erinnern, sind natürlich frei erfunden. Aber ebenso wie hier ist Bartsch auch sonst in der Erfindung der Wahrheit am nächsten gekommen. Mit wunderbarer Feinheit sind das alte Wien und der Schubertkreis gezeichnet.'
27. See Bernard Grun, *Kulturgeschichte der Operette*, Munich 1961, pp 401–2. Grun writes here that *Das Dreimäderlhaus* was the most performed operetta in the world

after *The Merry Widow* and *The Mikado*, had been translated into twenty-two languages and had been played *c*. 85,000 times in sixty countries.

28. Otto Erich Deutsch, 'Das eben ist der Fluch ... (Vom Drei- und Mehrmäderlhaus)', *Die Wage* 6 (4 April 1925): 84–7. Reprinted in Deutsch, *Wiener Musikgeschichten*, ed. Gitta Deutsch and Rudolf Klein, Vienna 1993, pp 110–13.
29. Otto Erich Deutsch, 'Schubert und das "Dreimäderlhaus"', *Illustriertes Wiener Extrablatt* (8 November 1925), p. 6: '[Schubert] ist auch selbst, wie ich bezeugen kann, mit dem Helden des "Dreimäderlhaus" weder verwandt noch identisch gewesen.'
30. Otto Erich Deutsch, 'Die zehn Ständchen (Schubert und die Frauen)', *Moderne Welt*, Schubert issue, Vienna (1 Dec. 1925): 17–19, especially p. 19.
31. Otto Erich Deutsch, 'Frauen um Schubert', *Kölnische Zeitung*, Beilage: Mode und Kultur (11 November 1928): 3.
32. Otto Erich Deutsch, 'Frauen um Schubert', *Hannoverscher Kurier*, Beilage: Die Frau 3/17 (1929): 1–3, 6–7, especially p. 1.
33. See Andreas Mayer, *Franz Schubert, eine historische Phantasie*, Vienna: Turia & Kant, 1997.
34. *Documentary Biography*, p. 47; *Dokumente*, p. 35.
35. *Documentary Biography*, p. 329; *Dokumente*, p. 227.
36. *Documentary Biography*, p. 364; *Dokumente*, p. 251. Caroline's name, spelt by Deutsch with a 'K' to conform with later 19th-century spelling changes, has been respelt using the historically-correct 'C.'
37. See *Documentary Biography*, p. 369, where Deutsch comments: 'It appears that Pepi Pöckelhofer, the "complaisant chambermaid," who may have gone to Vienna (? her home) on holiday, was still on friendly terms with Schubert. His father probably knew nothing of his earlier relations with her or did not take them seriously'; *Dokumente*, p. 254.
38. *Documentary Biography*, p. 413; *Dokumente*, p. 284, altered by Deutsch.
39. *Documentary Biography*, pp 658–59; *Dokumente*, p. 444.
40. *Documentary Biography*, p. 952; *Dokumente*, p. 607.
41. Otto Maag, 'Schubert-Feier,' *Der Basilisk, Sonntagsbeilage der National-Zeitung Basel*, 9 (18 November 1928). Deutsch also has a short report here entitled: 'Schubert's Jugendfreundin von Schweizer Abkunft'.
42. Dr Franz Köhler had also conducted extensive genealogical research on the Schubert family, to which he was related. In 1928 he owned the 'original' plaster-cast copy of Schubert's death mask. See Steblin, 'Neue Gedanken zu Schuberts "Toten-Maske"', *Schubert durch die Brille* 6 (Jan. 1991): 66–70.
43. See note 21 above.
44. *Memoirs*, pp 61–2; *Erinnerungen*, p. 72.
45. Kreißle, *The Life*, vol. 1, p. 35. See the original German, p. 35.
46. *Memoirs*, p. 182; *Erinnerungen*, p. 209.
47. *Documentary Biography*, pp 70–71; *Dokumente*, p. 49. This diary entry is discussed extensively in Steblin, 'The Peacock's Tale: Schubert's Sexuality Reconsidered,' *19th-Century Music* 17 (1993): 5–33, especially pp 6–8. Deutsch had apparently written the comment 'The thoughts on marriage do not seem to have been produced by any particular case' (*Documentary Biography*, p. 72) before he found the document from the Government at Laibach to the Civic Guard in Vienna, that establishes the significance of the 7 September date.
48. This law and its legal interpretation for Vienna (by Franz Herzog, 1829) are given in full in Steblin, 'Franz Schubert und das Ehe-Consens Gesetz von 1815', *Schubert durch die Brille* 9 (June 1992): 32–42. For a French translation of my article, see *Cahiers F. Schubert* 2 (1993): 17–26.
49. See my forthcoming article 'In Defence of Scholarship and the Historical Truth: New

Documents about the Schubert Family', submitted to *Current Musicology*. I also present here a facsimile of the impressive certificate with attached seal that Johann Baptist Bergmann, a 'bürglicher Bäckermeister' from the parish of St. Stephen's, was able to produce to claim his bride, Therese, in November 1820. Bergmann's title of 'Bürger' exempted him from having to meet the requirements of the marriage-consent law.

50. Kreißle, *The Life*, vol. 1, p. 35. See the original German, p. 35.
51. Rudolf Maria Enzersdorfer, 'Ein Autographenfund von Schuberts Liedern,' *Neue Freie Presse* 5 Jan. 1908; see also *Die Musik* Jg. 7, Heft 9 (Feb. 1908), Nachrichten und Anzeigen, p. III.
52. Otto Erich Deutsch, 'Schuberts Liederheft für Therese Grob,' *Neue Freie Presse* 10 Jan. 1908, p. 7, and 16 Jan. 1908, p. 8.
53. Franz Schubert, *Therese Grob Collection*, ed. Reinhard Van Hoorickx, private printing with permission from the Dr Wilhelm family in Bottmingen, Switzerland, 1967.
54. Maurice J. E. Brown, 'The Therese Grob Collection of Songs by Schubert,' *Music & Letters* 49 (1968): 122–34.
55. Ibid., p. 124.
56. Walther Dürr, 'Das Liederalbum der Therese Grob,' in: *Neue Schubert-Ausgabe, Kritischer Bericht*, series IV, vol. 1, Tübingen, typescript, 1972, pp 23–6.
57. *Memoirs*, p. 292; *Erinnerungen*, p. 336.
58. See *Documentary Biography*, Plate XXXI.
59. *Memoirs*, p. 206; *Erinnerungen*, p. 236.
60. *Documentary Biography*, pp 401–2; *Dokumente*, pp 275–76.
61. *Memoirs*, pp 265–6; *Erinnerungen*, p. 304.
62. *Documentary Biography*, p. 603; *Dokumente*, p. 407.
63. This material has now been transcribed and analysed in my book *Die Unsinnsgesellschaft. Franz Schubert, Leopold Kupelwieser und ihr Freundeskreis*, awaiting publication in 1998 by Böhlau Verlag.
64. *Memoirs*, p. 223; *Erinnerungen*, p. 255.
65. See my forthcoming article 'Schubert's Male Quartet *Das Dörfchen*, D598 and its Origins in the *Unsinnsgesellschaft*,' read at IMS-London in August 1997.
66. 'Verloren: Eine Mamsell verspüret daß sie vor 6 Wochen im Stadtgraben unter den Ruinen ihre Jungfräuleinschaft ganz verloren habe, und bittet den *röthlichen* Finder keinen üblen Gebrauch davon zu machen. *Elise von Antifi*.'
67. For an in-depth discussion of the tiny man on the left (Johann Carl Smirsch, code name: 'Nina Wutzerl') who is dressed in women's clothes and wears a huge hat decorated with peacock feathers, see my article 'Schubert's "Nina" and the true peacocks' in *The Musical Times*, March 1997, pp 13–19.
68. *Documentary Biography*, pp 87–94, 113; *Dokumente*, pp 59–63, 76.
69. See Steblin, *Babette und Therese Kunz. Neue Forschungen zum Freundeskreis um Franz Schubert und Leopold Kupelwieser*, Vienna: Vom Pasqualatihaus, 1996. This book, dedicated to the memory of Isolde Ahlgrimm, is also meant to be a practical guide, explaining what kind of information is to be found in the various Viennese archives.
70. 'Wie gefährlich die neue Erfindung der Rutschberge in Paris ist, beweist die neuste Zeitgeschichte aber auch die scheinbar unschädlichen Erfindungen des Kaleidoscops und der Draisine haben ihr Gefährliches wie uns das vorliegende Kupfer zeigt. Ein in das Anschauen des wunderlichen Farbenspiels im Kaleidoscop versunkener dicker Herr, welchem das dunkele Glas noch kurzsichtiger als gewöhnlich macht, wird von einem hitzigen Draisinenritter, der ebenfalls das Auge nur auf seine Maschine gerichtet hat, zu Boden geführt. Ein warnendes Beispiel für Andere. Bereits soll auch ein Polizeybefehl im Werke seyn, kraft dessen jedem Dalken [Dummkopf]

der Gebrauch beyder neuen Erfindungen als sehr gefährlich, aufs strengste verboten wird.'
71. 'Unterfertigter giebt sich die Ehre einem verehrten Publikum ergebenst anzuzeigen, daß bey ihm eine Gattung Schönsehröhre (Durchsehröhre genannt) zu haben sey, welche die sonderbare Eigenschaft haben daß man mit ihrer Hülfe durch alle Sorten Kleidungsstücke zu sehen im Stande ist. Wie groß der Nutzen dieser Gläser ist, wird jedermann leicht einsehen, da sie manchen Gegenstand zu Tage fördern, welcher bis jetzt mühsam verborgen gehalten wurde. Vorzüglich jungen Herren welche gern am Graben spatzieren gehen [...]'
72. '*L'observateur curieux* hat von der Verlegenheit in welcher sich *Madame Culronde* versetzt fühlte als der feurige *Chevalier Touchetout* unversehens einige physisch-anatomische Untersuchungen mit ihr vornahm und seine Hand zum Unglück der Dame und zum größten Erstaunen des *Chevaliers* statt der vermutheten natürlichen Erhöhungen einige Strumpfsöckel hervorzog, nichts weiter gemeldet, als daß sie gränzenlos gewesen sey.'
73. *Documentary Biography*, pp 106, 109; *Dokumente*, pp 72, 74 (with Schubert's pun in reply: 'Die Stadtfreunde sind liederlich').
74. 'Nach Berichten aus Spanien hat das dortige Inquisitionsgericht den berühmten Maler *Juan de la Cimbala* inhaftiren lassen weil er seinem eigenen Geständnisse zufolge, seit geraumer Zeit neben seinen Geschäften schwarze Kunst trieb. Man hofft indessen daß er mit dem Leben davon kommen werde, indem er sich bereits selbst vor seiner Verhaftung aufs grausamste verbrannt hat.'
75. Brian Newbould, 'A Schubert Palindrome', *19th-Century Music* 15 (1992): 209–10.
76. *Documentary Biography*, pp 93–94; *Dokumente*, pp 62–3.
77. *Memoirs*, p. 86; *Erinnerungen*, p. 100.
78. *Memoirs*, pp 233–4; *Erinnerungen*, pp 267–68. For the sources of other quotations in this section, see Steblin, 'The Peacock's Tale,' pp 14–16.
79. See Steblin, 'Schwinds Porträtskizze "Schubert am Klavier"', *Schubert durch die Brille* 10 (Jan. 1993): 45–52.
80. Walburga Litschauer, *Neue Dokumente zum Schubert-Kreis. Aus Briefen und Tagebüchern seiner Freunde* (Vienna, 1986), p. 68.
81. See Steblin, 'Neue Forschungsaspekte zu Caroline Esterházy,' *Schubert durch die Brille* 11 (June 1993): 21–34.
82. See Steblin, 'Le mariage malheureux de Caroline Esterházy. Une histoire authentique, telle qu'elle est retracée dans les lettres de la famille Crenneville,' *Cahiers F. Schubert* 5 (Oct. 1994): 17–34.
83. According to the marriage registry records in St. Pölten for the widower Carl Crenneville's second marriage on 5 April 1853. (Caroline died in Preßburg on 14 March 1851.)
84. Discussed in my article 'Neue Forschungsaspekte zu Caroline Esterházy,' pp 31–2. For a comprehensive study of the topic of key characteristics see Steblin, *A History of Key Characteristics in the Eighteenth and Early Nineteenth Centuries* (Ann Arbor 1981; reissued by the University of Rochester Press 1996).
85. See Steblin, 'Schubert à la Mode,' *The New York Review of Books* 41 (20 Oct. 1994): 72.

11 Adversity: Schubert's illnesses and their background
Peter Gilroy Bevan

> 'Adversity doth best discover virtue.'
> Francis Bacon (1561–1626)

A medical appreciation can only intensify modern wonder at the unique and prolific genius of Franz Schubert. His music is all the more marvellous when we consider the illnesses he faced throughout his life, and the difficulties and drawbacks, both personal and social, that affected him. During his last six years, his state of health was seriously undermined, and yet this was the period when many of his greatest works were composed.

An appreciation of Schubert's physical traits, character and temperament reveals the effect that his illnesses and handicaps must have had on him, and the manner in which he withstood them. His portraits show that he could not claim to be handsome, but was not unattractive although hardly charismatic, with a rounded face and cleft chin, dark curly hair and spectacles. He was short, with his height variously recorded as 4 feet 11 inches[1] or 5 feet 1 inch,[2] and was excused from military service on this account. Stocky in build and stout in his later years, his hyperactive personality qualifies him for inclusion in the *sthenic*[3] category. His output of musical composition was prodigious; his first work catalogued by Otto Deutsch is dated April 1810, and the listed titles of his works over the next 18 years fill 27 pages of the *New Grove Dictionary of Music and Musicians*,[4] the final entry being D998. Schubert died at the age of only 31 at the height of his composing genius, although it must be borne in mind that the average life expectancy for men at that time was only 38 years.

In temperament Schubert inherited traits from both parents – solidity of character and love of music from his father Franz Theodor, of peasant stock, and artistic spirit from his mother Maria Elizabeth whose family had an artisan background.[5] As a youth, he was described by one of his fellow students at school, Franz Eckel, later Director of the Vienna Veterinary Institution, as silent and uncommunicative, with his life 'one of inner spiritual thought ... seldom expressed in words, but almost entirely in music'.[6] However, he developed another side to his nature, portrayed by his father as follows: 'Even in his earliest youth he loved society and he was never happier than when he could spend his leisure hours in the company of gay friends'.[7] (Gay did not have its present homosexual connotation.) These two aspects of his temperament, inclined to alternation between high and low spirits, became more marked in adult life and have been appropriately termed cyclothymic;[8,9] these two extremes coloured his responses to his illnesses.

Syphilis

Schubert's serious illness which led to his death six years later started at the end of 1822 or in the early part of 1823. Previously there is no record of him suffering from other than minor ill-health. In a letter to Franz von Mosel, an influential supporter of his music, dated 28 February 1823, Schubert wrote of 'the circumstances of my health still forbidding me to leave the house'.[10] Although his illness is never named by him or his friends in their many letters collected by O E Deutsch,[11] it is now generally agreed that he had contracted syphilis during December 1822 and January 1823. Sams[12] discusses the detailed evidence in favour of this diagnosis which was first suggested by Deutsch.[13] Exact medical evidence is lacking and can only be inferred by studying Schubert's symptoms and their time-scale which appear in the letters. There are two reasons why confirmation of the nature of his illness must remain indirect; first, the cause of syphilis and its specific effects were not known until its causative organism, the spirochaete *Treponema pallidum*, was identified nearly a century later in 1905 by a German bacteriologist, Fritz Schaudin[14] and secondly, social conventions in the nineteenth century forbade the mention and discussion of venereal disease.

The spirochaete of syphilis was considered to have made its first appearance among the North American Indians and to have been brought back to Europe by Christopher Columbus and his sailors when they returned to Europe from their voyage of discovery to the New World in 1492.[15] By the beginning of the sixteenth century the disease was endemic throughout the countries of Europe. The name of the disease is derived from a poem published in 1530 by the Italian physician and poet, Girolamo Fracastoro, who was the first to give a correct description of the clinical features of syphilis.[16] At the turn of the nineteenth century 'lues' was the general term for venereal disease; gonorrhoea and syphilis were not distinguished from each other until Dr Ricord's notorious experiments on Parisian prostitutes in which he inoculated them with gonorrhoeal pus to study the course of the infection. Earlier John Hunter (1728–93) in London, generally regarded as the first scientific surgeon, contracted syphilis as a result of the foolhardy inoculation of himself with syphilitic pus to distinguish this condition from gonorrhoea.[17] His clinical description of a chancre (ulcer) of penis with bubo (abscess of groin) treated with mercury ointment and associated skin rash has never been bettered.[18]

There are three successive clinical stages through which the victim of syphilis may pass (Table 11.1). The infection is transmitted only by sexual contact with a carrier and the organism is very contagious, passing through the most minute abrasion. The suggestion that a contaminated toilet seat can pass on the infection, popular with those who suffer from the disease, is a fable without scientific support. Within one month of inoculation, a small papule (pimple) appears on the genital organs (mouth or throat in the case of oral sex), enlarges and ulcerates to form a typical chancre. It bleeds, discharges and becomes smelly, leading on to enlargement of the nodes in the groin which suppurate and form abscesses. By this stage the infection has entered the blood stream, and a generalized skin rash of rose-coloured patches appears. Septic spots may occur in the scalp with loss of hair.[19] The primary stage is usually relatively painless.

Table 11.1   The clinical stages of syphilis

Stage	Clinical features	Time scale
PRIMARY	An ulcer on the genital organs (chancre) with enlargement of glands or nodes in the groin sometimes with abscesses or fever.	Occuring within one month of contact, and lasting many weeks.
SECONDARY	Skin rash, inflammation of eyes, throat, larynx, bones, and internal organs such as liver and heart, and the nervous system. General malaise and loss of hair.	Starting within a few months of the primary stage and lasting many months or a few years.
TERTIARY	Formation of tumours (gummata) under the skin or in internal organs or the testicle; also structural damage to bones, eyes, main arteries, the brain, and locomotor nerves.	Developing years after the secondary stage and lasting the rest of life if not cured.

Within two or three months of the appearance of the primary sore, the stage of secondary syphilis follows, involving generalized dissemination of the infection and constitutional effects such as malaise, fever, headaches, loss of hair, pains in bones and joints, and anaemia. Redness and small superficial ulcers appear on the lips and in the mouth and throat. Rarely, the eyes, liver and kidneys may be affected at this stage.

The written reports of Schubert's movements in his letters and those of his friends are consistent with him developing primary syphilis early in 1823 and remaining indoors by order of his doctor to avoid contagion, and by reason of social unacceptability. It seems that he was out of the public eye for most of the remainder of 1823. In August of that year, Karl Beethoven, nephew of the composer, wrote that 'They greatly praise Schubert but it is said he hides himself'.[20] On 8 May Schubert wrote his despairing poem, 'My Prayer', with the desolate third verse as follows:

> See, abased in dust and mire,
> Scorched by agonising fire,
> I in torture go my way,
> Nearing doom's destructive day.[21]

This *cri de coeur* surely testifies to his realisation of the nature of the disease he had contracted, and would coincide in time with the advent of the secondary stage of syphilis, heralded by a generalised rash, and the symptoms listed above, presenting a few months after the primary infection. The rash which came and went over the next few years was, in all probability, particularly offensive as it would have affected his face, causing raised red nodules with a tendency to break down forming ulcers with surrounding inflammation. It is likely that he had suffered an attack of smallpox in childhood leaving scarring of his face; the Schubert family had been exposed to this infection as Franz's brother Josef probably died of smallpox,[22] which was endemic in the main cities of northern Europe for most of the last century. The advertisement for a soprano in the Seminary in 1808, with the post awarded to Schubert, specified that he must be past the danger of smallpox,[23] implying that he had suffered and recovered from an attack, leaving him immune; only in this way could he have been removed from the danger of the disease. Edward Jenner described his discovery of cowpox vaccination of humans to prevent smallpox in 1793,[24] but this was not adopted as widespread practice during Schubert's lifetime. His facial scarring, understandably not reproduced in his portraits, may explain his periods of withdrawal from society and his friends, as he must have felt humiliated by his appearance.

Schubert was extremely ill during the summer months of 1823 with clinical features strongly suggestive of the secondary stage of syphilis. Although the date is difficult to confirm, he was admitted to Vienna General Hospital (Allgemeines Krankenhaus) from May to July,[25] and must have been subjected to the only available treatments of the time – bleeding, purging and emesis. The principal medicament was mercury, given to all patients for every type of infection and disease. It is debatable whether the spartan conditions of the hospital conferred any benefit on him; in a letter to Schober (14 August 1823), presumably after leaving hospital, he wrote '... am fairly well. Whether I shall ever recover I am inclined to doubt.'[26] Perhaps the composition of his song cycle *Die schöne Müllerin* while he was in hospital and during the next few months[27] reflected his melancholy mood. It also represented the restoration of his creative powers, as his stream of music had dwindled and dried during the summer months.[28]

During the autumn of 1823 Schubert lost his hair owing to the combined onslaught of the syphilitic rash of his scalp, secondary infection, the effect of mercury, and the shaving which was the standard medical treatment for an infected scalp. This further insult to his appearance must have compounded his discomfiture, helped to some extent by wearing a wig.[29] In November his doctors reported that he was well on the way to recovery,[30] but in fact his health was permanently impaired and he suffered from recurring symptoms of secondary syphilis for the rest of his life – headaches, vomiting, aching bones, nausea and giddiness.[31] The bone pain that occurs in both the secondary and tertiary stages of the disease is intractable in nature, present day and night, and affects in particular the weight-bearing skeleton, the lower limbs and back.

Schubert's ill-health continued in 1824, although his hair re-grew. A new symptom occurred when he was unable to sing at a Schubertiad,[32] the loss of voice inevitably due to syphilitic laryngitis. Depression and disillusion were added to his poor health, resulting from the failure of his operas (even *Rosamunde*), the abandonment of the Schubertiads and the reading parties, activities that he had prized so much. On 31 March he wrote to Kupelwieser, 'My peace has gone, my heart is sore, I shall find it never and nevermore ... for each night on retiring to bed, I hope that I may not wake again, and each morning but recalls yesterday's grief'.[33] For the remainder of the year he retired to his father's school house at Rossau as a recluse. The medical régime advocated by his personal physician, Dr Bernhardt, had achieved little response – rest, fasting, hot baths and copious tea drinking, with applications of mercury ointment.[34]

The year 1825 started badly for Schubert with another period in hospital due to further symptoms of the same nature. In January he wrote the song 'Der Einsame' (The Recluse) while he was in hospital, according to Kreissle's biography,[35] perhaps reflecting his state of mind. During 1825 and 1828 he suffered repeated illnesses of the pattern already defined, but sometimes with new symptoms appearing. Inflammation of the eyes, particularly the iris, was a regular feature of secondary syphilis, with consequent photophobia (shrinking from light). Georg Eckel, a friend of Schubert from their schooldays, noted 'frequent screwing up of his eyelids' by Franz in his biographical letter dated 30 April 1858.[36] Syphilis attacks all tissues and organs and has been called 'the great imitator'. There is often mention of pains experienced by Schubert in the letters between him and his friends; 'pains in his bones' (Doblhoff to Schober),[37] and 'pains in his left arm so that he cannot play the pianoforte' (Schwind to Schober),[38] the latter most likely due to syphilitic peripheral neuropathy (neuritis).

Schubert's frequent absences on public occasions were noted by his friends. Eduard von Bauernfeld recorded in his diary on 2 January 1826 that Schubert was missing from the New Year's Eve party the previous night.[39] He also absented himself from a number of Schubertiads,[40] as noted by Schwind. Throughout this period, and indeed until his death, he continued to produce many of his greatest compositions, despite his persisting ill-health and the repeated hospital admissions. His portrait by Wilhelm Rieder (Plate 9), in 1825, said to be 'very beautifully painted' by fellow artist Josef von Spaun,[41] suggests some aspects of his deteriorating health; his face has a lean look, his cheeks are no longer chubby and he has lost much of his *embonpoint*, with his hair thinner than in his portraits before 1823.

Before we come to the last two years of Schubert's life it is of interest to review the circumstances in which he contracted syphilis. After he left the family home in 1816 at the age of 19, following three years as a master in his father's school, he never had a settled home but lived with various of his friends in succession. Although quiet and generally reticent by nature,[42] he had no difficulty in forming a circle of friends of his own age interested in music. The first Schubertiad is described by Josef Huber (with whom he shared lodgings in 1823-4[43]) on 30 January 1821,[44] with 'splendid songs by Schubert' after which plenty of punch was drunk and the merry party continued until 3 am. There are many references to Schubert's liking for alcohol,[45] and even the possibility of him smoking opium with Schober and sharing 'Persian pipes'.[46] Thomas De Quincey published his book *The Confessions of an English Opium-Eater* in 1822; opium was the popular social drug of the time equivalent to cannabis or Ecstasy today. A boisterous evening of music and songs, influenced by alcohol and/or opium, might in turn be followed by a night of promiscuity.

Schubert and Schober were close friends throughout their adult lives, and shared rooms from 1820-22, comparing notes and smoking their pipes in the evening.[47] Schober, a hedonist and man of the world according to Bauernfeld's diary,[48] exerted a bad influence on his younger friend and was luring him 'into loose living'.[49] This theme is described in more detail by Wilhelm von Chézy; 'Unfortunately Schubert, with his liking for the pleasures of life, had strayed into those wrong paths which generally admit of no return, at least of no healthy one'.[50]

In this connection an analysis of Schubert's sexuality is pertinent. His relationships with women were unsatisfactory, and he was 'shy of outward expression'.[51] He never married and the question of his possible homosexuality has been raised.[52] However, the evidence in this direction is unconvincing, and examples abound of his fondness for women. In 1814 Schubert's Mass in F was first performed and the soprano solo sung by Therese Grob, with whom he fell in love.[53] The affair collapsed the following year because of her parents' disapproval,[54] and he gave up for ever the idea of marriage.[55] In 1818 he was invited to Zseliz, across the Hungarian border, by Count Esterházy to teach his daughter Caroline the piano; the young Countess 'delighted him by her feelings for music and by her amiability', according to Spaun.[56] Schubert fell in love with her but she never realized the depth of his emotion and the affair remained platonic when he paid a return visit to Zseliz in 1824.[57] The charming thought has been expressed by András Schiff[58] that Schubert's feelings for his pupil explain why he wrote so many piano duets involving the crossing of arms on the second visit!

However, Schubert was no respecter of social class, and during his first visit to Zseliz, he had an affair with his chambermaid Pepi Pöckelhofer.[59] Numerous accounts are available of his appreciation of the other sex. Whilst staying with Anton Stadler in 1819, he wrote to his brother Ferdinand that 'there are eight girls, all pretty. There is plenty to do, you see'.[60] The evidence that he was normally heterosexual seems conclusive. Where and when he acquired his syphilis is in doubt. The course of his clinical condition places the responsible intercourse just before Christmas 1822, when he was in Vienna, and the incident does not seem related to his visits to Zseliz, as has been suggested by Kiemle.[61] Schubert quoted Martin Luther in a note dated 28 November 1822:

> Who loves not wine, maiden and song,
> Remains a fool his whole life long.[62]

He had just abandoned the Symphony in B minor (the 'Unfinished') and completed the Fantasia in C (the *Wandererfantasie*); exhilarated by this double achievement and having celebrated by a bout of drinking, he could well have sought the intimate company of one of the many prostitutes thronging the taverns of Vienna. This would be consistent with the quotation from Goethe on the back of the above note to Albert Schellmann ending 'And who stands, beware a fall'.[63]

Treatment

There were many forms of treatment for venereal disease in the eighteenth century listed by Dr von Rinna in his Encyclopaedia of 1833–6, and quoted by Sams.[64] Rinna took over Schubert's treatment from his previous medical adviser, Dr Bernhardt, during the last year of his serious illness. He was Court physician and had written two books on syphilis in addition to the Encyclopaedia.[65] All the *nostra* (quack remedies) advocated for syphilis had two features in common – none was effective and all were harmful to the patient. The main objective of all the measures used was to rid the body of the toxins or poisons produced by the disease. Purging caused dehydration, and fasting advocated by Schubert's doctors reduced energy and weakened resistance. Emetics were given to empty the upper gastro-intestinal tract, with the same consequences. Bleeding was the standard treatment for all infective conditions, and resulted in anaemia; the patient was usually bled when severely ill, frequently with counter-productive results, which probably happened to Schubert in his final illness (see below, and Plate 11).

Mercury was the panacea[66] for all conditions in the eighteenth and first half of the nineteenth centuries, and was known as quicksilver which indicated its spreading quality. It was used in the form of mercurous chloride or Calomel, and made up as a draught to drink, an ointment to rub into the skin or a poultice to apply to ulcers. The two latter methods led to high levels of mercury being absorbed through the skin into the bodily tissues, the dose related to the area of skin covered. In addition vapours were inhaled from ointment on the skin, thus increasing the total amount of mercury deposited in the body tissues. 'Volatile salve' prescribed for this purpose in the nineteenth century was considered to contain mercury, but on analysis only ammonia salts were found.[67]

Mercury has serious disadvantages when employed to treat human ills. It is very toxic to cells and organs; it remains in the tissues, as the body has difficulty in disposing of it; it is cumulative, repeated doses building up to a high concentration in the blood and throughout the body; finally, its therapeutic index is low with little effect on pathogenic organisms.

The main advantage of the medical use of mercury was that the ointment did help to clear the skin of rashes and pock marks from smallpox, and the draught acted as an aperient, emetic, diuretic, expectorant and sialogogue (to increase the flow of saliva), with the mistaken idea that this would rid the system of syphilitic toxins.[68]

As mercury becomes distributed widely in the body, it leads to protean side effects,[69] including inflammation of the mouth (stomatitis), ulceration of the gums (gingivitis), loosening and loss of teeth, excess salivation with a metallic taste in the mouth, a diffuse skin rash, kidney failure, tremor, diarrhoea and psychological disturbances (delusions and hallucinations – sometimes termed erethism). In the eighteenth and nineteenth centuries mercury was present in the medicaments mentioned above, often in containers inadequately sealed,[70] and in dentures and mirrors. Since the development of the mercury thermometer early in the eighteenth century, factory conditions of thermometer-making, and broken thermometers in homes have served to leave poisonous deposits of mercury in communities permanently.

In the present century there has been growing awareness of the dangers of mercury and use of the element has been abandoned in the West. Drugs containing mercury, such as Calomel, Neptal and Mersalyl (for kidney failure) are no longer used and omitted from the British Pharmocopeia. During the past ten years reports have been published on mercury poisoning in the home and in industry from many countries in addition to the United Kingdom – China, Finland, France, Israel, Japan, Puerto Rico, Russia and the USA. These reports describe a wide spectrum of clinical effects of mercury poisoning in those affected – dermatitis, hair loss, wrist and ankle pain, kidney damage, jaundice and liver damage, lung complications and neuro-psychiatric symptoms including tremor, ataxia (unsteadiness), forgetfulness, irritability and erethism. Consideration is being given by the medical profession to abandon mercury-containing thermometers[71] and sphygomanometers (blood pressure machines).[72]

Symptoms of mercury poisoning can thus resemble closely those due to syphilis. In Schubert's case it is difficult to differentiate the two main causes of his ill-health, as detailed descriptions of his clinical condition and treatment are missing, and allusions in his letters and those of his friends fragmentary. However, it seems most likely that many of his medical ills were iatrogenic[73] in origin.

After two centuries of use, the treatment of syphilis by mercury was given up in the mid-nineteenth century and bismuth prescribed, without improving outcome. Paul Ehrlich developed compounds of arsenic as anti-spirochaetal agents early in the twentieth century and discovered the beneficial effect of Salvarsan in syphilis, for which he was awarded the Nobel Prize in 1908.[74] Exact diagnosis of the infection was made possible by the development of the Wassermann blood test in 1907 by Fritz Schaudin, in which syphilitic antibodies are identified in the blood.

However, it was not until the discovery of penicillin in the laboratory in 1928 by Alexander Fleming and its clinical use pioneered by Howard Florey fifteen years later that a cure was found for syphilis. The disease has virtually disappeared from Europe and North America during the past two generations although occasional cases of primary infection still occur.

Depression

Schubert suffered from recurring bouts of depression during his adult life.[75] The first attested episode in 1816 when he was 19 years of age is deduced from a long entry in his diary on 8 September expressing feelings of disillusion and despair – while still young: 'Blissful moments brighten this dark life; ... Man bears misfortune without complaint, ... To be noble and unhappy is to feel the full depths of misfortune'.[76] A conjunction of events led to this crisis in his life. His love affair with Therese Grob had ended 'because he was too young at the time and without money or position' and because her parents disapproved.[77] He had just come to the end of three years teaching in his father's school which he had hated; Schober takes the credit for 'having freed this immortal master from the restraint of school'.[78] Although his three years as a schoolmaster at Rossau (1813–16) allowed him to compose almost half his musical output including his first five symphonies, it also led to a serious breach with his father, whom Mayrhofer had to console about his son's future.[79] Schubert was still affected by the death of his beloved mother in 1812.[80] He suffered disappointment at failing in his application for a new post as music teacher at the training college of Laibach (now Llubljana),[81] and later by his rejection for membership of the *Gesellschaft der Musikfreunde des Österreichischen Kaiserstaates* (Austrian Philharmonic Society).[82] (He was admitted some years later.) Finally he left the family home at the end of 1816 and moved in with Schober. Perhaps Schubert had these sadnesses in mind when he composed his last song of 1815, setting to music Goethe's tragic poem, *Der Erlkönig*.[83] His portrait at that time, by an unknown artist, shows an intense and introvert young man (see Plate 10).

Schubert left Vienna in July 1818 for his first visit to Zseliz. Initially he was well and happy, but soon depression set in; 'I am obliged to rely wholly on myself ... Not a soul here has any feeling for true art, or at most the countess'.[84] Returning to Vienna at the end of 1818, Schubert shared a room with Mayrhofer, but this arrangement did not help to combat depression as 'both the house and the room have felt the hand of time; the ceiling somewhat sunken, the daylight reduced by a large building opposite...'[85]

Schubert was always in financial straits. In Sidney Harrison's words, he had no friends and patrons among the aristocracy and lacked the business acumen to obtain reasonable prices from his publishers.[86] In 1821 Leopold Sonnleithner and other friends financed the publication of some of Schubert's works and cleared his debts, as 'he had no idea of domestic economy and was often led by his tavern friends into useless expenditure'.[87] However behind their backs, Diabelli, the publisher, offered Schubert a lower price for copyright and plates and Schubert unwisely settled. His dealings with Diabelli, and the other publishers in Vienna such as Steiner and Leidesdorf, were unsatisfactory, resulting in reduced income for Schubert and loss of valuable autograph manuscripts for posterity.[88] In a letter to Schober dated September 1824 from Zseliz, Schubert said of Leidesdorf, '...things have gone badly; he cannot pay, nor does a single soul sell anything'.[89]

His second visit to Zseliz marked a low point in his morale. In the letter to Schober just quoted, he reciprocates the despair expressed by his friend since 'such is the lot of almost every sensible person in this miserable world'. In an emotive poem, he reflects on the artist faced with falling standards, and observes that only the gift of sacred art can overcome grief and soften fate. The visit brought a final realisation to Schubert that his relationship with Countess Caroline must for ever remain platonic, in his reference to 'the attractions of a certain star'.[90] In the words of his friend Schönstein, this flame continued to burn until his death.[91] This state of dark depression led Schubert to the belief that he was being poisoned, and he persuaded Schönstein to return to Vienna with him.[92] He suffered from this delusion on other occasions, probably owing to paranoia resulting from his continuing ill-health, loneliness at Zseliz and unrequited love, or possibly owing to the toxic effect of mercury. In 1824 he must have felt his world crumbling, with the failure of his other areas of interest already mentioned.

The repeated dark moods and rages he experienced during the ensuing years were associated with his persisting illness, repeated doses of mercury and mental imbalance. One of these rages is described by Chézy when Schubert 'the juice of the vine glowing within him, ... liked to give himself up contentedly to silent rage ... and would demolish something or other, for example glasses, plates or cups.'[93] The contrast between the two natures of Schubert's cyclothymic personality became more marked in his latter years approaching the level of manic-depression, with a state of ecstasy alternating with 'the dark night of the soul'.[94] This was perhaps an extension of the sense of arousal induced by great music followed by the peace of relaxation, with the change between these two states of mind exaggerated by illness, mercury toxicity and alcohol. Macdonald has described Schubert's 'volcanic temper' in musical terms and suggested the possible background of psychological disturbance or even mental instability.[95]

A major change in Schubert's life-style took place after he left home in 1816. Previously he had been religious with a deep faith in God; Franz Eckel, a fellow student at the Seminary, noted that Schubert involved himself 'in matters which concerned the divinity to which he dedicated his entire life, and whose darling he was'.[96] During his schoolmaster years he joined the Bildung Circle,[97] a group of young friends pledged to self-improvement by education, including Spaun, Mayrhofer and others who remained friends for life. Schober, a recognised hedonist, became the leader of the group in 1819, which then indulged in pleasure-seeking activities to an increasing extent. Schwind wrote to Schober in November 1824, 'Schubert is here, well and divinely frivolous'.[98] It was against this background that Schubert contracted syphilis, and, in view of his religious upbringing, felt the greater shame. In July 1825 he wrote to his parents, 'I justly deserve the reproach which you made me concerning my long illness.'[99]

Schubert's recurring depressive state, which formed an important contributory factor adding to his ill-health during the last half of his life, sprang from a variety of causes. It was in part endogenous, starting at a relatively young age, but was also reactive in response to his physical illness and other problems; mercury poisoning played a part as did the religious dilemma; finally the social and environmental problems of the times must have formed a background favouring depression, made worse by his poverty as he was constantly faced with money difficulties.

Social and environmental conditions

In 1797, eight years after the start of the French Revolution, Napoleon took over as General of the French Revolutionary Army. During the first years of Franz Schubert's life, Austrian storm-troops marched past his house with military music to face the enemy. However, Bonaparte concluded peace with Austria, for the time being, and three weeks later the troops marched back.[100] In 1805 when Schubert was eight years old, and again four years later, Vienna was occupied by French troops,[101] with all that was implied for the civilian population – terror, summary arrest and executions. Napoleon's defeat at Waterloo was followed by the Congress of Vienna in 1815 which altered the map of Europe for most of the next century, with most of the territory captured by France returned to Austria, and the Austro-Hungarian monarchy established under Emperor Francis (Table 11.2).[102]

Table 11.2   Historical Chronology

1789	Start of the French Revolution
1795	Napoleon made Commander of the French Army
1797	Franz Schubert born
1804	Napoleon proclaimed himself Emperor
1805	Vienna occupied by French troops
1809	Vienna again occupied by French troops Metternich appointed Foreign Minister of Austria
1815	Napoleon defeated at Waterloo Congress of Vienna
1818	Metternich created Prince and ruled Austria until the Revolution of 1848
1827	March 26. Death of Beethoven
1828	November 19. Death of Schubert

This settlement placed Austria under the dictatorial control of Metternich who, supported by his secret police and informers, terrorised the citizens of

Vienna, filling the prisons with those who resisted the régime. Such political repression must have served to 'crib and confine' all creative spirits.

There were student riots in Vienna and Johann Senn, a friend of Schubert's, was expelled from their school, the Stadtkonvikt, for attempting to free another friend from prison. In March 1820, Senn, who was becoming recognised for his lyric poetry, was arrested in his lodgings for insulting the authorities; some of his friends were present, including Schubert, who received a black eye in the scuffle. Senn was imprisoned for 14 months and then deported.[103]

The reaction of the people of Vienna against the war, violence and the police state was idealised as the Biedermeier era, a time of *Gemütlichkeit* (pleasant cheerfulness), enjoying the superficial pleasures of surburban life expressed in the poems of the fictitious Gottlieb Biedermeier.[104] Schubert separated himself from this sentimental picture of Old Vienna by the intellectual and emotional depth of his music and his Bohemian life-style.

Living and surviving in Vienna, as in any large town in Europe at that time, had its many and special hazards. General standards of hygiene and sanitation during Schubert's lifetime were poor. There was no piped running water – the first European town to introduce such a system was Munich in 1840, more than a decade after Schubert's death. The supply of drinking water depended on polluted supplies from the Danube, water carts whose contents were often septic and the occasional spring. Sanitation depended on the bucket, termed the commode in better-class homes such as the Schuberts', and disposal was wayward. Flush toilets and a sewerage system came later in the century.

In these circumstances the high incidence of bowel infections, often with fatal results, is unsurprising. There was no recognition that these conditions were due to micro-organisms and treatment merely addressed the symptoms. It was not until fifty years after Schubert's death that Louis Pasteur, working in Paris, discovered that human infections were caused by bacteria and so laid the foundations for their rational treatment.

Health was also endangered by pollution in the larger cities of Western Europe, with houses crowded together and narrow streets enveloped by noxious gases. The hazards of alcohol, smoking and drug abuse have, of course, existed for centuries, and evidence has already been given of their use by Schubert and his friends.

Health care showed marked deficiencies in the first half of the eighteenth century. To enter hospital was to risk one's life, as whole wards were wiped out by hospital fever. Nursing was carried out by untrained and unintelligent skivvies and little attention was paid to avoiding cross-infection. It was only in 1854 that Florence Nightingale turned nursing into a profession by her determined introduction of nurse training into the hospitals of the Crimea. It is a great tribute to Schubert's consummate musical powers that he was able to continue composing during his admissions to hospital.

Malnutrition was widespread in Schubert's day, with little understanding of the principles of good health and no knowledge of proteins or vitamins. Neonatal and infant mortality were distressingly high, with only one in three babies surviving to adulthood. Franz Schubert was the twelfth of fourteen children, only five of whom survived,[105] in spite of his father's professional position and the relative prosperity of his family.

Life-spans were generally too short at this time to allow the development of cancer and degenerative arterial conditions – the main killers today. The most frequent cause of death at the time Schubert lived was infection, in the total absence of specific curative agents such as antibiotics and chemotherapeutic compounds. Infections persisted for weeks or months accompanied by fever, dehydration, loss of weight and general malaise, either burning out of the system slowly or killing the subject. Infective conditions resulting from the ingestion of contaminated food or water included conditions now recognised as gastro-enteritis, dysentery, typhoid, typhus and salmonella, although doctors in Schubert's time were unable to distinguish between them. Tuberculosis demanded much of doctors' time in the early nineteenth century and was dreaded by the medical profession and their patients, as suggested by its synonyms: consumption and phthisis.[106] The infection was endemic world-wide, and its incidence high in Western Europe; in London, physicians estimated that 14% of deaths in 1840 were due to tuberculosis, in Paris 18% of the population died of the disease. The rising incidence of tuberculous infection in Vienna reached a peak of 800 cases per 100,000 of the population in 1840 – a significant but lesser incidence than in London and Paris;[107] in Schubert's lifetime, the population in Vienna was about 300,000, and tuberculosis accounted for 2,400 deaths per annum.

Of Schubert's seven siblings who died in infancy or childhood, the causes of death are uncertain, but the pattern of disease in Vienna suggests that tuberculosis was responsible in some cases. The cause of this feared disease was not discovered until Robert Koch, the German bacteriologist, identified the tubercle bacillus in 1882.

Difficulties in the means of communications were added hazards of the times, especially for musicians who were committed to travel widely to bring their music to the peoples of many cities. The only means of land travel, the horse-drawn coach, was both slow and dangerous, with road surfaces consisting mainly of mud, or cobbles in the towns. John MacAdam, the Scottish inventor, pioneered an improved road surface in 1815, with small stones set in concrete, but macadamisation did not arrive on the continent for many years. The first railway train, the 'Active', built by George Stevenson, made its maiden journey in 1825 on the Stockton–Darlington line. Franz Schubert did not benefit from either of these two advances in communication, but had to rely on stage-coach journeys with frequent hold-ups due to damaged, lost or mud-bound wheels, and nights spent in draughty wayside inns. Schubert paid two visits to Zseliz (1818 and 1824) which was 125 miles from Vienna; he had to obtain a passport and the journey by *Postwagen* (mail coach), which was broken halfway with a stop at the 'Brown Stag' at Pressburg for the night,[108] was done in fourteen stages,[109] a tedious and tiring trip in which compositions may have been conceived, but not easily written down.

The background factors discussed above must have added to the discomforts of his illnesses for Schubert and reduced the time available for producing his peerless music, perhaps explaining in part why much of it remained unfinished.

The last two years

Schubert moved out of the Rossau schoolhouse early in 1825 into pleasant accommodation on his own; he was described by Schwind as 'well and busy again after a certain stagnation'.[110] During the summer he toured northern Austria for nearly five months with Michael Vogl visiting friends, and this holiday evidently improved his health and stimulated his muse.[111] However, his health deteriorated again during 1826, due to further depression[112] and a recurrence of syphilis. He failed to obtain the position he wanted – Deputy *Kapellmeister*.[113] He remained penniless, as recorded in Bauernfeld's diary.[114]

During the last two years of his life, 1827–28, Schubert's health became significantly worse, both physically and psychologically. 1827 has been called his climacteric year,[115] with a marked contrast between his behaviour as a man and his supreme achievements as an artist. According to Schober's Memoirs, 'Schubert then let himself go to pieces; he frequented the city outskirts and roamed around in taverns, at the same time admittedly composing his most beautiful songs'.[116] The two sides of his nature became even more polarised – in Bauernfeld's words, 'the pleasure-loving Schubert' and 'the black-winged demon of sorrow and melancholy'.[117]

Certain symptoms appeared more regularly in his letters and those of his friends. Josef Blahetka refers to Schubert's 'frequent pains in his head' in his obituary,[118] and Frost mentions his bodily weakness, headaches and giddiness during his last few months of life.[119] In a letter dated 12 October 1827, Schubert refers to 'my usual headaches assailing me again'.[120] On 1 September 1828, he moved to his brother Ferdinand's house in the Wieden suburb of Vienna on the advice of his doctor Ernst Rinna for health reasons, and because he was ailing and suffering from 'effusions of blood and giddiness'.[121] These symptoms strongly suggest that he had reached the tertiary stage of syphilis and was suffering from the early features of neurosyphilis.

Tertiary syphilis causes local lesions that ulcerate (gummata) in any organ or a diffuse type of chronic inflammation in any tissue resulting from closure of small arteries; the brain can be affected by the latter changes – neurovascular syphilis.[122] A latent period between the secondary and tertiary stages of the disease is common, and the time scale of the onset of tertiary syphilis in Schubert's case is appropriate (Table 11.1). The Oslo Study reported on the clinical course of a cohort of untreated patients with syphilis from 1910 to 1951 (as this was many years before penicillin was in general use); results showed that 33% of patients develop the tertiary stage of the disease, 15% die of it and mercury treatment does nothing to alter the course of the condition.[123]

Deterioration of Schubert's physical health during the two years before his death was accompanied by accentuation of his depressive state and unstable moods. The medical background of two of Schubert's major compositions during this period is of particular interest. The genesis of his 'Great' C major Symphony, D944, deserves mention in the context of his mental balance. Begun in 1825, it was ready to be put into rehearsal by the middle of 1827. When tried out by the Vienna Philharmonic Society Orchestra it was found to be too 'schwulstig' (over-inflated) and was put on one side as too lengthy and difficult to play.[124] It lay in the dust in his brother Ferdinand's house for ten years before it was discovered there by Schumann who persuaded Mendelssohn to conduct its first performance in Leipzig in 1839. Schubert had contributed so much effort and genius to the composition of the symphony that its rejection must have caused him further disillusion and depression at a time when his long-term survival was becoming endangered by ill-health. However, Schubert dedicated the work to the Philharmonic Society, received an award (not a fee!) of 100 florins[125] and was subsequently elected a member.[126]

1827 was also the year of the song cycle *Winterreise*, the story of the unlucky lover leaving the house of his fickle beloved, betrayed and broken-hearted. His closest friends were shocked by the 'sustained pessimism' of the cycle,[127] and Spaun wrote that, when Vogl performed the whole cycle, 'the entire company was moved to the very depths of its being by it'.[128] The work probably gave a true insight into its composer's state of mind at the time. A strong contrast is formed by the great instrumental music composed later that year, such as the two sets of Impromptus, D899 and D935, and the E flat Piano Trio, D929. Perhaps this demonstrated Schubert's fortitude in the face of his depression.

Beethoven died on 26 March 1827 and Schubert was one of the torch bearers at his funeral three days later.[129] After the ceremony Schubert and two friends, Lachner and Randhartinger, went to the Mehlgrube Inn,[130] and Schubert proposed two toasts – one to the memory of Beethoven, and the other to the first of the three friends to follow him into the grave. This has been interpreted by many commentators, Grove[131] and Hutchings[132] among them, as indicating a premonition of his coming death on the part of Schubert, but this interpretation seems unduly fatalistic.

The last year of Schubert's life was marked by continuing poor health, physical frailty, repeated headaches, attacks of giddiness and sickness, and recurring depressive episodes. Gastritis was an additional symptom appearing at this stage in his life.[133] Despite these hurdles, 1828 was marked by a frenzy of composing – his speed in composition had always been extraordinary.[134] 'His last twenty months alone were marked by an output comparable with the rich outpourings of Mozart's Vienna period ... as though the still young composer somehow knew that time was running out'.[135]

The piano was his favourite instrument, for Schubert was a pianist all his life,[136] and yet there is no record of his buying or owning a piano. Many of his compositions were created away from the keyboard. In his 'Notes on Franz

Schubert', Spaun describes the manner in which Schubert produced *Erlkönig*: after reading Goethe's poem aloud, Schubert 'suddenly sat down and in no time at all (just as quickly as one can write) there was the glorious Ballad finished on the paper'.[137] The composer's 'endless flow of music' and 'cascade of ideas'[138] continued until a few days before he died, although previously he had told Anschütz, 'Sometimes it seems to me as though I no longer belong to the world'.[139]

In view of the sense of urgency he must have felt as his health continued to decline, the beauty presented by the 'heavenly length' of his music (a term applied by Schumann[140]) can only be regarded as amazing. This feverish rate of production accelerated during the last few months of his life with the appearance of the E flat Mass, the last three piano sonatas, D958, D959 & D960, and many other pieces.

Through the summer of 1828 Schubert was under the care of Dr von Rinna, the eminent Court physician, who must have provided a very costly service for Franz's already strained pocket. He advised Schubert to move out of central Vienna with its polluted atmosphere, and he went to stay with his brother Ferdinand in the rural suburb of Wieden on 1 September, and was noted to be 'ailing, with effusions of blood (probably congestion of the head and chest) and giddiness'.[141] Unfortunately this move proved unwise as the district was near the river, wet and misty, with undeveloped sanitary arrangements. As a result Schubert's health deteriorated even further.

Schubert's final illness

Schubert had planned a holiday in Graz in October, 1828, but cancelled this ostensibly 'as money and weather are wholly unfavourable',[142] but perhaps also on account of the state of his health. Money was as usual short, and on 2 October he appealed to Probst, the music publisher, for payment of works he had given him and others promised.[143] Schubert was impecunious for most of his life, and this problem was noted by Spaun as follows: 'He [Schubert] was receiving payment for his works, even though this was miserable in comparison with their value.'[144]

Early in October Schubert undertook a three-day walk with his brother Ferdinand and two friends, on the advice of von Rinna, who believed in fresh air and exercise for his patients. The four walkers paid a visit to Haydn's grave at Eisenstadt and during the three days covered a distance of about 40 miles.[145] According to Bauernfeld in his obituary notice, during this journey Schubert 'was very bright withal and had many merry notions'.[146] How much of this was bravado will never be known.

On 31 October Franz and Ferdinand with some friends had a meal at Zum Roten Kreuz Inn in the Himmelpfortgrund, the Schubert family's regular tavern.[147] Franz wished to eat some fish but after the first mouthful, threw down his knife and fork, finding 'this food immensely repellent and felt just as if he had taken poison'.[148] From that moment he hardly ate or drank anything more and remained seriously ill. On 12 November he wrote to Schober, 'I am ill. I have eaten nothing for eleven days and drunk nothing. I totter feebly and shakily from my chair to bed and back again. If ever I take anything, I bring it up again at once.'[149] At this point von Rinna himself became ill and handed the case over to Dr von Vering, the leading venereologist in Vienna, who told his nephew, Gerhard von Breuning, that he had no hope of being able to save Schubert.[150]

On 14 November 1828 Franz Schubert took to his bed permanently; on 17 November he lapsed into coma, and died on 19 November. On his death bed he was correcting the proofs of the second part of *Winterreise*. His death certificate bore the term 'Nervenfieber',[151] a non-specific diagnosis denoting a feverish illness affecting the brain, and perhaps favouring the possibility of tertiary syphilis affecting the higher nervous centres. The death was officially registered in the City of Vienna as due to typhus.[152] In this century typhus has become recognised as a specific and serious infection due to a micro-organism termed a rickettsia, but in the nineteenth century, before the organism had been identified, typhus meant merely an acute febrile illness with clouding of the mind.[153]

The actual cause of Schubert's death has been the subject of many medical studies. There is general agreement that his illness dating from 1823 was syphilis, but there is no good reason to blame this condition on its own for his death.[154] It is evident that Schubert's death was the result of an acute infection affecting the abdomen and he described his final symptoms (above) as weakness (due to dehydration and starvation), fever and vomiting. There is no mention of abdominal pain and diarrhoea which he was unlikely to include in a letter to a friend, but which were probable additional symptoms. This clinical picture is typical of typhoid fever, a severe intestinal infection due to the typhoid bacillus, as a result of eating the contaminated fish, and quite distinct from typhus.

The remaining point of medical interest is a possible connection between syphilis and typhoid fever in Schubert's case. Syphilis has been a rare condition in Europe during the last fifty years as a result of modern diagnosis, the advent of penicillin and advances in venereology. Study of journals and textbooks of previous generations shows that syphilis does produce damage of the immune system, particularly in the secondary stage, and render patients more liable to succumb from infection, as with AIDS[155] today. Chronic infections in general are recognised as reducing immunity[156] but syphilis exerts an additional specific effect. The immune defences of the body comprise two main components – white cells in the blood (lymphocytes) which are carried to infected tissues and destroy micro-organisms, and special proteins (immunoglobulins) circulating in the blood and transporting antibodies. Laboratory tests have shown that syphilis reduces the number of lymphocytes in lymph nodes, thus weakening the cell-mediated immune response.[157] The effect of mercury would be highly toxic to immunoglobulins and also damage the production of lymphocytes in the spleen and bone marrow. Schubert's death was probably due to typhoid fever against a background of immunodeficiency induced by syphilis and mercury.[158] If he had not contracted syphilis and needed mercury, he would have stood a better chance of recovering from typhoid.

To add to his problems, Schubert lived and died beset by money worries, and financial instability must have been another threat to his peace of mind. He left debts totalling 1000 gulden or florins (10 florins were equivalent to one pound), and his total effects were assessed at 63 gulden.[159] Banking opinion today equates £100 in 1828 with £10,000 today.[160] However Schubert's debts were all discharged within a year of his death by posthumous publication fees, with the help of his friends.[161]

Six weeks after his death, Schubert's last completed piece was found among his papers – the profound String Quintet in C, D956; Thomas Mann, the German novelist and Nobel Prize winner for literature in 1929, said of the Quintet, 'It is music one would like to listen to on one's deathbed'.[162] Was Schubert foretelling his own death when he wrote it? The inscription by Grillparzer on his tombstone read, 'The art of music here entombed a rich possession but even fairer hopes', perhaps underestimating his genius but reflecting the shock of his friends at the sudden prematurity of his death.[163] Much of his greatest work remained unpublished, unknown and undiscovered for many decades.

Schubert was buried in the Wahring Cemetery in Vienna,[164] but was exhumed twice – in 1863 and again in 1887[165] when he was reburied in the Musicians' Grove of Honour in the Vienna Cemetery,[166] where his tomb is adjacent to the musician he honoured above all others, Ludwig van Beethoven. At both exhumations of his body, the pattern of decay of his bones confirmed changes characteristic of syphilis.[167]

When Hiller visited him the year before he died, Schubert told him, 'I write for several hours every morning; when one piece is finished, I start another'.[168] He was a prolific composer of beautiful music which lives on after him for all time. Schubert told a friend, 'I have come into this world for no purpose but to compose.'[169] A medical study of his life leaves us with the question, did his disadvantages and ill-health influence his compositions, or did he triumph in adversity and overcome them?

References

DOCUMENT refers to – *Schubert – A Documentary Biography*, (1946), ed. O.E. Deutsch, trans E. Blom. J.M. Dent & Sons, London.

MEMOIRS refers to – *Schubert – Memoirs by his Friends* (1958), ed. O.E. Deutsch, trans R. Ley & J. Nowell. A. & C. Black, London

Bevan, P.G. (1996), 'Schubert and syphilis', *Journal of Medical Biography*, vol. 4, no. 3.

Biba, O. & Matthews, D. (1989), 'The Age of Beethoven and Schubert', in the *Heritage of Music. The Romantic Era*, vol. 16, ed. M. Raeburn & A. Kendall. Oxford University Press, New York.

Biba, O. & Newbould, B. (1989), 'Franz Schubert', in *Heritage of Music, The Romantic Era*, ed. M. Raeburn & A. Kendall. Oxford University Press, New York.
Blumenthal, I. (1992), 'Should we ban the mercury thermometer?' *Journal of the Royal Society of Medicine*, vol. 85, Iss 9.
Capell, R. (1966), *Schubert's Songs*, Gerald Duckworth & Co, London.
Conybeare, J.J. (1943), *Textbook of Medicine*, 6th edn, 67, 120, E. & S. Livingstone, Edinburgh.
Dale, Kathleen (1946), 'The Piano Music', in *Schubert, A Symposium*, ed. Gerald Abraham, Lindsay Drummond, London.
Deutsch, O.E. (1946), 'Schubert The Man', *Schubert, A Symposium*, ed. Gerald Abraham. Lindsay Drummond, London.
Duncan, E. (1934), *Schubert*. J.M. Dent & Sons, London.
Frost, H.F. (1892), *Schubert*, in the Great Musicians Series, ed. F. Hueffer, 4th edn, Sampson Low, Marston & Co, London.
Gell, P.G.H., Coombs, R.R.A. and Lackman, P.J. (1975), *Clinical Aspects of Immunology*, 3rd edn, Blackwell Scientific Publications, Oxford.
Greenberg, J. (1996), 'Beethoven's mercury link', *BBC Music Magazine*, vol. 5, no. 3, p. 160.
Grove's Dictionary of Music & Musicians (1940), 4th edn, ed. H.C. Colles, Macmillan & Co, London.
The New Grove Dictionary of Music & Musicians (1980), vol. 16, ed. S. Sadie, Macmillan Publishers, London.
Guthrie, D. (1945), *A History of Medicine*, Thomas Nelson & Sons, London.
Harrison, S. (1947), *Music for the Multitude*, Michael Joseph, London.
Hudson, M.M. and Morton, R.S. (1996), 'Fracastoro and Syphilis: 500 years on', *Lancet*, vol. 348.
Hunter, J. (1818), *A Treatise on the Venereal Disease*, 2nd edn, Sherwood Neely & Jones, London.
Hutchings, A. (1967), *Schubert* in the Master Musicians Series, ed. J. Westrup, J.M. Dent & Sons, London.
Kiemle, H.D. (1996), 'What was the real cause of Schubert's death?', trans. D. Grey, *Brille*, 16/17.
Larkin, E. (1985), 'Beethoven's Medical History', p. 450, in *Beethoven – The Last Decade*, M. Cooper, Oxford University Press, New York.
Locksley, R.M. and Wilson, C.B. (1995), 'Cell mediated immunity and its role in host defence', *Principles and Practice of Infectious Diseases*, G.L. Mandell, J.E. Bennett and R. Dolin, Churchill Livingstone, New York.
McKay, E.N. (1996), *Franz Schubert – A Biography*, Clarendon Press, Oxford.
O'Brien, E. (1995), 'Will mercury manometers soon be obsolete?' *Journal of Human Hypertension*, vol. 9.
O'Shea, J. (1990), *Music and Medicine*, J.M. Dent & Sons, London.
Palferman, T.G. (1993), 'Beethoven: a Medical Biography', *Journal of Medical Biography*, vol. 1, no. 1, p. 41.

Pritchard, T.S.L. (1946), 'The Schubert Idiom', in *Schubert, A Symposium*, ed. G. Abraham, Lindsay Drummond, London.
Reed, J. (1987), *Schubert*, Master Musicians Series, J.M. Dent & Sons, London.
Rold, R.L. (1995), 'Schubert and syphilis', *Journal of Medical Biography*, vol. 3, no. 4.
Sams, E. (1980), 'Schubert's Illnesses Re-examined', *Musical Times*, vol. 121, no. 1643.
Schiff, A. (1997), *Omnibus*, BBC, Jan 22.
Storr, A. (1992), *Music and the Mind*, Harper Collins, London.
Wechsberg, J. (1977), *Schubert – His Life, Work and Times*, Butler & Tanner, London.

Notes

1. O E Deutsch (1946), p. 12.
2. E Duncan (1934), p. 71
3. *sthenos* = strength (Greek)
4. 6th Edition.
5. O E Deutsch (1946), p. 9.
6. Memoirs, p. 126.
7. Ibid, p. 212.
8. cyclothymic = *kyklos* (circle) + *thymos* (spirit) (Greek).
9. E N McKay (1996), p. 319.
10. Document, p. 270.
11. Memoirs.
12. E Sams (1980), p. 15.
13. O E Deutsch (1907), p. 227.
14. J O'Shea (1990), p. 187.
15. M M Hudson & R S Morton (1996), p. 1495.
16. Ibid, p. 1496.
17. D Guthrie (1945), p. 242.
18. J Hunter (1818), pp 331–3.
19. J J Conybeare (1943), pp 151–4.
20. Document, p. 288.
21. Ibid, p. 279.
22. Ibid, p. 6.
23. Ibid, p. 6.
24. D Guthrie (1946), p. 248.
25. J Reed (1987), p. 109.
26. Document, p. 286.
27. E Sams (1980), p. 15.
28. Ibid, p. 21.
29. Document, p. 314.
30. Ibid, p. 295.
31. J Reed (1987), p. 110.
32. Document, p. 342.
33. Ibid, p. 339.
34. E Sams (1980), p. 17.
35. J Reed (1987), p. 133.

36. Memoirs, p. 51.
37. Document, p. 342.
38. Ibid, p. 343.
39. Ibid, p. 502.
40. J Reed (1987), p. 134.
41. Memoirs, p. 357.
42. O E Deutsch (1946), p. 13.
43. J Reed (1987), p. 273.
44. Document, p. 162.
45. Memoirs, p. 327.
46. Document, p. 231.
47. Ibid, p. 195.
48. Ibid, p. 428.
49. Ibid, p. 230.
50. Memoirs, p. 261.
51. O E Deutsch (1946), p. 15.
52. E N McKay (1996), p. 159.
53. J Reed (1987), p. 20
54. For further details, see Chapter 10, pp 231–2 (Ed.).
55. O Biba & B Newbould (1989), p. 82.
56. Memoirs, p. 134.
57. Ibid, p. 100.
58. BBC (1997).
59. Memoirs, p. 104.
60. Document, p. 121.
61. H D Kiemle (1996), p. 10.
62. Document, p. 246.
63. Ibid, p. 247.
64. E Sams (1980), p. 17.
65. E N McKay (1996), p. 322.
66. E Larkin (1985), p. 450.
67. T G Palferman (1993), p. 41.
68. S J Greenburg (1996), p. 160.
69. J J Conybeare (1942), p. 251.
70. H D Kiemle (1996), pp 10–12.
71. I Blumenthal (1992), pp 553–5.
72. E O'Brien (1995), pp 933–4.
73. Caused by medical treatment – *iatros* = physician (Greek).
74. J O'Shea (1990), pp 11–12.
75. Memoirs, pp 137–8.
76. Document, p. 71.
77. Memoirs, p. 70.
78. Ibid, p. 208.
79. Ibid, p. 14.
80. Document, p. 61.
81. Ibid, p. 53.
82. E N McKay (1996), pp 74–6.
83. R Capell (1966), pp 108–9.
84. Document, p. 99.
85. Memoirs, p. 13.
86. S Harrison (1947), pp 180–1.
87. Memoirs, p. 108.
88. E N McKay (1996), pp 174–7.

89. Document, p. 375.
90. J Reed (1987), p. 119.
91. Memoirs, p. 100.
92. Ibid, pp 101–2.
93. Ibid, p. 261.
94. A Storr (1992), pp 97–8.
95. H Macdonald (1978), pp 949–52.
96. Memoirs, p. 50.
97. E N McKay (1996), pp 45–6.
98. Document, p. 383.
99. Ibid, p. 434.
100. Document, pp xxii–xxiii.
101. J Wechsberg (1977), pp 25–6.
102. Document, pp xxii–xxiii.
103. Document, pp 128–30.
104. J Wechsberg (1977), p. 28.
105. Memoirs, p. 34.
106. *phthisis* = to waste away (Greek).
107. J O'Shea (1990), pp 89–90.
108. E N McKay (1997), p. 79.
109. Document, p. 92.
110. Ibid, p. 401.
111. Ibid, pp 434–7.
112. Ibid, pp 528–9.
113. Ibid, p. 521.
114. Ibid, p. 548.
115. J Reed (1987), p. 164.
116. Memoirs, p. 266.
117. Ibid, p. 234.
118. Ibid, p. 10.
119. H F Frost (1892), p. 97.
120. Document, p. 679.
121. Ibid, p. 803.
122. J J Conybeare (1943), pp 154–7.
123. J O'Shea (1990), pp 6 and 12.
124. Memoirs, p. 431.
125. Document, pp 559–60.
126. Memoirs, p. 457.
127. J Reed (1987), p. 164.
128. Memoirs, p. 364.
129. Document, p. 624.
130. Ibid, p. 623.
131. 4th edn, p. 611.
132. A Hutchings (1967), p. 75.
133. J Reed (1987), p. 193.
134. Memoirs, p. 21.
135. O Biba and D Matthews (1989), p. 13.
136. Kathleen Dale (1946), p. 111.
137. Memoirs, p. 131.
138. T S L Pritchard (1946), p. 238.
139. Memoirs, p. 224.
140. O Biba and D Matthews (1989), p. 12.
141. Document, p. 803.

142. Ibid, p. 807.
143. Ibid, pp 810–11.
144. Memoirs, p. 136.
145. Document, p. 811.
146. Memoirs, p. 37.
147. Document, p. 818.
148. Memoirs, p. 37.
149. Document, pp 819–20.
150. Memoirs, p. 256.
151. Document, p. 823.
152. Document, p. 24.
153. E Larkin (1985), p. 442.
154. R L Rold (1993), pp 232–5.
155. Acquired Immune Deficiency Syndrome.
156. R M Locksley and C B Wilson (1995), pp 137–8.
157. P G H Gell et al (1975), p. 812.
158. P G Bevan (1996), p. 184.
159. Grove, 6th edn, p. 771.
160. Personal communication.
161. Document, pp 898–9.
162. J Reed (1987), p. 205.
163. Document, p. 899 and Memoirs, p. 143.
164. Memoirs, p. 369.
165. Document, p. 926.
166. E N McKay (1996), p. 338.
167. J O'Shea (1990), p. 116.
168. Memoirs, p. 283.
169. Ibid, p. 77.

Index of works by Schubert referred to in the text

Orchestral and Instrumental (including stage works)

Adagio and Rondo Concertante for piano quartet, D487   63
Alfonso und Estrella, D732   3–14, 67
   Overure   157
Allegro in A minor for piano duet ('Lebensstürme'), D947   28
Arpeggione Sonata, D821   69, 84–91 (incl. Exx. 3.6, 3.7, 3.8, 3.9, 3.10, 3.11, 3.12), 109, 110

Claudine von Villa Bella, D239   12
Concerto in D major for violin and orchestra, D345   110n

Der Graf von Gleichen, D918   91
Die Freunde von Salamanka, D326   12, 111n
Die Zauberharfe, D644   65, 181, 190n, 210, 236
Divertissement à l'hongroise for piano duet, D818   157, 231

Écossaises (various)   86

Fantasy in C major for piano, D760 ('Wanderer')   50, 156, 181, 191, 192, 193, 197, 207, 250
Fantasy in C major for violin and piano, D934   63, 65, 68, 69, 101–8 (incl. Exx. 3.21, 3.22, 3.23), 109, 111n, 238
Fantasy in F minor for piano duet, D940   133, 156, 161, 222, 237, 238, 239n

Fierabras, D796   xi, 12, 67, 233
   Overture   157

Grand Duo for piano duet, D812   885, 91, 157, 207

Impromptus for piano, D899   143, 167, 168 (Ex. 7.1b), 190n, 191, 258
Impromptus for piano, D935   101, 156, 191, 197, 201 (incl. Ex. 8.14), 258
Introduction and Variations on 'Trockne Blumen' for flute and piano, D802   69

Lazarus, D689   161
'Lebensstürme' – see Allegro in A minor

Moments musicaux, D780   86, 121, 156, 191

Notturno in G major (arr. of Matiegka)   225

Octet for wind and strings, D803   65, 69, 91, 157, 161
Overture in the Italian Style in D major, D590   51–2
   arr. for piano duet, D592   233
Overture in the Italian Style in C major, D.591   51–2
   arr. for piano duet, D597   233
Overture in E minor, D648   66

Piano Sonata in E major, D157   45
Piano Sonata in E major, D459   73

268　*Index of Works*

Piano Sonata in A minor, D537　12, 55, 81, 192, 197, 205–6 (incl. Ex. 8.22)
Piano Sonata in A flat major, D557　45, 81
Piano Sonata in E minor, D566　81, 199 (incl. Ex. 8.12)
Piano Sonata in E flat major (D flat major), D567(568)　45, 52, 61n, 81, 192, 199 (incl. Ex. 8.11)
Piano Sonata in F sharp minor, D571 (fragment)　52, 81, 191, 192
Piano Sonata in B major, D575　51, 81, 188n, 192, 199–200 (incl. Exx. 8.13a, 8.13b)
Piano Sonata in C major, D613 (fragment)　55–6 (incl. Exx. 2.18a, 2.18b)
Piano Sonata in F minor, D625/505 (fragment)　191–2
Piano Sonata in A major, D664　49–50 (incl. Exx. 2.16a, 2.16b), 58, 192, 197 (incl. Exx. 8.6, 8.8)
Piano Sonata in E minor, D769 (fragment)　52, 55
Piano Sonata in A minor, D784　50, 56, 207
Piano Sonata in C major, D840 ('Reliquie')(fragment)　55–6, 57–8 (Ex.2.19), 121, 191, 198 (incl. Ex. 8.9), 207
Piano Sonata in A minor, D845　73, 98, 189n
Piano Sonata in D major, D850　94, 98, 181, 188n, 189n, 192, 206 (incl. Ex. 8.23), 207
Piano Sonata in G major, D.894　94–5 (incl. Ex. 3.15b), 98, 121, 156, 193 (incl. Ex. 8.1a), 203
Piano Sonata in C minor, D958　166, 169–179 (incl. Exx. 7.3, 7.4, 7.5, 7.6, 7.7), 184, 187, 188, 196 (incl. Exx. 8.4, 8.5), 205 (incl. Exx. 8.19, 8.20), 207, 259
Piano Sonata in A major, D959　166, 179–186 (incl. Exx. 7.8a, 7.8b, 7.8c, 7.9), 187, 192, 197, 202–3 (incl. Exx. 8.17a, 8.17b), 205 (incl. Ex. 8.21), 207, 259
Piano Sonata in B flat major, D960　21, 23 (Ex. 2.5), 56, 121, 187, 188, 191, 192, 194, 198–6 (incl. Exx. 8.2, 8.3), 197, 201–2 (incl. Ex. 8.16), 204 (incl. Ex. 8.18), 207, 259

Piano Trio in B flat major, D898　16, 20–1 (Ex. 2.3), 56, 59n, 68, 157, 164n, 201 (incl. Ex. 8.15)
Piano Trio in E flat major, D929　59n, 64, 65, 68, 101, 108, 157, 158, 160 (Ex. 6.2), 164n, 204, 238, 258

Quartettsatz in C minor, D703　21, 22 (Ex. 2.4), 46, 48–9, 56, 84
Quintet in A major for piano and strings, D667 ('Trout')　52, 54 (Ex. 2.17b), 69, 83–4, 102

Rondo in A major for piano duet, D951　141
Rondo in A major for violin and string orchestra, D.438　63, 72
Rondo in B minor for violin and piano, D895 ('Rondeau brillant')　63, 68, 69, 91–101 (incl. Exx. 3.13a, 3.15a, 3.16, 3.17a, 3.17b, 3.18, 3.19, 3.20), 109, 155
Rosamunde, (D797)　3, 157, 220, 230, 248

Six Grandes Marches for piano duet, D819　156
Sonata in D major for violin and piano, D384　45, 61n, 62, 69, 72–8 (incl. Exx. 3.1a, 3.1b, 3.1c, 3.1d, 3.1e), 80, 84
Sonata in A minor for violin and piano, D385　45, 62, 69, 72–3, 78–80 (incl. Exx. 3.3, 3.4)
Sonata in G minor for violin and piano, D408　45, 62, 69, 72–3, 80
Sonata (Duo) in A major for violin and piano, D574　62, 80–4, 85, 86, 109
String Quartet in mixed keys, D.18　29, 30 (Ex. 2.7a), 31 (Ex. 2.7b)
String Quartet in C major, D32　30
String Quartet in B flat major, D36　30
String Quartet in C major, D46　30–1, 33, 35 (Ex. 2.10a), 36 (Ex. 2.10b)
String Quartet in D major, D74　33, 36 (Exx. 2.11a, 2.11b), 37 (Ex. 2.12a), 38 (Ex. 2.12b), 41
String Quartet in E flat major, D87　41–5
String Quartet in D major, D94　29–30, 31 (Ex. 2.8), 32–3 (Ex. 2.9a), 33, 34–5 (Ex.2.9b)
String Quartet in B flat major, D112　33–7, 39–41 (Ex. 2.13), 45, 69–70

Index of Works 269

String Quartet in G minor, D173   45, 46, 47–8 (Exx. 2.15a, 2.15b), 48, 58, 69, 70
String Quartet in E major, D353   51, 70–2
String Quartet in A minor, D804   65, 84, 91, 141, 153, 155, 157, 197
String Quartet in D minor, D810 ('Death and the Maiden')   59n, 64, 84, 91, 153, 157, 160, 197
String Quartet in G major, D887   16, 19 (Ex. 2.2), 56–7, 59n, 65, 68, 91, 92, 93, 94 (Exx. 3.13b, 3.14a, 3.14b), 133
String Quintet in C major, D956   xi, 16, 17–8 (Ex. 2.1), 46, 55, 56, 58–9, 68, 153, 157, 158, 238, 261
String Trio in B flat major, D581   45
Symphony in D major, D2B (fragment)   130
Symphony No. 1 in D major, D82   38, 43–4 (Ex. 2.14b), 45, 130
Symphony No. 2 in B flat major, D125   46, 69, 130
Symphony No. 3 in D major, D200   46, 130, 136
Symphony No. 4 in C minor, D417 ('Tragic')   52, 72, 130
Symphony No. 5 in B flat major, D485   129, 130, 132
Symphony No. 6 in C major, D589   51–2, 53 (Ex. 2.17a), 67, 68, 130, 140, 141, 189n
Symphony in D major, D615 (fragment)   130
Symphony in D major, D708A (fragment)   130
Symphony No. 7 in E, D729 (sketch)   127, 130, 132, Plate 2, 133, 135, 141, 142, 145, 150, 190n
Symphony No. 8 in B minor, D759 ('Unfinished')   xi, 22, 24–7 (Ex. 2.6), 56, 118, 129, 130, 132, 133, 157, 164n, 192, 221, 250
Symphony No. 9 in C major, D944 ('Great')   xi, 22, 46, 68, 70, 127–150 (incl. Exx. 5.1, 5.2a, 5.2b, 5.3, 5.4, 5.5a, 5.5b, 5.6a, 5.6b, 5.7, 5.8, 5.9a, 5.9b, 5.10, 5.11, 5.12, 5.13, 5.14, 5.15, 5.16, 5.17, 5.18, 5.19, 5.21, 5.22, 5.23, 5.24, 5.25, 5.26, 5.27, Plate 1, Plate 3, 157, 158. 161, 166–7, 168 (Exx. 7.1a, 7.2), 169, 189, 189n, 258

Symphony No. 10 in D major, D936A   68, 130, 148–9

'Trout' Quintet – see Quintet in A major for piano and strings, D667

Variations in A flat major on an original theme, for piano duet, D813   85, 91
Variations on a theme of Anselm Hüttenbrenner, for piano, D.576   81
Variations in E minor for flute and piano on 'Trockne Blumen', D802   102

'Wanderer' Fantasy – see Fantasy in C major, D760

Church Music

Deutsche Messe, D872   3

Hymnus an den heiligen Geist, D948   67

Mass in F major, D105   249
Mass in A flat major, D678 xi
Mass in E flat major, D950   xi, 157, 164n, 238, 259

Salve Regina in C major, D811   84
Stabat Mater in F major, D383   72

Solo songs and partsongs

Songs (general)   2, 64, 66, 91, 161, 208, 212

Amalia, D195   64
Am ersten Maimorgen, D344   229
Am Meer, from *Schwanengesang*, D957   112–126 (incl. Exx. 4.1, 4.2a, 4.2b, 4.5), 156, 207
An die Musik, D547   118–120 (incl. Exx. 4.3, 4.4a, 4.4b, 4.4c, 4.4d)
Aufenthalt, from *Schwanengesang*, D957   156

Das Dorfchen, D958   66, 233
Das Fischermädchen, from *Schwanengesang*, D.957   120
Das Wirtshaus, from *Winterreise*, D911   121

Der Atlas, from *Schwanengesang*, D957 207
Der blinde Knabe, D833   156
Der Doppelganger, from *Schwanengesang*, D957 153
Der Einsame, D800   248
Der Herbstabend, D405   111n
Der Hirt auf dem Felsen, D956   156
Der Leidende, D432   230
Der Leiermann, from *Winterreise*, D911 153
Der Lindenbaum, from *Winterreise*, D911 156
Der Müller und der Bach, from *Die schöne Müllerin*, D795   156
Der Musensohn, D764   61n
Der Neugierige, from *Die schöne Müllerin*, D795   156, 158
Der Pilgrim, D794   156
Der Post, from *Winterreise*, D911   156, 158
Der Taucher, D77   207
Der Tod und das Mädchen, D531   59n, 197
Der Wanderer, D489   156, 214
Des Baches Wiegenlied, from *Die schöne Müllerin*, D795   121
Die böse Farbe, from *Die schöne Müllerin*, D795   156
Die Bürgschaft, D246   207
Die Forelle, D550   156
Die Gesellgkeit, D609   210
Die junge Nonne, D828   156
Die Nachtigall, D724   210
Die schöne Müllerin, D795   116, 118, 158, 161, 207, 221, 226, 239n, 247
Die Stadt, from *Schwanengesang*, D957 120
Drang in die Ferne, D770   2

Erlkönig, D328   67, 153, 156, 193, 207, 211, 221, 252, 259

Gesang der Geister über den Wasser, D484 67
Gott der Wettschöpfer, D986   157
Gott im Ungewitter, D985   157
Gretchen am Spinnrade, D118   156, 158, 214

Hymne an den Unendlichen, D232   157

Im Frühling, D882   86, 116

Klage, D.Anh.I.28   229, 230

Liebesbotschaft, from *Schwanengesang*, D957   156

Mailied, D503   229
Morgengruss, from *Die schöne Müllerin*, D795   116

Nachtgesang im Walde, D913   157

Rastlose Liebe, D138   64

Schwanengesang, D957   112, 153, 212
Sei mir gegrüsst, D741   102, 104–5, 238
So lasst mich scheinen, D877/3   121
Ständchen, D889   158
Ständchen, D920   157

Trockne Blumen, from *Die schöne Müllerin*, D795   158

Ungeduld, from *Die schöne Müllerin*, D795   156, 138, 225

Wandrers Nachtlied, D224 and D768 197
Winterreise, D911   153, 187, 212, 258, 260

General Index

Abbado, Claudio   129, 149, 151n
Abendunterhaltungen   66, 210
Abraham, Gerald   154, 155, 163, 164n, 165n, 262n, 263n
Ahlgrimm, Isolde   242n
Akademien   67, 68
Amalia, Duchess of Saxony   216
Anderson, Emily   211, 219n
Angermüller, Rudolph   219n
Anschütz, Eduard   232, 233, 235, 236
   Gustav   232, 233, 235
   Heinrich   64, 216, 232, 259
Arnim, Bettina von   216
Artaria, Domenico   93

Bach, Johann Sebastian   110n, 155
   Brandenburg Concerto No.5   198–9 (incl. Ex.8.10)
Bacon, Francis   244
Badura-Skoda, Eva   59n, 151n
Barth, Josef   64
Bartos, Frantisek   164n
Bartsch, Hans Rudolf
   Schwammerl   225, 240n
Bauernfeld, Eduard von   91, 223, 224, 226, 227, 231, 237, 238, 240n, 248, 249, 257, 259
Beach, David   61n
Bean, Hugh   167
Becker, Jean   155
Beethoven, Karl   247
Beethoven, Ludwig van   2, 4, 10, 12, 13, 14n, 15n, 37, 64, 66, 67, 73, 74, 80, 83, 93, 140, 141, 153, 154, 155, 189n, 191, 192, 194, 207, 258, 261
   Bagatelle, Op.126, No.4   122
   Cello Sonata in G minor, Op.5   66

Missa Solemnis   211
Overture, *Die Weihe des Hauses*   110n
Piano Concerto No.4 in G major   193 (incl. Ex.8.1b)
Piano Sonata in E major, Op.14, No.1   78 (incl. Ex.3.3)
Piano Sonata in F minor, Op.57 ('Appassionata')   197
Piano Sonata in E minor, Op.90   52
Piano Sonata in C minor, Op.111   237
Piano Trio in B flat, Op.97 ('Archduke')   105, 108
Quintet for piano and wind, Op.16   158
Septet, Op.20   2, 66, 158
String Quartets   2, 92
String Quartet in E minor, Op.59, No.2   140
String Quartet in E flat major, Op.127   92
String Quartet in B flat major, Op.130   102
String Quartet in C sharp minor, Op.131   93
String Quartet in A minor, Op.132   93, 123
String Quartet in F major, Op.135   93
Symphony No.1 in C major, Op.21   2
Symphony No.2 in D major, Op.36   2, 136
Symphony No.3 in E flat major, Op.55 ('Eroica')   2
Symphony No.5 in C minor, Op.67   138, 140
Symphony No.7 in A major, Op.92   66, 197–8 (incl. Ex.8.7)
Symphony No.8 in F major, Op.93   123
Symphony No.9 in D minor, Op.125

('Choral')   3, 110n, 145, 157, 211
Violin Sonata in D major, Op.12, No.1
   74–6 (incl. Exx.3.1a, 3.1b, 3.1e, 3.1g,
   3.1h)
Violin Sonata in A major, Op.47
   ('Kreutzer')   97 (incl. Ex.3.17b)
Bellini, Vincenzo   158
Bendl, Karel   158
Bennett, J E   262n
Bergmann, Johann Baptist   229, 242n
Bernhardt, Dr   248, 250
Berthé, Heinrich   208, 225
Bevan, P G   261n, 266n
Beveridge, David   164n
Biba, Otto   110, 150n, 261n, 262n, 265n
Bilding Circle   253
Blahetka, Josef   257
Blangini, Giuseppe   211
Blom, Eric   239n, 261n
Blumenthal, I   262n, 264n
Bocklet, Karl Maria von   64, 65, 68, 93,
   94, 95, 101, 102, 108
Bogner, Ferdinand   102
Böhm, Josef   68, 93
Bonaparte, Napoleon   254
Borodin, Alexandre   185
Boulez, Pierre   194
Boyd, Malcolm   28, 59n, 61n
Brahms, Johannes   60n, 129, 137, 151n,
   154, 158
Branscombe, Peter   59n, 151n
Breitkopf & Härtel   91, 129, 143
Brendel, Alfred   191, 204
Breuning, Gerhard von   260
Britten, Benjamin   208
Brown, Clive   14n, 15n
Brown, Maurice J E   129–30, 132, 133,
   135, 143, 229, 230, 242n
Brusatti, Otto   61n, 110
Burgtheater   64, 232
Byrd, William   194

Čapek, Josef   158
Capell, Richard   262n, 264n
Cappi & Diabelli   3
Castle, Eduard   219n
Cavett-Dunsby, Esther   61n
Chailley, Jacques   187, 190n
Cherubini, Luigi   158
Chézy, Helmina von   220, 239n
   Wilhelm von   220n, 239n, 249, 253
Chopin, Frédéric   192, 194

Christalnigg, Graf   214
Chusid, Martin   60n, 61n
Clapham, John   163n
Clark, Suzannah   110
Colles, H C   262n
Coleridge, Arthur Duke   239n
Columbus, Christopher   245
Cone, Edward T   126n
Concerts spirituels   67, 68, 110
Conybeare, J J   262n, 263, 264, 265n
Coombes, R R A   262n
Cooper, Grosvenor W   140, 151n
Cooper, Martin   262n
Cornelius, Peter   216
Cortot, Alfred   194, 208
Covington, K   59n
Crenneville, Carl   237–8, 243n
Czerny, Karl   2, 14n, 191

Dale, Kathleen   262, 265n
Das Dreimäderlhaus (Berthé)   208, 225,
   240n
Deas, Stewart   15n
Debussy, Claude   189n
Deutsch, Gitta   241n
Deutsch, Otto Erich   110n, 218n, 223–4,
   225, 226, 227, 229, 231, 232, 233,
   239n, 240n, 241n, 242n, 244, 245,
   261n, 262n, 263n, 264n
Devrient, Ludwig   219n
Diabelli, Anton   84, 252
Doblhoff-Dies, Anton Freiherr von   248
Dolin, R   262n
Donizetti, Gaetano   219n
Doppler, Josef   222
Dörflinger, Ferdinand   233
Duncan, E   262n, 263n
Duport, Louis Antoine   111n
Dürr, Walther   3, 11, 14n, 230, 242n
Dvořák, Antonin   59n, 153–63
   Quintet in A minor, B7   154–5
   String Quartet in A major, B8   154–5
   String Quartet in E flat major, B92   155
   Symphony No.9 in E minor ('From the
      New World')   156
   Violin Sonata in F major, B106   155

Eckel, Franz   244, 253
Eckel, Georg   248
Ehrlich, Paul   251
Elgar, Edward
   Symphony No.2 in E flat major   144

General Index

Ense, Varnhagen von 216
Enzersdorfer, Rudolf Maria 229, 242n
Erdmann, Eduard 191
Esterházy, Johann Karl 210, 249
  Karoline 221–3, 225, 226, 227, 237–8, 249, 253
  Marie 226

Fallersleben, Heinrich Hoffmann von 227, 231, 232
Fauré, Gabriel
  Nocturne No.13 189n
  Violin Sonata in A major 189n
Ferguson, Howard 61n, 189n, 208n
Fétis, F J 218n
Fibich, Zdenek 160–1
  'Tak mne kovzlem ondy jala' 161
  Piano Sonata in D minor 161
  Quintet in D major, Op.42 161, 162–3 (Ex.6.3)
  Symphony No.2 in E flat major, Op.38 161
Finck, Henry T 163n
Fischer, Edwin 194, 208
Fischer-Dieskau, Dietrich 208
Fischl, Viktor 154
Fleming, Alexander 251
Florey, Howard 251
Forgács, Baron 209, 211
Fracastoro, Girolamo 245
Frankl, Ludwig August 231
Frederick William IV of Prussia 216
Frisch, Walter 126n
Fröhlich, Kathi 226
Frost H F 257, 262n, 265n
Furtwängler, Wilhelm 167, 188–9

Gell, P G H 262n, 266n
Gesellschaft der Musikfreunde (see also *Musikverein*) 62, 65, 66, 67, 68, 73, 93, 133, 150n, 211, 219n, 234
Gluck, Christoph Willibald 126
Goethe 64, 81, 216, 217, 250, 252, 259
Goldschmidt, Harry 120, 126n
Golitsïn, Prince Nikolai 92, 93, 102
Gounod, Charles 156, 157
Greenberg, J 262n, 264n
Griffel, L Michael 130, 132, 133, 137, 139, 143, 144, 145
Grillparzer, Franz 216, 234, 261
Grob, Bartholomaus 228
  Heinrich 63, 230
  Johann Heinrich 227
  Therese 63, 72, 220, 224–5, 226, 227–30, 242n, 249, 252
  Wilhelmine 228
Grove, George 258
Grun, Bernard 240n
Grünwedel, Gusti 231–2
Gulasch, Johann Alois von 234
Guthmann, Friedrich 1, 14
Guthrie, D 262n, 263n

Hackelberg-Landau, Baron 209
Hals, Frans 204
Handel, Georg Frideric 67, 110n, 155
  Israel in Egypt 110n
Harnoncourt, Nicolaus 150
Harrison, Sidney 252, 262n, 264n
Hartmann, Fritz 232
  Moritz 217, 232
Hartwig, Otto 218n
Hascher, Xavier 28–9, 59n
Haslinger 2
Haydn, Joseph 2, 45, 63, 66, 69, 141, 155, 158, 166, 187, 189n, 259
  String Quartet in C major, Op.54, No.2 140
  String Quartet in G major, Op.76, No.1 140
  Symphony No.101 in D major ('Clock') 140
Heine, Heinrich 112, 120, 121, 124, 125, 217
Heissenstamm, Graf 214
Hellborn, see Kreissle
Herzog, Franz 241n
Hilmar, Ernst 14n, 189n
Hinrichsen, H J 61n
Hoffmann, E T A 231
Hollpein, Heinrich 227
  Leopold 228
Holz, Carl 14n, 92, 93
Holzapfel, Anton 224, 228
Hölzel, Heinrich Josef 232
Hönig, Therese 226
Hoorickx, Reinhard van 229, 242n
Howat, Roy 143, 189n
Huber, Josef 249
Hudson, M M 262n, 263n
Hueffer, F 262n
Hummel, Johann Nepomuk 2, 66
Hunter, John 245, 262n, 263n
Hutchings, Arthur 258, 262n, 265n

274 General Index

Hüttenbrenner, Anselm   81, 210, 220, 224, 226, 228, 233
  Der Abend   210
Hüttenbrenner, Josef   3, 11, 210

Jäger, Franz   68
Jeitteles, Ignaz   219n
Jenner, Edward   247
Jiránek, J   164n
Joachim, Josef   157, 207

Kalkbrenner, Friedrich
  Septet, Op.32   158
Kärntnerthortheater   67, 212
Karvin, Anna Karvinski von   211
Kempff, Wilhelm   191
Kendall, Alan   261n, 262n
Kenner, Josef   237
Kerman, Joseph   111n, 120, 126, 126n
Kiemle, H D   250, 262n, 264n
Kirnberger, Johann Philipp   3
Kinsky, Charlotte   64
Klein, Rudolf   241n
Koch, Robert   256
Köhler, Franz   227, 241n
Kramer, Richard   112, 126n
Kreissle von Hellborn, Heinrich   221, 222-3, 227, 228, 229, 237, 239n, 240n, 241n, 242n, 248
Krejči, František   154
Kuna, Milan   164n
Kunz, Babette   233, 234
  Michael   234
  Therese   233, 234
Kupelwieser, Johann   233
  Josef   233, 235, 236
  Leopold   233, 234, 236, 248
Kyas, Vojtěch   164n

Lachner, Franz   68, 231, 234, 258
Lackman, P J   262n
Lamartine, Alphonse de   217
Landhaussaal   67, 101
Lange, Aloisia   211
Langer, Suzanne   126, 126n
Larkin, E   262n, 264, 266n
Lászny, Katharina von   231
Léhar, Franz
  The Merry Widow   241n
Lehmann, Lotte   116
Leidesdorf, Maximilian Josef   253
Lenau, Nikolaus   213, 215, 216, 219n

Léonard, Hubert   157
Lewy, Josef   68
Ley, Rosamond   239n, 261n
Lilac Time   166
Linke, Josef   64, 68, 92, 93
Liszt, Franz   153, 155, 156, 157, 158, 191, 192, 207
Litschauer, Walburga   243n
Locksley, R M   262n, 266n
Longyear, R M   59n
Löwenthal, Max   216
  Sophie   214, 215, 216
Luib, Ferdinand   210, 222
Luther, Martin   250

Maag, Otto   227, 241n
MacAdam, John   256
Macdonald, Hugh   253, 265n
Mackerras, Sir Charles   151n
Mainville-Fodor, Joséphine   209
Mandell, G L   262n
Mann, Thomas   261
Mandyczewski, Eusebius   154, 158
Marston, Nicholas   110
Marty, Jean Pierre   2, 14n
Matiegka, Wenzeslaus   225
Matthews, Denis   261n, 265n
Mayer, Andreas   241n
Mayrhofer, Johann   81, 84, 221, 252, 253
Mayseder, Josef   66
McCreless, Patrick   111n
McKay, Elizabeth Norman   60n, 219n, 262n, 263n, 264n, 265n, 266n
Mendelssohn, Felix   1, 140, 153, 155, 158, 258
Metternich, Prince Clemens   190n, 229, 254
Meyer, Leonard B   140, 151n
Meyerbeer, Giacomo   216
Michelangelo   192
Mitz, Christine   227
Mollo, Stefano   129, 149
Morton, R S   262n, 263n
Moscheles, Ignaz   160
Mosel, Franz von   245
Mosel, Ignaz von   64
Mozart, Franz Xavier Wolfgang   212, 219n
Mozart, Wolfgang Amadeus (jnr)   216
Mozart, Wolfgang Amadeus   2, 10, 12, 45, 63, 64, 66, 67, 69, 73, 74, 80, 110n, 141, 154, 155, 158, 187, 192, 237

Così fan tutte 212
Davidde penitente 110n
'Haydn' Quartets 61n
Piano Concerto in G major, K453 176
Piano Concerto in C major, K467
Piano Sonata in D major, K576 74
Serenade in C minor, K388
String Quartet in G major, K387 41, 42 (Ex.2.14a)
String Quartet in D minor, K421 140
String Quintet in D major, K593 140
Violin Sonata in E minor, K304 74–5 (incl. Exx.3.1c, 3.1d)
Violin Sonata in A major, K305 74–6 (incl. Ex.3.1f)
Violin Sonata in F major, K377 79 (incl. Ex.3.4)
Mozatti, Josef 211
Müller, Wilhelm 226
Musgrave, Michael 60n
Musikverein, see *Gesellschaft der Musikfreunde*

Nejedlý, Zdeněk 164n
Nestroy, Johann 210
Neumann, Philipp 3
Newbould, Brian 51, 59n, 60n, 61n, 150n, 151n, 161, 163, 165n, 167, 181, 187, 188n, 189n, 190n, 236, 243n, 262n, 264n
Nightingale, Florence 255
Nowell, John 239n, 261n

O'Brien, E 262n, 264n
Onslow, George 158
  Quartets 158
O'Shea, J 262n, 263n, 264n, 265n, 266n

Palferman, T G 262n, 264n
Pascall, Robert 151n
Pasteur, Louis 255
Paumann, Johann von 221, 222, 239n
Paumgartner, Sylvester 102
Petöffy, Sándor 217
Pichler, Karoline 64, 211
Pierron, Jeanette Cuny de 226
Platen, August Graf von 217
Pöckelhofer, Pepi 226, 227, 230, 241n, 249
Pougin, A 218n
Pritchard, T S L 263n, 265n
Privat-Musikverein 64

Probst, Heinrich Albert 91, 108, 259
Pry, Paul 164n
Pugnani, Gaetano 1

Quincey, Thomas de 249

Rachmaninov, Sergei 191
Raeburn, Michael 261n, 262n
Randhartinger, Benedict 258
Reed, John 59n, 61n, 130, 133, 135, 136, 143, 144, 152n, 263n, 264n, 265n, 266n
Rehm, Christoph Peter 218
Reinbek, Emilie von 219n
Rektorys, A 165n
Rellstab, Ludwig 217
Rettich, Julie 216
Ricord, Dr 245
Richter, E F 160
Richter, Sviatoslav 195, 208
Rieder, Wilhelm 248
Rink, John 189n
Rinna, Dr Ernst von 250, 257, 259, 260
Ritter, William 165n
Rode, Pierre 1
Roitzsch, F A 128, 150n
Rold, R L 263n, 266n
Romberg, Bernhard 66, 102
Rosenblum, Sandra 14n
Rossini, Gioacchino 1, 2, 158, 211
Rössler, Josef 226
Rückert, Friedrich 216, 217
Rudolf, Max 208n
Rudorff, Ernst Friedrich Karl 156
Rutter, John 189n

Sabatier, Francois 211, 226, 218n
Salieri, Anton 72, 74, 211
Salis-Seewis, Johann Gaudenz von 81
Sams, Eric 245, 250, 263n, 264n
Sand, Georges 217
Schaudin. Fritz 245, 251
Schelling 216
Schellmann, Albert 221, 250
Schick, Hartmut 164n
Schiff, András 249, 263n
Schiller, Franz Ferdinand von 64, 207, 219n
Schindler, Anton 92
Schnabel, Artur 191, 194–5
Schober, Franz von 81, 216, 217, 223, 231, 232, 236, 238, 247, 249, 252, 253, 257, 260

Schönstein, Baron Carl von   64, 68, 216, 222, 230, 237, 253
Schott of Mainz   108
Schreier, Peter   208
Schroder-Devrient, Wilhelmine   219n
Schubert, Carl Daniel Friedrich   10, 15n
—, Carl   227, 229
—, Ferdinand   8, 11, 63, 110n, 227, 229, 235, 249, 257, 258, 259
—, Franz Peter
  Schubertiads   64, 237, 2248, 249
  S's accents   195, 206
  S. and the dance   203–4
  S. and depression   252–4
  S. and dynamics   128–9, 135, 148–150, 194, 206
  S's father   63
  S. and Freemasonry   187, 190n
  S. and 'golden section'   185–7, 189
  S. and metre   140–3, 146–150, 167–179, 189n
  S's ornaments   207–8
  S's pianos   64, 194–5, 258
  S. and the piano pedals   207
  S. and repeats   197
  S's smoking   249
  S's social and environmental conditions   254–7
  S's syphilis   230, 245–254
  S. and tempo   1–14, 127–8, 187–7, 190n
  S's time-signatures   128
  S's transitions   16–59
—, Franz Theodor   244
—, Ignaz   63, 227, 229
—, Johann Friedrich   9, 15n
—, Josef   247
—, Maria Elizabeth   244
Schumann, Elisabeth   116
Schumann, Robert   1, 153, 155, 158, 161, 258, 259
  Piano Quintet in E flat, Op.44   158
  Symphony No. 2 in C   145 (incl. Ex. 5.20)
Schuppanzigh, Ignaz   14n, 64, 65, 68, 92, 93, 111n
Schuster, Vincenz   84, 111
Schütz, J A P   3, 4, 15n
Schwarzenberg, Prince   64
Schwemminger, Heinrich   227
Schwind, Moritz von   215, 26, 231, 237, 248, 253, 257
Senn, Johann   255

Serkin, Rudolf   191
Shakespeare, William   219n
Slawjk, Josef   65, 68, 93, 95, 101, 102, 108
Smetana, Bedrich   156, 157, 158, 159–160 (Ex. 6.1), 160, 161, 164n
  Piano Trio in G minor, Op.15   158
  Triumph Symphony   158
Smirsch, Johann Carl   242n
Sonnleithner, Leopold   252
Spaun, Josef von   63, 64, 221, 223, 231, 232, 237, 248, 253, 258, 259
Spohr, Louis   1, 12, 13, 66, 157
  Jessonda   11, 12
Spontini, Gaspare   2
Stadlen, Peter   14n
Stadler, Abbé   211
Stadler, Anton   249
Stadtkonvikt   69, 25
Stapleton, Karl   164n
Staufer, Johann Georg   84, 111n
Steblin, Rita   241n, 242n, 243n
Stein, Jack M   112, 116, 126n
Steiner & Co   253
Stevenson, George   256
Storr, A   263n, 265n
Stradner, Gerhard   238
Strauss, Johann   203
Suk, Josef   164n
Sullivan, Arthur
  The Mikado   241n
Sulzer, J P   15n
Suppé, Franz von   221, 222, 237
  Franz Schubert   221
Swieten, Baron Gottfried van   110n

Tartini, Giuseppe   1
Tchaikovsky, Peter Ilyitsch   139
Tennstedt, Klaus   150
Theater an der Wien   67
Tibbets, John C   164n
Tichatschek, Joseph   219n
Tieck, Ludwig   216, 219n
Tietze, Ludwig   68
Toeplitz, Uri   14n
Toller, Nicholas   150, 152n
Tomášek, Václav   163
  Eclogues   163
Tovey, Donald Francis   61n, 138, 144–5, 151n, 152n
Truscott, Harold   59n
Türk, Daniel Gottlob   15n, 197

Tyson, Alan   111n, 126n

Uhland, Johann Ludwig   217
Unger, Carl   209–219
  Caroline   209–219
Unsinnsgesellschaft   232–7

Vering, Dr Josef von   260
Viotti, Giovanni Battista   1
Vogl, Johann Michael   64, 68, 81, 93, 211, 221, 257, 258
Vogl, Kunigunde   231
Vogler, Abbé   110n
Voříšek, Jan Václav   66, 163

Wagner, Johann Jakob   238
Wagner, Richard   107, 155, 158, 219n
Waidelich, T Gerrit   111n, 219n, 239n
Wallace, William Vincent   158
Walter, Bruno   116
Weber, Carl Maria von   158

Euryanthe   11, 13
Webster, James   59n, 78, 111n
Wechsberg, J   263n, 265n
Weiss, Franz   68, 92, 93
Westrup, Jack   61n, 262n
Whaples, Miriam   29, 60n
Wilson, C B   262n, 266n
Winter, Robert   60n, 130
Wintle, Christopher   60n
Wolf, Hugo   126n
Wolf, Nanette   219n
Wolff, Christoph   59n
Wollenberg, Susan   59n, 163n
Wurzbach, C von   218n

Zaslaw, Neil   14n
Zimmermann, Carl Friedrich   233
Zum römischen Kaiser   64
Zum roten Krenz   259
Zumsteeg, Johann Rudolf   219n